The Attic

A Novel

Fran Caldwell

THE ATTIC

A LULU BOOK: ISBN 978-0-9920523-0-0

Distributed by Lulu Press, Inc.

This novel is a work of fiction, although some characters and events are based on archival fact.

For Pat, with love and deepest appreciation.

This book could not have been written without you.

My thanks to:

Historian and novelist Melissa Marsh, whose own knowledge of WWII is far greater than mine, and Sarabeth Purcell, whose poetic novels are so enviably 'now'. Both were so supportive of "The Attic", along with my daughter, Kim, and my best friend, Judy, ever-patient and enthusiastic manuscript readers, and agent Kae Tienstra, who gently pointed out that times have changed, and self-publishing could be a very positive experience.

The BBC website was a huge resource for my research, but ultimately it was my sister, Pat, who inspired me with her own story.

ONE

I first noticed the light in August, last year. It was just a dim light in the attic, but I could see into the room, through the pretty maple tree outside, and make out a cupboard on the far wall and some sort of patterned wallpaper, despite so much grime on the little window. I'd been in this apartment at Jarvis and Wellesley for just over a month, and finally finished unpacking all my boxes. Of course, I'd noticed the house opposite right from the beginning, when I came to check this place out before I signed the lease, and I was impressed then.

It's a fine old building, early Victorian, Queen Anne style, three storeys with the attic. It's empty, did I say? The ground floor windows are boarded up, and there's a 'Keep Out' sign nailed to the front door. It's a shame, because it's a great old house and I feel sorry for it, so neglected and sad, with bits of crud lying around in the overgrown front garden.

Anyway, my bedroom looks straight across to it and I am exactly level with that attic window. And I've seen this light more than once now - and it intrigues me. I can sit here for ages, on my bed, with Rupert purring beside me, just staring over.

Rupert was a stray I found in the back lane after I moved here. I was taking my garbage down, and he was hiding behind some boxes, just sort of peering at me, very nervous. He looked pretty skinny, so I went upstairs to get him some tuna, which he devoured, once I stepped back a bit. I kept this routine up for around ten days, buying real cat food for him by then, and one day he allowed me to stroke him.

I don't know how it happened, but I kind of fell in love with him. He looked up at me with his huge eyes, and there was such love there and I instantly bonded with him. It was a stronger feeling

1

than any I'd ever had before. I just picked him up and took him up to the apartment. I'm probably not meant to have any animals, because most landlords are unforgiving about that from what I've heard, but no one knows he's here, and he is so clean and quiet. Rupert has become my best friend.

Does it sound as if I don't have a lot going for me right now? I have a rather good job, working for a marketing company at Bloor and Bathurst. I got into a lot of trouble some time back, just after high school—well, before I graduated, if that's important. A social worker who came to the house to speak to my mother about me came up with this training scheme, because of my interest in art, and I learned graphic design. I enjoy the work, and it pays fairly well, although I could make more if I went to a place that didn't know my background. Because the training scheme was affiliated with various small companies, and mine was one of them, I was taken on with a sort of 'she should be grateful for the opportunity, forget the money' attitude. Oh, Dylan, my boss, is fine with me, but I know I'll never get much of an increase. He has other artists working there making a hell of a lot more than I do.

As was expected, I am grateful.

And I love where I live. Of all the areas in Toronto, I like the Parliament Street enclave best. We call it Cabbagetown, but I have no idea why. There's a small-town feeling about it, as if the natives are unaware that they're in the heart of a large city. There are cuter neighborhoods, posher ones, more hip ones, but Parliament is natural, just being itself with absolutely no effort. Young professionals have moved in, of course, and spruced up some of the houses, but the street seems to yawn back at it all. You can buy a feather boa, a vampy satin dress, or a Victorian chamber pot filled with bright beads (an accent piece, right?) in a little boutique nestled next to an almost irrevocably neglected house, its porch all askew, and with its windows boarded up, while on the other side is a beautifully restored brick mansion, all amber glass, with a lovingly stripped front door with shiny brass hardware. This mish-mash of form, this incongruity, the total unlikelihood of it all, delights me. Even the people seem to have been dropped randomly by some humorous god – black, white, Asian, Indian, dirty-haired old guys clutching bottles of something loosely akin to booze, Porsche-driving so-called success stories, hookers and panhandlers, corporate go-getters and artists, straight and gay – all for me to share. It's like living on the Left Bank. I imagine.

So I started to see this light fairly regularly. One night it was on, and then a couple of days would pass with nothing, and then it would be on again. It's always quite late when I see it, just as I'm climbing into bed. Anyway, I got the distinct impression that it appeared brighter more recently, as if it was getting stronger.

During the day, thinking about it, I put it down to some caretaker or security guy checking the place out. Not that I saw a light in any other window, and that was weird. Then I decided it must be a bum, settling in for the night. I just couldn't figure out why he'd want to be up in the attic. I mean, why wouldn't he doss down on one of the lower floors?

The mysterious nocturnal coming and going started to bother me in the end.

I'm sitting here tonight, on my bed, clipping my toenails – not a beauty regime; it's just that they hurt if I don't keep them pruned. Rupert is curled up beside me, ignoring my movements which must be disturbing him; he could move if he wanted, but he doesn't; he just loves physical contact with me. When I glance up, for no reason I can think of, other than I feel compelled to look, the light is on over there again. This time I develop goose bumps. They worry me, because they came with this feeling that some one called me – told me to look. Shit, that's scary.

Yet the attic doesn't look scary; that glow makes the room seem cozy, somehow. Anyway, I don't believe in ghosts, although I enjoy a good ghost story – I mean, who doesn't? Right now I am only considering *who* is responsible for that light, not *what*.

I finish my nail-pruning, rub some hand cream into my feet, climb into bed and switch off the lamp. After a bit of tossing and turning, thinking about that damned light, I fall asleep.

The old hot water radiator wakes me around two, clanking and gurgling as if it's ready to take off somewhere (this is a very old apartment building). I am completely awake again, and sit up to look out of the window. This area is an interesting one, a gay neighborhood, mostly. You get to see some interesting stuff late at night if you know what to look for. I'm not implying it's disreputable; but it can be entertaining in a spicy way.

It's been snowing and the street is hushed and beautiful, everything uniformly covered with the soft sparkly stuff. Now the house across the road looks as if it's set in the countryside somewhere, with its big, now-bare trees and the vacant lot transforming it. I half-close my eyes to the high-rises in the background. The scene could be from a Christmas card.

The light is still on in the attic, of course. I try to figure out what the rest of the room looks like. Sleep is finally making my eyelids droop and I give into it and wriggle back down under the covers, to the waiting Rupert.

This time, probably because the room is now overheated (the radiator can't be adjusted), I have a very erotic dream involving some security guy. I won't go into details about it, but it's a juicy one. For someone with so little experience with sex, I manage superbly in my dreams.

Jimmy, the super in my building, is changing a light bulb in the hallway when I get home tonight. He's a New Yorker, and never lets you forget it, especially during the Stanley Cup Playoffs. He gets particularly sneery during Canadian elections, which – come to think of it – seem to occur with astonishing regularity.

I asked him once why he hadn't gone back to the States after his (Canadian) wife went (I don't think anyone has been brave enough to clarify *where* she went – whether it was to Heaven or some less ethereal plane, like Belleville, where she came from), and he shrugged his shoulders, rubbed hard at his nose and said, "Nothing much there anymore. It kinda hurts to walk down your old block and not be recognized, you know?"

At the time, this struck me as an odd reason, because Jimmy seems to know few people here, too, from what I've seen. I think he must be lonely, because he is always alone, whenever I've seen him on the street, or in the local coffee shop. He's old, of course, fifty-ish, and I guess it's harder to make friends at that age. I quite like talking to him because I'm very interested in New York, especially writers from there; they have such a distinct voice, impossible to confuse with writers from other places.

Jimmy's not that friendly with me, in fact, probably because of the age difference. To tell the truth, I do most of the talking and

4

Jimmy replies most times with monosyllables. I think he's a bit shy, too. But I'm working on him.

Jimmy is a member of AA. It doesn't seem to help much, because at least once every six weeks or so he's plastered. When you live in our building, you have to hope nothing much goes wrong with the john or the heating or anything, because it takes him two or three days to recover after one of his binges. Of course, when he's sober, he tells everyone how well he's doing since he joined the local Chapter; I don't think he remembers the binges at all. Anyway, probably because he sympathizes with them, he seems to have a soft spot for the poor old winos who doss in our hall on particularly frigid nights; he never throws them out.

Tonight is the end of one of Jimmy's super-dry days; he doesn't look at me when I speak, but I can see he's feeling pretty good.

"Hey, Jimmy," I smile brightly, "do you know who lives in the old place over the road – you know, the empty house? Sometimes there's a light on?"

"Bums, I guess," he replies good-naturedly, still not looking down at me from his stepladder.

"It's just that it looks all boarded-up downstairs. How would they get in?"

"Those guys will find a way in somewhere," he replies, stepping down from the ladder and scratching his ass thoughtfully.

My one girlfriend, Katie, told me that guys *never* do things like that in front of her. We'd been talking about things guys do, you know, and I mentioned ass-scratching and crotch-adjustment, because they are things that guys do in front of me all the time. Katie was horrified. She is more feminine-looking than me, so that's probably the reason. I guess I look more like one of the boys, you know. And it's true that I follow the Maple Leafs with a passion. Higher testosterone levels, or something. Anyway, it's okay for a man to be himself with me – I mean, it's no skin off my teeth if he has an itch.

Jimmy's scratching finished, he picks his nose. "Maybe they found a loose board on a window, or something." He balls the result of his nostril-delving, inspects it, and flicks the little rascal towards the fire escape.

5

"It doesn't sound right that people can just wander around other people's property," I say, somewhat envious of the intruder's freedom to check out that attic room.

"Ah, no one's lived in that dump for years. They're waiting to put up another high-rise as soon as they pick up the land on the other side."

"They're going to pull it down?" I am filled with sadness at the image of the house torn apart and flattened.

"I told you, they have to get more land. It could take years. So they'll just sit on it until they're ready."

'I thought it might be a security guy or something, in the house."

"No security guy. Just a bum, is all."

"Well, I don't think it's right that they can just break in like that." I wish Jimmy would look at me, just for a second. I'm beginning to think I'm not here. I get that feeling a lot with people, I admit. I have this urge to wave my hand in front of his eyes to get his attention.

Jimmy folds the ladder, which he's been wiping off with a rag to remove the salt and muck his own boots left behind; it's messy out there, slush and ice all over. He turns to leave, and looks briefly at me. "You haven't emptied your mailbox for a couple of days." His eyes are absolutely without expression. I don't know what I expected to see there – warmth? Understanding? He leaves without waiting for my response.

I'm not a worrier; I can't recall giving much thought to the economy or terrorism or stuff like that. For me, it's the little things, the dumb niggles that no one else ever seems concerned with. My music is too loud; my TV is too loud; salespeople don't seem to see me; sometimes they don't even *hear* me, for God's sake. I find myself wondering what people honestly think of me, even as I convince myself that I don't give a shit.

It was probably my mother who started this in me when I was a kid. She always said it was important to be able to walk down the street with your head held high. I never asked her why. She also said, proudly, that one should keep oneself to oneself. I *never* worked out what that meant. She was a bit strange, my mum, and I guess some of her hang-ups rubbed off on me. I know people see me as out-going and confident, but, deep inside, I'm not.

I'm pretty straight, especially compared with how I was. I'm twenty-six years old and I can't say that I've ever done one adventurous thing in my life. I would have graduated high school, but when I got into that bit of trouble, that was the end of that. Mum got sick around that time, too, and I spent a lot of time with her, helping her.

After I learned the computer graphics program and started working for Dylan, things improved quite a bit. My life seemed to take on more meaning, as they say. I have cash to spare, as well, because I don't spend much on myself anyway. And Mum left me money when she died, although that's all tied up in Canada Bonds for the time being. When I'm ready to spread my wings, as Dylan sometimes says, I'll have plenty to finance it. Come to think of it, isn't twenty-six a bit old to be spreading fledgling wings?

I consider myself bright; I read heavier stuff than most of the people I know. Some find me witty, although I don't often get the chance to display it. I'm not very sociable, I think I mentioned that. I just don't enjoy going out that much. The truth is, most people don't seem interested in the same things I am. The women mostly talk about clothes and guys. It's exactly the same as when I was in high school; nothing changes.

And when the conversation veers around to love and sex, it's not that it's boring, it's just that I have nothing much to contribute on the subject. I also think it shouldn't be discussed casually; it's very personal stuff. Hey, I'm not saying I'm a virgin, or anything. I did it once, when I was seventeen. I can't say it was memorable.

I've done a few radical things; got involved with an animal rights group, went picketing –"*Vivisection is Morally Wrong!*"– that sort of thing. I always smile at demonstrators, whatever their cause, because it takes guts to put yourself and your opinions out there for everyone to see.

I never got hooked on tobacco or booze. A lot of the kids at school did, but I just couldn't afford it. Where did those guys get the money for it? By the time I had a little extra cash, I wasn't interested. I honestly think most of those kids did it just to spite their parents. I liked Mum; I didn't want to spite her.

7

Oh, then how did I get into all that trouble? Mm, this is unsavory, but needs to be opened up. I was in this girl gang. Hey, I was only fifteen when it started, but it got kind of bad. Girl gangs can be evil. I don't talk about it, even now. I'm just lucky that I got out before things became serious for me. A couple of those girls are in prison now. They just went right on doing stupid stuff. I stopped.

So, at the end of my youth, one foot firmly heading towards middle age, almost a virgin (I figure it grew back), I need something to get me motivated. I don't know what falling in love is like; I read an article about someone losing a child, and I can't imagine having a child in the first place, let alone grieving over it, although I guess it would be like that for me if something happened to Rupert.

TWO

I did a dumb thing: I allowed this guy, Charlie, to stay with me for a while. I met him at a dull party a while back, and he was desperate for a place to stay. I looked at his dirty hair and bad skin, and I wondered why the hell I said what I said, but I said it anyway. "Okay," I said. *Okay?* It was meant to be for a month, until he'd saved enough to get first and last month's rent together for his own place, but it's been six weeks now. I'm not happy about it, because he's a messy bastard, never cleans up after himself, but I'm not good at confrontation.

The one advantage I see in the arrangement is that I have to keep myself more or less presentable. I'm not much on grooming, but try a bit harder knowing he could walk in on me at any minute, so I shower and get dressed in the morning, you know, on weekends, and of course I have to do that through the week because I work. That's the good thing about having Charlie here, the self-improvement part of it all.

Charlie doesn't get in my way; he's out a lot, and that's good, because I like my space to myself. I read a lot, a book every couple of days, on average; I think I'm a speed reader. I like to draw, my only passion, to be honest. I work mostly in pen and ink, street scenes, buildings, interesting people, things like that. I use photographs that I take on the weekend for my material. I upload them to my computer, and just start drawing away. I watch the usual TV shows, take care of my house plants, and spend a lot of time just sitting with Rupert.

Back to that light thing. I didn't tell Charlie about it. He doesn't go in for that mystery/fantasy stuff much. About the only spiritual experience he has is with the help of a little weed. Not that I have anything against that; I used to use it myself, but not anymore. Once I cleaned up my act, discovered other ways to deal with things, I didn't seem to need it anymore. Occasionally, at a party, if it's being passed around, I'll take a drag, but that's just being sociable. I mean, I don't need it, you know?

I'm an inwardly happy person, an optimist, and I have nothing to complain about. Honestly. It's not that my life is dull, but it *sounds* dull. Saturday nights are the worst.

The apartment is freshly cleaned and cozy. I nearly always waste a few dollars on fresh flowers on Saturday morning. I've washed my hair, and it smells wonderful. I might have shaved my underarms and legs. I make a special Saturday night dinner, because I have time to fuss with it. I've washed the dishes, I'm sitting in my favorite chair, gloating over how nice everything looks, and then I turn on the TV.

It's that stupid TV that does it every time. I will not learn. I just know, sitting there, trying to find something intelligent to watch, that I am *the only single girl in the whole of Toronto, perhaps the whole Eastern seaboard, watching TV alone.* It's not that I mind doing it, but it's what people would say if they knew; that bothers me.

The people at work always ask if I enjoyed my weekends and I tell them I did, because I did. But then they sometimes ask me *what* I did, and I begin to mumble a lot. It's embarrassing to admit that I got a lot of pleasure from shopping for groceries; going to the library to change books; washing and ironing my clothes; vacuuming and dusting the apartment; scrubbing out and refilling Rupert's litter box, making a superb casserole; re-potting three of my bigger house plants; playing on the computer for four hours; weeping over an old Meg Ryan movie; and having the apartment completely to myself because Charlie didn't come home until late Sunday night.

Nobody decreed that we should be deliriously happy all the time. I think today's expectation of instant gratification in all things is wrong. My mother never expected to be happy *any* of the time – well, after Dad died, anyway. She often seemed startled by her own laughter, as if it sneaked up on her. I'm not like that. I have a very well-developed sense of humor. In fact, I laugh at myself all the time. Perhaps that means that I'm a bit of a joke, but that's okay. I'm a realist.

Anyway, the house across the road has given me an additional interest. My mind goes wild conjuring up stories to fit that crazy light, which is on every night now. Once I find the answer to it, there'll be no excitement left for a while. If it does turn out to be some old drunk holed up over there, the way Jimmy said, I'll be disappointed. I'd rather imagine some terrorist cell, using it for their planning meetings, stuff like that.

So, in a way, I don't *want* to find out any more about it, in case it's a dull explanation. But I *need* to know.

Of course, there is no way that you would ever catch me going *into* the place. Excitement is great, but creeping around in a creaky old house is going too far. But I will just check over there to see if someone has forced a window. I can do that. I won't go inside. Shit, there would be lots of spiders in there; I'm not too fond of spiders.

Tomorrow, on the way home from work, I'll just take a quick look. There's no harm in that. It's almost my civic duty.

I knew it would be easy to get in. The whole house is rotting. The boards on the lower windows are hanging by rusty nails and the exposed panes have been broken. I have to climb over a pile of old packing crates outside the back door (the front door would be too conspicuous). The floor of the back porch is spongey-feeling, but it takes my weight. The door feels equally sodden, as if it had soaked up all the moisture of Toronto's current winter, and it easily opens with the gentlest of hip nudges. However, I am certain that no one else came in this way, just looking at the dirt on the back porch, with no scuff marks or foot prints; whoever is coming in, they must be doing it through the front door or through one of the windows.

Okay, I'm in. I honestly didn't plan this. It's just that now I'm here, it seems necessary. The first spider I see, I'm leaving, of course.

There's still enough light from outside coming through the windows so that I don't need the flashlight I brought with me; the days are becoming longer now that spring is on its way; it doesn't get dark until almost 6 pm. It's a good flashlight, a big one. I bought it to take to the Muskokas two summers ago. One of my friends asked me to go camping with them, but then at the last minute she had to cancel, as there wouldn't have been room in her car after all. I was relieved, in fact. I'm not much of an outdoors-ey type. I do still have the sleeping bag, the little tent, and this flashlight, that I bought, though. I figured they could come in useful one day.

No spiders yet. I'm not afraid of the dark shadows in the corners or under the stairs, as long as I don't see a spider. I don't worry about the dark - in fact, I couldn't scream to save my life. I tried a couple of times, just to practice, and all that comes out is a sort of croak. No wonder they hire actresses just for their scream ability; it's a talent.

I'm not your typical girly-girl, if you know what I mean. I never was much good at flirting, or saying the right stuff to make a guy like me. I guess I always figured it was just too damned hard, keeping all of that up. I'm too lazy - or very liberated. Not that I ever consciously worked at being liberated; I seem to have been born this way.

I told you I live in a gay neighborhood, well that's deliberate on my part. I figured I could walk around freely at night or whenever I liked (a lot of girls won't, you know) without worrying about guys stalking me. Not that I expect to be stalked, but it is a funny old world these days, and better to be safe than sorry. The irony is that a couple of nice guys I talk to on the block told me they thought I was gay. Isn't that cute? It's because I don't dress in a girly-girl way, see? And I always wear Doc Marten's; they're just so comfortable.

I can only remember being scared once, in the dark. My sister, Patty (have I mentioned her?), locked me in our unfinished basement and then went off to play. I didn't yell, or anything, although I peed my pants. I figured yelling would just get me into more trouble – if not from my mother, then from Patty, for telling. No one missed me until supper, about four hours later, although I wasn't much good at judging time then; I was only about four or five, I think. My legs were chapped from the urine, and my nose was all snotty from crying. I tried to climb up to the top of the workbench that ran under the high window; there was a flashlight there somewhere, I knew, but I couldn't reach it. In the end, Patty snuck down and opened the door. She gave me that look that said I would die if I told Mum.

That basement was the spookiest place I've ever been in. Probably some kids would have been permanently affected by the experience, but not me. I guess, even then, I was too strong-willed to be psychologically damaged. I've never trusted Patty since, of course. Sometimes I catch her looking at me, and I see it: she knows I remember what happened, but she never mentions it.

I don't take much notice of the rest of the house. I'm inside, and heading up the stairs for that attic. It's strange that I'm not even a tiny bit nervous. The house is so still, and the floorboards don't even squeak, and no rodent scitters across my path. The house feel as if it's been waiting for me; how crazy is that? But I believe in good and bad vibes in a place, and this house has nothing but good ones.

At the top floor, I have a choice of two doors – there are two separate attic rooms up here – but I see the golden light under the door of one of them. It *was* waiting for me.

The door sticks a bit as it opens, and then I feel the tiniest chill. Who might be waiting on the other side? This could be my final moment of life. But it's the briefest of thoughts, because now the door is open. There's no one here.

I knew it would be a charming room. The glow from the overhead bulb, no more than 25 watts, I'm sure, has always made the room welcoming. The wallpaper is green-striped, with tiny pink rosebuds running evenly between each stripe, and it seems new, not at all faded. There is a rose velveteen upholstered sofa under the window, obviously an antique, or a very good reproduction, but also oddly fresh and new-looking. There is a small lady's desk and chair, in walnut, I think, nicely polished, and the upholstery on the chair seat is perfect. Two books, '*The Fountainhead*', and '*The Grapes of Wrath*', sit on top of the desk, between two figurine bookends. I've read '*The Fountainhead*', but I don't know the other book, although I think they made a movie of it. I know both books are old, and yet they are in pristine condition…reprints, I guess, with no sign of the yellowing that happens so quickly with books.

The cupboard on the wall opposite the window is empty, except for a crocheted throw in a cream color, draped over a hook on the inside of the door. There is a calendar for 1947 over the desk, a complimentary one from The Dominion Bank, and it doesn't look old either. This is nuts. Even the floor is clean, without a sign of dust. And now I look close up, the windows are clean. They certainly don't look clean from my bedroom; how strange is that?

Then I take a look at this square chest thing, positioned on the side table next to the sofa. I see now that it's not a box, but an old style record player. It says '*Gramophone*' on the front in gold lettering. It's an odd piece of equipment, with a sticking-out handle on the side and I give it a tentative wind. There is a simple On/Off switch next to the turntable, and, when I switch it on, the turntable does what it's meant to do: it turns. I turn it off and quickly look at the paper sleeved old records sitting in the compartment under the turntable. '*The Dancing Years*' on both sides of the first disc, obviously a ballet; '*Cornish Rhapsody*' and '*Warsaw Concerto*' on another; '*I'll Be Seeing You*' and '*We'll Gather Lilacs*', on the third record; '*As Time Goes By*' and '*All the Things You Are*', on the fourth; and the fifth has '*Down the Road A'Piece*' and '*Pine Top's Boogie Woogie*' on the reverse. I put side one of '*The Dancing Years*' onto the turntable, and carefully get it running, with the brass arm in place. It takes a bit of fiddling, and the disc seems to spin impossibly fast, but then the music fills the room, sweetly romantic, in ¾ time (I know music; I took flute at high school).

Whoever stays in this room must be very old. They must be very gentle too, I think, judging by their taste in music – although I'm not sure about the boogie-woogie one. This room is just too well-kept, to homey-looking, to be inhabited by a vagrant or a thug. I might just sit here on the sofa and wait for them to come back. I don't think they'll mind, so long as I explain how I came to see their light. This music is making me feel a bit sleepy: I'll just stretch out on the sofa for a bit. This is such a lovely room. I feel quite at home here.

THREE

I get on well with the people I work with, although they're a very mixed bunch – creative types, for the most part, and more interesting than the average. Of course, not everyone is friendly; I'm thinking of Sandra here. She pronounces it 'Sondra', you know? Totally snobby-sounding. Sandra is our office manager, handles the pays, keeps track of our hours, our sick days…stuff like that. She's very beautiful, in that well-polished look some women have – an impossibility for me, of course, but I admire it in others.

I am nothing much to look at, and I certainly can't be considered even slightly buffed, let alone polished. I do try sometimes, but I don't have the knack. Katie tried to teach me some tricks over the years…how to emphasize my cheek bones with blusher, how to apply eyeliner, but I'm just no good at it. My look is Urban Tomboy, I guess. My sister, Patty, says it's Punk, but it's not; I have never had a piercing in my life, and my hair isn't spiky; in fact, I couldn't get my hair to spike if I wanted to, as it's curly, and refuses to be anything but curly. I wear a lot of black – only black, in fact – it's easier to dress on a budget that way because everything matches. I guess that's why Patty thinks it's Punk. If I were a bit more feminine-looking, I would call it Goth. That can look quite romantic on the right girl.

Sandra doesn't like me, although I'm not sure why. Perhaps it's because she knows how I came to get this job, and feels I don't deserve it. Either way, when she's being a bitch to me, which is often, no one else seems to see it; it's as if she is speaking to me in a foreign language that only I understand. She can spoil my day with just a couple of words, or even with one raised, well-plucked eyebrow.

I like to read during my lunch hour. I'm not a chatty type in the lunch room, particularly as I have little in common with the women here; they all have lovers or husbands or children, and I only have Rupert and my plants, so I have nothing to contribute. The guys here all go out for lunch. Funny that. I think it's because they make more money than the women do.

Nell Roberts is okay. I sometimes talk to her. She's unmarried, too, an older lady – at least forty-five or fifty – but she knows a lot about gardening. She's been tremendously helpful to me with my houseplants…advising about leaf-drop, and brown spot, critters making webs and then eating the leaves, things like that. Sadly, she takes a different lunch hour to me, so we only get together briefly at coffee breaks.

But that Sandra… she worries me so much that when I hear her voice in the hallway, or see her heading towards me, my stomach knots up...I sort of cringe. She knows she has this effect on me, too, and that makes her try even harder. It's downright sadistic, in fact. As I said, she never says anything that anyone else would interpret as nasty, but I know; even when it sounds like a compliment, it's meant to stir me up.

It always does.

I hate confrontation of any kind, and also because I figure, practically, that with her clever mouth she'd be bound to win anyway, I do my best to appear unruffled. Of course, she sees through that.

Her comments are almost always about my appearance (brains are more important in the long run, don't you think?).

"Oh, Strachan," she says, all dimples and *Eternity*, "are you losing weight?"

And I'm not, but everyone turns to examine me anyway. Thing is, I'm not overweight, but my ass is a little larger than I'd like, and, by now, everyone is studying my ass. She always throws things like this at me when everyone is here.

"Oh, Strachan," she says, flashing her newly-whitened teeth, "what a difference eye liner makes on you...you look so pretty!"

The implication here is that I look like shit most of the time – which is probably true, but do I need to be reminded? All the eyes devour me again, and this time someone offers a beauty tip – how to make my mouth look fuller by using lip liner. So I guess I have an over-developed butt, and under-developed lips. What a loser.

All this sounds as if I'm a bit prickly, a touch paranoid, right? Sandra made me this way. I was like an innocent puppy when I first started here, all smiley and friendly to everyone. I just wanted to be liked, because this was my chance to turn my life around. I bought doughnuts for every one each Friday morning; ran down to refill the meter for Dylan's car; taped episodes of *Desperate Housewives* (which I absolutely hated) for Jackie, the art director, while she was on vacation; stayed late numerous times waiting for the Fedex guy; and delivered artwork to clients on the way home – all because I wanted to be accepted. If we hadn't ended up hiring an office junior, I would still be doing those things.

I guess I should be flattered that Sandra bothers with me at all; my mother tried to convince me when I was still in school that girls did this sort of thing when they were jealous. Of course. That's what it is. Sandra is jealous of me. I wish.

Finally – and I'll say no more about it – everyone loves her. She's "so vivacious", "so striking", "so personable", and the office couldn't survive without her. So, on top of being emotionally obliterated by her most days, I can't say anything about it to anyone. They'd think I was nuts. Or a bitch.

Maybe I am. Both. But I wasn't before I came to work here.

I've considered looking for another job. I already said that I think I could earn more somewhere else. But I feel comfortable with everyone else and I've been here such a long time; I get a bit nervous at the idea of starting over with new faces, especially with the possibility of lots of Sandra's in a bigger company. I'd need new clothes, for a start, just for the interview. It's all a bit daunting. I should have more confidence, I know.

But today, after that strange visit to the attic room last night, no one – not even Sandra – can spoil my mood. I've been humming that music…'*The Dancing Years*' theme…all day. I'm not usually a hummer. If anything, I'm more of a whistler, but they don't like me doing that at work; I found that out the first week I came to work here. Dylan pointed out that not everyone was familiar with the scat version of '*How High the Moon*' and to some it could be irritating. I agreed, of course. It might have been worse. I've been known to whistle the full '*Concerto in F*' by *Gershwin*. That would sound pretty odd to unfamiliar ears.

I am full of energy. I don't usually have much of what you could call zest when I get home at night, so something is happening. I take a bath and wash my hair. I haven't been able to stop thinking about the house. I dozed off last night for at least an hour, and no one came. Perhaps they realized I was there and kept away. I'm going back tonight. I want to see this person. I have to understand what that room is all about.

It's very odd that the person who uses this room hasn't returned. Everything is just the same as it was last night, neat and shiny, happy to see me. I feel as if I've just come home. I could move in here, if I had a bathroom and kitchen; that's how comfortable I feel. If I lived here, there would be no Charlie messing up the kitchen, no rap blasting through the thin walls from the next apartment, no bums peeing in the hallway, no rent to pay. Tomorrow, I think I'll check out the rest of the house properly.

I've put on 'Warsaw Concerto' tonight. It's a wonderful piece of piano music, full of passion and longing. That makes me sound as if I know what I'm talking about, doesn't it? Well, you don't have to experience these things to recognize them, do you? In fact, the imagination probably can conjure up more raw emotion than the real thing ever could.

I kneel on the sofa and lean my elbows on the windowsill to press my face against the cold, clean glass. There's my apartment across the way, plants rampant at the windows. It's like looking across at another world. This must be how astronauts feel when they look back at earth from space. This place, right here, is all that counts; this dear room, so quiet and still, is all that matters. The rest of Toronto, wars, recessions, the world...even Sandra – all of it seems light years away.

I'm a secular person, with no experience of the sacred. My parents were the same, and brought me up this way, and then I went on to read all kinds of philosophies that seem to reinforce this in me, so I manage without the usual God or gods. In saying this, I am explaining that I don't believe in the supernatural in any form, pragmatist that I am. Yet standing here, looking out of the window, I am filled with such a feeling of warmth, a sort of spiritual thing, and for a moment I wonder if this is what *Born-Agains* experience when they accept Christ.

Words seem to be forming in my head, strange words – a vocabulary that I'm not familiar with in my usual day. I'm trying to tune in to snatches of memory that I can't quite focus on. I feel I could write some poetry – and I haven't done that since I was fifteen. If I had a pen with me, and some paper, I think I could write it down, these bits of ideas, these half-thoughts, these elegant, tiny phrases.

It's not a poem at all. It's a story. I really could write it down if I had a pen. It's a story about a girl in love. It's not me though – the girl. I know it's not me. This girl is very innocent, unspoiled; I'm neither of those things. Inexperienced? Yes. Innocent and unspoiled? No.

This girl seems to be speaking to me, although that sounds crazy. But you know when you're suddenly reminded to do something last minute - say when you're about to leave the house? It's that little voice that says something like, "Strachan, you forgot your library books." Something like that. Well, it's that kind of voice, coming from inside me, but it doesn't stop talking. It sort of prattles on. Well, prattle is a bit rude. More like meanders on, gently, non-irritatingly.

I'm guessing this voice is what they call the writer's muse, this thing I'm hearing; I've read about it, about how it arrives and takes over the writer's hand as they work. But I'm not a writer. My English is only good because I read so much. It doesn't mean I'm any good at arranging words on a page.

This story, this poetry – whatever – is from this girl's viewpoint. It's starting to become clearer now, and the words are beautiful. She's English. She comes from a place called Boscombe. That weird name just jumps out at me, as if I just read it on a sign. I know nothing much about England, other than the obvious stuff I've seen on TV. And I've read about it in novels, of course. I don't know why, but I imagine this to be Hardy country. I always think Hardy first, ask questions later. I'll eventually get to Dickens.

I love Thomas Hardy, so romantic, so tragic. I guess his is the only writing about love that makes sense to me, where it all leads inevitably to a dismal conclusion. '*Far From the Madding Crowd*' was surprisingly upbeat, though; it had a reasonable ending after all the bodies had hit the dust; and at least Bathsheba ended up with that nice shepherd. It's a shame all of Hardy's books couldn't have been more optimistic, but then I always seem drawn to cynical, realistic books. I did say I wasn't a girly-girl.

19

So I guess this is some sort of historical story. Where on earth is it coming from? I've been reading all of the Harlan Coben thrillers, including those with that detective character I don't care for, and I do like a good thriller. I haven't read any Hardy or other writers of his era for years. I'm trying to remember what movies I've watched lately, but I'm sure there's been nothing related to these ideas teasing around in my head. I'm just not a romantic, and I avoid films that are sentimentally sweet.

But this isn't Hardy's England, after all. The more I concentrate on the little voice, the more I can feel that. It's later. I sense trains – well, they had trains in Hardy's time, didn't they? Perhaps not. But I can picture newer kinds of trains, speedier-looking. And the stations are packed with modern day people – not exactly modern, perhaps from the Thirties because the women's skirts are short, to the knee. It could be the Twenties. But now I see soldiers, many, many soldiers. And there are long lines of children, waiting for something. And now there are sailors, and women in uniform, and lots of hugging and kissing goodbye everywhere. There are men wearing metal helmets, and the children are all getting on the trains. There's a loudspeaker and the woman's voice is garbled and robotic, the words indecipherable. And there are piles and piles of sandbags everywhere.

This is the 1940s, I'm certain. This is war-time Britain.

My sigh is so loud that it wakes me up. I'm lying on the sofa, although I don't recall moving down here from my earlier position at the window. It's late. I've been here almost two hours. I must have napped. The record player has long lost its crank, or whatever you call it, and is silent. I can't remember what I was thinking about. I know there was a girl, in some sort of romantic situation, but I can't remember any of it now.

I wonder if it will come back to me. I must remember to bring pen and paper tomorrow.

As I turn out my lamp, back in my own room, I can't help noticing a new sort of warmth inside me. Rupert snuggles up against me; he missed me tonight. The feeling inside me is like when I was a kid, the night before Christmas – that sort of delicious warmth. Perhaps this is how love feels. Can I be falling in love with a room?

FOUR

As soon as it's dark, I head back to the house. Jimmy commented that he'd seen me in the garden over there, so I have to be more careful; darkness should hide my unorthodox visits. All day, I've been itching for five o'clock to come; it felt like a twelve-hour day.

I have a notebook and pen tonight. I thought I could make the attic into a sort of writing room. Perhaps I was always meant to be a writer, but simply hadn't found an inspirational place to do it. Of course, if the owner does come back, I'll just have to brazen it out.

I've been thinking about that owner. It's weird that someone would just leave a place like this for anyone to walk in. Perhaps they died, or are in hospital.

The minute I open the notebook, after I've put on the record, 'Cornish Rhapsody', the thoughts just start flying. Even as I start scribbling the words down on the page, I am surprised by myself. Who would have thought I had this in me? The date I write at the top is *September 22, 1942*. It must be the old-fashioned music I'm listening to. I don't know where that date came from, but there it is.

The girl's name is Celia. I don't think I've ever met anyone with that name, but I haven't time to think about the strangeness of it, because the pen is rushing across the paper, and I can barely keep up with what's appearing.

She is pretty and she is in love. His name is Alex, and he's a sergeant in the RAF, a Halifax rear gunner. She lives with her parents in Boscombe, Hampshire, although she's in the wafs(?) now and lives in a camp nearby, but she does try to get home when she's not rostered on. The camp where she's billeted is under the jurisdiction of the Boscombe Down air base, although that's over an hour away, and no air ops take place at her camp. It seems to be purely a service depot of some sort. She enjoys her job driving lorries(?), sometimes to remote air bases, delivering supplies, and once or twice having to take shelter beside the lorry because of an air raid. She has chauffeured some military VIPs to London – even an American General! This life is certainly exciting for her, especially compared to the job she had as a secretary to a solicitor in civvy (?) life.

When she first joined up, she believed that it would be fun. There were dances in the camp every Saturday, and that's where she met Alex. She doesn't mind the war; it's brought purpose into her life; she's doing her bit for the war effort. Her mum and dad worry about her of course, but they are proud of her too, understanding that it's something she wants to do – needs to do.

I stretch and re-read the page. I must find out what some of those words are, but it reads wonderfully, so far. Come to think of it, a 'lorry' is a kind of truck I think. Of course it is. 'Civvy' is civilian, I guess. 'Wafs' is strange. I'll look that up on the internet.

The record needs turning over, and then I settle back to the writing again. This time I try not to analyze as I write, because that seems to slow down the flow. This time I just go with it, letting it lead me where it will…

Still being a virgin in this day and age is blooming stupid, Celia thinks. Some might think it's amazing she's hung on so long, because it's not for the lack of opportunity. It seems as if everyone is doing it. Live for today, they say, because tomorrow might never come. Most of the girls in camp are at it like rabbits, and they talk about it, too, which is a bit rude. But she listens in, without looking as if she's too interested, because she needs to know more about it, obviously.

"Don't forget to do a wee after he's pulled it out," Gladys says seriously.

"Oh, I do," replies Martha. "I know all about that."

"Because it will wash it all away," continues Gladys.

"Well, that and a good wash," Doris says. "Weeing is just the first thing."

Margaret joins the group sitting on Gladys's bed. They are a pretty bunch, these girls – and they are barely more than girls. Gladys has a box of Black Magic chocolates, a gift from her American sergeant, and she's sharing with the others, a rare treat for all of them.

"Mum says you should put in a little sponge, just before," Margaret says.

"What's that for then?" asks Gladys.

"It stops his stuff from getting right up inside."

"Haven't you lot ever heard of rubbers?" Evelyn asks, looking a bit bored.

"Rubbers?" Gladys stares at her.

"She means French Letters...*you* know, " Yvonne calls from five beds down.

"Condoms!" Evelyn says firmly. "You *must* have heard of condoms."

Martha and Doris burst out laughing, but stop abruptly when they see Evelyn's expression.

"Thought they was just to stop the clap," Doris says tentatively. She is standing, with her shoes on, in a bowl of warm water. The shoes don't fit, apparently. Out of the water, the shoes will stay on until they dry, however long that takes – she'll probably wear them to bed. In the morning they'll fit perfectly.

Margaret glances towards Celia, who's lying on her bed, pretending to read.

"Are you getting all of this, love?" Margaret calls to her.

Celia looks up, feigning mild surprise. "Pardon?"

"Are you picking up everything we're talking about? It might come in handy for you soon, what with your new bloke."

Celia smiles at them wanly. "We're not like that," she says quietly. "It's different with Alex."

Margaret laughs, and the others join in. "What's different? You mean he doesn't want to do it? What is he then - a pansy?"

"Oh, stop teasing her," Pamela says.

She's the only one in the hut that Celia admires. Pamela was at university when war was declared.

"He's a gentleman," Celia says quietly. Her face is very red.

"Blimey, do you believe that?" Margaret looks at the others who giggle in response.

"They're the worst, if you ask me," Marion says. "While they're being all gentlemanly in the street, they can 'alf get saucy in the back of a cab."

"Well, Alex is always a gentleman. He's not like that." Celia turns over so that her back is to them. As she tries to find her place in the book, she half wishes they were right.

She dies a little every time Alex has a mission. Rear gunners have the most dangerous job, because they're so vulnerable on the plane, which can arrive back at base with all the crew alive, except the gunner. He's positioned at the back, behind the tail of the plane, with no protection, just a glass bubble to sit in.

The doctor told her that her nose bleeds were caused by nerves. He gave her a tonic that's supposed to help. She only has the nose bleeds when Alex is flying. The tonic can't help with that.

When she first met him, he was ground crew, and then in training, but still safe, but then he went into Bomber Command, the 35th Squadron out of Graveley, North of London, and that's when the nose bleeds started.

Her parents have no idea how she feels about him. They're 'going out', her mum tells people, but she doesn't use the more formal word 'courting', which would imply something a bit more intimate. But there is no intimacy, not yet. He is such a nice young man, barely touching her except when they dance, or to put her arm through his when they're walking.

He's kissed her, of course, but it's innocent, just a quick peck on the mouth when he says goodnight. If he knew how she felt, he would be mortified. He's old-school in his manners, not like the new young chaps out there, all mouth, and whistling and hooting as girls walk by. Totally common, they are. Uncouth, her mum says. Alex is always totally couth.

Alex is twenty-five, just right, she thinks, for her nineteen years. He was just completing his degree at Cambridge when the war got going in earnest. He didn't wait to be called up; he enlisted. He could have applied for officer training, but he wanted to be with the "real chaps", he'd said. And even though he is based so far away, he goes to great lengths, hitch-hiking sometimes, to get down to see her. He is a decent man, and you see it in his eyes. He's all serious and sensible one minute, talking about books he's been reading, and the next he's laughing like a schoolboy. When he visits for tea at her parents' on Sundays, they always listen to Arthur Askey on the wireless, because Alex asked them to turn it on specially. Alex laughs so hard that they all join in, whether they think Arthur Askey is that funny or not. Alex is infectious that way. She's laughed so much more since she met him.

Of course, she cries a lot more, too.

September 30, 1942

"Don't forget to take your cardy, Celia," Mum says. "It could turn a bit nippy when the sun goes down."

"Right, Mum," she says.

Her father looks up from his newspaper. "Where's he taking you tonight, then?"

"Concert at the Town Hall. Some pianist," she replies.

"Oh," he says, "all highbrow is it?"

"I expect so," she replies. "Alex likes classical music."

"Funny how he took such a shine to you, isn't it?" Her mother tucks a stray wisp of Celia's hair under her cap. "It's not as if you have much in common, him being from Winchester."

"I don't know," Celia replies. "Are they that different from us in Winchester?"

Her father holds out his hand and rubs his first two fingers and thumb together. "Money, love. That's the difference."

"How do you know that?" She stands in front of the mirror over the mantelpiece, and applies her lipstick sparingly. There is so little left in the tube, and she wonders when she'll be able to get more of the same color.

"The whole area is toffs. Always has been. You'll see, if he ever asks you home." He turns back to his newspaper.

She knows Alex is upper crust, because he speaks so well, so clearly, and he never uses slang. She speaks well, too, because she went to the Grammar school, and they were very pushy about it there. But she knows that her speaking voice is not the same as his. They're a different class, but he doesn't seem to notice.

"They're coming up next week – some business his father has to attend to. Alex wants us to have lunch together, if I can manage the time."

"Ooh," her mother responds, "you're going to meet them. That sounds serious then, doesn't it?"

"Well, best behavior that day, girly," her father says. "Want to make a good impression."

Even as he says it, Celia knows that he doesn't doubt her. Over and above her attractiveness, which he constantly reminds her of, Celia is always charming, even if she does say so herself, and it comes naturally to her. She feels oddly refined, more than her mother probably. Mum tries to be careful with her pronunciation and vocabulary, and she is fastidious with her dress and grooming, but it takes more effort for her, but it had immediately impressed her father when he met her back in 1922. He told Celia once that he had seen her mother across a dance room floor, and decided, right there and then, that she was for him. He had never regretted it. And he constantly reminded Celia that her mother had certainly made a good job of raising their daughter.

"Cold?" Alex asks, touching her hand.

She jumps at the touch. "Oh, no, I'm not," she said.

They sit in the little park near the Town Hall. A lot of the people who'd been at the concert are strolling around; it is a balmy night for so late in the season.

"Dashed good concert! Did you enjoy it?" He turns a little, so that he can see her face.

"Oh, I did," she breathes. "The music was lovely. Say the name again?"

"Debussy. A Romantic if ever there was one."

"It was very sweet, almost sad," she says.

He smiles at her. "A bit like you, in fact."

"What?"

"You. You come across as sweet and almost sad. It's the sort of face you have. You're so pretty, Celia."

She blushes, but he can't see it. The lamps in the park will remain permanently dark until the end of the War.

"Celia?" He leans forward, and reaching out with a gentle hand turns her face towards him. His hand shakes a little. He looks at her for a long moment, and then leans forward and kisses her fully, in a way that she has only imagined.

A warmth spreads through her from her stomach to her chest, and she feels breathless as he moves away from her.

"I've wanted to do that for so long." He seems to be apologizing.

"I wanted you to," she replies.

He puts his arm around her shoulders then, and pulls her closer to him. They stay that way for a very long time, until Celia finally has to admit that she's cold, and he takes her home. At the

26

door, knowing her parents are just inside, she kisses him goodbye quickly on the cheek and lets herself in.

"Nice night was it, dear?" her mother calls from the sitting room.

"Yes, Mum," she replies.

It was the most amazing night of her life.

October 8, 1942

"Mother has been so looking forward to this, Celia." He holds the door open for her. "You'll get on like a house on fire, don't worry."

The restaurant is a bit posh, for Celia's taste. She is never entirely comfortable having waitresses bowing and scraping for her. She prefers to feel that she's one of them, not better than. But it is beautiful, with its crisp white tablecloths, fine china and sparkling silver – real silver, she thinks. Of course, the menu will be tiny, what with the rationing.

She is surprised at how young Alex's parents look, although probably in their mid-forties. Her own father is fifty-eight, and her mother at forty-six looks much older. Alex's mother is glamorous. Alex's father is elegant.

"Ah, at last, Celia," Alex's mother extends her hand, "there you are."

Her hand smells vaguely perfumed, wafting up to Celia as she takes it.

"It's a pleasure to meet you, Mrs. Briard," she says.

"Oh, for heaven's sake, call me Patsy. Even Alex does sometimes, don't you, dear?" She smiles indulgently at her son, then turns back. "This is Alex's father, Harvey."

Harvey is very handsome. He has a small moustache and slicked back dark hair, like a film star. Celia's mother would find him charming.

"Lovely to meet you, Celia. I won't say that Alex has told us a lot about you, but then he's always been a bit of a dark horse." He pats her cheek, but doesn't take her hand.

"Well," Alex says, "I told you she was lovely. That's all you needed to know. I didn't lie, did I?" He stands beaming at her as he pulls out the chair for her to sit down.

"And you're in the WAAFs, Celia. Are you enjoying it?" Harvey asks.

"I am. It's exciting. A bit frightening sometimes, but I'm getting braver. But we all have to be brave now, don't we?"

"Amen," says Patsy. "Remember that poster they used to have in the post office before it all started? 'Keep Calm and Carry On'? It still applies, I think. Although the bombings seem to be getting closer all the time."

"Our next door neighbors had their windows blown out the other night from a bomb in the street behind us," Celia offered.

"Oh, my God, dear girl," Harvey pats her hand. "But you were all right, and the neighbors...?"

"Oh, they're in Scotland. I think they're staying there until the end of the War. And I was at the barracks, on call. Mum says the cat was a bit upset, though. But Mum and Dad were all right."

"Poor animals," Patsy says. "We don't stop to think about how it's affecting them do we? So many must have died."

"Mum's a bit of an animal lover," Alex says.

"Oh, and I am, too," said Celia. "I can't bear to think about them, after the All Clear. They must be so frightened."

"No evacuation for them, is there?"

"Well, some places allow you to take your pets, but I don't think it's too common," Harvey says, pouring weak-looking tea for them all.

"And you were a secretary before, and now you're a driver?" Patsy adds milk to her tea, giving it the appearance of – to use her father's expression – 'pee-water'.

"And a mechanic," Celia laughs. "We have to be able to mend our own lorries. I'm very good at it now."

"I say, well done!" says Harvey. "I could use you on my old Riley. Not that it's much good to me these days, with no petrol."

"And they're threatening to confiscate it for the war effort," Patsy says.

'Not if I have any say in it, they won't. I still have some pull!" Harvey slams his hand down on the table, but Celia sees that he's not genuinely angry.

"Dad's on the Council."

"Oh?" Celia is impressed. She's never met anyone on the Council before.

"But are you safe in Boscombe? I mean, honestly?" Patsy leans forward to study Celia's face. "Harvey says they're after the aerodromes every time they come over."

"Mum and Dad did evacuate early on, but he thinks it's his duty to be at home. And he's a Warden now, so he feels necessary."

"And he was wounded in the Great War, yes? That's why they wouldn't take him this time?" Patsy nibbles on one of the bread rolls. She ignores the pretty curls of margarine on the tiny silver tray.

"He has a bad chest."

"Well, we're luckier," Patsy says. "It's not that Harvey isn't fit enough, but the company he runs is considered necessary to the war effort, so they left him to it. I must say I'm glad. I couldn't bear it if he had to go too. It's bad enough knowing that Alex is out there." She smiled at Celia. " '*For men must work, and women must weep...*' yes?"

"Kingsley, Mother?" Alex asks dryly.

"Oh, I don't know who it is. I just appreciate the sentiment."

Harvey laughed. "Well, don't forget this girl works as well, as hard as any damned man, if she can strip an engine."

And she did work hard. She had developed muscles in her arms she'd never seen before, and took to wearing long sleeves when she wasn't in uniform. The last thing a girl needed was to appear muscular, after all.

I have to stop now, because I am so tired. I can't believe how much I've written. What an era the 40s must have been. Everyone seemed so bright and chipper (?), always with a ready laugh, despite the bombs each night. There was always an excuse for a party, dancing and singing around an old piano. I wish I didn't have to leave – I know that I can only write this story here, in this room. But now I must go home and sleep.

FIVE

Celia, dear, what a joy you are to me. What on earth did I do with my time before you came along? I'm fascinated by the things I'm learning about you and your life. You and Alex are so perfect together, and I can't wait to find out what happens next.

When I was young, I used to imagine this kind of romance. I've become cynical; I've seen some bad stuff. You don't mean it to rub off on you, but it does. Women have a hard time, generally speaking. I'm not a hard and fast feminist, but I do think we still have a long way to go, whatever the law says. I don't need to go into details. I guess we all know what I'm saying.

But listening to Celia, I find myself thinking, just for a little while, that it might be possible. True Love. The Right Man.

Alex seems like the epitome of the hero to me. The Americans say that gunners are a dime a dozen, and the British call them expendable. Such a nasty word, that. How could Alex ever be that?

And off Alex goes on another mission. And Celia again holds a bloody towel to her nose.

"St. Peter wouldn't know what to do with me, if I turned up too soon," he said once, in a pub with some friends.

"As long as I don't have to hose you out when you get back..." one of his friends countered, straight-faced, and the rest of the airmen laughed loudly. The women in the group remained silent.

It was a joke, Celia knew, but she didn't like the sound of it and asked him about it later. He told her it was based on a tiny poem, *"Death of the Ball-Turret Gunner."* He didn't recite it for her. She made a note to look it up at the library.

I checked out the rest of the house tonight. All the rooms are hideously empty, beer cans on the floors, garbage bags filled with God-knows-what, the remains of a tiny fire on the floor of one room, as if someone lit it to keep warm. The toilet in the one bathroom was utilized long after the water was turned off, and is absolutely

30

disgusting. Whoever used it would have been smarter just shitting in a bucket, but Christ knows what kind of people dossed down in here. But it all happened a long time ago. The filth is dried and caked on in the bathroom, and the house is just too dusty and full of cobwebs to have been lived in recently. Yeah, cobwebs. Even so, I've seen no spiders.

I opened the electrical box in the hall on some whim, as I came in. Now this is strange – as if everything else hasn't been - the meter isn't registering. I mean, the power isn't flowing through it. It's only natural that a derelict house would have no power, but to see that little meter, its dial unmoving, frightened me. I have light upstairs, so how is it possible? But then I calmed down. The room itself isn't possible, is it? I have accepted that I'm involved in some sort of supernatural thing. It doesn't spook me, because Celia's story is so sweet, and I know there's nothing evil there. Whatever the reason, the room wants me to know about her. I am delighted that it chose me.

October 20, 1942

Alex is flying tonight. Another night mission. Celia checks under the blackout curtain above her bed, just a crack, to see if the moon is out. The moon is an unwanted, dangerous thing now, and she is relieved to see that there is too much cloud cover for it to be harmful. She doesn't know if she can take much more of this. Each time is becoming harder and harder. Perhaps she'll develop anemia and die, although tonight her nose hasn't bled. It's possible she's becoming stronger, but she doubts it.

She is writing a letter to her mother. She doesn't know when she'll get home again for a while, and likes to stay in touch. Lucy Harrison is regaling some of the other girls with a story, complete with actions, about what happened with the American Air Force colonel she was with last night when he discovered, first hand, so to speak, about cammy knickers (?) Apparently he had tried unsuccessfully to remove said underwear, and, for fear of damaging them irreparably, she had to direct him to the little buttons (?) in the crotch. He was amazed, she says, bloody amazed. She guesses that American women don't wear them.

Of course, Celia can't tell her mother this story. Instead, she writes about Janine's pet white mouse, which she keeps in a biscuit tin with holes punched in the lid in her locker. She lets it out for a run around her bed each night, and strokes and cuddles it. It's escaped more than once, which caused a bit of fuss in the hut; some of the girls aren't too fond of mice, white or otherwise. Someone will report her soon, she's sure. She wonders what will happen to the poor mouse then.

Celia wishes she could tell Mum about her feelings when Alex is away. Did Mum ever feel like this about Dad? Her parents are so placid with each other, so undemonstrative, it's difficult to imagine that they were ever in love. And as for doing it together – well, that's impossible.

She always assumed that sex was a relatively simple thing, believing her mother's offhand, if shy, comments on how it would all come naturally on the night, and having read a few books that seemed to indicate a fairly swift interaction, after some kissing and gentle caressing. As these books mostly indicated the act itself with a series of asterisks, she was left with her own interpretation of how things proceeded.

But since she's been eavesdropping of late, she's come to realize that there might be more to it than she'd imagined. She's certainly heard one of the girls speak about how impossible it was for her to do it standing up. Why on earth would someone want to do it that way? No film she's ever seen showed the heroine leaning up against a wall, or standing in a doorway, just as the scene faded to black. That's why people spoke of "going to bed", wasn't it? So that they could be horizontal, as nature intended.

She does have a lot to learn. Alex will teach her. Of course, that's assuming that Alex knows these things.

"It suits you, Strachan. You should get it." Katie is squeezed into the corner of the fitting booth, her head on one side.

I look at my reflection. The dress is a pretty color, and the fabric feels very nice on my skin, but I'm not a frock person. For the life of me, I can't imagine how Katie talked me into being here, in this tizzy up-market shop. I never go to the Eaton's Centre, let alone a boutique-y place like this. I buy a lot of my clothes at Goodwill, because there is such a huge variety, and it's not because I'm trying to save money, but for the recycling aspect of buying there. I am quite Green.

"I haven't worn a dress since Dad died." I twist round so that I can see my rear view. My ass looks rather sexy, in fact. But I need different shoes. My Doc Marten's give me an 80s Madonna look, a bit too dated even for me.

"Oh, come on, Strachan," Katie pats my shoulder, "you're getting too old for that grunge thing. It's time to be more womanly." She catches her own reflection in the mirror and tips her face on an angle the better to admire herself.

"I don't know where I'd wear it." I like the way it buttons down the bodice. Celia has a dress very similar to this, not that she gets to wear it much as she always seems to be in uniform, but she wore it the last Sunday that Alex visited for tea.

"Spring's here. It will be getting warm soon, and you always complain about being hot. It's all that black. It holds the heat in." Kate reapplies her lip gloss.

"It does feel nice." My face seems paler against the green of the dress, my eyes darker. Even my hair seems to have a reddish cast which I've only ever noticed in bright sunlight.

"Get it!" Katie stamps her foot. "And we'll find some other stuff. And shoes, proper shoes."

"All this money..." The dress is worth a whole day's pay, I notice.

"You never spend anything on yourself."

She's right, I don't. I buy treats and toys for Rupert, or things for the apartment, but rarely for me. I don't seem to need much.

"Well," I say, "let's not go overboard."

"You should get one of those cosmeticians to do your face too, just to show you."

"You tried to show me, remember?" Katie's face is always perfect, right down to the minute swish of glaze across her lips.

"Well," she replies, "that was using my makeup. We have different coloring. Yours is more European, and mine is California."

Katie is a golden-skinned blonde. Both colorings are artificial, but they suit her. When we were kids at school, her hair was as dark as mine. Her skin is enhanced to the 'California tan' with some cream from a bottle. She is very pretty, all the same. I haven't seen her in weeks, because she is always off limits to me when she has a new guy in her life; come to think of it, Katie always seems to have a new guy in her life.

In the end, despite my protests, we bought quite a lot. I don't know what happened to me. But I certainly have the cash, even a credit card that I never use, and it felt good, if I'm honest. I had a sort of butterfly feeling in my stomach the whole way home.

I hate having to wash the makeup off tonight, because it does make me look a bit more interesting. Perhaps I should practice on the weekend. The cosmetics cost me over a hundred dollars, so I'd better be able to put them to some use.

"What are you up to over there?" Jimmy faces me in the hallway as I come in from work tonight.

"What do you mean?"

"Over at the old house. What are you doing over there?"

He's been eating some sort of garlicky food, and his breath reeks of it. I step back a bit.

"Why is it any of your business, Jimmy?"

He glares at me. "It's not, I guess. But it's dumb, being in a place like that all hours."

I search for my earlier version of an excuse, which I'd concocted casually some days before.

"I'm doing a sketch of this apartment building, of my place, from there. Drawing it, you know."

His face crinkles in disbelief. "Drawing it?"

"Just for a keepsake. One day I can look at it and remember it."

"You could take a photograph from downstairs. Why do you need to draw it? And why from inside the house?"

I shrug. "Well, after all, it's still a bit chilly at night. I do it inside to keep warm."

"And what's wrong with a photograph?"

"It's not the same. I like to draw. A drawing is a piece of art."

"It must be a weird drawing, if you're doing it in the middle of the night."

"I capture the play of light – you know – light and shadow." I'm beginning to sound lame. I didn't think I'd need to continue my lousy excuse for this long.

He scratches his chin, studying me. "You're a weird one, I'll say that."

"How so? Just because I like to draw?"

He shakes his head. "There aren't too many broads who would go into an empty building at night, especially around here. That's weird."

"I don't scare easy." I meant easily, but he didn't notice. "I'm not your usual woman."

He studies me with obvious disdain, taking in my black jeans, my black raincoat, my Doc Marten's and my somewhat wet hair. It's raining tonight. Ah, spring is springing.

"No, you're not, are you?" He turns to walk away, and then stops and looks back. "You're not doing dope with your buddies over there, are you? I mean, I have to live here too, you know. It wouldn't look right, you being a tenant and all. Give the place a bad name."

Sure, but bums can sleep in our hallway, right, Jimmy?

I tut at him. "Oh, for fuck's sake, Jimmy – no, I'm not! I don't do that shit." I push past him up the stairs, wanting to say more, but he's silent, and I realize I've shut him up – perhaps for good on that subject. I've always been very polite to him. He's probably in shock.

December 4, 1942

Alex and Celia's romance is heating up. He's kissed her quite a lot since that first night, and now she enthusiastically kisses him back. I find myself squirming in the chair as I write this, because it's actually exciting me – talk about not getting any. I mean, I don't miss sex; they say you can't miss what you've never had, and I've never had it in any truly fulfilling way. But this thing of theirs...well, it feels real to me, as if I am Celia, and Alex has his hand on *my* breast – on the outside of my uniform, of course. No man has ever touched my breast (you can't count Russell). I put my hand down and cup myself as a man might. It does feel good, but only because I'm imagining that it's Alex.

"We could go next weekend. I'm off until Sunday night," he says, his mouth against her ear.

She wipes the film of perspiration from her upper lip and sighs. "I don't know if I can swap with anyone..."

"Please, Celia. Try for me. Every time I go, I think it's the last time I'll see you. I can't stand it." He rolls away from her and sits up, fumbling in his pocket for his cigarettes.

They are in the wooded area above the promenade, not far from her parents' house, a place for walkers and their dogs, for children to run, but they are hidden deep within the trees, well back from the path, sitting on a carpet of damp, cold pine needles. He lights two cigarettes and hands her one.

"Lucy might do it," she says. "Her colonel is leaving next week, and she wanted a couple of extra nights with him."

"Try, darling," he says urgently, leaning in to her and kissing the side of her mouth, one hand lingering on her thigh.

Alex is losing his gentlemanly attitude. That's what wars can do, I guess.

I wear my new dress to work today, with the beige Mary-Janes. I even put on the tiniest bit of makeup and clip a barrette in my hair where it always falls down over my eyes. When I first considered doing this, I decided I couldn't go through with it, but then I looked out of the window, which is now open a few inches, and I could hear the birds, and see the leaves forming on the trees outside, and feel the slightly warm breeze. I suddenly couldn't bear the idea of putting on my usual black gear.

"Strachan!" Peter is standing at the door of my alcove. Peter is one of our sales guys. He's quite handsome, but not my type. What is my type, I wonder?

I shake my head at him. "What?"

"What have you been doing to yourself, babe? You look like a girl."

"I am a girl."

He laughs. "You know what I mean. You look like a regular girl."

"Thanks, Peter. I'll take that as a compliment."

He raises his eyebrows, and bounces his head a bit, side to side. "You look good."

I swivel round on my chair and stretch out my legs towards him. "Look, girl shoes, too."

"Oh, my God. You've abandoned the Doc Marten's."

"I felt like a change."

"Brave you," he says. "I can imagine what a hard time everyone's going to give you." As he walks away, he calls back over his shoulder, "You'll give Sandra a run for her money now."

I reach down to my bag, and pull out the little compact that came with all the other stuff I bought for my face. I look at myself in the mirror. I do look good. My face seems brighter, lighter, as if it's under one of those golden lights that Bruce uses in Photography. This makeup thing is quite miraculous. But compete with Sandra? I don't think so.

SIX

I'm at home, sitting on the couch in the living room, reading the newest pages for the second time, when Charlie walks in. I can't remember when I last saw him, but it's been over a week, and on that occasion he was dashing out the door as I was coming in, so we hardly spoke.

"How come you're still up?" he asks, throwing his jacket over the back of a chair and kicking off his shoes.

He never hangs his jacket up in the hallway, although I just put up a nice coat hook that I bought at Canadian Tire. He never takes his shoes off at the door, either, regardless of the weather outside and the amount of slop that comes off them onto the rug.

"Reading," I say, indicating the pages, and fuming about the jacket. "Will you hang your jacket up, please?"

He flops down in an armchair. "Yeah, later." He eyes my notebook. "What is it?" He lights a cigarette.

"It's a book I'm writing," I reply. There, I said it. I told someone.

He coughs a bit, and pulls himself awkwardly erect. "You're what? Writing a *book*? You gotta be kidding me."

"Why is it so odd? Don't you think I'm smart enough?"

He is checking out my face, gauging what he should say.

"It's not that. I guess you're pretty smart. You sure read a lot. But...you know, you're not the type." He reaches sideways for the ashtray.

"What type is that, Charlie?"

"Well...you know – the artsy type. Like Rhonda." He gets up and walks out to the kitchen where I hear him plugging in the electric kettle.

I knew he'd say her name. My teeth almost grind when I hear it. Rhonda Harrold is a friend of Charlie's, – in fact, I think she's a regular lay of Charlie's, but I've never asked. She is a patronizing, snobby, sharp-eyed superbitch. Without doubt, she's worse than Sandra, who is, after all, not particularly bright from what she's revealed by her TV viewing habits. But Rhonda is a 'talented newcomer', as they say, having written and published two non-fiction books (non-fiction, for God's sake!), '*China – The Only Certainty*', and '*Jesus – Hebrew Hustler?*' (She's fond of titles with dashes in them.) Both books got rave reviews, although not in any mainstream magazine or paper, but certainly in alternative publications. From what I can gather (I refuse to read them), they are very clever. When you consider that Rhonda is just twenty-four years old and only two years out of York University, it's a bit deflating. When you meet her face-to-face, it's downright alarming, because she is very pretty with a great figure, and long, blonde, tossable hair – you know the kind that is swept back with languid fingers and which falls perfectly back to the original face curtain?

I squint evilly at Charlie as he sits down again.

"Rhonda isn't typical of any particular profession, Charlie. And, anyway, she writes non-fiction." I point to my notebook. "This is more your literary fiction, if you're interested. It's a whole different game."

"You're just jealous of her, Strachan. She gets to you."

Rhonda has won all sorts of scholarships and awards, which she is currently 'considering', unwilling to rush to accept something that might prove detrimental to her career down the road, and she is pursuing (her word) a Masters in political science. She never includes inferior mortals in her conversations, once turning to me during a particularly boring discussion about the Shah of Iran, and saying, "Oh, poor Strachan, don't bother trying to follow us, pet. We're just talking shop."

I glare at Charlie. "If you know that, then why bring her up? I mean, if you know how much she bugs me."

He has made a cup of instant coffee. He didn't offer me one, although I prefer the properly-brewed kind. Perhaps he remembered that.

"Dunno, Strachan. You sort of bring it out in me." He grins. "It's like you're always expecting a put-down – waiting for it."

"Like a loser, right?"

"I guess," he says, and sips his coffee.

"I took you in when you had nowhere to go, Charlie."

He stares at his feet. "I know you did. I appreciated it."

"You have a funny way of showing it." I realize that I have tears in my eyes.

He looks up at me then. He's not an unattractive man, although he's a bit too thin, and the way his longish hair falls into his eyes make his nose a bit beak-like. He cultivates this effect. He thinks he looks intellectual.

"In fact, I'm moving out," he says. "I found a place over on the Danforth."

"Oh," I say. "Well, that's good then, isn't it?"

"Yeah, nice to have a place of my own where I can do what I like, you know."

He already does what he likes here, but he doesn't see that.

"When are you moving?"

"First of the month. It gives me time to pick up some bits for the place."

I nod at him, no longer angry. I realize that it will be strange not having him coming and going at all hours. I can't believe it, but I've gotten used to having him around.

"So," he settles back in his chair, "what's the book about?"

I stand up then, and turn towards my room.

"You wouldn't be interested, Charlie. It's all about love."

Most girls are prettying themselves up on a Saturday night, preparing for a date. Well, I have a date of sorts tonight – but not with a man – with my attic.

The now familiar warmth greets me as I enter the room. I hang my coat and scarf on the hook behind the door and remove my boots. I won't need boots for much longer, because most of the snow is gone, and there's nothing much forecast. Soon it will be proper shoes weather all the time, because I'm beginning to like the Mary-Janes I've been wearing at the office. I'm going to buy some more girl shoes, in different colors. I don't know what's come over me, clothes-wise.

Within moments of starting to write, I notice that I'm breathing shallowly; it always happens. I've gradually moved closer to my notebook, too, leaning in to it, my nose is only a couple of inches away from the page. Concentration or short-sightedness? Perhaps I need glasses.

In just twenty minutes I've completed three closely-written pages. I stretch and lean back, rotating my stiffening shoulders, as I read:

December 8, 1942

Celia is close to losing her virginity. She's certainly thinking about it a lot these days. She's allowed Alex to reach beneath her skirt a couple of times, and became quite breathless as he touched the soft skin of her thigh above her stockings. He moved his hand no further than that, but she found she had wanted him to. She has started to imagine his body against her, moving against her, but can't picture the act itself. She has no idea what to expect, but thinks it must be the most delicious feeling ever, somewhat like sliding slowly down into a hot bathtub, with soft foamy water caressing every body crevice.

I've got news, Celia. It's not a bit like that.

Betty Friedan had a sizeable impact on me when I was 16. I absorbed her doctrines religiously, although a few kids pointed out that Friedan was old hat. It's true the book I borrowed from the library was first published in the 60s and probably had more relevance for my mother, who had never read it, but it still made sense to me. I wanted a career and, just maybe, a man – in that order. No vegetating in suburbia for me, no sir. It wasn't difficult to follow Ms. Friedan's teachings because I was such a blob, so unappetizing, and unlikely to fall victim to the prison of marriage. There was no temptation to speak of. All the other girls in school seemed so formed by then, more or less the way they would look and act as adults. I was formed too, I thought, with a round, blank-looking face that seemed to indicate a lack of intelligence. This was humiliating to me because I considered myself very smart, and no one could see that by looking at me. I wanted wise eyes, a knowing smile, a cool, appraising expression. I had none of these, although I did practice a lot with a mirror.

But Russell James didn't seem to mind. He was in my home room and I would catch him looking at me. Well, to be honest, I would catch him looking at my breasts. This in itself was clever of him, because I wore such bulky sweaters or oversized shirts, that my boobs were quite overwhelmed by fabric. But somehow he knew -

41

or seemed to think, by his expression - that wondrous mysteries lay just under the thickish surface of my clothes.

I was very curious about sex. Many of the girls I hung around with had already tried it, or at least touched a penis. I'd only seen a penis in art magazines, and flaccid, uninteresting things they were, too. Anyway, I started to get excited at the prospect of Russell's hands on my breasts. From there, it was easy to take the fantasy the next step.

Russell was a smart boy, went on to become a computer programmer. His drawback was his stammer. He was terribly shy, and the speech impediment didn't help, or vice-versa.

Nothing would have happened if I hadn't made the move.

I arranged to study with him – history, as I recall, which wasn't a difficult subject for me, but I told him it needed polishing to get my grades up. As he'd never followed my grades, he had no idea I was already getting straight As.

Once we were in his living room, with his parents out at their regular Friday night Bingo, we didn't even open the books, because Russell sort of jumped at me. In an instant, his hands were on my boobs, rubbing them around and around violently. I stopped him and showed him how to do it gently and slowly. It felt so good then, that I quickly took off my top and bra and let him get stuck right in. Oh my God, I had no idea how wonderful someone's hands and mouth could feel! Of course, it was all completely out of control by then and the next thing I knew, my jeans were off, and then my pants, and I was flat on my back on the floor, and Russell was trying to do what boys like to do best. And I saw his penis! He seemed to enjoy me looking at it and kind of wagged it at me.

It hurt. No one had ever mentioned pain. He prodded hard, and I moaned; he thought the moan was joy and prodded some more. I wriggled and he thought I was getting off on it. And then Russell came, in a shuddering, jerky sort of movement. I didn't have to be told what had happened; recognition of the human orgasm must be instinctive. It had taken about two minutes; I also instinctively knew that it was meant to take a bit longer.

Russell pulled away then, without looking at me. In fact, he'd barely looked at my face during the whole thing. His face was all washed-out and blank, and he was breathing a bit heavily.

I pulled up my pants and jeans where I lay, and then reached for my shirt and pulled it over me, suddenly feeling terribly vulnerable.

"Are you all right?" he asked, as he zipped himself up. He didn't stammer. I had cured him.

"Of course I am," I replied.

"I mean, can you take care of it...?" he nodded towards my nether area.

He was worried I might get pregnant. Shit, I hadn't even thought about that, but I needed to sound cool. He didn't realize I was a virgin, after all.

"I'll be fine. Chill," I said.

And then Russell picked up the history book, after pushing the coffee table slightly forward to cover the damp spot. The thing is, the James's aren't the kind of people who replace floor coverings too often, so his sperm, long dead and desiccated, is probably there still, deep in the tufts of the wall-to-wall carpeting in their living room.

I wonder if he ever thinks about that when he goes around there for Sunday lunch with his wife and two kids.

Anyway, I digress. Celia has no idea how much this is going to hurt...

"What's happening to you, Strachan?" Katie asks, running the tip of her little pink tongue along her upper lip to remove the slick of cappuccino foam there.

"You mean the clothes? – You started it!"

"Well, it's not just the clothes, is it? You're wearing the eyeliner, and it looks good. And lipstick. I can't believe I had that much influence over you. Is it a guy?"

"No," I say, and sip my coffee.

We are sitting outside a nice place on Wellesley with a patio area out front, and the sun, although not strong yet, warms us all over, radiating over our bare arms. It's the first day we've been able to go out without a jacket. Katie still doesn't have a new man, so this is a treat for me, seeing her twice in one week.

"So, why the change? In all the years we've known each other, I've never seen you like this."

I brush a fly away from my cup. Ah, Spring! "It's complicated, but I think my life's taking a new direction."

"You're leaving Dylan's! Oh, wow, Strachan, that's fantastic! I knew you would in time..."

"I'm not leaving the job – well, not yet. It's something else. I'm writing this book. I think I might be able to get it published."

Katie puts her cup carefully onto the saucer. "You've written a book." It wasn't a question.

"It's early days, yet. But it's looking pretty good to me. I have to get someone to read it – you know, someone who knows about that kind of thing."

"An editor?"

"Well, I was thinking of Nell at work. She reads hugely. I figure she could say whether or not it's any good."

"What's it about?"

"I know you'll think it's weird, but it's about England during the Second World War, about this guy and girl who fall in love. It's a love story, I guess."

Katie starts to laugh, and then stops suddenly, and frowns. "Strachan? How could you know about that stuff? No, I didn't mean that - I meant, *why* would you write about that stuff? You've always been so practical and down-to-earth. You never see chick movies, I know that. You've told me lots of times you don't believe in all that romance crap – and *that's* what you call it, so don't deny it."

"It's complicated..." I say again. "When it's finished, I'll show you, and tell you how I came up with the story."

"And that's why you're changing your look? So you seem more like a romance writer?"

I hadn't considered that. "I don't think that's why. But I'd like a change. I don't feel quite so cynical, you know? Somehow my clothes made me that way, I think."

"They certainly depressed me." Katie smiles. "And you look nice, girl. You'll be finding your own romance if you keep this up."

"Yeah, like *that's* ever going to happen..."

"You never know. I don't know how you live without having a guy in your life. It's shitty being alone. I'm going nuts myself."

"I've always been alone. It's not shitty at all."

"But no sex! I don't know how you do it..." Katie sighs.

"That's because you get so much of it. You're addicted."

Katie laughs. "I am, aren't I? Nothing wrong with it, is there?"

"I guess not. Better than booze or drugs, anyway."

"Oh, right, and you'd know all about that, too, yeah?" She squeezes my hand where it rests on the table. "Get yourself laid. Do you a whole heap of good."

"Toss one of your cast-offs my way, and I might consider it. I mean, how else would I find someone?"

"You should come out at night more. You never go anywhere. I've met most of my guys at parties and bars."

"Don't think so, Katie. Thanks all the same. You know I'm not into the bar scene."

"Yet you don't seem to have much luck at the library, either, for all the time you spend there."

"Mm, guess I just don't look available."

She smiled. "Well, you do today. You're learning how to be a girl. Who knows what else you're capable of?"

December 14, 1942

Alex never speaks of his missions. Of course, he can't; *Loose Lips Sink Ships, Careless Talk Costs Lives,* as they say. Celia wants to know how he feels when he flies, longs to find out what his experiences are, so that she can feel even closer to him. But Alex isn't forthcoming. If he had close friends, she would have spoken to them, but he seems close to no one, except to her and to his parents. She'd asked him once about one chap he knew, another flyer, Martin; they had gone out together with him and his girlfriend. She was interested. Where was Martin from? Where did his parents live? Alex replied that he didn't know, that he'd never asked him. Yet they'd appeared chummy enough, like friends.

"They can't form close friendships. Didn't you know that?" Margaret tells her when she mentions it back in their hut.

The rest of the girls look a bit uncomfortable, she notices, and they look away.

Gladys looks over at her, strangely sympathetic in that moment.

"They don't know if they'll ever see each other again, don't you see? So many blokes dying each day. It's not worth the effort."

Celia frowns. "I hadn't thought about it..."

"They have some soppy ideas. Some of them think they have better odds for the next time, each time they make it back." Gladys looks around the room and then back to Celia. "I think that's a load of codswallop." So much for sympathy.

"Anyway, don't get too involved, if you know what I mean," Margaret says. "It's all a bit of fun. Keep it that way."

Gladys is still studying her. "I think she's got it bad, poor bitch."

Celia looks squarely at her. "I love him. I can't just switch it off like you do."

"God love you, then. You're bound to get hurt."

Celia drops her eyes, because they are filling with tears.

It's time for me to go home. I suddenly have a need to cuddle Rupert, safe and sound in my own bed.

SEVEN

Nell looks up at me with a somewhat confused, wondering, expression. "Can I take them home?" She pats my notebooks in front of her. "I can't read them all here."

I gave them to her when I first arrived at work. I've filled four so far, and I know there's a lot more to come.

"Of course, I didn't mean you to read them now. You got a quick look, didn't you?"

She shakes her head. "I don't know what to say, Strachan. I just read a random dozen pages, but I'm so impressed. I can't believe it, knowing you all this time, talking to you. You never said a word..."

"Well, I only started a few weeks ago. I mean, I only just started writing."

"But it's so beautifully crafted, dear. You must have done other things, perhaps when you were younger? No one just starts out this well. They say it takes years to become a good writer."

"Well, I wrote a few poems when I was in school, but they were pretty shitty. I mean, I didn't show anyone. They were teenage crap – all doom and gloom and wallowing in self-pity. The usual."

She sighs heavily. "I'll read as much as I can tonight, and let you know what I think tomorrow, is that all right? I don't think I'll feel any differently, though. From what I've seen, you should be able to find an agent for it." She shakes her head again. "I just can't believe it. How secretive of you."

"Do you think it's that good, that someone might want to publish it?"

"I'd be surprised if someone doesn't jump at the chance. You've got a great story, as far as I can tell, and you're so young yourself, which would be of enormous interest, and you've never even been to England, let alone have any knowledge of that war. It's amazing. I suppose the internet is as great as they say for researching. I should reconsider getting it at home."

Nell is our bookkeeper and deals with all the intricacies of the company's accounting system, using the most up-to-date program, yet she's done nothing more than play on the internet here at the office, once or twice, she confessed to me ages ago. It's funny how many people have no urge to get involved with it. I guess, like sex, if you've never known it, you have no idea what you're missing.

"By tomorrow, I should have more," I say. I have an appointment with the room tonight.

"Ah, the writing urge is upon you, yes?"

"Mm," I respond.

"Good for you, Strachan. I'm very proud of you. It must be wonderful to be a writer. I always wanted to be, when I was younger, but I just didn't seem to have enough passion for it. I'd start things, and then just let them slide."

"Well, as I said, I never thought of myself as a writer, either." After all, it's not *me* who makes up all the wonderful words and sentences that fill the notebooks on Nell's desk. I'm not sure I want to know how I do it. Perhaps it's an obscure kind of madness, or some kind of savant autism that's never been diagnosed. I've always known I'm not what you would call conventional. I'm definitely oddball, even as I try to fit in with the mainstream.

"Tomorrow, then." Nell turns back to her computer. "I must get on, dear. Month-end's coming up, and Dylan gets very stressed if it's not finished on time."

"Thanks for doing this, Nell. You're the only one I trust to read it."

She turns back to me. "Am I? How sweet of you. I hope I can live up to your faith in me."

"Oh, you will. You're one of the few people I know who cares what I think."

She smiled. "Strachan, I've told you before – you must have more confidence in yourself. You have such a good mind, and yet you don't let anyone see it. You're what's known as a dark horse, with hidden talents."

I laugh. "Well, if we get this thing published, it might be hard to stay a dark horse, right? I'm not sure how I feel about that."

She pats my arm. "Come on, let me do my work. We'll talk tomorrow. I'll change my lunch hour and we'll go to the park, all right?"

I return to my alcove feeling very good. I've shown someone Celia's story. It's very exciting to think that Nell will soon be sharing it. I have a hard time getting back to the cereal box graphic I'm working on. It sounds like creative work, right? It's not. It's just me manipulating a program, doing a bit of tweaking, turning Jackie's draft into a file that's ready for printing. I might just as well be working on Nell's month-end.

December 19, 1942

"*We'll meet again...*" the girl at the microphone sings. Celia listens to the words carefully, awed at how much they affect her. She checks to see if Alex has seen the tears forming in her eyes, but he is watching the singer, a small smile on his face. Men are so practical and she longs to be that way herself, at times. It's a terrible burden, this love she has for him. Sometimes, dreamlike, she tries to imagine that she had never met him. Life would be so much easier for her.

The singer finishes and nods at the crowd's applause and steps off the tiny stage. The pub they're in is just one of many in the area. It's small, with perhaps twenty tables, but has become a haven for the WAAFs and their friends, being so close to their camp.

Alex turns to her. "So, if you can't swing the time off this weekend, when do you think?"

"Not until after Christmas. The girl I was swapping with got *jankers (?)* for coming back late from leave. *And* she'd lost her cap. Sergeant in Charge Kilpatrick is a real bugger, I told you. He had her cleaning out the lavatories this morning. He's always looking for an excuse to put someone on a bloody charge. No one else will do it, because they want to try to get home for Christmas Day."

Funny how she curses now. Before she joined up, she'd never so much as used 'damn'.

"Little Hitler, is he?"

"Bus driver in civvy street, can you believe it? It's a wonder he taught any of us to drive the way he handles a lorry. Rides the gears the whole time." She shakes her head. "Bus driver..." She pushes a loose strand of hair back into the coiled roll at the back of her head – *must keep the hair off the collar*. "Of course, it's obvious he hates women."

"Pansy?"

She looks at him and frowns. "No, I don't think so. He likes looking at Gladys when she has her jacket off – you know what I mean. He stares at her bosom. It's just that he seems to hate her, the way his eyes are, even while he's looking..." She shivers. "He's a bit creepy."

"As long as he doesn't look at you like that." Alex touches her cheek with a finger. "He doesn't, does he?"

"Not that I've noticed." She smiles and glances down at her chest. "Of course, Gladys has a bigger chest than I have." She knew he would look.

"You have a lovely chest," he says, leaning in to whisper it.

She blushes and her heart does that silly flip-flop.

"But the first week in January is certain," she quickly says. "I've already seen the roster. So you can go ahead and arrange it – but in Bournemouth, Alex. Not Boscombe. Just in case someone sees me."

"Leave it to me. Shouldn't have too hard a time getting a room."

"Don't forget that new lot from the Canadian training course. They're all billeted around there."

He frowns. "The new chaps, yes. But I can't believe they'd take up all the rooms. They're are dozens of hotels."

"Just reminding you. It's not just Canadians, either. Aussies, South Africans – they were all in Canada for training. Can't remember how many...Margaret was telling me about it."

"If the worst comes to the worst, we can always go up to Winchester. Mum and Dad wouldn't mind."

She stares at him. "Stay at your parents? Alex! I couldn't do that!"

"They're very broadminded. They like to see me happy."

"Well, they're not going to see you happy with me. At least, not that way." She glowers at him. "For God's sake, Alex, how can they be so casual about such things?"

"Generation they're from, I suppose. You know – the naughty Twenties."

Celia doesn't know. Her own parents describe the era in more serious terms, often mentioning how poor they had been. Her own parents aren't toffs, have never been to a night club in their lives, while Alex had told her that his parents go regularly to a particular West End club to meet up with friends.

Celia studies him. "Do they truly like me, Alex?"

He laughs. "They *love* you, Celia. They think you're the sweetest thing."

"And they think I'm good enough for you?"

"What's brought this on?" he asks, signalling to the waiter for more drinks.

"I just don't understand why they wouldn't want someone from their own circle going out with you. Some of their friends must have daughters."

"But it's you I want." He squeezes her hands in his. "You silly girl, Celia. You don't see how happy you make me, but they see it. They dote on me, bless 'em."

She withdraws her hands from his, and sits quietly as the waiter puts their drinks on the table.

"Anything to make you happy, is it?" she asks then.

"Well, within reason, sweetheart." Alex says. "I mean, they'd draw the line if I bought home some tart."

She smiles. "Thank goodness for that, then. " She sips her drink.

"They love you, Celia. You have nothing to worry about there."

But Celia isn't convinced.

I've managed to find out quite a lot on the internet to explain those odd words that I've used. I've corrected my spelling in my notebooks, too, where I could. Anyway, I've done this summary – Nell is going to need it too:

- *WAAF*   Women's Auxiliary Air Force
- *Lorry*   Truck
- *Cami-knickers*   Camisole/pants in one, *accessible by unfastening crotch buttons (ouch!)*
- *Jankers*   Nothing on this - disciplinary action?

I think the worst is over for the need to translate. As I get into sync with the voices, I seem to be able to understand what's being said more and more. Oh, and when Lucy left her cap on the train, she called it her *"titfer"*. This is Cockney rhyming slang - *Tit for Tat* = *hat*.

I'll have to be careful with this new vocabulary. I'd look a right twerp if I started using their funny expressions around the office. Like that...*right twerp*?

Celia went to the library and got help from the librarian about the ball-turret gunner poem that Alex wouldn't explain. She wrote the words down carefully from the little volume of poetry she was given, and shivered at the last line. I've already checked it out and it made my eyes well up.

Poor Celia.

I am whistling very quietly in my alcove, when Rod Brewer suddenly sticks his head over my screen.

"What's that tune, Strachan? Was that *'We'll Gather Lilacs'*?"

I look at him, trying to judge what words I should produce. Dummy, Strachan! This has got to stop.

"Yeah, it was one of my Gran's favorite songs."

"And you know it?"

"Yeah – well, it looks like *you* know it, too."

"I was in our local theatre group's production of *'Perchance to Dream'* a while back. It's hard to forget something you rehearsed a hundred times." He studies me over the screen, his chin resting on the top.

"Oh," I say. "It's pretty, isn't it?"

"Not quite you, I'd have thought..."

"What, you figure me for *Metallica* or something, right?"

"Something like that." He moves around into the alcove and stands beside me. "Although, you've changed lately. Not so in-your-face as you were. What happened? You gotta a new guy?"

I never had a guy, new or otherwise, but I'm not telling him that.

"Yeah, I guess..." I pat my hair. "Guys like a more feminine look, right?"

"Good for him." He smiles. "You look nice, Strachan. It suits you." He turns to leave, then looks back. "I'm not sure about that music though. People will start thinking you're a bit strange." He laughed. "Your grandmother's favorite song...that's so funny."

"I liked my grandmother."

"Yeah, me too mine. But I'm not about to start singing Sinatra classics around the office. Gran is a big Sinatra fan."

"There's nothing wrong with old music," I say. "Some rapper does a re-mix and suddenly everyone's into it."

"Yeah, I guess." He walks away, calling back, "Cute, Strachan. Very cute."

January 5, 1943

Alex has booked a room at the Excelsior Hotel right in the heart of Bournemouth. It's a spectacular looking building, all columns and balconies, painted cream, with formal landscaping in front, although that's marred by the sandbags piled along the sides of the short drive. Celia is impressed, realizing that it's far posher than anywhere she's been before.

"Like it?" Alex asks, as they walk up the steps.

"It's beautiful," she says. She thinks the foyer looks a bit like the Victoria and Albert Museum, but doesn't think the comment would go over well with Alex.

The whole vast reception area is filled with servicemen and women, with very few civilians – and those are elderly. Kitbags and helmets and gas masks are littered around the banquettes and chairs and some people are stretched out on the tiled flooring, using their kits as bolsters.

"It's terribly crowded, Alex," she whispers, as they reach the desk.

"Just wait over there, Celia." He points towards the lifts. "I'll just be a minute."

A group of American flyers makes way for her as she tentatively walks to the lifts, murmuring among themselves. One of them makes kissing noises as she passes him.

"Ooh, Momma!" one of them coos after her.

She finds she takes such things in her stride now. Once she would have blushed, but now she finds it flattering. She's a Momma, is she?

She lights a cigarette while she waits for Alex, the lighter swiftly extended by a very young Canadian flyer. He looks both excited, looking at her, and frightened, at the same time. He's too young to be away from home. She thanks him and moves away.

"Right," Alex is beside her, "come on, pet. Fourth floor."

The room is down an interminable corridor, and she wonders if Fate is reminding her that she still has time to turn back. But she wants this. Like the Canadian, she's both exhilarated and scared. She glances at Alex. His face is bright with anticipation, and she feels the familiar throb for him. He loves her so much.

He checks out the room, pops his head in the bathroom, as she sits down cautiously on the bed.

"I'll run you a lovely bath, sweet. It's one of those huge claw-footed things."

She moves to the window while he's in the bathroom. There's a surprising amount of traffic on the road, mostly military vehicles, some commercial vans. It's a perfect sun-filled day. If she half-closes her eyes, it could be just another weekday, with people going about their business. Just to her right, barely half a mile away, although she can't see it, the sea rolls onto the beach as it's always done. It's as if there is no war at all, except that now the beach is heavily-strung with barbed wire.

"All right?" he asks, emerging from the bathroom.

She looks at him. "It's just like an ordinary day."

"Well, it is, isn't it – mid-week and all?"

"I mean, it's as if there's no war here."

"Oh, I see." He strokes her head. "It is, though – like it or not."

He turns to put his bag on the bed and unpacks pajamas, a robe, slippers, some other bits, shaving things.

"Hungry?" he asks. "I might be able to rustle up something from the kitchen. With all this lot here they must have stocked up a bit."

"I could manage something, but I don't know what." She had baked beans on toast in the NAAFI (*canteen*) for breakfast. She had baked beans on toast for breakfast yesterday. And the day before. Her appetite seems to have gone down as a result.

"Leave it to me," he says.

She watches him as he leaves. She suddenly feels terribly alone in this big empty room. The furnishings are too elaborate, the furniture too imposing, the bed far too large and *expectant*. She misses her mother, and tears come into her eyes.

She turns off the taps in the bathroom and undresses. The huge mirror over the sink has been taped across diagonally, to prevent shattering, and she sees the reflection of the upper half of her body strangely divided into four. Her face is pale, and she looks more drawn than she once did. She's not sure if this is because she is maturing and losing her baby-face, or whether recent events have taken their toll. She normally has pink cheeks.

She slides down into the bath, studying the water as it rises up over her navel. She takes the tiny guest soap from its holder and begins to wash herself carefully, almost as if she is participating in a ritual. She smiles, thinking that this might be called, for some grand oil painting, "The Preparation of the Virgin". She places both of her hands between her legs, an unfamiliar place, never deliberately explored, except, perhaps, when she was very young. The touch makes her gasp, and she pulls her hands quickly away. But she is no longer anxious, despite breathing faster. It will be all right, she realizes, the time she'll spend with Alex in that huge bed. She can barely wait for him to return.

She doesn't think she'll want the food he's bringing. Food is the last thing she wants at this precise moment.

Then she hears the plane.

EIGHT

A lone German *Messerschmitt* has slipped through the lines of defense along the south coast. Whether on whim, or deliberately, the pilot aims low at the hotel, strafing the ground floor and then the upper floors as he veers away.

Alex is returning along the fourth floor corridor when the attack occurs. He drops the tray of food in stunned reaction to the sound, trying to understand what's happening, even as he recognizes the high pitched scream of the fighter. Although the sudden influx of servicemen in Bournemouth would hardly be ignored by the enemy, he's never heard of fighter attacks in broad daylight on anything but a military target. The fact that no *109* has ever been reported so far from London is confusing too, as he knows this fighter has limited range, barely twenty minutes flying time from its base.

When he rushes into their room and on into the bathroom, Alex at first can't see Celia, but he hears her voice.

"I'm here, Alex."

She is hunched down in the corner, between the wall and the head of the bath, a tiny gap she's squeezed into, naked and shivering. He kneels down and makes sure she's not injured and then grabs her dressing gown from the rail next to her and awkwardly wraps it around her wet body and gathers her to him, pressing her head against his chest. She doesn't cry, which surprises him. His eyes take in the even, shoulder-height line of bullet holes running around the wall facing the window.

"Can you stand up now?" he asks her.

"I think so." Her voice sounds normal.

She leans heavily on him as she stands, momentarily supporting herself on the edge of the bath.

"All right?" He looks into her pale face.

"Just give me a minute. I feel a bit wobbly."

"You've had a shock," he says, unnecessarily.

After a moment, she reaches for his arm and allows him to lead her back into the bedroom where she sits down on the side of the bed – on the lovely bed where they were meant to be together that night. It now supports her as if she's an invalid.

He pries her hand from its grip on his arm. "I'm going to pour you a drink," he says.

Her eyes follow him as he walks to the table to pour whiskey for her, but then she notices the walls, and her mouth opens in surprise.

"Oh, Alex, look at the walls. Look at the walls."

The same even line of holes run around the bedroom directly across from the ruined windows, and shattered glass covers the floor.

"It's over now," he says, hoping he's right. He hands her the drink. "Drink it straight down, Celia."

He's suddenly aware of the amount of noise around them – sirens blaring, police vehicle bells, people shouting, and he looks through the remains of the window. People are running everywhere, some away from the building, others towards it.

"Injuries?" The urgent voice belongs to an Air Raid Warden standing in the doorway to the hall.

Alex looks at him blankly, surprised to see him. "No. No injuries."

"Good, good," the man says. "Stay put for a bit. Mess down there," he says, nodding towards the hallway, and leaves.

Celia touches Alex's hand. "People must be hurt."

"Yes." He sits down next to her, pulling her to him. "We'll do as he says. Just stay here for a little while, and then I'll go and check it out."

"I was having such a lovely bath," she says.

'Were you?" He pushes a strand of hair back from her forehead.

"I thought it was one of our boys flying over, being a smart-Alec." She looks at him. "They do that sometimes, you know."

"Yes, I know." He is looking at her breasts as he speaks. Her gown has slipped down.

She follows his gaze, but doesn't cover herself.

"You're so lovely, Celia," he says, his hand reaching forward to stroke her.

She draws a sharp breath as he touches her. "I want to go to home, Alex," she says, removing his hand.

"Of course you do. It's only natural." He sighs, and stands up. "I'll be back in a minute," he says. "Get dressed now, Celia."

He can't calculate the number of dead or injured in the lobby, but is only aware of the amount of blood he sees and smells. He steps carefully through the crowd of people tending the wounded, trying not to impede them, knowing he is superfluous to the activity there. The aging porter who had offered to take up their luggage (they hadn't needed him) is sitting in a wing chair next to the desk. He appears uninjured, but his face is ashen.

"You saw it all, did you?" Alex asks him.

"Yes, guv. Saw it all," the man says, without looking up. "Bleeding Hun. Who'd have thought it?"

"You're all right?"

The man looks at him, trying to place Alex's face, but failing. "Think so." He glances down at himself. "Bleeding shock, though." He looks at the crowd around them. "Some of them copped it, right? Terrible thing. Just lads, most of them." He sighs, shaking his head. "All over in less than a minute, that's all. In less than a minute."

"Well, as long as you're all right," Alex says.

"Just sit here a bit, I think. Get my legs back."

"Best thing, yes." Alex looks towards the shattered doorway. "Do you think I'd be able to find a taxi out there?"

"Worth a try. Can't hurt."

"Look after yourself," Alex says, squeezing the man's shoulder.

It will be more than two months before Alex can recount to anyone his own experience of that day.

They manage to find a taxi to take them back to Boscombe. The cab driver talks excitedly non-stop for the whole trip. He'd seen it all from the other side of the street, he tells them. Never seen anything like it before, he says. Celia remains silent until they arrive at her house.

When they picked their way carefully through the hotel lobby to get outside into the daylight, into the real air, away from the sights and smells inside, she saw her young Canadian flyer propped up against a wall. She saw by the loll of his head that he was no longer alive, and she wasn't surprised. She was only upset that no one sat with him. He was so alone. He was just a boy, after all.

It's not been easy for me, today. I have a new project at work, and this involved a staff meeting, which I always hate. Just tell me what you want, and I'll do it. Don't make me sit down with everyone else and have to listen to you all go on and on about the process and the deadlines. I'm not a good team player. I'm more your support staff, happier in the background.

Add to the work thing the fact that Celia has gone through hell. I was crying by the time I'd read the pages last night. What a shitty world we live in, to have that sort of thing happen. And to think it's still going on, even now, two generations later, in Afghanistan, Pakistan, and all those other countries. We never learn. If Celia's story hadn't more or less forced itself on me (well, I *could* have stayed out of the house), I would never touch anything related to war, or any sort of violence. I don't like books about it, never watch films about it, and think of myself as a pacifist. If this is true, how can I produce a book about World War II? Celia's words certainly don't glorify war, but the era is beguiling and so profoundly moving that her romance with Alec would have little significance except for that time and setting. I am a hypocrite.

"I absolutely love your story, Strachan," Nell says. "I sat up so late last night finishing it. I can't wait for more."

We're sitting in the park, surrounded by anxious pigeons waiting for sandwich scraps. It's a very warm day, and Nell has removed her coat, tentatively, not certain she trusted her decision. It's only early May.

"You really like it?" I ask her, still hardly believing she's read it all.

"It's a wonderful read. I knew that from those pages I looked at earlier, but I had no idea how clever it is. I really think you'll get this published."

I look hard at her. "How do I go about that, Nell? I don't know anyone who's published before. Well – that's not true. There is one girl I know – I can't stand her – and, anyway, she writes non-fiction. It's probably a whole different publishing field."

"No, not necessarily. Publishers take all kinds of genres. Most of them. But if you don't like this girl, well…you wouldn't want to ask, I suppose."

"What would you suggest?"

"We have to find you an agent, I think."

I sigh heavily. "And how do I do that?"

She smiles then, and pats my hand. "You should look it up on the internet. There will be some kind of list somewhere. Perhaps a writers' site?"

"Oh, of course. I could do that. What else would I need?"

"I think we need to get the whole thing re-typed, because it isn't properly separated into chapters, or even paragraphs, here and there. I could help you with that. I'm a good typist."

"But on the computer, right? I mean, you wouldn't be using a typewriter."

She laughs. "No, I'm not that old. I know how to do word processing."

"Good. Although it seems like a lot of work."

"I don't mind. It would be my pleasure. I could probably scribble all over the pages and you could do it yourself, but you'd still have an awful time with it. Just give me a few days, and I'll see what I can pull together."

"Am I going to be famous, do you think? I don't fancy that much."

"Well, I don't know about that. Perhaps in some circles."

"I don't like the idea of being interviewed, on TV – you know, things like that."

"I don't suppose you have to do anything you don't *want* to do, if it all happens for you. You can be mysterious and secretive."

I smile then. "I like that."

I imagine a headline, "*Strachan Marshall, the elusive and mysterious writer of* – what? – '*Celia's World', was awarded the Booker Prize today.*"

"What are you thinking about?" Nell asks.

"Just trying to imagine how it must feel to be famous," I say.

"Well, as I said," Nell replies, "perhaps not famous, but at least published. Not many writers get to say that, even after years of hard work."

I feel a bit guilty as we head back to the office. I've done no real work at all, although my wrist aches sometimes after a long writing episode in the attic. I've been thinking about buying a laptop. Should have thought of it from the start. Save Nell a lot of typing.

February 11, 1943

"I can't get the same night off as you for a month," Celia says simply, as she sits down next to Alex in the pub.

"Oh, well…it's only a month," Alex responds. "Where do you want to go?"

"Not Bournemouth. I never want to go back there."

"What about Poole?"

"Whatever you decide."

"Leave it to me," he says. "I think I know just the place."

Not that the place would make any difference to Celia. She just wants to get on with things, now that the horror of Bournemouth is fading somewhat.

He holds her hand on the way to the bus stop. She can smell his shaving soap, and she raises her head a little to smell it better. He glances at her upturned face and misinterprets it, bending quickly to kiss her. He pulls her into a doorway so that he can press against her, and she becomes light-headed at the feel of him. He pulls away and glances out from the doorway and then looks back at her.

"Celia, darling, I can't stand it. I say I can, but I can't wait."

"I know," she says.

He studies her for a moment, then takes her by the hand and leads her away from the doorway, past the bus stop, to the small unfenced parkette there, and he pulls her into it.

"Alex?" She knows the park is unsavory, has seen men relieving themselves in the shadows once or twice.

"Shh," he responds. He takes off his overcoat and puts it down on the grass, in a dark area behind a large tree.

He glances around. "It's all right. There's no one else here."

She sits down awkwardly on his coat, and stares up at him silently.

"I know it's not how we planned it," he says, kneeling beside her.

"Nothing is, these days," she replies quietly.

"Do you trust me?" he asks, stroking her face.

She nods.

"Honestly?"

"Yes."

He unbuttons her jacket and then her blouse, staring down for a time and then pressing his face to her breasts. After a moment, he pushes her gently back. He watches her face closely as he slides her skirt up.

"You want this, don't you?" he asks her hoarsely, his face bright against the darkness around them, as he lowers himself to her. "Tell me you want it."

"I want *you*, Alex. I've always wanted you."

But it's not the way she'd imagined it.

NINE

I cleaned out Charlie's room today. He didn't say goodbye, just didn't come back. Then I saw that all of his stuff was gone, including some food from the fridge, which I guess he figured was his. There was junk in the room, of course. It's hard to imagine Charlie tidying up after himself at the best of times, let alone when he no longer has to face me. He'd piled it up in one corner, probably shoving it with his foot, mostly. Old magazines, a couple of left-wing newspapers, one running shoe, an empty condom box, two ripped T-shirts, and three odd socks. And a lot of dust. This room has never been vacuumed since he arrived. I stuffed everything into a couple of garbage bags and took them down to the bin room. I found I was thinking of my mother.

Patty was too upset to help me when Mum died. I went home to an empty, cold house and cleaned out everything, so Patty wouldn't have to see it all again. I loved Mum, more, I think, than Patty – in a different way. Quietly, you know? Unlike Patty, who is physically demonstrative, I never showed it. I think it would have embarrassed my mother if I had suddenly thrown my arms around her the way Patty did, and kissed her on the cheek. Our relationship was more sedate, formal. Mum always said I was Dad's girl. Perhaps she was right. But I did love her. Her death hurt more than I ever let on. I hid my grief behind my sensible, calm exterior. I was a "pillar of strength" everyone said. Good old Strachan – turned out all right after all, didn't she? Always smiling.

I've often wondered if my mother loved me back. I suppose all parents must, but it was never evident in Mum. She was such a silent woman, always serious. Did she think I said cute things when I was young? I don't remember. I know my father did, because he told me, laughing at me as he said it. Dad died when I was twelve, a bad time, I've read, for a girl to have that loss. I still remember his smell, and the warmth of him. He was always piggy-backing Patty and me, bringing birthdays with him when he got home every day,

63

and I always expected something, some little goodie in his pocket, because he did things like that.

When Dad was killed, Mum became even more withdrawn. She behaved like a lunatic at the inquest, cursing and screaming at the truck driver whose rig had skidded sideways into my Dad's old pickup truck. Even after the verdict of accidental death was handed down, she wrote letters to the man – God knows how she found his address – telling him he could never hold his head up in town again and that he was a murderer who had orphaned her two girls. He took her words to heart, it seems, because he and his family moved down to Toronto the following spring.

Patty and I mourned Dad in our own way. Patty wept throughout the day, and had constant nightmares; I remained more or less silent for weeks, just barely able to deal with school, and spending all of my time in my room when I came home. Old man Marshall, my grandfather, died a year later. It hurt him a lot, I guess. Dad was his only child.

My mother had been sweet-tongued and happy once, surely, enough to attract my father. A year after they married, Patty was born. They swallowed their disappointment (why *is* that?) at not having a boy, because, by all accounts, she was so cute and loveable. When I came along six years later, there was no excuse. My mother had a rotten time in labor with me, because I came feet first, and I was big and ugly as well. My parents didn't bother making any more babies. Well, none as far as I know.

When I was nine I squeezed past my mother one day, to go out into the yard. Mum was standing on the back steps and, as I shoved, she overbalanced and sat down hard on the bottom step, injuring her coccyx – her tail bone. She had to stay in bed for about a month with evil-smelling pads on her back to relieve the pain. I was never forgiven.

Years later, she and Patty would remind me of it, whenever my mother had the slightest twinge of back pain.

Mum: "I have a backache again."

Patty: "Oh, dear, is that from when Strachan pushed you off the back step?"

I spent most of my childhood with this awful guilt. Every time Mum would wince, in stooping for something, or putting on her coat, say, I would feel this wave of remorse – my own shame, and pity for her at the same time. All our neighbors knew what I'd done. To this day, in the old neighborhood, there are probably a few people who could give you the details of Mum's "accident."

I still feel guilty. I probably started something which contributed to her death. She was never a strong woman, not sturdy like me. I guess I take after my father's side of the family. Menopause (far too early) was hell for my mother. She got so weird that at one point she refused to drive, because she was frightened of blacking out at the wheel. Our doctor told her it was "all in her mind" but she underwent some kind of treatment at Toronto General for a while, although I'm not sure what it entailed. This was all around the time I got into trouble with those girls. Deep down, I think my behavior was a sort of protest against how stressful my life was at home. Patty was already married, and I had to deal with this sad-eyed, gaunt woman, with her awful sallow skin, who winced when she stooped. She was only forty-nine years old when she died – a massive kidney infection they said. Probably bought on by all the tonics and drugs they'd given her, I bet.

Anyway, I'm not demonstrative. Had Dad lived longer, perhaps he would have rubbed off on me somehow. Mum and I shared that house alone for nine years after Patty married, and I don't recall that we once held each other. She treated me as her equal from the time I got my first period. "You have to be careful, now," she told me. "You can get pregnant." And that was it for the sex talk. She never questioned where I went, or who I saw. She knew I was doing all right at school and seemed satisfied with that. We lived like a couple of middle-aged spinster ladies, sharing everything, not talking much, always with that odd wall of formality between us. Of course, this was after my trouble with the law. I became very conservative after that close shave. Patty, meanwhile - silly, charming and ever-cuddly - was Mum's joy, even if I was the one who did everything for her. Serious, reliable Strachan, eternally capable, was left to her own devices.

In that old house where I had grown up, I sat on the floor with Mum's mementoes around me. There were several boxes and cookie tins, my father's old expanding a-z file where he kept all the family documents. There were the usual certificates, and very old photographs – some of people I didn't even know – and a little box with a lock of dark brown hair. My father's I guessed, because

Mum's was fair before she went prematurely grey. Both Patty and I have dark brown hair. Looking at Katie sometimes, I wonder how it must feel to be fair. Totally different I should think, like being a complete other person.

I sat there desperately wishing I had known Mum better. All that she had been was reduced to these few odds and ends – no journals or love letters – just three shoe boxes, two cookie tins, and an expanding cardboard file.

I climbed onto their bed – Mum's bed – and wept.

After I finished cleaning out Charlie's room, I dragged my big desk in there and filled the bookcase with my own books. With Charlie's old rug (which will need cleaning because his pungent smell is still in it), and my second best cover for the bed, it will make a cozy study. I've always wanted a study.

I've decided not to look for another room mate. I don't need that extra money, after all. I mean, the apartment was mine alone before Charlie came along. I don't think I'm the sort who shares easily, and I'm too old for it, to be honest. There's something decidedly juvenile about sharing, isn't there?

So now I'm curled up on the bed in my new study (well-sprayed with air freshener so it smells like lemons) and I'm having these daydreams about the past. It's not something I would choose deliberately, because it tends to be depressing. One thing's for sure, I know I will never write in this room. I can only write in the attic. This will be a reading room. But it's a shame about the view from Charlie's window. It's ugly with that blank red brick wall without one window to relieve it.

Rupert refuses to come in here with me. It must be the lemon smell.

I haven't been to the house since Tuesday night. I feel a bit miserable about that because I had enjoyed those times so much, swearing I'd go back for ever, if necessary, and now I've managed to push it completely out of my head. My attic doesn't seem to hold the same joy for me any more.

I'm pissed off with Alex, if you want to know. The way he got poor Celia in that park was horrible. She deserves better than that.

When they finally stood up and straightened their clothes to leave, Celia saw the blood on one sleeve of Alex's overcoat, even in the dark. She blushed, for Christ's sake. What's that about? I mean, she was a virgin, so there was bound to be a little blood. Alex quickly picked up the coat and put it on as if nothing was wrong. He offered his other arm to her as they left.

The only thing he said to her, as they reached the street, was, "Are you all right?"

Is this some kind of standard line that all guys use on girls the first time they nail them? It's exactly what Russell James said to me all those years ago. What does it mean? Has our hymen been irreparably broken? Was there a huge amount of pain involved here? Are babies forming even as we speak?

Funny thing - remembering that day with Russell - there was no blood. Now that's odd. I should check that out on the internet.

"Shit, Strachan, you're looking good!" Jay Connor appears beside me. He is our music guru. He handles all the tracks for our productions, clears the copyrights, stuff like that. I admire his musical knowledge, although I don't know anything about him personally. Everyone says he's very cool. He has never spoken directly to me before, although we've worked at the same place for years.

I look at him as he stands peering over my screen. He's not bad-looking, although he wears his hair in one of those tiny pony tail things, way too dated, and wears suit jackets with jeans. I guess he considers himself alternative. I suppose I shouldn't criticize, considering my old taste in clothes.

"Thanks, Jay," I say. I feel a bit awkward. What else can I say to him?

"Guess you're on a new path, getting ready to climb the corporate ladder – something like that?" he says, nodding at my outfit.

I don't understand how my blue dress and red Mary-Jane's can make me look corporate, but figure he moves in those circles more than I do, so perhaps he's right.

"No, nothing like that. Just felt like a change."

"Change for the better, I say." He leans his elbows on the top of the screen and rests his chin on his arms. "What are you doing for lunch?"

I am so astonished that I blink, and my head jerks slightly.

"Lunch?" I sound like a simpleton.

"Just across the road at Domenic's. I can only spare an hour."

I study him. Does he have any idea how strange this is for me?

"Well… when were you thinking?" I can feel my cheeks getting warm, and I have a hard time looking at him.

"One? There's a whole bunch of us. We go there most days."

"Oh, sure. One's fine." I smile quickly and turn back to my computer. I can handle a bunch of people. It was the thought of being alone at a table with him that unnerved me.

"See you then," he said, and turned and left.

Jay Connor asked me to lunch! What on earth is happening to me?

February 22, 1943

"How are you feeling these days, Celia." Pamela sits down on the edge of Celia's bed. "Are you over that awful day in Bournemouth?"

"Oh, I'm over it. Won't be the last time we have to face something like that, I suppose."

"Awful, though. How's Alex?'

"He's all right. I'm meeting him tomorrow night. Just for a drink."

"You ought to get him to the church, Strachan. Make a decent man of him."

"We don't talk about it. I think he'd prefer to wait until the war's over."

"Well, that could be years!" Pamela laughs.

"It's just the way he thinks. That people should wait and start their lives fresh in peacetime." In fact, Alex has never spoken of marriage to her, only stated his opinion on the subject once or twice when they were out with friends.

"Don't know how you can wait. Anyone can see how much you're in love with him."

Celia looks at her. "I do love him. But I can wait." She has to lie. She knows that "waiting" implies not having sex. Pamela assumes that decent people don't have sex outside of marriage. She is from a very conservative family, more so than Celia's own.

"He must have a very strong character, to be so patient." Pamela glances around the room at the other girls. "Shame more people can't be like that."

"Mm," Celia agrees, deliberately not looking at the others.

Pamela stands up. "Anyway, dear, I just wanted to see how you were feeling. I'm glad you're a bit better." She turns to walk away, and then turns back again. "Why were you there, anyway? At the Excelsior?"

"We thought we might be able to have a nice lunch, with so many people staying there. Before the new trainees came back from Canada, most of the hotels didn't offer anything." The lie was perfect. In fact, she had already used it several times – the first time with her parents.

"Oh, of course. How dreadful. Looking forward to a nice meal, and then that happens. I don't suppose you'll go back there now. I couldn't."

Celia smiled wanly. "I don't want to go to Bournemouth again, ever."

Even as Alex had mentioned another hotel there, close to the Esplanade. He'd been irritated when she refused to go. It was so hard to find decent accommodation these days, he'd said.

"We do this every Friday, Strachan," Jay says, as we all walk back to the office. "You'll have to make it a regular thing, now you've gotten to know everyone a bit better."

He doesn't realize that I've worked for Dylan for years – longer than many of the people we've just lunched with. It's as if I didn't exist until he spotted me in my new blue dress.

"I sometimes meet Nell for lunch. I'm never sure what day."

"Nell..." He looks puzzled. "Oh – yeah – the bookkeeper. "Whatever. Just as long as you know the invitation stands."

It pleases me that he found my musical knowledge quite interesting. The hour flew by as we talked about our favorite artists, tracks, videos. He was stunned that I like Meade Luxe Lewis (the pianist on the Boogie Woogie record at the attic). I've added to my tastes since I've been writing there. Of course, being single, and not terribly sociable, I've always buried myself in music. I have just three things that I'm passionate about: books, drawing and music. Oh, and, of course, Rupert. But he's not a thing.

February 23, 1943

"I wish you'd talk to me about this, darling. I have the feeling you're always trying to make excuses lately." Alex lights another cigarette, then taps it rapidly on the side of the ashtray – three taps always - in that familiar way he has, even as no ash has accumulated.

"I'm not, Alex. It's just that I'm still nervous about staying in a big hotel. And I certainly won't go back to Bournemouth."

"Well, I don't know what you want, then." He gazes across the room, watching the people standing at the bar, his face stony.

"Perhaps a Bed and Breakfast somewhere. In the country." *(Somewhere that wouldn't appeal to a lone German pilot.)*

He turns to her, and reaches for her hand. "I'll see what I can find. It's been nearly two weeks, Celia. Try to understand what it's like for a chap. I sometimes have a pain from wanting you."

She wonders if it is anything like the pain she felt that night, under the tree.

"I'm off next weekend." She tries to sound brighter, because his face is so serious.

"Righty-oh. Leave it to me. Countryside, eh?" He smiles then. "*Far From The Madding Crowd*' and all that?"

She smiles. She likes it when she recognizes Alex's quotes. She read a lot of Thomas Hardy at the Grammar.

TEN

February 26, 1943

"He's always a gentleman, isn't he? No hanky-panky?" Celia's mother asks brightly, as she pours the tea.

"Oh, mother!" Her father is embarrassed. "You can't ask the girl that!"

"I can." She is firm. "I've a right to know how he's treating our girl."

"It's all right, Mum," Celia says. "He's very considerate. He'd never do anything to upset me."

"That's not what I meant, and you know it." Celia's mother sits down and begins slicing bread.

"You can't talk about this with her." Her dad doesn't look at Celia as he speaks, but concentrates on stirring his tea. "She's her own woman, now, what with the war. You can't treat her like a child."

"In my day, it was up to the parents to keep an eye on such things. The last thing I want to hear is that she's in the family way."

" – Mum!" Celia is mortified.

"It's the age we live in. All these American blokes over here, getting all the young girls excited. Our own chaps are being saucier as well, they say. I was talking to Mildred up the street, and she mentioned it. Mark my words, there'll be lots of unwanted babies when this war is over." She sniffs loudly. "Just don't come crying to me if he gets you into trouble."

"I just don't know why you're bringing this up," her father says. "What's got into you?"

Celia's mother chews the corner of her mouth. "Intuition. I can't help it. I've always had it." She looks directly at Celia. "Are you going to say anything?"

"We're in love, Mum." She drops her eyes. "We can't help it." She didn't intend to sound petulant.

"There!" Her mother jumps up, slamming her hand on the table, making the cups and saucers rattle. "I knew it!"

"Celia?" Her father's face is pale.

"I'm sorry, Dad. I love him."

"This damned War!" Her mother walks to the window and stares out. "Of course, he's going to marry you," she turns to Celia. "He's said it, I hope."

"After the war's over, Mum. He doesn't see the point now with all the upheaval going on."

"Oh, is that so? He doesn't see the point? We'll see about that. We didn't raise you – put you through the Grammar, and you a secretary and all – to see you stuck with an unwanted kiddy."

"You won't say anything to him, will you, Mum?"

"I knew it," her mother mutters, ignoring the question, sitting back at the table. "I noticed the difference in you. It's a mother's intuition."

"He's a decent enough chap, your Alex," her father says. "He'll see you right."

"I never thought I'd see the day…" her mother says, to know one in particular. "I did the best I could for you, teaching you how to behave properly."

Her father reaches over and takes his wife's hand. "There, there, love. Don't get yourself all worked up. Celia's not silly. I'm sure she knows how to look after herself." He looks uncomfortable, not certain what women actually did to "look after themselves".

"I'll worry about you every time you're out with him, now," her mother says, withdrawing her hand from her husband's.

Celia tries a tiny smile. "I should think my work would cause you more worry, Mum," she says dryly.

"Don't be daft," her mother says. "Of course I worry about that. But it's not nice to imagine you two fumbling about somewhere. It's …" she seems to struggle for the word, "– smutty."

Celia stands up the, pushing her chair noisily back. "There's nothing smutty between me and Alex. He's a lovely man. I'm lucky to have him." She turns to the chair behind her, reaches for her jacket. "I won't stay, Dad," she says, forcing a smile. "I think I need a bit of time to myself."

"Oh, now, Celia," her father says. "Don't go. Your Mum's just a bit upset. Sit down and finish your tea."

She walks around to him and bends to kiss his cheek. "I'll pop by again soon." She looks at her mother, whose head is bowed. "Sorry if I upset you, Mum. Try to see things my way."

Her mother looks up at her then. She is crying. "Oh, Celia, love. How could you?"

Celia guesses that she could and would many, many times over.

I found a good site on the internet devoted to finding literary agents. Nell suggested that I look by genre. Both of us were perplexed over this, because we couldn't work out what the book is. We decided on two: historical romance and memoir. Somehow we'll incorporate this into the letter I'll write to the agent. In fact, Nell says I'll probably have to write several before I get the right response. Nell gave me a draft of how she thought the letter might be worded. She's halfway through the typing of the book so far, but I figure I'll have at least that much again before the story is finished.

How will it end? Each night I'm over there, I find myself wondering where it's all going. Celia needed to tell this story for a reason, I think. Why else would it be coming to me this way?

I looked up automatic writing on *Google*. It's also called 'trance-writing', which is accurate, because I do feel as if I'm in a trance when I'm scribbling away. It suggests that it can be caused by a spirit, or the unconscious mind – some psychotherapists utilize it in their sessions to release repressed memories. All of this makes sense to me. It's possible that Celia's story *is* a memory. Perhaps my grandmother (who *was* from England) told me stories when I was tiny, and I'd forgotten them, and now they've re-emerged. I know little about Gran, because she died so long ago and Mum hardly mentioned her. But this appeals to me as an explanation far more than the spirit thing. No one wants to think they've been visited by spirits.

Of course, this doesn't explain the attic, especially the records and the calendar.

"Lunch?" Jay is standing behind me this time, and leans around to speak to me.

"Oh, yes." I grin at him. " I'll be there."

"No," he smiles – a nice smile, "I meant just you and me today. We'll go somewhere different."

"Oh." Jay fancies me. Oh, my...

"There's this seafood place at Harbourfront – Conroy's. Do you know it?"

I've been to Harbourfront, but not to eat. "No, I can't place it."

"You'll love it," he says, patting my shoulder – in fact, not patting, more like stroking. Nice.

I've been thinking about Jay quite a lot lately.

"So what's he like?" Katie asks as she sits down on the couch. She glances around. "Your place is looking cool."

"Thanks. I've been working on it." I pour wine for both of us. It's the first bottle I've bought since I moved here. I don't get a lot of visitors. "He's lovely. Really nice. I feel very comfortable with him."

"Has he kissed you?"

I stare at her. "Christ, no! We just had lunch together."

"So? He could have kissed you there, or on the way back to work."

"Well, he didn't."

"But you wanted him to, right?"

I smile. "I wondered what it would be like."

She studies me with that naughty look she gets, and I can almost see her brain working. "Strachan's going to have sex soon," she says, in a sing-song voice.

"Maybe."

"I can't believe it's been so long. When was it, ten years ago? Russell Frigging James!"

"He wasn't so bad."

"He was a dead loser. He couldn't get anyone to do it with. He must have flipped when you showed up."

I frown. "There's something I wanted to tell you." I drop my voice a bit, quite unnecessarily. "You know how you're supposed to bleed when you do it the first time? Well, I didn't. I've been researching it."

Katie bursts out laughing. "Oh, that's *so* what I'd expect of him. He didn't finish the job! He didn't even get it in properly!"

"It's possible. I don't suppose there's a way to find out, unless I ask a doctor."

She stares at me. "Could you tell by looking, do you think – you know, with a mirror?"

"Ee-ooh! I don't think so. I mean – what's it supposed to look like, after you've done it?"

"Bigger?" she says helpfully.

"I don't think *he* was very big." (I've since familiarized myself with average stats on penises, through a medical site I found. Not that I was looking deliberately. I was checking out 'Psoriasis' in the 'Ps' and came across it. I keep getting this funny red rash under one arm. Nell thinks it's caused by nerves. Me with nerves?)

"A bit ragged-looking around the edges?" Katie asks thoughtfully.

"Shit, Katie. What do I know? It's been so long, I think it might have all healed up as if it never happened."

She laughs. "I don't think it works that way."

"I just wondered about it. I know it's not important, but I can't help thinking about it. It did hurt, you know. but maybe it didn't hurt as much it should have. Or maybe it hurt because he was just poking at me, and just making me sorer."

"Poor Strachan. You deserve a good fuck with a nice guy with a big one."

"Ouch!" I say. "I don't know about that."

"What, that Jay might not have a big one?"

"That I could handle it. It was bad enough with Russell."

"You're gonna love it, sweetie. You don't know what you've been missing."

I can't tell her that the lovemaking between Alex and Celia has been turning me on. How do I explain that? She'll laugh, of course. I'll have to tell her in the end. She is my best friend, after all.

February 26, 1943

Even as Alex flops back on the pillow, Celia longs for more, and aches with the emptiness she now feels. She loves having him inside her, almost moans out loud at times, but it's fleeting, that hint of ecstasy – like a tiny gnat buzzing around, and you wait for it to land so that you can swat it, but it never does, just hovers, sometime near, then far away. She isn't unhappy. The huge pleasure she feels just having him touch her, stroke her, is greater than anything she's ever experienced. But she knows there's more.

"Happy?" he asks her, reaching for his cigarettes.

"Yes, Alex. This is much better than the park."

She looks around the little room they've rented for the night, with its simple furnishings, the chintz curtains at the window, the view out over the fields. She accepts the lighted cigarette he offers her.

"Lucky to hear about it, this place," he says. "Barnes told me about it."

She hates to think that other couples have been in this bed, their bed, more or less sinning to the same degree. Alex signed the guest book as Mr. and Mrs. and she liked that, but she guesses that everyone does it – every unmarried couple who wants to make love in a bed, that is. Certainly more have done it on the grass, anyway. Not everyone can afford to rent a room.

"We could go for a walk before it gets dark," she says.

"That would be nice," he replies.

"There's a river over there. You can just see it." Perhaps there will be ducks, or even swans, something from the old world to make them forget the time they are living through. She sighs. With rationing the way it is, she doubts ducks and swans have survived this long.

"We'll go in a bit." He is stroking her breast, his other hand still holding the cigarette.

"Do you think there'll be any ducks on the river?"

"Oh, I don't know, sweet. Perhaps they're for dinner tonight?" He chuckles, not realizing how much he's wounded her.

"My dad used to take me to feed the ducks," she says, as his head moves lower over her.

He reaches back and stubs out his cigarette, then does the same with hers.

"We used to take bread down. They love bread." She is still staring out of the window.

His mouth is on her now, and she closes her eyes. She might get it right this time. Perhaps there's some trick to the way she holds her body.

"Trout or Haddock?" the landlord asks, as he puts down their ales.

Celia smiles at Alex. No duck, then.

"Whatever you recommend," says Alex. He smiles at Celia as the man leaves. "This is perfect."

"It's lovely." She glances around at the old timbers of the room, the brasses and porcelain decorations. It's a Dickens-style house.

"You're lovely," he says, taking her hand. His arm brushes her breast.

"You make me feel lovely." But it wasn't quite true. If she could just get the knack of it, things would be different.

He pulls her hand under the table to his groin, and presses it close. "See what you do to me, just looking at you?"

She pulls her hand away, glancing back towards the kitchen. "Alex! Someone might see."

He laughs then. "I'll wait. We've got all night."

She would definitely get it right then.

"Yanks went in yesterday, did you know?" The landlord, Bill Edmunds, puts their breakfasts in front of them.

No baked beans in sight, Celia registers. An egg, a sausage and a few slices of fried tomatoes are mouthwateringly beautiful on the Willow pattern plate.

"Went in...?" Alex responds.

"Yank Bombers went into Germany at dawn yesterday. On the BBC this morning."

Alex leans forward. "Good run?"

"Naval Yards. Got the bastards, didn't they?"

"Losses?"

"Didn't say. But if they didn't mention it, perhaps they all made it back."

Alex smiles. "Berlin, here we come," he says softly.

"All be over soon," the other man responds. "A couple of months I'd say. Then the Yanks will claim they did it by themselves, you'll see."

Celia straightens up. "The war's nearly over?"

"Could be," Alex says. "Things seem to be moving quickly."

Celia smiles as she picks up her knife and fork. Perhaps they would have a June wedding. People always said a June wedding was best.

The knack – that elusive buzzing gnat – might be possible when they're married. Perhaps that's how to get it right. It was the tiny bit of guilt she felt with him, she knew, that was messing everything up.

"Christ," Alex says, after Bill leaves them, "I can't believe it. Things will go back to normal."

Celia has long forgotten what 'normal' is.

ELEVEN

I'm going to dinner with Jay tonight. It's the first time in my whole life that I've been out at night alone with a guy.

As I fiddle with my hair, trying to tame it into some sort of style, the terrible void in my life hits me. I have never dated. How is it possible, in the 21st Century, for a cheerful, outgoing girl of my age to have achieved this? Katie has always encouraged me, to no avail. Patty has smirked about my solitary state a number of times, and that didn't help either.

I'm not shy. I've always been totally comfortable with most people. I fancied the *idea* of sex when I was young, but I guess Russell screwed that up. I must have a low libido. In the olden days they would have called me frigid. But I'm not scared. I talk to guys all the time, evaluating them as possible date material, if they're reasonably viable. I mean, I wouldn't date a married guy, or someone who's caught up with another girl. To a certain extent, that limits choice, doesn't it? Everyone seems to have someone these days. I fantasize over movie stars like Daniel Craig and Brad Pitt, but then who doesn't? And Justin Trudeau looks interesting. But it's just that – fantasy. I'm not like those girls who constantly talk about finding the Right One.

At one point, I wondered if I was a latent lesbian. In fact, a couple of time I attracted one or two, because they thought I was too, and they started getting a bit too chatty with me, and I just *knew*. But at times I've looked at women more closely, trying to imagine doing things with them, you know. It didn't work. There would be some poor girl talking away at me, and I'm getting this slightly *ick*, just-swallowed-medicine expression on my face at the thought of touching her *there*. After a while, she'd excuse herself from the conversation, probably figuring me for a total nut. Anyway, it's clear that I have no interest in women's sexual apparatus, and I'm quite relieved about that. It's apparently not easy being gay. I certainly don't condemn women who love women. Everyone has to do what's right for them, after all.

However, the male body is interesting. Not the obvious phallus, because we're bombarded with the idea of that, but more specific spots. I'm very fond of the area just below the stomach, above the pelvis, where that little crease is. I've never seen this in the flesh, as it were, but lots of pictures. It seems like a delightful place to rest a hand, to gently stroke, because the skin always looks so soft right there. The other place is the back of the neck, just where the hairline ends. I've often stood on the streetcar behind some guy and longed to touch that spot. So, I'm eccentric, right? The girls I used to hang with back in high school were always going on about penises. They had a huge knowledge of the subject, describing size, shape, warts, peculiar angles, and loved talking – and laughing – about them. Nobody ever mentioned less obvious parts.

So I know I'm straight. Just deprived. As I finish getting dressed I realize that I'm feeling quite horny. This is so unusual for me that I burst out laughing and Rupert is startled by it. Is it wrong to think about sex with a guy before you've actually dated? I don't know if our little lunches count as dates, after all. Either way, I've shaved all the obvious parts, and tidied some others. My hair is soft, and smells good. I've lotioned my skin with something Katie gave me at Christmas, and there's a sheen to my arms and legs. I'm wearing a floral print dress in blues and mauves. It has little buttons up the bodice and a tie belt and it looks good with my red Mary-Janes. I look girly-girl enough to impress Jay. It's evident he prefers that.

"You're a puzzle, Strachan." Jay reaches for a bread roll.

"I am?"

"It's like you're a magician's assistant. You went into the box one way, and came out completely different. What made you switch styles? Was it a guy?"

I can't tell him about Celia. I think she's responsible for a lot of this.

"It was time. I'm getting too old for that youth-angst look".

"Cool." He butters his roll. "It suits you. I'm sorry we didn't get to know each other earlier."

"That's okay. We're doing it now." I sip my drink.

"But it's embarrassing. All that music stuff you know. I could have used you once or twice."

"Well, I'm here now. For next time."

He sits back to allow the server to set our food down, but he is watching me the whole time although I pretend not to notice.

"I would never have picked you for the piano concerti type," he says, starting to eat.

"Me too…it came out of the blue. I just heard something and got hooked." The Celia thing is bound to make things complicated. My clothes, my hair style, my taste in music – even my vocabulary sometimes, if I'm not on guard – they've all started to lean towards the 40s. Katie loves that I have my own style, totally unique she says. It does take a while to hunt down clothes that I think are right, but the charity shops are always good for that, most times. I've resisted those vintage boutiques so far, because they tend to be a bit expensive.

"What do you do in your spare time?" Jay asks.

"I like drawing." Not that I've been doing much lately. "I read a lot, play on the computer." I take a quick breath. "I'm writing a book."

He looks suitably surprised. "You are? What kind of book?"

"Romance, set in World War II"

"Wow! I'm impressed. Can you tell me about it, or do you like to keep that stuff under your hat?"

I find I can't wait. "It's about a girl and guy during the war. He's a flyer and she's…(*he won't know what a WAAF is*) …a driver in the Women's Air Force. It's set in the south of England."

"World War II? Hey, Strachan, that's amazing. How did you come up with the idea? Was someone in your family over there?"

"No, at least, that's not where the idea came from. My great-grandfather was a soldier, but I don't know where he was."

"And you've always wanted to be a writer?"

"No, but I love reading, and I've always thought it must be cool to see your own name on a book."

"Will you get it published – is it easy?"

"I don't know. We've only just started figuring out that part of it. Nell's helping me with letters to agents, and how to format the book properly."

"So, that's it. I wondered what you two had in common. She's quite a bit older than you."

"She's been fantastic about it. She believes in the book. I realize now that I didn't have a clue what I was doing, but she's helped me pull it all together."

"A writer." He studies my face. "You're a woman of many parts, aren't you?"

I smile. "Guess so. But then everyone has sides to them that no one knows about."

"You have more sides? Skeletons in the closet?"

"I got into trouble when I was a teenager. I almost went to a detention place for juveniles." I have no idea why I'm telling him all this, but he seems so interested in me. This is new, from a guy. From anyone, in fact.

"What did you do?"

"I belonged to this sort of gang of girls who did a lot of bad stuff, and I just went along with everything. I wasn't popular in school, but I liked being with them because they included me. They thought I was smart, and seemed to find me useful."

"What sort of bad stuff – or don't you want to say?"

He has taken my hand where it rests beside my drink. It's such a warm hand, gently holding mine, and I stare at it for a moment, and then look back up at him.

"They used to steal cars, stuff from stores - sometimes they got money from old guys."

"They? Not you?"

"I never went with them when they were taking things. I was the one who negotiated the price with the guys who bought it from us. They said I was good at talking, that I sounded like I knew what I was doing."

"A sort of middle-woman." He smiles. He has such white teeth.

"I guess. They got caught one night – four of them, anyway – taking stuff from this electronic store. They didn't mention my name to the police, and I would have been all right, but a couple of girls who weren't there told everyone in school. It got to the principal's office, and then to my mother. I was lucky they didn't go further with it."

"And what did you mean, *"money from old guys"*?"

"Sometimes they'd give blow jobs to guys they'd pick up coming out of bars. They did that when they were bored. The guys were usually so drunk they didn't know how much money they were handing over. Sometimes the girls would convince them they hadn't paid in the first place, or they'd threaten to call the cops and report them for having sex with minors."

Jay's mouth is open now, his fork halfway up to it, and his eyes are wide. He puts his fork down. "They were hooking."

"They never called it that. They did it for kicks, to laugh about it later."

"And you never...?" He shakes his head slowly.

"No. I was too chicken. I loved being a part of it when they brought stuff back to the house. We'd go through it and decide where to try and flog it. It was fun working out how much it was all worth."

He sighs then, releases my hand and sits back. "You kill me." He studies me, as if he's searching my face for some clue to my state of mind.

"I'm not crazy, Jay. You asked me, and I told you. I don't tell people about it usually."

"I guess I should feel flattered," he says. "I just never expected anything like that. You always seemed so quiet, so reserved."

"Oh, yeah, well that started after Mum died. I sort of withdrew from everything. I upset her a lot with the gang thing. I probably had something to do with her getting sick. My sister says that, anyway."

"You have a sister?"

"Patty, yes. She lives in Peterborough. I don't see her much. She's married. She's older than me."

He smiles then. "You know, when I asked you out, I figured we'd have a lot to talk about, because of your interest in music and stuff. But I had no idea we'd end up talking about your dissolute youth. You crack me up. I don't think I've met anyone like you before – not the street stuff – I've met a lot of people who get away with shit like that. I mean that you're so friendly and honest in the way you approach people, that you don't seem to have a cynical side. Everyone's a cynic these days. Somehow you come across as fresh and new, as if you've been in a convent or something."

"A convent? Oh, wow – that's good." I laugh then. The mood had started to get a bit deep.

"Not that you're nun-like – I didn't mean that. Just that you're…sweet. You're sort of unspoiled. Haven't guys told you that?"

I smile. "No guys. I'm a wallflower. I don't date."

"You don't date." He shook his head. "What's this, then?"

"First time. I haven't been with a guy since high school."

"Oh, my God, Strachan!" He leans back and laughs so loudly that the people at the next table turn to look at him. He leans forward. "You're too much! I can't take it in."

"Are you saying I'm entertaining?"

"Jesus, yes!" He pushes his plate away. "I want to get out of here. Let's find a club somewhere. I'm in the mood for some really cool jazz." He looks at my plate. "Have you finished? Did you want coffee?"

"No. The jazz club sounds good."

It's after one a.m. when we get back to my place. This is where I feel awkward, with no prior experience at the goodnight-at-the-door thing. I don't have to worry for long. As soon as I start to put my key in the door he is pressing up behind me, and *kissing my ear!* Fresh and new, he called me. Well, someone kissing my ear is certainly that. I almost faint at the feeling of his breath there, the softness of his mouth. I take a huge breath and turn to him as I back into my hallway.

You know those movies where the couple barely gets through the door and they start ripping off each other's clothing, and then have wild sex up against the wall? I've seen that kind of scene so often, it's boring. Well, Jay is different. I knew he would be.

He follows me into the living room, without touching me. He waits until I've hung up my jacket and put the coffee on. He sits easily listening to the Miles Davis CD I put on. He sips his coffee slowly, comments on the music, looks around at my décor – which is looking quite smart these days, with a lot of bamboo and my big plants – all Asia/Pacific, you know.

Only when we've finished our coffees and I've taken the cups to the kitchen does he make a move. I feel as if I am watching him in slow motion. He walks over to me, takes my hand and leads me into the bedroom, where he undoes my buttons and the little belt, and lets my dress slide to the floor. But *he picks it up*! Definitely my kind of guy. He hangs it carefully over the back of the armchair, and then he turns to me and unfastens my bra.

He helps me step out of my pants, and then he stands well back from me so that I can *see him* properly. He's *so* ready for sex. Well, I'm ready for sex by now, or course, and my mouth has gone dry from looking at him, but not my other girl bits. He undresses himself, deliberately, slowly, watching me the whole time. And then – there it is – a man's naked body. I stroke his belly, allowing my hand to fully savor that smoothness I had always imagined.

To say that Russell was a bit uninteresting in the organ department is an understatement. Now I realize just how good my intuition was. Of course, penises are meant to be larger, meant to be harder, and definitely meant to be inside you a whole lot longer than Russell's was.

The pain is excruciating (I knew it had grown back), but only for a minute or two, and then the hurt turns into the most incredible pleasure. Jay is everything I could have hoped for in a lover. How does he know exactly how I like it? Even *I* didn't know until now exactly how I like it.

I think we made love three times through the night, although I am a bit muddled about that, because at times it seemed like he never withdrew from me, that his body had become an extension of my own. Now I understand that fleeting thing that so bothers Celia. She hasn't had an orgasm. Yet little old Strachan, so stupidly inexperienced, managed it more than once. Well, it turns out it had nothing to do with me. It had everything to do with Jay, and his stubborn refusal to give up on me.

It's a shame I can't return the favor and pass some of this pleasure on to Celia, explain what's involved. She's changed my life. It would have been nice if I could have changed hers.

"Guess you're not a virgin anymore, lover." Jay glances towards the bed as he dresses.

I'm astonished to see so much blood on the sheets.

"Oh, I didn't realize." I am embarrassed, just as Celia was. "But I had sex once before. This isn't the first time."

He bends over and kisses me gently on the mouth. "It fucking-well was, you dumb-ass. Whatever you did last time, it wasn't a done deal."

Jay is forty, he told me tonight, but he looks much younger, more like a guy in his twenties. But it was the forty that made me come twice, I'm sure. Thank God for older men.

TWELVE

Nell's apartment building is a surprise. From outside, it's all modern high-rise glass, scary in its multi-resident capacity; I've never been a fan of large buildings. The whole area at Finch and Yonge is awash with the same architecture.

But inside–well–it's cozy. The living area is brimming with furniture and knick-knacks - paintings, vases, pot plants, embroidered cushions, mirrors and footstools. I am reduced to that ungainly feeling I get sometimes, picking my way carefully to one of the sofas. The view through the bank of sliding windows is incredible, but I couldn't live here. The building actually creaks with the wind – like a tree. Really.

"How long have you been here, Nell?"

"It was Mother's – she moved here in 1984. She left it to me when she died in 1990. I thought about selling it at the time, but I didn't want to be unkind to her memory." Nell's gaze hovers over the assorted accessories. "A lot of this was hers. It's not my taste, but I can't seem to get rid of it."

"Well, she was your mum. It's to be expected." But there was no way I would have lived in our old house, after Mum died. The fact that she left it to Patty was more or less fine with me, although it has gained in value far more than the cash she left me, and it would have been fairer had we shared in its proceeds.

"We never get over our mothers, do we?" She blinks. "It doesn't matter how old we are."

I smile sadly. "I wasn't that close to mine. I wish I had been."

"Oh, I'm sorry. My mother doted on me. I think her biggest pleasure was that I never married. She couldn't have managed sharing me with anyone. I was terribly spoiled growing up."

"And your dad?"

"I was five when he died. I don't remember him at all." She pours coffee, and offers me the sugar.

"Mine died when I was twelve. It hurt a lot." Not too many people know this about me.

She looks hard at me, frowning. "Oh, it would. Of course. At that age..."

"He was lovely. I was close to him." I feel tears coming into my eyes, which Nell sees. What a useless subject to introduce. I've been in enough emotional turmoil since Jay the other night, without dragging poor Dad into it.

She sighs. "Your sensitivity shows in your writing, Strachan. I see that."

"Do you? You think it shows?" Of course, it's Celia she sees, not me.

"Such vulnerability. I wept once or twice. You have a poet's touch."

Shit, this is tough. I hate being a fake with Nell.

"Nell, there's something you need to know about the book – about how I came to start writing it..."

Her eyebrows arch in encouragement. "Yes?"

So I tell her.

It takes me about twenty minutes, explaining it all, especially as she interrupts constantly while I am talking, but in the end she doesn't seem too shocked.

"So now you can see the dilemma I'm in. Can I morally try to publish it as my own?"

"How amazing to have such a problem," she says. "*I* should be so lucky! You've got to show me this room, you know. I won't rest until I've seen it."

I look at her. "Oh, I don't know...I go after dark, so that no one sees me. Would you really like to see it?"

"My goodness, yes. And I have a friend – you'll like Ida – who's a Spiritualist. She's a lovely girl, and I think she could help us solve the question of *why* you were chosen to write this book."

"What do you mean, a spiritualist?"

"She belongs to the Spiritualist Church – surely you've heard of them?'

"What about them?"

"They believe in the continuation of souls – that it's possible to communicate with spirits of the departed. It's an old established church. It's not considered weird, or anything."

Not considered weird or anything. Talking to dead people. But then, here I am, writing journals of dead (probably) people. "And you believe it, too?"

"I'm not sure what I feel about it. I don't dismiss it out of hand. I've known Ida since I was a girl, and she's charming, very kind. I've been to a couple of meetings with her, and they were intriguing, but I can't say it convinced me. I suppose it's like any religion – you have to have faith in it. I've never been a very good Christian, I'm afraid."

"But you think she might be able to help...? I don't understand. If you don't believe in it all..."

"Oh, I don't *disbelieve* it. I'm open to the *proof* of it. This might be the opportunity to see if it has any substance. Could I ask her - for you?"

"You're not convinced about what she does, and yet you accepted what I just told you about the room. What's that about?"

She laughs then. "Oh, I'm a firm believer in the energy that's left in old places. You only have to walk into some empty houses – ones that are for sale, I mean – and you can just feel the previous lives, their energy still in there. You must have done that. It's the same thing, more or less, as believing what Ida does. Except she claims she can *see* those lives." She stands up and turns to the kitchen. "I'll just get the cake."

I sip my coffee. I never once though of Nell as a crank. There she was, doing the banking, making up our pay cheques, and all this time she was a bit crazy. Yet, all this time I was doing my job, tweaking the latest ad image, sitting with the art director and going over things, having coffee with Katie, screwing Jay, and not once did I consider that I was a nut job. I was writing this ridiculous story in a derelict attic, and not once have I questioned my own sanity.

"So, what do you think?" Nell asks, placing an incredibly rich-looking cake on the coffee table.

"I don't suppose there's any harm in it. I've been thinking about it a lot lately – why me? But it still won't answer the question of whether or not I can say it's my book – that I wrote it."

"But that doesn't matter." She hands me a plate with a rather large slice of cake on it. "From what I've read, a lot of writers claim they don't know where their words come from. They say that another power takes them over, or that they felt like they were under some sort of influence as they wrote. It's common, apparently. So what's so different about what happens to you? It's the room that makes it so unusual. And Ida might be able to clarify that."

I can't eat the cake, after all. "If you think so. We can give it a shot."

"I'll phone her later. She works at the hospital on Saturdays. She reads to the patients."

I reach for my bag, and pull out the envelope. "Here's the latest, anyway. It's type-written this time. I got a lap top."

"Oh." She takes out the pages. "This is lovely. So neat. I'll give you a diskette so that you can just back up next time. Save you printing it off, and I can work directly with your file."

"My computer only takes CDs."

"Oh, well, probably mine does, too. I should look."

After we've cleared away the coffee things, we move out onto the balcony. It's not too windy. It feels rather like sitting on the deck of ship. Come to think of it, I've never sat on the deck of a ship, but this is how I imagine it would be.

"It's nice to have you here, Strachan," Nell says. "I don't have many visitors, and most of those are old friends of my mother's."

"I don't have many visitors either. Guess you and I are a bit alike that way." And then I remember how different I've become. "I slept with Jay the other night." It just pops out.

"Oh, Strachan – did you?" She hardly changes expression. "I don't know if that's such a good thing. Working together... They say you shouldn't mix business with pleasure. He seems like a nice boy, though." She is oddly unimpressed by my confession.

"Well, a bit more than a boy. But he is nice."

"I didn't picture you as the sort of girl who...you know...has affairs."

I smile at her. "It's not an affair. Isn't that when one of you is married or something? We're both single."

"Oh, right."

90

"It's more or less the first time for me. I've never been involved with anyone before this." (You certainly can't count Russell.)

"Well, then. How lovely for you. We all need affection in our lives."

"I didn't know how much I needed it." I laugh a bit loudly. "Now I can't stop thinking about him."

"I understand. Love is all-consuming."

Love? Is that what it is? "I don't know if it's love, but I like being with him."

"If you can't stop thinking about him, it probably is." She smiles at me. "I've been in love. I know what it's like."

"Who was it?"

"Oh, just a lovely man I knew years ago. We met at a Christmas do. We were immediately drawn to each other. He died."

"I'm sorry."

"Oh, so long ago, it hardly seems real now. Mother was nearly out of her mind the whole time I was seeing him. 'You can do better,' she said. 'Don't rush into anything.' She wanted me to establish my career first, before I got married. That's what she *said*, but, were she honest, she just didn't want me to marry at all. I don't think she cared for my father much. I'll never know why, but she didn't seem to believe in marriage."

I can't think of anything to say here. I don't find her mother's attitude particularly wrong. What *is* so great about marriage, anyway?

"How did he die?" I finally ask.

"Motor bike accident. He had one of those big Harley-Davidson things."

I stare at her. It's impossible to picture Nell on the back of a Harley. "You were a biker's girl?" I laugh.

"Yes, for a short time. I wasn't always a boring accountant, you know."

"Well, I'm impressed, Nell. And you're not boring...there's more to you than meets the eye."

"As it is with most of us, isn't it?"

"I guess."

I wonder if Nell has more skeletons in her closet?

March 4, 1943

"Oh, dear Lord, have you heard?" Pamela rushes into the hut, wild-eyed. She flings her cap angrily onto the nearest bed.

"What? What's happened?" Evelyn sits up from her nap.

"Terrible accident in London last night. Hundreds were killed." Pamela's eyes are filled with tears. "In a tube station – don't know where. They were going down there to get away from a raid, and there was a panic, and all these people were trampled. Mothers, babies – all crushed. It's the worst we've seen. Worse than any bombing."

Celia is holding Pamela's hands, rubbing them. "Pam, Pam. Sit down, love. Tell us slowly what happened."

Doris and Martha join them. The rest of the girls are out tonight.

Pamela brushes the tears away and swallows. "There was an air raid – retaliation against our raid on Berlin on Monday, they're saying. The silly blighters at some anti-aircraft battery used a new rocket that made a different sort of sound, like a bomb going off or something – and all the people walking down the stairs to the station just panicked. They're saying over 170 people died, a lot of them women and children. God, I wish I hadn't heard. You don't always hear, do you?"

She bursts into tears and flops back on the bed. It's not even her bed. Celia has never seen Pamela overcome with any emotion. She has always been the calmest person in the hut.

"Pammy, did they say which station?" Martha asks. Her family lives in Putney.

Pam shakes her head against the pillow. "No. It's under wraps. No one's saying anything. It was our mistake, wasn't it? Can't blame Gerry for this one."

Celia sits down on the side of the bed. "Pamela? You said there was a big raid on Berlin on Monday? Do you know what squadrons?" She hasn't heard from Alex in three days.

Pamela sits up and looks at her, grabbing her hand. "Oh, I'm sorry, Celia. That was a rotten thing to throw at you. I don't know who went. It was big though, I know that much."

Celia gently releases Pamela's hand and stands up. "I'll try to reach him on the phone. Sometimes I can get through."

She waits for what seems ages for the operator to connect her to Alex's HQ. The telephone is outside the NAAFI, and she can see people laughing and chatting inside, as they eat their evening meal. Probably baked beans, she thinks, bleakly.

"Hello?" He sounds normal.

"Alex? It's me."

"What's happened? I thought we weren't meeting until Saturday."

"I heard about the raid on Monday – Berlin. I wanted to make sure you were all right."

"I thought we agreed you wouldn't listen to BBC News. It's better if you don't know what's going on."

"I know that. It was Pamela. She heard about this terrible thing that happened in a tube station in London. All these people killed. She said the London raid was retaliation against the Berlin one. Were you in it?"

"Look," he is trying to be patient, "I've said this to you before. I'm not going to discuss what I do, or where I go. You don't need to know this, Celia. You've been better, you said. No more nose bleeds, right?"

"No, they seem to have gone."

"That's because you can't get all worked up about something if you don't know about it. Be a good girl, now. Go back to your hut and try to forget all of this. I heard about the station. Bloody awful. But there's nothing that can be done for them now. Just remember that we're targeting Berlin. We're closing in on the bastards."

"I love you, Alex." She has never said this to him before.

There is a small silence before he speaks. 'There, there, sweet. It will all be over soon." His voice is gentler.

"I don't think I could bear it if something happened to you. I try to be strong, think like the other girls, but I can't." She wipes her eyes with her handkerchief, trying to ignore a group of WAAFS leaving the mess hall who look at her curiously.

"You know how I feel, silly. I won't let anything happen. We've got too good a thing going here, haven't we? Now go and put your feet up. Make a cup of tea. I have to go. I'll see you on Saturday at the pub."

He doesn't say that he loves her too. But that's only natural. These Air Force chaps are careful not to say too much. Wouldn't want to jinx anything, would they?

I go online just before I get ready for bed. I've been doing this a lot lately, as more historical events occur. In a way, it's confirming the work. It's a validation that the writing is not just a work of my imagination.

173 people died at the Bethnal Green tube station that night. The name of the station was withheld because of the censorship of the time – it might have been hushed up because of the location of that new anti-aircraft weapon they'd used – but there was still a huge government enquiry. The accident caused the largest loss of civilian life in the UK in one single night of World War II and the greatest loss of life in one incident in the history of the London Underground network. The largest number killed by a wartime bomb was 68 at Balham. But Gerry did that. Bethnal Green was our fuck-up.

I have difficulty falling asleep tonight.

THIRTEEN

It's time for the Katie Confessional.

"I knew it, you naughty girl!" She claps her hands like an excited child. "I knew it'd happen the first night."

"I was a pawn of love," I say dramatically. I can't believe how pleased she is.

I head out to the kitchen to make coffee, but I can see Katie from here. She can't stop grinning. If anything, she's more excited about my sexual adventures than I am – and I'm very excited! For Katie, it means I'm part of her club now. Friends do much the same things, don't they? They're meant to have a ton of things in common. But Katie and I have never been similar. I think the only reason we're still friends is because of the link to our past – to school and family. She certainly doesn't like the same books that I like, or movies, for that matter. Her political attitudes (which she doesn't even recognize she has) are totally different to mine. I'm definitely socialist – I mean, I care about the way people live, that they have an equal piece of the pie. Katie doesn't give a shit about anyone but herself, most of the time. I love her, of course. She's my one and only friend. Without her, Nell would have to step in, because there's no one else. Much as I like Nell, there is a slight difference in age. After a while, I'd be bored with her interests, and she'd probably be bored with mine, although I can't think what right now. In fact, Nell's interest in reading and movies is much closer to mine than Katie's.

"Did you come?" she asks practically, as I put down her coffee.

"I did! I couldn't believe it. More than once, but they sort of rolled into one another, so I lost track."

"Multiples! Oh, that's amazing. He must be fantastic."

Her eyes are wide and shiny as she speaks. I know Katie of old. I'll have to keep an eye on her if Jay's ever around when she's visiting.

"Oh, Katie. He's so lovely. I can't believe how lucky I am. He tries so hard, you know, to make me feel wonderful. It's like an art form with him. I've read enough books to know he's unusual."

"And to think you hadn't noticed him up till now..."

"Oh, I noticed him. But always from a distance, and just the occasional nod, the usual stuff. He always seemed so unapproachable, because he usually has this little entourage with him when he *is* in the office – he's out a lot. But when he's in he's got the receptionist running after him with some delivery, or one of the artists asking him stuff, or he's in Dylan's office in a meeting. He's like a star around there. Of course, he never noticed me, tucked way down the back – and wearing my usual gear."

"He's noticing you now." Katie is very impressed, I can see. "When are you seeing him again?"

"Saturday. There's a harbor cruise he likes."

"Romantic!" Katie says.

"He does it a lot. There's a different jazz group each week."

"Oh. So no holding hands in the moonlight..."

"Bit cold yet for the moonlight thing."

"Mm, suppose so."

"Oh, and I *was* still a virgin up to that night, after all."

"Oh, there! I told you. No wonder he got such a kick out of you. Men are always impressed with that, being the first."

"He didn't seem surprised." Or impressed.

"Oh, he was. They like that kind of scoring, believe me."

"Well, it's all over with now. I'm looking forward to the next time without all that mess."

Katie grimaces. "Ooh, right."

"It was embarrassing."

"It is. (It's a wonder she can remember.) Some guys have a hard time with that side of things." She munches on one of my home-made cookies. Yes, I do things like that sometimes.

"Then again," she continues, "some guys get off on it. You know, even doing it during your period."

I stare at her, and can't control my expression. "Oh, Katie. That's terrible. You mean some guys *like* it?"

"I guess."

"You've known guys like that?"

She shrugs. "Oh, yeah. A couple, actually."

I have so much to learn about men. Katie explained the foot-fetish phenomena years ago. She knew a weirdo who liked to lick her feet and suck on her toes. He preferred her feet to her boobs. She stopped seeing him after a couple of weeks, although she said she'd quite enjoyed it, but felt it didn't bode well for a long-term relationship, because she was quite fond of having her boobs touched, and he never did that.

We're listening to Nora Jones. We do seem to share the same taste in *some* music. I knew there had to be something.

"You know that book I'm writing?" I roll over onto my side so that I can see her properly. We're both sprawled on the rug. The one couch I have is a bit short for sprawling.

She looks at me. "Yeah. How's that going?"

"Good. I don't think I have much more to do. You'll be surprised when I tell you how I did it."

She grins. "I know what you're going to say. It's your Gran's story. You found some old diaries, right?"

"What? How did you come up with that?"

"Well, it makes sense that you wouldn't just make up a story about that War, would you? You've never said a word to me about being interested in that time. Fuck, you hated that *English Patient* thing, remember?"

"So you always figured it wasn't me. That I couldn't write it?"

"Come on, Strachan. I know you. If you were that good at English, it would have come out by now."

I study her, somewhat hurt. "Well, it wasn't anything to do with my Gran. It all happens – all my writing – in that attic room over there." I point through the window, although we're too low on the floor to see from here.

"What?" She struggles into a sitting position and stares out. "What about that attic?"

"It makes me write. It's such a beautiful room. When I'm over there I can't help myself. It's like being hypnotized or something. The words just seem to come to me."

Her mouth is a little open. Katie loves horror movies. I can see she thinks this is in the same mode as *Stir of Echoes* or something.

"What do you mean? What does it feel like?"

"I can't explain. I get sleepy, listening to the music, and then I start writing. Sometimes I fall asleep while I'm writing. But there are all these pages done when I wake up. I've nearly finished the book."

She closes her mouth, and then opens it again. Her lips are dry-looking.

"What music?"

"There's and old record player over there and some old 78s."

She frowns then. "Whose place is it?"

"I don't know. The house is empty. It's been empty for years."

"And you go in there by yourself." It's a statement.

"Only at night. Otherwise someone might see me."

"And you sit on the floor writing?"

"Not on the floor. There's a little sofa."

"A sofa…" She looks a bit pale, in fact.

"The room where I write is furnished."

"Jesus," Katie says softly. "You never said anything."

"It might have stopped, and then everyone would think I made it all up."

"I wouldn't. You know me, Strachan. You should have said something."

"Well, I'm telling you now. And you'll see the book."

"Can I see it?"

"Do you want to see it tonight?"

She makes a silly face, but grins. "Fuck, yes, of course I do."

"We can go later."

"Oh – no, I didn't mean that. I meant - can I see the book?"

"It's not here. It's with Nell. She's formatting it for me."

She's disappointed, but recovers. "But we could go over tonight, as you say, and see the room. That would be good." Although she doesn't sound truly enthusiastic.

"We have to wait until it's dark."

"Wow. We haven't done anything like this since we were kids."

She's right. I'm looking forward to taking her over there.

She's not going to believe it. I'll put on *Pine Top's Boogie Woogie*. Katie will get that sound. She could get hooked on it, like me.

"When you said it was derelict, I didn't realize how bad it would be getting in. Are you sure there aren't any crack heads in here?" Katie picks her way carefully through the debris on the back porch. As usual, she's wearing rather nice shoes.

I hold the flashlight higher, so she can see better as she follows me up the stairs. "It's all right, Katie. I've never seen anyone in here. And once we're upstairs, you'll see how pretty the room is. It's incredible, you'll see."

As we reach the top floor, I'm a bit startled to see no light under the door. There's always a light showing. Without fully considering this, I throw open the door to give Katie the full impact of it. And then I jump back, treading on Katie's foot.

"Shit, Strachan! Ow! What's wrong? Put the light on, for Christ's sake."

"I can't." I say, barely able to breathe. As I scan the room with the flashlight, it's obvious that something terrible has happened.

The room is hideous, like something from those fake haunted houses that people set up for Halloween. There is thick dust everywhere, on everything. The smell of damp and decay hits both of us, and I can hear Katie's labored breathing beside me as she peers in.

My dear couch, where I've napped so many times – well, its innards are hanging out from deep tears in the shabby fabric; the books are green with mildew; the veneer has started to peel off the gramophone cabinet, and the top of the desk isn't much better, its top wavy and buckling. A large pool of water lies in one corner, beneath a yawning hole in the ceiling. The wallpaper has fallen away from the wall directly beneath the hole, and the rest is so faded with age that the print is almost unrecognizable. The records are where I last saw them, but their paper covers are now a pulpy mess. The calendar is on the floor, yellowed and curled with age, covered with specks of mouse droppings.

And then I see the thing that is most shocking to me, if anything *could* be more shocking at this moment. The little window, where I'd so many times pressed my face to look out, is covered, as if from the beginning of time, with the thickest cobweb I've ever seen. At its heart, obvious even by the flashlight, is a fat, nasty spider. I almost pee myself right there.

That's when I remember poor Katie.

I turn to her. "Ok, Katie. It's terrible. This isn't how it looks usually. It's lovely, this room. I can't believe how ugly it all is." I am beginning to cry, because it's suddenly occurred to me that I have nowhere to write now. Celia's book will never be finished.

Katie is looking at me very strangely, looking into my face. She puts her hand on my arm and says, "Come on, babe. Let's get out of here."

I allow her to take me down the stairs, and out into the street. As we cross the road, I glance back, truly hoping the light will be on again up there. But it's not.

Even now, sitting on my couch back home, while Katie makes me a coffee, my skin is still prickling over what's happened. I realize I'm shivering, and that's when Katie comes in with our drinks, just as I reach for the throw.

"I put some vodka in it, is that okay?"

"I don't have any vodka." My voice doesn't sound right.

"It's mine. I had a little flask in my purse."

The coffee tastes good, and warms me very quickly. I look up at Katie.

"What am I going to do now, Katie? The book? I won't be able to finish it."

"Don't worry about that now. I think you should take a hot shower, and then go to bed. You're shattered, look at you."

"But I can't write without the attic. It means she's gone – Celia. I can't finish her story."

Katie stands in front of me and takes my hands. "Listen to me, Strachan. I don't know what you thought happened when you went over there, but it's over, whatever it was. You can't go back there again, okay? You're not yourself – look at you. Writing a book in an attic – shit! I thought you were odd at times, but this is too much. There *was* no story. There *was* no Celia. You can see that now, can't you?"

I frown at her. "What d'you mean, *no Celia*? Of course there is. She's a WAAF, and she's in love with Alex. She's going to marry him soon. When the War is over." I pull away from her hands. "Wait until you see the manuscript, when Nell gives it back to me. You'll see."

"Right, of course I will." She sits down next to me. "I think Jay had more of an impact on you than you realized." She straightens up. "There *is* a Jay, isn't there?"

"Oh, Katie! I can't believe you think I'm crazy and made all this up. Look how long I've known you."

"I know, but it's not like we've spent that much time together, is it? I don't see you that often."

"And so you think I've gone nuts…"

"Not nuts. Just…exhausted. And you're so alone all the time. Too much time to think. People start believing all sorts of funny things when they have too much time on their hands. You had a tough few years, didn't you? What with your mother. It can take a long time to finally come to terms with things."

I hadn't realized that Katie had such depths to her. I don't think she's ever spoken to me in such a serious way.

"I'm not mad, Katie. I'll show you the book. You'll see."

"Do you want me to stay tonight? I can, if you like."

"There's no need. I'll be fine."

She takes a tissue from her pocket and wipes my eyes. I didn't know I was still crying.

"If you're sure. I'll phone you as soon as I get home." She studies me.

"I might be in the shower. Don't bother, Katie. I'm just going to feed Rupert and go to bed."

"I'll call you tomorrow, then." She hugs me, then goes to the door, standing there for a moment. "Perhaps you could phone Jay. That might make you feel better."

"You weren't sure there even *is* a Jay." I smile.

"Oh, fuck it, Strachan. All that stuff you told me about him. There's no way you could make that up. Unless you are a crazy writer, after all." She blows me a kiss and leaves.

I get the distinct impression that she couldn't wait to get out of here.

I take my shower, and make a hot chocolate. I'm standing at my window looking at the darkened house. An old man shuffles by below me, walking like one of those fifties movie robots, not lifting his feet, scuff, scuff along the footpath. It's very late, and quiet outside. A squad car glides into my line of vision, halting in front of the house. I can hear the radio clearly. A light goes on inside the car and I see two young cops bending over their radio, or something. For a moment, I wonder if they'd had a report about me and Katie in the house. All this time without detection, it would make sense for all hell to break loose tonight, but after a minute the light goes out and the car pulls away.

Where do I go from here? My room has rejected me. I missed something somewhere when I was writing. Alex must have died, and perhaps Celia has too. There's no other explanation for it.

As I try to fall asleep, it occurs to me that I might be able to finish the book myself. I don't think there's much else to come, considering that the War is coming to a close. I stop mid-thought – wait a minute. I last heard from Celia in 1943? World War II didn't end until 1945.

But it doesn't mean they survived until then, does it?

Dear Celia. How did it all end for you?

FOURTEEN

Jay's pleasant face hovers above my screen. There's such concern and sympathy there, and I feel loved.

"Poor Strachan, what's up?" he asks. He doesn't say "'ssup." He's not like that. He doesn't have to sound cool. He *is* cool.

I manage a smile. "I'll be fine. Just a bit down today."

"Anything I can do?" He doesn't make it sound in the least suggestive, but I hear it that way.

"I don't think so. I'm just tired."

"I should come over tonight and make you some soup. I'm good at soup."

I consider this. He could make a difference to my mood. "What time?"

"I'll drive you home after we've finished today. You don't want to deal with the subway feeling like that. Okay?"

I nod. I receive this kind of concern so rarely that I'm overwhelmed by it. Katie can be kind, when I have a cold or something, but only when she's not involved with some guy, so it's sort of hit and miss. My mother was good at it, although I always imagined I was putting her out, spoiling her schedule, so that I didn't appreciate it as much as I should have. Patty is useless. There's nothing soft and tender about that girl. I blink away some tears that are forming.

He reaches over the screen and strokes my cheek. "Hey, sweetie, don't get upset. Shit, you *are* feeling bad, aren't you? Do you want to stop off at your doctor on the way home?"

I shake my head. "No. I'm not sick. It's been a heavy week. I guess I'm exhausted."

"Well, I'll do the soup, and then we can curl up on the couch and watch a funny movie. We can eat potato chips and ice cream, whatever you want, if it makes you feel better. We can't have my girl all upset now, can we?"

His girl. I'm *his* girl. "Lovely," I say, grinning like a fool.

I'm starting to feel better already. Perhaps I can tell Jay about the room. That would help.

"So, do you think I'm nuts?" I ask him. We are wrapped around one another in my bed, both naked. The soup, potato chips and ice cream are a distant memory. Recent lovemaking is evident by our very moistness.

"I'd never think that about you. Anyway, I've heard things like it. My mother used to tell us stuff – my sister and me – when we were kids. She always made it sound real. If there's a whole church devoted to the idea, and a lot of the world believes in it, why shouldn't it be possible?"

"Now that it's gone – the nice room, I mean – I half-think I did imagine it. But Nell's working on the book. That's my proof that it all happened."

"When will she be through with it?"

"She's going to try to get it finished tonight. She saw what a state I was in today."

"And you're sure you couldn't have dragged this up from your subconscious yourself – you're convinced it wasn't you doing the writing?"

"No way. I didn't do it, Jay. I'd probably freak out even more if all that came from me. When you read it, you'll understand."

He leans over and kisses me then.

"Do you want me to stay tonight?"

I realize he's ready for me again. He is always ready for me. "Maybe not all night. I have to get *some* sleep." I reach for him, enjoying the little gasp that escapes his mouth.

Strachan Marshall, twenty-six, never been kissed until last week, now makes a guy as amazing as Jay gasp. What else am I capable of?

"You've done over 400 pages, Strachan." Nell hands me the CD. "According to my program, your word count is more than one hundred and twenty thousand words."

"It sounds like a lot."

"It's probably a bit long for a first book, in fact. You might want to check that online. I have a hunch it should be shorter, but then – for goodness' sake – what could you cut out?"

"Well, I couldn't, could I?" I turn the case holding the CD over and over in my hands. It's all here, every word to date. "I can't think of any bits that aren't important."

"That's what I thought. Of course, a good editor would sort it out. I wouldn't worry about it now."

"And I haven't finished it yet."

"At least you *can* finish it, without waiting for that ending to come to you. If Celia isn't able to get through to you any more, you'll have to do it yourself – I could help you with that, if you want."

I look up into her face. This woman absolutely trusts me. She believes every word I've told her about Celia. I don't know if everyone will. "I'm not hopeful. The light wasn't on last night."

"Ida will know what to do."

Weird Ida. The ghost-hunter. The spirit-chaser. We're meeting at Nell's tonight. With everything that's happened, can she be considered any more eccentric than I am?

Ida is older than Nell. She has the sort of wrinkles which look more obvious with too much makeup; she is, of course, wearing too much makeup. Her hair is that harsh straw-color that results from extreme economy, rather than a preference for the shade; no hairdresser would permit her to leave the salon that way. She is overweight, and pants from the sheer effort of moving her chair closer to the table. In contrast to these shortcomings, she has a very pretty face. She reminds me of Good Queen Glinda in *The Wizard of Oz*.

"When can I see it, Strachan?"

"Any night. You decide." I need to pee. We have consumed an enormous quantity of Nell's tea during Ida's interrogation.

"I think Monday would be good for me," Ida says. She glances at Nell and raises her finely penciled eyebrows.

"Oh, yes. Monday's good." Nell seems a little in awe of her.

"Will it make much difference if the light is still off?" Nell asks, as she wraps the last of the cake in some plastic wrap. "It's been a few days since she saw it."

"No difference at all," Ida says, holding up her tote bag to receive the wrapped cake. She's a regular visitor here, I suppose. "Thanks, Nell. I'll make something the next time." She pulls on her white angora knitted hat. "The Grangers hadn't heard anything for months, remember? I was still able to make contact."

"Oh, that, yes. I'd forgotten," Nell says.

"Well, I must fly." Ida smiles at me. "Don't worry, dear. We'll get to the bottom if it."

She looks like a giant pom-pom in her white coat and fluffy hat. I watch her with interest. Perhaps, like Queen Glinda, she will just up and fly right out of the kitchen window.

She smiles again. "See you on Monday night. I'll let myself out." She makes her exit in the normal way. I'm a bit disappointed.

"That's a very nice desk," Ida says, running her hand over its dusty surface. "Probably worth a bit." She turns to continue her examination of the room. "Hmm." She nods at everything, taking it all in. "You were right to call me, I think."

She is wearing a bright red pantsuit tonight, with black high-heeled boots, and a black fedora with a red band. She looks rather sharp, and certainly wouldn't be overlooked in a crowd. She points to the sofa. "Let's pull that out into the middle of the room. It will do."

Nell and I drag it forward. It looks pretty disgusting, as if mice have nested in it, although there's no sign of them now.

"And clear that record player off, and we'll use the table," she orders.

As we're doing this, she produces a canvas sheet from her huge tote bag. It looks like a painter's drop cloth to me. She spreads it over the sofa so that we can sit down. She lights a small candle and places it on the table, then nods to me, and we both turn off our flashlights. The candle and the draft from the window produce an array of moving shadows around us, although it's still quite bright in the room, of course. This is downtown Toronto, after all, surrounded by highrises.

She holds out her hands to us as we sit either side of her. "Whatever happens, don't release my hand. It's important to maintain contact." She wriggles her plump body into what I assume is a more séance-comfortable position, and closes her eyes. "Close

106

your eyes," she says. She has a firm, kindergarten-teacher sort of voice, as if she's telling the kids their naptime isn't over yet.

Alice begins to breathe shallowly. I open one eye and see that her face is perfectly at peace. She wears a lot of eye makeup.

"Close your eyes!" she hisses.

How did she know?"

After a few minutes, during which I try not to fidget, her breathing becomes harsher, and then she speaks. "Is someone there? Can we help you?"

I hold my breath for a while at that point.

"We are here to help you," Ida continues. "Strachan is here to help you."

Christ, don't bring me into this.

"Yes?" Her voice is sharp. "Yes?" she asks again. She is breathing rapidly now. A full two or three minutes pass and then her breathing starts to sound normal again. She releases a huge sigh. "You can open your eyes now," she says. She releases our hands.

Nell and I look at her expectantly as she turns her flashlight back on. I quickly switch mine on.

"There's nothing more I can do here, Strachan." She smiles gently at me. "She will only communicate through you."

My mouth drops open a little. "You *spoke* to her?"

"It's not actual speaking. It's a sort of understanding. A *knowing*. She doesn't want anyone else but you. She's upset that you've brought strangers here. This must be the last time." She stands up and waits for us to stand so that she can fold the drop cloth.

"She said that? She only wants me?" I look at Nell. "That means I can still finish her story, doesn't it?"

Nell strokes my shoulder. "I knew Ida would be able to help."

I look at Ida. This round dumpling of a woman is a miracle to me. "I never believed you could do anything."

"Oh, I knew that. I can always tell. But it made no difference. She likes you."

"Did you find out why? Why me?"

"It's amazing in this day and age, but apparently you're both virgins. She thought you would have more empathy for her." She looks directly into my face. "Is she right?"

"Until last week, yes."

"Well, then. You have – or had – something in common. Mythically, an important symbolism - virginity."

Nell shakes her head. "But it's no longer true, is it? Strachan is sexually active now."

I love the way Nell puts things. She means I fuck a lot.

"And so is Celia," says Ida, a wide smile appearing. "Apparently she's quite enjoying herself."

How did she know Celia's name? We never mentioned it. It must be all part of the *Knowing* thing.

"Thank you, Ida," Nell says.

"Oh, yes, Ida," I say, rather breathlessly. "Thank you. This was amazing."

"Only to newcomers," she says. "After a while, the amazement goes, and it's all very ordinary. You should come to one of our meetings."

She stuffs a business card in my hand.

"I'll see." For all Ida's help, I don't think I'm ready for that kind of thing on a regular basis. Once Celia's story is finished, I doubt I'll ever dabble in the occult again.

Because that's what it is, isn't it? *The Occult.* Scary-sounding. Katie would love it – all of this.

I just want to get back to normal. Whatever 'normal' is.

Hey, that's what Celia said.

As Nell and Ida pull away in Ida's car, I spot Jimmy by the corner. He's just standing there, looking at me. He's holding a bucket of take-out chicken in his arms.

"Hi, Jimmy." I can't pretend I haven't seen him.

"You said you just went in there to draw."

"Mmm," I murmur. "Just wanted some friends to see the view, too."

"Not what I'd expect – your lady friends." He turns towards the entrance. "Didn't look like crazy druggies, at least."

"Oh, you're right, Jimmy. They're just normal ladies. I told you there was nothing weird going on."

He's satisfied. He *smiles* at me. How odd is that?"

"So, the one in the red suit – is she married?"

It seems Jimmy likes ladies with a little flesh on their bones.

"I'm not sure. I only just met her. I'll find out."

"Yeah, please. She looked approachable, easy to talk to. I like that in a woman."

If he only knew.

Around three, Patty phones. She never calls me at the office. She went into labor two days ago – a false alarm. She just got home.

"They should have kept me in, Strachan, to be on the safe side."

"But you're not due for a while. Would you like to be stuck in there for ages?" She's my sister. I love her, but I have a hard time dealing with her. I want to get back to my work.

"I've had three miscarriages, remember? You'd think they'd take that into account."

"Well, if they did all the tests, I'm sure they know what they're doing." But I'm not sure of that. You see these news reports about the terrible mistakes made in hospitals these days. "Do you feel normal?" There's that word again.

"As normal as you can be when you're as big as I am. I feel fine, Strachan. I haven't had a twinge since. It just pissed me off that they were so casual about it."

"Well, there. As long as you feel all right..."

"Can you come up this weekend? That's why I rang. I tried you a couple of times at home, but you always seemed to be out. Anyway, it'll be the last chance before the baby."

Oh, wow, a yummy weekend in Peterborough. We'll probably do the malls. Be still my beating heart.

"I suppose." I'd vaguely thought that the room would be okay again by this weekend. But I haven't seen Patty in months.

"I'll meet you at the bus station," she says, encouraging me.

"When?"

"Saturday? There's a bus that gets in around 11:00. We can do some shopping, although I can't walk too much. We can grab lunch at this new place I saw."

"Okay, sounds good. " At least it will be only for one night.

"What have you been up to lately?" she asks.

"Oh, this and that."

"Still drawing? I was thinking you could do one of our house. I'd like that."

I'd forgotten I used to draw. "Oh, right. I'll bring a pad and pencils with me."

"Only if you feel like it."

"No, I'd like to. I haven't been doing much drawing lately."

"So what have you been doing?"

"I have a boyfriend." I've been doing him a lot.

There is silence at the other end, and then Patty takes a breath. "A guy? You have a guy?"

"Yep. I have. He's nice." How can you describe Jay to anyone? They have to see him to believe him.

"I can't believe it. All this time. We never thought you'd find anyone. Is it serious?"

"Don't know. It's all new, but he seems keen."

"Strachan with a guy. Eric will be surprised."

Her husband probably always thought I was gay.

"I surprised myself."

"Well, we *will* have a lot to talk about. I'm quite stunned."

Wait until I tell her about the book…

FIFTEEN

"It's good that you'll be away on Saturday. I'm going to be out of town." Jay is massaging my back. He's very good at it. I suspect he's massaged a lot of backs in his time.

"Oh? Where are you going?"

"Music thing in Chicago. Some client schmoozing. I go every year. I won't get back until Tuesday."

"The office won't function without you."

He stops massaging me. "What do you mean?"

"Just that everyone seems to slow down when you're not around. Even Dylan is brighter when you're in the office. I notice these things."

"From your little secret cave, way over in the corner?"

He stands up, leaving me spread like a reddened cadaver on the rug. I pull my robe around me. I am wearing underwear, but I still get self-conscious in bright light. "I get lonely. I peer over the top of my screen a lot."

"Anyway, I don't understand what you said about the office. I don't *work* for Dylan – you knew that, didn't you?"

I turn over, twisting to look at him as I sit up. "You don't *work* for him?"

"I mean I'm not an employee. I provide a service, that's all. I'm a contractor. It's a wonder Nell didn't tell you – she pays my monthly bill and expenses."

"We haven't discussed you that way." I pull myself up onto the couch. "It's the same thing, isn't it? You're like the freelance artists - billing by the hour?"

"It's not the same. I have a lot of clients. Dylan just happens to be one of them."

"Oh." I look at him closely. "So you're a company."

"I am. JayCee Enterprises." He smiles sheepishly. "I came up with the name when I was much, much younger."

"Well, I don't know what difference it makes that you're not an employee."

"Just that you might wonder where I get to a lot of the time. I have my own office on Avenue Road."

"Oh. I figured you have places to go, people to see…the usual."

"How did you think I could work full time for Dylan? Researching music tracks, or hiring musicians or jingle writers for the occasional marketing blitz could never take up so many hours."

"I hadn't thought about it."

"I'm involved in a whole bunch of stuff. I see a lot of Dylan because he's a good friend. We more or less started out in this business at the same time."

"I didn't realize…"

He straightens up. "Hey, you didn't say what's happening with the room. Any light, yet? And you were going to show me the book. I almost forgot."

"You'd have to read it on my computer – it's not printed off." I don't fancy Jay just reading for the rest of the evening. I haven't decided yet whether to tell him about Ida. I'm still uncomfortable with that.

"It's probably not your kind of book, Jay."

"What kind is that?"

"Well, I don't know. You've mentioned a couple of writers you like."

"And you didn't respond. I remember that. Guess we have different tastes in reading."

"I don't care for thrillers much, or most sci-fi. I read a lot of it when I was a kid, and I guess I burned myself out on it."

"So you've matured, and I haven't. What do you like now?"

I shrug. "Whatever appeals to me at the moment. I don't have just one interest."

"Eclectic tastes, eh?" He is curling a strand of my hair around his finger. He does sweet things like that all the time.

"What is it about me you like, Jay?" I know I shouldn't ask, but I'm curious. "You must meet so many women…"

"Oh, yeah – *here* we go. The questions."

I'm hurt by this. "What, because everyone asks that – all those other girls you've known?"

"No, idiot. If anything, it's because you *never* ask questions. I've never met a girl who didn't want to know my life history within the first week. You've waited this long."

"So?"

"So, you're different. The women I meet are usually ambitious, pushy, obsessed with their looks, and demanding. My relationships don't seem to survive long. I get fed up with them, or they dump me because I travel a lot. Either way, I like not feeling suffocated by you. You're a good girl, Strachan. I like listening to you – to what you have to say. It's always interesting. You make me laugh, too. I feel good around you. Someone should have snapped you up years ago."

I am unable to speak. In my daydreams of late, I imagined Jay saying something like this to me, but I always dismissed it with the conclusion that he is way too sophisticated, that he'd soon become bored with me.

"Hey," he pulls me close to him, "don't you start getting all weepy on me, okay?" He smiles his rude smile, the one that gives me a jolt in my belly. "I prefer getting you wet the other way, sweet."

Oh, and doesn't he do that well?

I spot Patty as soon as I step off the bus. Considering that I rarely think about her, or talk to her, it surprises me how emotional I get. Tears are in my eyes. It must be the childhood association, the link to our parents. We don't have anything else in common.

"Strachan, you look lovely." She holds me at arms' length to see me properly. "What have you done to yourself?"

"Katie took me shopping. I never knew what I was missing."

"Good for her. At least I can walk down the street with you and not wonder what the neighbors are thinking."

"Did you do that?"

"Oh, yeah. We don't have a lot of alternative types on our street. You should know that."

"But typical of you to give a shit about it. Why do you care what they think?"

"Oh, and you don't? What do you think the Punk clothes were about anyway? You wore them to shock the old biddies, admit it."

She's probably right. It was a way of giving them the finger, I guess.

"You're so fat," I say.

"Thanks for noticing."

She's huge, and although I don't know too much about it she looks ready to drop her bundle at any minute. "Are you sure you're up to this weekend? Shouldn't you be putting your feet up?"

"I'm going mad with boredom. Eric won't let me do anything when he's around. I have to wait until he goes to work to get out of my chair. He was so cranky with me yesterday, because I decided to move that armoire we have in the second bedroom – the baby's room. It wasn't hard to shift, and I had so much energy. He was furious when he saw what I'd done."

"You should be more careful, all the same. You've been waiting for this baby for so long."

"It's natural to want to do physical things towards the delivery date. I was reading about it. It's the nesting urge. It's deep within our biology." She starts the car and heads for the parking lot exit. "I was thinking about painting it – the armoire, I mean, but that would involve a lot of stooping. I don't stoop well these days."

"How's Eric?"

"Oh, he's fine. Very nervous. I think being sent home from the hospital the other day was harder on him than me. He got quite argumentative with the doctor." She glances at me. "What's new with you?"

"Quite a lot."

"So? Don't keep me in suspense. What have you been up to?"

"Well, first, I have this guy now. Jay's so good to me, Patty. I didn't know men could be thoughtful. Well, I never gave them the chance one way or the other."

"Jay, eh?" She laughs. "You with a boy friend... And here Eric thought you were gay. This will put his nose out of joint. He never believed me when I said you weren't."

"How come you were so sure I wasn't?"

"Well, you're not, are you? So I was right. I don't know how I knew. You just do, don't you?" She pulls into a small plaza and stops the car. "Shall we be bad and get something decadent to just take home? Chips and dip? Ice cream? I've had this craving for them all day." She waddles ahead of me into the store. "Of course, you get what you want. You don't have to eat mine."

It's fun being back with her. How strange to have this sisterly feeling, all warm and concerned. It must be her pregnancy. I can't remember ever giving a shit about Patty until today.

I guess I'll wait until she's finished stuffing her face with all the crap she bought before I tell her about the book. The shock might be too much for her digestion. Hell, I could send her into labor.

Well, that's what she wants, doesn't she?

Rupert is pissed off with me. Along with having Jay here all the time, I added insult to injury by disappearing for a whole night. He's fine without me, because he has a bowl of dry food and fresh water, but he enjoys the regular wet (yukky) stuff from a can, and he missed out on that. He sleeps most of the day anyway, but he does expect those night time cuddles and I haven't been as forthcoming with those the last couple of weeks. It's a good hour before he sidles over to me and fixes me with that wide-eyed look of disapproval.

"I'm sorry, chum. I have to go places sometimes." I pick him up and hold him close to me. "You big baby. Mummy's home now." I don't know how I came to start using such silly expressions with him. If Patty's wardrobe-moving can be considered a biological imperative, then I guess being a mum to a cat is reasonable for a childless woman.

I set him down on the floor. "Come on, ugly. Let's open a can of something really, really smelly."

As I walk around the couch to go to the kitchen, my eyes are drawn to the window in my bedroom – the door is always open. I draw a sharp breath. The light is on in the attic!

I run to the kitchen to throw Rupert's disgusting food into a bowl.

If the light is on, she must be back. I grab my jacket and the laptop, and head for the door, remembering at the last moment to get the flashlight.

"I'll be back soon, Rupert," I say to his self-absorbed back.

I take a huge breath, and open my door. Please, please, don't let Jimmy be around. If he were to see me at this moment, he'd know by my face that I do more than draw over there.

It's just the way it always was – that warm, golden light, everything in its place as it should be.

"Thanks, Celia," I say, as I sit down on the couch. For the first time, I believe she can hear me. I am almost overcome by the feeling of peace that's enveloping me, as if I've just smoked weed.

I consider what music to put on. It's becoming a little monotonous now. How many times can you keep playing the same old records? I should research the era, and see what I can find in the used record shop. Time for a change.

Celia won't mind. She's probably as tired of it as I am.

"Oh, I'm so pleased for you, dear." Nell gives me a quick hug. "I know what a worry it was for you. Ida must have been right. Celia only allows *you* to be there."

"I did a huge amount last night, Nell. Can you run your eye over it and do your thing? It looks better, because I followed the way you set the rest of it up, so it shouldn't be as bad as last time."

"Leave it here. Dylan's off to his golf this afternoon, so I'll do it then."

"It's good to get back to it. I was lost without it."

"Is she all right?"

"Oh, yes. You'll see. But I can't help thinking that something is going to happen soon. It's as if it's building up to a climax, the way real books do."

"Well, it is a real book, isn't it?"

"You know what I mean."

"It would be good for you to finish it. Much as I'm impressed with it, the idea of you poring away over it, late at night in that awful room, is sad."

I smile. "The room isn't awful now."

"Oh," she smiles. "Of course it's not. I wish I could see it that way."

"I should take a photograph. I never thought of it before."

"Of course! Oh, do that for me, Strachan. I could give one to Ida. She'd enjoy that."

I am uncomfortable. "Nell…I didn't ask the other night…but what's the usual fee for her work?"

"Oh, silly. She won't take anything from you. First, she's my friend and it was a personal favor. Second, she enjoyed herself. She likes doing house calls with some serious history to them. Apparently, some are quite dull."

As I head back to my work, I can't help wondering how many house calls Ida gets. It's intriguing to imagine people across Toronto dealing with the same kind of situation I'm in. Were they embarrassed to talk about it? Did they think they were losing their minds? And what do spiritualists usually charge for their services? Do they have a sliding fee structure to accommodate people on lower incomes? Do they charge by the hour, or by the quality of the presence?

If I become famous, and rich, I'll donate some money to Ida's church. I can't believe she earns very much from ghost-hunting.

Oh, dear. *There's* a word you don't toss around lightly – not in my usual world, anyway.

SIXTEEN

March 23, 1943

It's one of those indoor nights, when all the girls seem to be off at the same time, but not a duty night when they are all expected to clean the hut top to bottom. Nights like this remind Celia of all the boarding school books she'd read when she was young. She'd always thought it sounded like fun to be in a dormitory with lots of girls, sharing food hampers, getting up to all kinds of innocent mischief. She had sometimes resented the fact that her parents would never spend good money on that kind of school, even if they'd had that sort of money. They are devouring a fruitcake that Lucy's mother made for them. She used up a lot of her ration book coupons on the ingredients, they were solemnly told.

Celia finds herself telling Pamela about her affair with Alex, very quietly, sitting on Pam's bed, which is farthest from the door, and away from the racket the rest are making. She doesn't know why she's telling her, even as she's speaking about it, but has this terrible need to share what she's been feeling lately, and there is no one else.

"You should have been more responsible, Celia," Pamela replies, at the end of her little confession. "All these chaps are the same, you know, however different they seem. It's the way men are, isn't it? He won't marry you now. You've ruined any chance of that."

Celia frowns. "But why? He loves me." She hadn't expected to be made to feel uncomfortable, but had hoped for sympathy from the other, wiser, girl.

"Oh, they all say that."

But Alex had never said it. "Alex is different."

"That's what I'm saying, pet. They're all the same, don't you see? All men need sexual intimacy. It's their nature. It drives them. It's quite beyond their control. And that's why it was up to you to stop him. You should have told me what you were going through. We could have talked all this out before it was too late."

"Too late for what?"

Pamela fixes patient eyes on her. "You've spoiled yourself for anyone else, haven't you? I mean, what well-brought up fellow will want you now?"

Celia is stunned. "But I don't want anyone else. Just Alex. I would never go with anyone else."

Pamela sighs. "You'll see. By this time next year, it will all be over."

Celia shudders despite herself, because she'd thought this herself, but had believed that Alex's death would be the reason. "I just wanted to tell someone...how I'm feeling about it all."

Pamela puts an arm around Celia's shoulders, and squeezes her. "Look, pet, I'm sorry to be so unkind about it. It's just what I believe. You should have saved yourself for after the wedding." She reaches for her mug of almost-cold tea. "I don't mean to be dismissive. It must be awful to be in love with someone so much that you lose control, especially now, with so many chaps going missing, or dying. I know I couldn't do it."

Celia looks at her. Pamela is not a pretty girl, by any standard, with a nose that's impossibly large for her thin face, and skimpy, lack-luster hair. Perhaps it's this fact that's protected her from temptations of the flesh, a phrase Pamela has used once or twice in the past. "I don't regret any of it," Celia says quietly. "I want to be with him that way all the time. It's getting worse, rather than better. I thought..." she hesitates, "...doing it, you know...would somehow make it easier, but it's just made me want him more."

"Oh, yes," Pamela sighs, "that. It's all to do with biology and procreation. It doesn't last, you see? It's Nature's way of making sure you do it enough times to produce offspring." She says it dispassionately, patiently, as if explaining something to a child.

The noise from the far end of the hut is becoming louder. Gladys is dancing to a Benny Goodman record on her table-top record player. It's quite a smart-looking machine in its fine wooden case and must have been expensive once, although it's a bit dated with the old brass speaker – probably made in the 30s. Gladys is wearing only her brassiere, knickers, suspender belt and lisle stockings, having shed her uniform when she came in, but she's put

119

on her dress-wear high heels. She looks like a showgirl as she jitterbugs alone, Celia thinks, while the girls clap in time.

She turns back to Pamela. "In any case, I just wanted to tell you. I didn't want to have to fib anymore."

Pamela is still watching Gladys. "Best to be realistic, anyway. Enjoy it, now you've started. I expect you knew it couldn't last forever."

The door suddenly flies open, banging loudly back against the wall, and everyone turns to it. Marion darts forward and turns off the record. Gladys falteringly stops dancing and reaches for her dressing gown. The flight sergeant stands there, his face a mottled mauve and red, the eyes taking in Gladys's still-exposed body, lingering on her breasts, and her rather large thighs, the soft white tops of which show above her stockings.

"Sorry for the noise, Sarge. Just a bit of fun." Gladys is now completely covered, although her thin gown does little to disguise the body beneath.

He glowers at her. His voice is thin when he speaks. "You women don't give a tinker's curse about anyone but yourself, do you?" He is still looking at her body. "I suppose you don't give a toss that twenty-seven of our ships have just been lost, do you? Too bleeding busy having a good time, eh?"

No one speaks, although a few of the girls move slowly away towards their own beds.

"What ships, Sarge?" Doris remains where she is.

"Merchant Navy. North Atlantic again. German U-Boats wasn't it? The bleeders…" He finally pulls his gaze from Gladys to look at Doris. "You've got a brother doing that run, haven't you?" There is the tiniest smile on his face as he says it.

Doris turns away then, biting her mouth, shaking her head from side to side. Martha moves to her, and puts an arm around her.

"You'd never know there was a bleeding war on, the way you lot carry on," the sergeant says. He looks at Gladys. "My office, 0900 hours." He leaves without another word.

"Oh, bollocks," says Martha. "He's going to have it in for all of us now." She looks at Gladys. "You'll be cleaning out the lavatory block for a month."

Gladys's face is white. Celia feels sorry for her. Everyone else is huddled around Doris, who seems dazed.

"Try not to worry, love," someone says to her. "His ship's likely not involved and there's nothing you can do tonight. Things will seem better in the morning, you'll see. "

That's what people always say, but it isn't always true. It's only in the light of morning that the true ravages of the night before are evident. Celia shivers as she walks back to her own bed. She wishes now that she hadn't told Pamela about the things she'd done with Alex. She wishes that Gladys had not played the music quite so loudly, and that she hadn't undressed before she'd started to dance.

"Imagine you an aunt," Katie says. "Auntie Strachan." She tries it out. "I think it would be great. I'll have a kid one day. You will, too, probably." She finishes the last of her coffee, and signals our server. We're back at our favorite coffee shop, sitting on the patio.

I smile at her. "We both will, I suppose, although it's hard to imagine, isn't it? I can't picture you with a huge belly." I glance down at myself. "I can picture myself though. People always said I had childbearing hips."

"More like Jay-bearing hips the way you two have been at it lately." Katie laughs at herself.

"He's wonderful to me, Katie. All these years I'd never given a thought to what it would feel like, the whole love thing, I mean. Now it's all I ever think about. Well, that and the book."

"Oh yeah, the book. So tell me when it happened – when did it call you back again...is that how you put it?"

"Sunday night. The light just appeared again and when I got there, the room was back to normal."

"Normal. Right."

She still thinks I'm having a breakdown or something.

"And I'm catching up on the writing. I think things are coming to a head. I can't explain it, but I just feel it – that the book will end soon."

"Well, I'll take your word for it." She sits back to allow fresh coffee to be poured.

"And I have a good list of agents to write to now, so I'll be all ready to go."

"You think you have a chance at getting this thing published?"

"I do. It's good, Nell says. I read a lot, Katie, and it's better than most things I see."

"Aren't you worried about them prying into your life, asking you about how you wrote it – I mean, you won't tell them about the room, will you?"

I nibble on my lower lip. "I might. Everyone is into fantasy these days. Look at all the hype that angels got a few years back. People want to believe in things like that."

"Not me. Hate that shit. But I know what you're saying. Could make for a best-seller with what people read." She sighs. "And all that paranormal crap in the movies! It's getting to where you can't find a serious, reality-based film. What's wrong with everyone?"

"It's because we've lost our religion, lost faith in God. That's what Nell thinks. People need something to replace it."

"More fool them. " She looks squarely at me. "Yet you don't believe all that crap, and you still claim this…thing…this girl is making you write it. Doesn't that sound crazy?"

"I know. It does."

"I've always thought you were one of the smartest people I know, Strachan. It just seems so weird…"

"I know," I say, trying not to sound whiney. "I wish I could think of another explanation, Katie. It would make things so much easier for me. I'm dreading those interviews that writers have. I'll suck at it."

"It should have been me in your attic," she says. "I was always a bit of a ham, you know. I'd have some fun with it."

Katie would be perfect as a successful writer, basking in fame, adoring TV interviews and guest spots. I study her. "Perhaps you could be me. If it happens."

She looks at me. "You mean, pretend to be you. Pretend that I wrote it?"

"Why not? You love that sort of thing. It's a thought, anyway."

She is very moved, I can see.

"Do you think we could? Who else knows about it?"

"Only Jay and Nell. Oh, and I told Patty, although she was so shocked I don't think she absorbed what I was saying. I didn't mention anything about the room. She'd understand if you took the credit. We could call it a collaboration."

"Hell," Katie says. "I'd love it. Me on TV! Instead of always the other side of the camera!" She grabs my hand. "But you'd resent that after a while. Why wouldn't you want credit for it?"

"Credit for what, Katie? I'm not the one writing it. It would be just so satisfying to have the book out there for people to understand about the War, to learn about people like Celia. I don't know what other reason there was for me to write it. Perhaps it will become clearer at the end. You'd be doing me a favor."

"You say that now…"

"Well, there's time to talk more about it. It won't be finished for a while. And then I have to find an agent, and a publisher. It could take months."

"It could take years," Nell says. "I hope you understand what the odds are against getting published these days. I've been reading a lot online, and the chances are so remote, although I suppose you could always self-publish it. But the conventional publishing market is at an all-time low, with companies only wanting tried-and-true writers who won't let them down."

"But if I do, the idea of having Katie say she's the writer…do you think it would work?"

"I don't see why not. I do understand your thinking, Strachan. I know I'd have a hard time dealing with all that publicity. It's far worse today, from what I can see. Your life would barely be your own, if you did well with it."

"There! And Katie would love that. She always fancied herself as a TV star, or a presenter. When we were in school she used to get the lead in all our theatre productions. And she's so pretty and full of confidence."

"And you wouldn't mind?"

"No, I don't think so. I've been scared shitless at the thought of reporters knocking on the door, or whatever they do."

"But you'd get the money. You'd have to arrange the financial thing, so that it's fair." She leaned back in her chair, and stared out of the window above her computer. "I think we just need to get this thing to an agent, before you start making any decisions.

See how you feel when you get that positive response – *if and when you get it."*

If and when I get it…

SEVENTEEN

When I open the door to my apartment building tonight, I am startled to see an old bum sitting on the steps. He's not peeing, thank Christ, which I've seen before, but the smell of whatever it is he's been drinking hits me. He looks at me apologetically as he pulls himself up to leave. He sweeps his arm towards the stairs in a chivalrous gesture, and I almost expect him to bow. I shove past him, and then some sort of pity takes hold of me, and I turn back.

"Take care," I say. He looks pleased. And then I run up the stairs two at a time. There are worse things in life than winos, after all.

The phone is ringing as I enter.

Eric's voice, higher than usual, greets me. "You should have a cell phone, Strachan, for fuck's sake. Everyone has a cell phone except you."

I know right away. "It's Patty, right? Is she okay?"

"Yeah, she's fine. A girl. We have a baby girl."

Goose bumps spread over me. "How big. Are they healthy? When, Eric?"

"An hour ago – I tried you at work, but you'd left. Patty and the baby are fine, just fine. I forget how much she weighs, sorry. But she's fine."

"I'm so happy for you both, Eric." In fact, I never liked Eric much. I always secretly thought Patty could do a lot better, but at this moment I feel a great rush of affection for him. "You made it finally. Have you got a name yet?"

"Sarah Margaret. You know, Sarah after my mum, and Margaret after yours. I've never seen anything like it – you knew I was in the delivery room, yeah?"

"Patty told me you wanted to do that." I only realize I am crying when a large fat tear drops down onto the phone.

"We're a real family now, aren't we?" And he's crying too, the way his voice breaks.

"Yeah, Eric. You've done it. I'm so happy. Tell Patty I'll be up soon, but I don't want to get in the way."

"No, that's fine. She'll be home in a couple of days, I think. She can phone you when she's ready, okay?"

"I can't wait," I say, sniffing. "Give Patty and the baby a kiss for me."

"Take care, Strachan."

"Aunty Strachan from now on, please."

He laughs. "Yeah, that's right. Sounds good."

"Tell Patty that I love her, okay?"

"Sure. But I guess she knows that. She's your sister, after all."

I replace the phone and stand for a while, staring at it. Yes, she's my sister, my only living blood relative, until now. And I'm an aunt. An old, almost-maiden aunt. Lucky you, Sarah Margaret. Everybody deserves relatives.

I take off my jacket and hang it up. As I walk to my room, I begin to remove my clothes, tossing my dress on the armchair as I pass, kicking off my shoes near the sofa. A nice hot shower would go down well about now. In a dumb kind of impulse, I go to my mirror to remove my underwear. I never look at myself naked, well, hardly ever. A healthy-looking, well-nourished (as a pathologist would put it) woman looks back at me, still somewhat unfamiliar because of this new-found makeup that seems to transform me. The eyes are bright and the skin clear, but I never much fancied my ugly snub nose – *retroussé*, my mother called it. Of course, my shoulders and backside are way too broad, but the waist indents nicely. My breasts are fuller than is fashionable, which means I can never wear tank tops without embarrassment, but then I haven't worn a tank top since I was eleven, so that's not a big deal. I could have done worse with my body.

Jay seems to enjoy it. I guess that's all that matters.

March 26, 1943

"Well, Doris's brother is safe," Lucy says as she comes in. "She just heard from her mother. His ship *was* in that convoy – you know, all those ships that went down – but he was late getting back from leave, and missed it. "

"Doris must be relieved," Celia says.

"He was all scared because he thought he'd be in real trouble with the captain. He'd have been in worse trouble – he'd have been dead - if he hadn't been late. He's not 'alf upset though. They had to call the doctor." She laughs. "Of course, his mother was a bit put out by it because his boat used to do the Buenos Aires run, and he'd bring back boxes of butter and sugar, and other nice stuff. Probably pinched it – he's a steward, isn't he?" Lucy looks around the room. "Has anyone seen Gladys? We're going to the pictures tonight."

"She must have an extra shift." Pamela has just come back from her bath and her hair is wet.

"I haven't seen her since Tuesday night." Marion glances up from her shoe polishing. "Does anyone know what Sarge gave her for jankers?"

Celia looks up then, and sees the girls exchanging strange looks.

"What are you thinking?" she asks them. "He can't do too much to her, can he? I mean, it's not like civvy street, where you could be fired."

"I'm going to ask around," Lucy says and leaves the hut.

"It's just that he is such a bastard," Marion says. "I wouldn't trust him as far as I could throw him."

Ten minutes later Lucy returns. They all know immediately that something is wrong.

"He's been transferred," she says, a little breathlessly.

"Transferred? Where?" Pamela walks over to her. "Why did they do that?"

Lucy takes a deep breath. "There's to be an enquiry. It'll all be hush-hush, of course, and we won't hear anything about it, but that filthy pig fucked Gladys – raped her. He walked her over to the lavatory block on Wednesday morning and started to tell her what she had to do for jankers – knowing him, he'd have wanted her to clean it with her toothbrush – and then he just suddenly grabbed her and threw her over one of the sinks. Everyone was on duty, so no one came in. The sad bitch waited until he'd gone and then she went over to the medical officer. She was in a bloody mess."

No one responds, but the sound of their breathing seems overly loud.

Pamela crosses herself. "Poor thing. I like Gladys. She can be a bit silly, but she's always been kind to me."

Marion is still staring at Lucy. "He hurt her?"

"Yes, he bleeding-well hurt her. He did her up the arse, didn't he? What kind of animal does that?" She turned to look at all of them. "I'll tell you what, if he came near me, I swear I'd bleeding kill him. And I doubt anyone would stop me."

"He always used to look at her in a funny way, did you notice?" Celia speaks up. "It was like he fancied her but she disgusted him, too. It used to give me the creeps – that look."

"Well, we're shot of him now." Lucy flops down on her bed. "They've sent him up north somewhere to a men's camp. The word will get out though. He won't get away with it. Once the blokes up there get wind of it, they'll give him a proper seeing-to, you wait and see. They should cut his dick off."

"Where's Gladys now?" Marion asks.

"Home on sick leave. It's a shame, because her Yank is back this weekend. She was dying to seeing him, too. She won't want him to know, will she?"

"Who told you all of this, Lucy?" Pamela asks.

"I know one of the nurses over there. We worked in the same factory when we got out of school. She's an old friend – tells me everything that's going on. Never anything as bad as this, though."

"She's a sensible girl, that Gladys. She's strong. She'll get over it." Marion sat down limply on one of the beds. "I know what you mean about wanting to kill him."

"He bit her when he was doing it." Lucy screwed up her face as she said it and rubbed at her eyes. "He made her bleed. How could someone like that be in charge of women? What kind of bloody stupid war is this, to let something like that happen?"

"He should be up on a charge." Pamela's face is pale.

"Oh, Lord love her, she thinks they could charge him." Lucy shakes her head. "You'll never hear another word about this, not at this camp. The things that go on you wouldn't believe. Even with the brass. It all gets swept under the mat."

"She's right, of course," Celia says. "I worked for a solicitor. There were lots of things on civvy street like that never taken any further. It stands to reason it would be her word against his. He probably said she led him on."

They look gloomily at one another. Lucy is the first to move.

"I'm going out. I don't care if I don't have a pass. Bugger the lot of them. Let's just see what the bastard's replacement will do about that." She pulls on her cap and looks back at them. "One thing's bloody sure. The next Sergeant-in-Charge had better be a woman. If they bring in another bloke, I'll write to Churchill himself."

"To think, it could have been any one of us," Pamela says.

She doesn't see the amused glances the rest of the girls exchange.

"So where's the manuscript?" Jay asks, as he opens the wine.

"I still haven't printed it off. Nell works from my disk. I could burn a CD for you, if you like."

"Oh, right. Is it finished?"

"Not yet, but close, I think." He has lovely shoulders, very broad, considering how slim his body is. I have this urge to run my hands over him now, before we've eaten, and feel his immediate response.

"Should I wait until it's done? Is that better?" He hands me my glass.

"Probably. I'll definitely be printing it then. Nell says we need to proofread a hard copy before we contact anyone. She thinks we'll still have missed errors working with it from the screen."

"She's right." He sits down next to me and puts his hand on the back of my neck, lightly massaging at the hairline. "You all right? Miss me?"

"Of course. I hate not seeing you."

"Are you very hungry?" His hand has moved around down my throat, and hovers at my neckline.

I realize what he's getting at. "Not exactly."

"Great. Come on, then." He puts his glass down and grabs my hands, pulling me up off the couch. "I've got something for you." He glances down at his groin. "I've been saving it just for you," he says, with a villainous chuckle.

He is a bit rougher than usual, probably because of our separation. There is no preliminary stroking, or kissing, and he is already inside me before my bra is off. He moves against me almost with anger – rapid and forceful, without his usual lazy, preliminary rhythm, and I have no time to respond myself before he comes.

He opens his eyes and looks down at me then. "Sorry, hon. I did sort of warn you. I haven't stopped thinking about you. Give me a minute and I'll make it up to you."

After a while, he does – twice – very slowly, with his eyes open, watching me the whole time, whispering to me. I love when he does that. He says it's a Tantric Yoga thing.

We don't eat dinner until after eleven.

Katie wants to get pregnant. Ever since I told her about Sarah Margaret, she won't shut up about it. She's says she doesn't need a husband because marriage is old-hat, but now she wants a child. This isn't the first time I've heard this. When we were still in school, the topic often came up between us. It makes sense, when you consider it, with so many broken marriages, and kids all screwed up because of it. By having a Significant Other outside of marriage, the kid would never become accustomed to the usual domestic arrangement, and therefore wouldn't be upset when it ended. Because it always ends, doesn't it? I don't know what the stats are on it, but I think it's up to one couple out of three who divorce within five years. Not much fun for a kid, that.

"It's just a question of who I'd like as the father," Katie says, lifting her head from the sofa arm just enough to drink her wine. "It can't just be anybody."

"You could run an ad," I suggest wickedly.

"That's not so funny, you know. It's probably the best way to deal with it, although not on Craig's List." She laughs then. "I could interview them, and get to know them, keep it all business at first. Of course, I'd have to fancy him, as well. This guy will be in my life, even from a distance, for a long time, I should think. I'd have to respect him."

"Not a sperm bank, then?"

"I don't think so. I mean, fucking is fun, and I think that must somehow influence a kid, don't you think? I wonder sometimes if those sperm-donor babies might be a bit too conservative, or boring, because of the way they were conceived. I wonder if anyone has done any studies on that."

"Well, you seem to have it all worked out. I'm behind you. You know how I feel about marriage."

She grins at me. "I know, sweetie. You're my biggest supporter. Christ knows, my parents don't like the idea."

"What did you expect? Whole different generation..."

"But you'd think, from all their years of seeing it, they'd understand about marriage being a crock of shit. I know my mum secretly does, but she'd never say anything for fear of hurting Dad."

'Women are always wiser about that stuff."

"And you still feel the same, even now you've met Mr. Wonderful?"

I raise my eyebrows. "I guess so. I hadn't thought about it." I grab another scoop of tortilla chip, salsa and sour cream. I've made burritos to follow.

"I guess we're a lot different from our mums. They ached to be married."

"I know, poor things." I wipe a great blob of red and white yumminess off the front of my shirt. "It was even worse for our grans. They weren't even expected to enjoy sex."

"I know!" Katie sits up properly to eat. "How weird is that? They didn't even know about the clitoris until the Seventies. What the hell did they think that little knob was there for?"

We both laugh, more at her name for it than anything else.

"I still can't see marriage in my future," I say then. "It just seems too un-me. As far as I can tell, the only difference would be that you'd go grocery shopping together, check out hardware stores, stuff like that."

"But you'd do that now, if you lived with someone."

"Oh, I won't do that, either. I just like my own company. I mean, it's wonderful having Jay here, and I hate it when he leaves, but then, within about half an hour, I think of all these things I love to do that he isn't a part of, or isn't interested in – you know, like going to the library, or flea market shopping. And at night I like to just hang out on the couch, watching some old film – probably one he wouldn't like. And I don't always feel like shaving my legs as often as I should, and that's a bit of a nuisance – having to do it."

"Yeah, and sometimes on the weekend I don't even shower – just grub around all day in my PJs. It's nice to be a slob sometimes. No guy would put up with that."

131

We finish off the tortillas in relative silence, except for the munching, each of us thinking about the secret pleasures of single life; I know Katie feels as self-satisfied about it as I do.

"I was meaning to tell you, Strachan," Katie says, reaching for the wine bottle. "I think I'll pass on taking the credit for your book. I've given it a lot of thought, and it just wouldn't be right. It *is* your book, however shy you are. You're the one who has to publicize it."

"That's cool," I say. "You don't have to explain. It was a lot to ask."

"What I will do, if you want — I could coach you, show you how to deal with questions, how to sit properly in an interview so you look comfortable – that sort of thing. I know all that. It's a skill that can be taught. By the time I've finished with you, you'll look like you've been doing it forever."

"I love that, Katie. Do you honestly think you could help me? I mean, could you teach me how not to freeze up, or get tongue-tied – because I'm sure I will if I have a TV camera on me."

She nods. "I'm certain. We'll do it on a regular basis, so that it becomes second nature." She laughs. "Shit, Strachan, you haven't even finished the book yet, and we've already got you on TV!"

It should be funny, but it's not. I have always believed, deep inside, that it could happen. It's just a question of when.

EIGHTEEN

June 25, 1943

Celia is overwhelmed by '*The Dancing Years*'. Alex had promised her that they would go, but hadn't managed the tickets until now. They took the train to Waterloo and then a taxi to Drury Lane. She rarely sees London these days, and is appalled at the destruction, but the show almost makes up for it, and the sweet story will stay with her for a long time. For Celia, the songs from the show, in particular, '*My Dearest Dear*', will be Alex's and hers for eternity. She knows she's foolish to think it, but it's as if Ivor Novello wrote it just for them.

"I'll buy you the record, if I can get hold of it," Alex says, as they ride back to Waterloo. "You can play it on Gladys's Gramophone."

The reference reminds her of the night Gladys did her wild jitterbug, and she shivers, despite herself.

Alex touches her hand. "Are you feeling all right, darling? A bit tired?"

"No, Alex. I was just thinking about Gladys."

"You should try to put it out of your mind," he says. "I'm sure she's managing very well. Look, she got some time off, which is more than a lot of us get, and we've had some pretty rotten experiences too, remember."

"It's different to the War," Celia says. "This is personal. She won't forget it, even when she's old."

"Well, Celia – look, you don't know that. Some of these women are a lot tougher than you realize. They aren't all from nice schools, good families. A lot of them already knew a lot about life long before this War came."

She looks at him. "You think Gladys is a tart? Is that it?"

"Well, not a tart, exactly. But she's probably seen a thing or two. You said she was seeing some Yank, and they have a reputation for getting what they want, believe me. I doubt she's some innocent girl, with no experience."

"Like me and you, in fact." Celia gives him a little humorless smile. "You got what you wanted, too, like her Yank, and I'm certainly not innocent. So it's the same thing."

The taxi has pulled up in the station concourse, but Alex continues to stare at Celia, his face flushed with anger.

"That's two bob, guv," the taxi driver says.

Alex looks blankly at him, then recovers and fumbles for change. He takes Celia's arm as usual as they walk to their platform, but the grip is firmer, and she suspects there will be a bruise there tomorrow.

He hardly speaks to her on the way back to Bournemouth. There is an air raid nearby during the trip, and they are stationary, without lights, for over an hour before continuing. Celia stares blindly at the windows with their drawn blackout shades. Her face is set, her mouth tight. Why had she been so unkind to him? She tries not to cry.

When their taxi draws near to Celia's camp, Alex instructs the driver to pull over near a group of darkened shops, and pays him off. Celia looks at him questioningly, but takes his hand as he helps her out.

"We'll walk the rest," he says to her. "I could do with some air."

"I'm sorry, Alex, for what I said," Celia says, trying to see his eyes. "I don't know what came over me. I know you're not like those other men, chasing girls every night, just out for a good time."

"But you said it." He stops and turns to face her. "I think that you half-believe it – that I took advantage of you. Isn't that so?"

She looks up at him, at his handsome face, sees the way his fair hair – even here on the darkened street – gleams softly from the Brylcreem he uses to control it. "I do sometimes, when I'm in one of my moods," she says. "We all get blue, Alex. I can't help thinking awful things. I shouldn't have said it."

He pulls her to him, quite violently, and she gasps at the suddenness of it.

"No, you bloody-well shouldn't have!" Alex rarely swears.

And then he kisses her, bruising her mouth with his, forcing her lips open too wide, probing for her tongue, not in a gentle, Alex-sweet exploration, but in a kind of hungry animal way. Celia is at first repulsed, but then finds herself excited as she's never been before, and she allows the kiss and fully engages herself in it, wanting him to devour her, to consume her. She takes his hand and pushes it between her thighs, pulling her skirt up with her other hand, and stepping back into the shadows of a shop doorway, dragging him with her. Using both of her hands, she holds him so hard against her that he can barely manage to unbutton himself.

And so it is on the night that Celia sees '*The Dancing Years*' that she finally captures that elusive gnat, the mysterious thing that had so often teased her with the promise of pleasure beyond her experience. Shuddering, she understands that her tentative pursuit of it was always bound to fail, that only this almost-brutal thrusting of both their bodies could conquer it. It is exactly this kind of bliss that she's been longing for, the moment she'd imagined when she was alone.

It isn't quite the setting she pictured. It isn't in a great, soft marriage bed as she expected. But in a doorway of the tobacconist's on the High Street, up against the protective boards on the glass door, next to a large poster advertising Players cigarettes, Celia finally cries out at her first orgasm, although she doesn't know its name.

And Celia now knows how people do it standing up.

"Penny for them," Nell says, leaning over my partition.

"Oh, the book, of course."

"How's it going?"

"I bought some records today at the little used record shop – you know the one up the street. I was going mad listening to the same stuff over and over, but I needed it. If I don't have music, nothing much seems to happen. It's all linked somehow. Anyway, I bought some ballads from that time, and a bunch of swing bands, because I thought they'd help lift the mood. I'm hoping it's coming to an end, Nell. I know that sounds mean, but I'm getting tired of it all. It's exhausting, all the bad stuff that keeps coming at me. I used to enjoy it, but now, when I'm re-reading everything, I just feel so tired."

"It stands to reason those years would be emotionally draining. People dying, disappearing, being maimed, families never sure if they'll see one another again. It's a natural reaction."

"People getting raped," I say dryly, not looking at her, but my voice breaks a bit as I say it.

"What?" She looks at me sharply. "Not Celia?"

"No, a girl in her hut. I went online last night and fished around. Apparently there was a lot of it going on. If you think about it, women weren't like us back then. It was way before the Feminist Movement, and they would have still been pretty much polite and obliging, I guess. Hard to imagine some girl telling some guy to fuck off if he started getting too pushy."

"It still happens today though, so it wasn't just that they were more compliant."

"Not just that. It was the attitude that said it was okay. That men will be men, that they couldn't help themselves. No one was ever charged, unless he killed the girl. It was as if they felt it was bound to happen, and what could you do about it, anyway?"

"Women have been mistreated since time immemorial. They don't have it much easier in the military today."

"Yeah, I've heard that, too." I sigh. "Anyway, it's all a bit depressing. I wish something sweet would happen to cheer me up. As it is, I think Alex will die, and that doesn't bode well for a light ending, does it?"

"There's so much of you in this book now, isn't there?"

Nell has such a gentle face. She's motherly, and yet she's never had a sniff at motherhood, unless she came close with her biker.

"Hard to keep myself out of it. I sometimes think I am Celia – I've told you that before. When she's said, I'm sad. When she's happy, I'm happy." *When she's randy, I'm randy.* But, of course, I don't say that to Nell.

"It will be over soon," she says. "Once this book is done you can get back to your normal life. All writers experience this, you know. And actors. It takes time to reclaim themselves after being immersed in their character's life for a long time, but in the end they do. You'll see."

"You okay for more editing?" I ask her, reaching for the CD in my bag.

"Yes, of course." She looks at it. "Rape in this lot, is there? I might need a sip or two of Scotch tonight to get through it."

I laugh. "Have a Scotch anyway, but it's not that bad. There's very little detail. It's sad, that's all. I liked Gladys."

"Oh, no. Gladys?" She stares down at me, frowning. "The one with the lovely American sergeant? I like her, too. She's very funny."

"Not these days. She's gone home to recuperate. But everyone says she's tough, so I guess she'll be back." I smile at her. "We sound like a couple of crazy ladies, discussing these people as if they're real."

Nell is quite serious now. "But they are real, Strachan - or *were*. Somewhere there's a record of these people's lives. Ida and I were talking about it."

"She is clever, isn't she? How on earth did she get this ability, Nell?"

"She doesn't know. She always said she could do it when she was a girl, but she didn't because people would have said she was mad. Her own mother thought her mad. She was the only one Ida told – at least, until she joined her church."

"I still have a hard time with it myself, and yet she knew things she couldn't have known unless she really is psychic." I hear myself say these words, but it still sounds like a crazy lady talking.

"Oh, she's psychic all right." Nell is firm. "I've seen lots of things, believe me. I've been telling her for years to promote herself more. She could be famous. And she definitely could be richer."

"I didn't think she could make much money at it. I mean, how many people like me are out there?"

"You'd be surprised. No, she doesn't do it for the money. She believes it's a gift she's meant to help people with. She won't change now. She'll be cashiering at Loblaw's until she's too old to see the cash register."

"Loblaw's?" I start to laugh until I see her face.

"Yes, didn't I say? She's been with them for over twenty years, same branch."

I smile at her. "Isn't that funny, Nell? Can't you see how funny that is? The mysterious and amazing Ida, making change at a supermarket?"

Nell smiles too. "I suppose it is funny. I've never thought about it. A job is a job, after all, and she's the senior one there. She likes it."

"I only know she made feel better. If someone else believes me – I mean, someone professional – I don't have to wonder if I'm losing my mind." But a profession implies certification or degrees, doesn't it? I don't suppose Ida has any of those. It's not like you could pick up some credits at your local community college, is it?

July 2, 1943

"Meeting Alex?" Pamela asks, as Celia tidies up in front of the mirror.

Celia smiles. "Going home for tea with Mum and Dad. I'm meeting Alex at the cinema later."

"He's not going to your parents' for tea?"

Celia shrugs. "Not since that blow up I had with Mum that time. I don't want her having a go at him."

"Well, that's a shame. Perhaps he could win her over. I'm sure if she were to get to know him better, she'd see what you see in him."

"Not my Mum. She's as stubborn as a mule. Once she says something, she sticks to it. Dad's been trying to talk her around. Perhaps he'll do some good. Not yet, though." She dons her cap, and adjusts it to the correct angle.

"Will you be back tonight? I thought we could play cards." Pamela's evenings are often spent alone. She explained once that all her close friends were in Bath, where her family home is.

"Should be, unless Mum insists I stay over and do something with her tomorrow. There's a nice jumble at the local church on Saturdays."

"A jumble. I love those. Mummy was on the church committee before the War and used to arrange those. I found some lovely things there."

"Perhaps next time you could come with us. You could stay over one Friday. When Alex is flying. Would you like that?"

She is delighted. "Oh, Celia, I'd like that so much! I look forward to it."

"Right, then. I'll tell Mum. She'd like to meet someone from my hut. She's always going on about it."

"And perhaps you could come to Bath one weekend. You'd enjoy it. It's quite a big house, and Mummy is always inviting people to stay."

"Done! I'll check Alex's roster, and we can work something out."

"Are you eating properly?" her mother asks. "You look a bit piqued."

"I'm all right, Mum. We get a lot of beans, dried eggs, some sort of porridge that isn't a bit like yours – oh, but Lucy got some strange meat stuff called Spam from her Colonel. It wasn't bad. It's some sort of American thing. Most of the time, everything's thick and awful. I'd put on weight if I ate it all, but I get full quickly. I look forward to your salads." Her mother was growing lettuces, beetroot, spring onions and tomatoes at the back of the garden. At first she used to curse the neighbors' cat, who she swore was weeing on it, but then saw how well the plants were doing, and encouraged it.

"Alex isn't joining us?" her father asks, as he sits down at the table.

Her mother gives him a look, which he ignores.

"Not today, Dad. Other things on his plate."

"Because he shouldn't feel like a stranger around here. I like the lad. I enjoy a good natter with him." He looks pointedly at his wife.

She drops her eyes, busying herself with tea-pouring.

"I'll ask him for the next Friday he's off, shall I?" Celia says, looking at her father, but intending it for her mother.

Her mother bangs the teapot, now thankfully less than half full, down on the table. "Oh, for goodness sake, Celia, just ask him! I'm not going to eat him, am I? I've had my say, and you know how I feel. He's just a chap doing what chaps do if they get half the chance, after all. I can't hold a grudge against him forever. It's this bloomin' war, that's what's done it. I just wish you could have waited until you were married."

Celia blushes. "No one's said anything about marriage, Mum. I told you. Once the war is over, then we'll consider it."

Her mother frowns at her. "Consider it? What's to consider? Of course he has to marry you."

Celia smiled and shook her head. "Mum, I'm not having a baby. Isn't that the usual reason blokes *have* to marry a girl? It's the

Forties, for pity's sake. Women don't think the same way as they used to."

Her mother looks at her blankly. "It's turned all you girls into tarts. That's what I heard at the grocer's. Things will never be the same again."

"Of course they won't," her father broke in. "This bugger of a war has seen to that, hasn't it?" He looks at Celia. "Don't worry about it, love. It's hard for your Mum to get her head around everything that's been happening. The world seems to be speeding up somehow. Ask Alex around, and your mother will be perfectly nice to him." He winked. "She told me she thought you were lucky to catch him, and that if she was twenty years younger she'd go after him, so there."

"Oh, Bert, don't!" Her mother is embarrassed. "It was just a joke."

Celia looks closely at her mother. "I shall have to keep my eye on you, then, won't I?"

"Oh, Celia," her mother says, "you know I think he's a nice boy. I am trying to understand, really I am."

"Good," her father says. "That's settled then." He lifts a corner of the bread on his plate and peers at it. "What is it in these sandwiches? It's never fish paste. It looks like something the cat left behind the settee."

"I can't just give you dates off the top of my head," Alex says. "It's meant to be top secret, you know. Things are getting more involved every day, now. I've told you all of this before, Celia."

They have just seen the film, "*Suicide Squadron*", which has left Celia feeling particularly sad and vulnerable. It was a poor choice, she realizes, although Alex seemed unmoved by it. Too late now, the story, overly sentimental but endearing, and the background music, which she discovered is called "*Warsaw Concerto*", is indelibly etched in her brain.

"Well, just the dates around a weekend, that's all I was asking for. I don't expect to know where you're going, or what's happening through the week. I'd like to invite Pamela to my house one Friday, and I'd like to see where *she* lives. I think they own an estate, from what she's said."

"I'll think about it." He strokes her face, and stoops to kiss her quickly. "I wish we could get away somewhere again. You've been affecting my sleep."

"I'm not doing it in a doorway again, and that's that, Alex. You'll just have to wait."

But she had to wait too, and it was unbearable. Perhaps a doorway, or even that nasty little park, wasn't completely out of the question.

NINETEEN

"Hey, Strachan, got a minute?" Dylan pops his head around the kitchen doorway, where I'm pouring coffee.

"Sure," I say. I take my cup with me. No formality here.

"You've been with us for a long time now, haven't you?" he asks, as he flops down on the sofa in his office. "What is it – over nine years, going on ten?" He likes to sit on his sofa to work, bringing his papers with him. He only moves to the glass and chrome desk to use his computer.

"Ten years in August."

"Mm, right." He studies me. "It's time for more responsibility, I think."

"What?"

"You're not a kid anymore. I sometimes forget that. Jay and I were chatting and he mentioned your writing. It seemed to me that you would probably do quite a nice job working with Kelly on some copy and scripts. It would mean more money, and you'd get to meet clients. What do you think?"

I cannot speak. I sit there clutching my coffee, my face slowly reddening, and I inwardly curse Jay. What was he thinking?

"It's a lot to take on now, I know." He can't ignore my scarlet face, but drops his eyes politely.

"I don't know, Dylan. I don't write that sort of thing."

"Writing is writing, isn't it? You obviously have a knack for grammar and spelling, punctuation – all that. If you brought some literary excellence to the work, that wouldn't go astray either. People are more astute these days, and expect more."

"When were you thinking?" I like Kelly Hogan. When we have office parties, she's the one person (Nell usually leaves early) I can sit easily with, talking. She's into the same writers I read, and has suggested others I've come to enjoy. I don't see her through the week, because she's on another floor, but whenever there's a birthday or at Christmas, we gravitate towards each other.

"First of the month? I have someone in mind for your position, if she's interested. It shouldn't be a difficult transition."

"Kelly's a nice girl. I'd enjoy working with her." It will be the first time I've worked side-by-side with a colleague. I'll lose my safe, quiet little corner.

"Another eight thousand a year? How does that sound?"

I stare at him. What an earth will I do with so much extra money? I manage fine on my current pay. "It sounds like a lot."

"You'll clear an extra $500 a month I should think. It's what I was paying Vanessa when she started there. Of course, it will increase once we've established it's the right fit for you."

"I don't know what to say, Dylan. Thank you? It doesn't seem enough for a chance like this."

"You won't miss the graphics stuff? You've done a good job with it over the years and you've learned a lot."

"I don't think I'll miss it," I say, casually, inwardly excited to finally be rid of it.

"Because everything you learn here is part of the marketing experience, a great highlight on your resume. It won't go astray. You'll be confident about all aspects of the business, especially when clients ask questions. Soon, you'll know as much as I do." He chuckles.

My career is set for a giant leap. I'm entering the world of marketing executive internship. I'm also expecting to publish my book. I look rather cute, and I have a wonderful lover. And I'm an auntie.

Last year, around this time, I was a junior artist working on someone else's designs. I grunge-dressed and rarely shaved my legs. I was a virgin who had never seen a naked man. Any orgasms I experienced were by my own fair hand. I never went anywhere, and rarely had people over. I was a loner trying to convince myself I wasn't lonely.

Isn't it amazing what a year can bring?

"I was a bit pissed off at first," I say to Jay, as he takes off his jacket. "But then it all turned out so well, that I can't be mad at you."

"You could never be mad at me, could you?" He puts on his little-boy face, and ruffles my hair.

"I wasn't expecting it, Jay. I was in shock for a minute. And what if I can't do it? I mean, I don't remember the technical rules of English, but I just know them. If someone starts talking about conjunctive verbs, or participles, I'm going to look like an idiot."

"No one's going to throw that stuff at you. Kelly's a nice girl. She'll support you. I see you working well together."

"And I'll be meeting clients, Dylan said. I'm definitely nervous about that."

He pulls me down onto his lap, where he sits on the sofa. "You'll knock their socks off, you'll see. You have a lovely openness to you, girl. They'll get sucked in by that."

I look into his nice eyes, thinking how wonderful he always makes me feel. "Is that what you saw in me, openness?"

"You were like a very young girl, the first time I really noticed you. No posing, no cynicism. I was bowled over by you at that first lunch."

"And now I've been deflowered, is the young girl still there?"

He nuzzles my neck. "Mm. Yummy. I could be charged."

I laugh then. "Should I go put on my gym slip?"

"Your what?" He stares at me.

"Oh…um, from my book. Pamela was talking about her sports uniform and that's what she called it."

"Ah, a school uniform. Those parochial school girls have a reputation for naughtiness."

"Well, sorry, but I don't have one. Perhaps for Halloween…" I stand up to get coffee.

"I've read the first ten chapters, Strachan," he calls to me. "Do you want to run by me again just how this stuff comes to you? Because it's brilliant."

I put my head around the door. "You like it?"

"It's great. I'm having a hard time putting the light out at night. Just one more chapter to go, I think. You've got something, I think. Nell was right."

I bring the coffees in and sit down next to him. "Do you think I need to tell an agent, of a publisher, about the room? Can I convince people that I got all that information by researching?"

"Of course you can. It would have taken a long time to pull it all together, but I'm sure it's all available if you know where to look. It might be worth browsing around online, in case someone asks for your source sites."

"So I won't have to mention how weird everything's been?"

"Look, Strachan. I think it's a great book, and probably won't need any other gimmicks to sell it. But if you wanted to really make a splash, you could admit to the room, because it will bring huge publicity, probably world wide. Everyone loves that stuff these days. But you probably don't need it, that's all I'm saying. If you're more comfortable saying it's all your own work, then go for it."

"You're very cool about the attic, Jay. How come you don't think I'm crazy?"

"Dunno." He looks hard at me. "I think I'd know by now if you were some sort of crank, wouldn't I? If you say this is how it happens, I believe you. Of course, we have to find out more about this girl Celia. You can't just record her story and then forget about it. You should check out the records for the house at City Hall. There'll be deeds on file, and perhaps she owned the house, and you'll find her that way."

I shake my head. "No one else would go along with this. I've never known a guy who would consider anything paranormal, unless he was a total geek."

"Why should a guy be any less fascinated by the idea than a woman? The occult has been studied throughout history, and you can bet they were mostly guys doing it."

"You just seem so practical and modern-thinking."

"And you're not? Come on, I could picture Nell being involved, but not you."

"Ida thinks it's because Celia and I were both virgins, and that's why she trusted me."

He tips his head on one side. "Ida? Another member of the coven? Interesting. And Celia doesn't mind that you're not an unspoiled maiden anymore."

"Well, she's not either, so she can't make a big deal of it, can she?"

"Right, I get it." He finishes his coffee and puts his feet up on the coffee table. "There's a site you can go to that lists British census statistics through history – well, for as long as they kept records. Glenn, one of my squash buddies, is into it. He said the census is sealed until it's – I think – about a hundred and twenty years old, to protect people who might still be living, but both Alex and Celia's grandfathers should be listed. I mean, you've got their surnames, and you know where they lived. Most people don't move far from their parents' old stomping grounds. I'll get more details from him, next time I see him."

"Wouldn't it be amazing if we could do that?"

"And there's always Births, Marriages, and Deaths, in England. I don't know how we'd go about it, but we have names and places, and approximate ages, it's do-able isn't it?"

I smile at him, tears pricking my eyes. I've never known anyone I could rely on before. If I had a problem, there was no one to share with. Mum had enough of her own, and she was gone, anyway. Patty was never the sensitive type. Nell is fantastic, of course, but there's nothing like the man in your life just taking charge. It's a brand new experience for me.

"Wanna do it?" He says then, jumping up and grabbing me around the waist. He's no longer talking about genealogical research.

"You romantic fool, you," I say. "What a way to sweep a girl off her feet."

"You love it. A bit of rough, that's what you need." And with that, he pushes me to the floor, fully dressed, and begins to tug at my underwear.

A bit of rough? It certainly worked for Celia.

Babies are so wonderful. I'm feeling much brighter today. In fact, I can't remember why I was depressed. Sarah Margaret is a wonder.

When I bent over her crib, saw her for the first time, I thought I'd never seen anything so exquisite. That sweet, soapy-fresh smell, unlike any other fragrance, made me want to bury my face in that soft body, squash her ever so gently against me.

What were you dreaming as you lay there? What was going on in that perfectly-shaped head with its dark cap of hair? They can tell us when the fingernails began to form on those tiny fingers, and when the heart took its first detectable beat, but I bet they don't know when the first thought comes. Or maybe they do.

I watch Patty with her, when she finally picks her up. I have never seen such an expression on Patty's face before. It's not the bliss you'd see on the face of a woman with a lover. It's different.

It's a look of enormous peace, of complete satisfaction. Patty looks as if she and Sarah Margaret are the only two on the face of the earth. They are independent of all other life. That's the look.

Of course, Patty lets me hold the baby. Not for long, though, because Sarah Margaret starts to fuss, but enough for me to know that I will be a mother myself one day. This hype about motherhood is not hype at all. It's a deep primal urge that can't be restrained. Perhaps, for some women, it never presents itself, or never fully develops, but for me, and especially for Patty, it's almost a religious experience.

Patty and I are sprawled on her couch. My feet are on the coffee table, and hers are tucked up beside me. We watched a nice movie, a bit of a tear-jerker, but Patty told me that she cries at anything anyway, even a comedy. She admits to being ridiculously hormonal, but she doesn't make it sound unpleasant. Eric has gone to bed.

"I should have tried acting at school," she suddenly says. We'd been talking about great actors, who our favorites are. Both our tastes have changed over the years.

"Seriously? You used to talk about it, but you never auditioned for anything."

"Mum thought acting was trash. That's what she called it."

"I never knew that. I thought you just weren't that keen after all."

"No, it wasn't that. You know Mum. What she said wasn't questioned. I just went along with her. Life was easier that way."

"She would have loved the baby."

Patty smiles. "Yes, she would have. She wasn't too satisfied with me, but Sarah Margaret would have won her over."

I turn to her. Her blouse is still unbuttoned from feeding the baby, and one breast, although more than adequately covered by the nursing bra she wears, sit lazily exposed, a perfect white orb against the navy blue of her shirt.

"What do you mean, wasn't satisfied with you?"

She smiles at me. "Well, you know. You were her favorite, let's face it. I never got away with a thing."

I frown. "I wasn't her favorite, silly. She did everything for you, took you shopping, taught you to cook, and to sew. She never bothered with me. I bored the shit out of her."

Patty laughs. "That just proves how dumb you were about Mum, Strachan. She did those things with me because she guessed I'd need them. She figured I'd be married before I was twenty, and I was." She swings around and puts her feet on the floor, and then stretches. "I'm going to bed. I might get a couple of hours before madam wakes up."

"Hang on a minute. Tell me what you mean – that you needed to be taught that stuff. What about me?"

She is standing now, looking down at me, and I see how much she looks like Mum. I've never noticed that before. It must have something to do with motherhood.

"She expected more from you. She thought you were the one who would go on to do something else with your life – you know, a career. She told Grandad she thought you'd be a good teacher, or a journalist, and that you shouldn't waste that time tying yourself down with a husband and kids. She always knew you were the clever one."

I stare at her. "She thought I was clever? She never said that to me."

"It might have gone to your head. She was already having trouble with you, remember, being a smart-ass, arguing about stuff all the time."

"And I was expected to find my own way, without any encouragement from her, is that it?" I realize I'm getting angry, but it's such a stupid response, with Mum gone.

"Whatever she said to you, you would have done the opposite, wouldn't you? She knew that."

Patty is right, of course. If Mum had suggested taking additional courses, after I'd left school, I would have laughed at her. It's only lately that I've been considering what I'm meant to do with the rest of my life. Deep down, I always knew it wasn't manipulating *PhotoShop* on a computer.

I now understand what my mother had tried to do. But did she have to be so disconnected from me the whole time she was doing it?

TWENTY

July 30, 1943

"How are things with you and Alex?" Pamela sits down on the bed next to Celia, who's trying to finish the Norah Lofts library book her mother had lent her, due back on Monday.

"Oh, everything's all right. I haven't seen him for over a week, though. He needed some rest. They had a huge mission last weekend, and again a couple of days ago, but I suppose you heard."

"Where would I hear anything?" Pamela raises her eyebrows. "No one seems to gossip with me, except you."

"I probably don't know much more than you do, Pam. Alex never goes into details, but Lucy said there was a massive raid on Hamburg. Thousands of civilians killed, and a lot of people evacuating the city."

"Perhaps it won't be long now…" Pamela says, gazing out of the window towards the adjacent field, where a group of airmen are half-heartedly kicking a football around.

"We keep saying that, don't we?" Celia sighs. "Dad says we're no closer to the end of it now than we were three years ago."

"I can't remember what my life was like before the War," Pam says, studying her hands, as if the past might be imprinted there. Like Celia's, they are rough-looking.

Celia glances down at her own hands. "I know. To not be afraid every time you hear a loud motor, or a plane go over. To know your mum and dad are safe all the time. To go shopping and know everything on your list will be in the shop, and that you don't need coupons to buy them." *To be with Alex, and not have to keep saying goodbye.*

"I used to have such nice hands. My best feature, really," Pam says, massaging hers.

"Mm. It's that awful soap they have for the laundry. And that smelly stuff for cleaning the shower block. We should have gloves."

149

They sit for a moment in silence, both knowing how inane the mention of gloves is in the world they inhabit.

Katie flops down on the chair opposite me, and waves to the server. "I have to eat right now, Strachan. I'm starving."

"Have you been dieting again?"

"Shit, no. It's just that I missed breakfast." She gives me a wicked grin. "I found him, the guy that's going to knock me up. Of course, he doesn't know that yet."

"Who is he, Katie? Where did you find him?

"He's a new weather guy at the station. He just got divorced and he's totally out there. He's as randy as a dog in heat and we've been at it the whole weekend."

"He's a good choice?"

"Oh, Strachan, he's hot-looking, dark, but with blue eyes – whatever that's about? –and he's built like Matthew McConaughey. I can't get enough of him." She looks up at our server and orders a burger and fries.

"But he's smart, too? You don't want someone who's a moron." I am thinking about some of the TV weather people I've seen, and they weren't too impressive.

"He got his degree in meteorology and then his Master's in oceanography. He's dynamite!" She giggles. "And I don't just mean his brain…"

"But you'll keep it business like – you know what you said."

"Oh, that's fine. I'm going to tell him my plan this weekend. We're going to Montreal for the weekend. That way he can't just run off."

"What's his name?"

"Kyle," she breathes, and then sees my look. "Kyle Sheppard. You can see him yourself on the 11:00 news."

"You sound as if you're a bit too involved, Katie, if this is meant to be a practical arrangement."

"Oh, it's just a bit of fun. You know me. It never lasts." But her face reflects the bliss of a woman who wishes it would.

August 7, 1943

"Don't ask me any questions, Celia, there's a good girl." Alex looks into her face, waiting for a response.

"I won't. I know you get upset." She sits down at the beer garden table, and removes her cap. "A Shandy, please."

"Right." He goes into the bar, ducking beneath the low doorway of the ancient pub.

Celia looks around at the other customers. They are mostly in uniform, and there's an even mix of nationalities. She wonders if they all feel as deeply about this war as the British servicemen and women sitting there, laughing and joking, but who are more personally affected here at home. She knows that Alex is obsessed with his part in the War because of his own ties to England, but could an Australian or a Canadian ever feel this dedication, this need to retaliate for all the death and destruction wrought on the tiny island? One of the Australians catches her eye, and nods to her. She smiles back, but he sees she isn't flirting with him.

"There you are." Alex puts the drinks down and sits opposite her.

"Thank you," she says. He looks tired, the skin under his eyes oddly translucent and inadequate, minute blue veins visible.

"It's been a while," he says, sipping his ale.

"Too long, Alex," she says, wearily. "I haven't known what to do with myself this past week."

"I'm sorry, sweet. I was buggered, truly. I wouldn't have been very good company."

In fact he rarely is, these days. Alex doesn't laugh as much as he did when they first met. At first she thought she was to blame, but then she noticed that a lot of the men she'd seen around the camp seemed equally somber. It wasn't her; it was the War.

"Any chance of a weekend together?"

He looks at her, surprised. "*This* weekend?"

"This weekend, next weekend. Whenever you can do it."

"We've been busy," he said simply.

"I know that, Alex."

"I can stay tonight, if we can find somewhere. I don't have to be back on duty until 14:00 hours tomorrow."

"Where?"

He looks at the pub building, at the upstairs windows, and smiles at her. "Wait here a minute," he says.

They manage to get a small room at the back of the pub, the bed hastily made up by the landlord's wife.

151

"I don't let rooms now," the woman says, as she puts a pillowslip on.

"We appreciate it, really," Alex says, grinning at Celia.

"It's the licence, you see?" The woman finishes smoothing the quilt, and stands back to check. "We don't have a residential licence." She glances at them. "You'll have to keep this to yourselves, you know. I don't want the coppers around here."

"Oh, we won't say anything," Celia says. "It will be our secret."

"When my husband comes home after the war – he's in the Army - we'll apply for the licence again."

"It won't be long now," Alex says.

"We'll decorate all the rooms, and I'll put vases of flowers in each of them, and lovely soap in the bathroom." She whisks a dust cloth across the dresser, and moves to the hall. "We'll serve meals out in the garden, too, when he comes home. He likes to cook."

Celia looks at the woman's gaunt face, the empty eyes. "We just want to get back to normal, don't we?" Celia says. "To be proper families again."

The woman gives her a quick smile. "Yes, we're all in the same boat, aren't we?" She takes one last look into the room. "If you need anything..." She laughs. "– *If* I've got it – just call me. I'm Connie."

They follow her back down the creaky staircase. If they are to eat, they need to find a grocer's shop before it closes. Connie doesn't do meals.

Celia takes Alex's hand as they walk along the narrow path beside the road. The fields on either side are lushly green, and clumps of blue, pink and white wildflowers bob at the bottom of the hedgerows.

"She's luckier than most," Alex says, reading her thoughts. "At least she can have a Scotch or a gin whenever she feels like it."

Celia smiles. "I've needed that a few times lately, after an air raid, but I made do with a couple of aspirin. Our new woman sarge says aspirin cures anything, from headaches, to bad nerves."

"No more nose bleeds?"

"No. I don't know why I had those, but they've gone."

"Good, glad to hear it. And good that you've got a woman in charge now."

She feels silly, complaining about the infrequent air raids close to her camp, considering all the things Alex sees. She's also lucky to be with him as often as she is. Connie, and all the other lonely women out there, live for the day when their men will come home for good.

They are silent for the rest of the walk, but Ivor Novello's song suddenly begins to tease her. She would sing it out loud, but doesn't think she could do it justice, so she hums it instead.

And Alex starts to hum along, and then to sing. His tenor voice is strong and confident. She has never heard him sing. He should be on the stage.

"My dearest dear, if I could say to you..."

Celia doesn't notice she's crying until he stops and pulls her to him.

"Celia, you silly goose! You're such a cry-baby. I won't sing anymore it if makes you sad."

"I'm not sad. I haven't felt this happy for a long time," she says, looking up at him. "I just want the bloody war to be over, so we can get on with our lives."

"Not long now," he says.

For a split second, she believes him.

"Want to come to New York with me?" Jay asks, pulling the cork out the wine bottle.

"*Do* I? Jay, seriously?" I've never been, but all the best writers are from New York, aren't they? Perhaps we'll see one".

"I have to be down there for Friday morning, but I'll be free by lunch time and we can do the town, come back on Sunday night? Yeah?"

I look hard at him. "You're amazing, Jay, thinking of me. I've always wanted to see New York, but I never got round to going."

"I know you're a writer-nut, so I'll book the Algonquin."

My mouth drops a bit. "The round table Algonquin? Where all those famous writers used to meet?"

"The very one." He hands me my wine.

"Oh, God, I can't believe it." I suddenly remember. "What about Dylan?"

"Don't worry. I already cleared it with him. I told him about us. Is that okay?"

"I thought you already had. I thought that's why he promoted me."

"No, it wasn't that. I mentioned your book, and suggested he take a closer look at you. That there was more to you than he was giving you credit for. He's a busy guy. He doesn't always notice things."

"What do they wear in New York?" I wonder if 40s style dresses are in vogue there.

"What we wear in Toronto, girl. We're almost next-door neighbors, for God's sake."

I hug him. "Thanks, Jay. You have no idea how impressed I am. New York!"

"Get used to it. The agent for your book is probably going to be a New Yorker."

I frown. "Really? Why?"

"Because that's where most of them are. New York is *the* place for agents. Ask Nell."

"So I could become a regular down there? If they buy the book?"

"Oh, I don't know about that. Everything happens online these days. The only reason I'm going down this time is because this guy wants to meet me face to face, and he won't move his ass to come up here. Musicians!"

"What guy?"

"Guitarist/composer. John Williams wannabe. I've got a new client who needs a sort of rhapsody – you're more than familiar with *that* music" I've told him how many times I've listened to the *"Cornish Rhapsody"*.

"I wouldn't expect that kind of music behind a commercial."

"Not for a commercial. For a feature-length film. Toronto production company, a lot of U.S. money."

"You're involved in a movie?" Jay is always surprising me.

"Well, not me, personally. But I get to sit down with the director." He nibbles on my left ear as he speaks, and I lose concentration momentarily.

"What's the film about?"

"A love story, naturally, with the kind of music they want. It's set in Chicago – Toronto streets look so much like Chicago's, right? (He says this sarcastically. Jay constantly gripes about Toronto's lack of visibility in film.) I don't know much more, but I'll have the synopsis by Friday. If I can sell this guy, I get the contract."

"You're always coming out with new things about yourself," I say. "My mother would have called you a dark horse."

"Oh, I don't know about that. It's just that I assume you know these things already... that someone at the office tells you what I'm doing."

"I don't really talk much to the people at work. Nell's the only one, really. And she minds her own business, so I don't think she knows too much about you."

"My life is an open book. Ask questions, if you want." His hand is idly stroking my breast, so gently that it barely registers with me for a moment.

I study his face and that open, easy expression in his eyes. Jay is *trustworthy*, that's the word. I've never been too good at trust, because I'm afraid of screwing up and giving it to the wrong people.

"Why aren't you married? Most guys your age are."

"I was, in fact. We broke up over ten years ago." He smiles at my widening eyes. "All you had to do was ask."

"What happened?"

"I don't know. I still haven't figured that out. We just seemed to get bored with each other. One minute we were totally involved, doing everything together, and the next we found excuses to do things alone. It wasn't her fault any more than it was mine."

"But you loved her?"

"Of course, at the beginning. We were crazy for each other. It just didn't last."

I chew on my lower lip. "So you don't believe in it lasting, right?"

"Marriage? I wouldn't say that. I'm smarter now, and I'd recognize the signs, I think. I quite liked it at the beginning. I wasn't happy about it falling apart."

"I meant the being in love bit."

"Well, there are a lot of people who seem to think it's marriage that kills that. But what do I know?" He strokes my hair. "Are you asking me if I'm commitment-phobic?"

"I don't expect anything from you, Jay. I'm happy just the way things are."

"Because I think I'm in love with you, Strachan, if that's what you want to hear. I certainly have a hard time getting you out of my mind, when I'm supposed to be doing something else."

He kisses me then, that lovely Jay kiss that has spoiled me forever for any other man. Of course, I've nothing to compare it to, but it always takes the breath out of me.

His words are what all women want to hear, aren't they? These are the words that are included in all great songs and novels. I should be overwhelmed by them, I know, but I'm not. It's nice that he might love me, but it was never essential. Kissing him like this is.

"When do you figure you'll know for sure if you love me or not?" I ask, when we draw apart. I'm searching for something to say that won't hurt his feelings.

"Christ knows," he mutters, pushing me back on the sofa, and unbuttoning my shirt. "Ask me again later." His mouth is at my breast, like a hungry infant, and it's impossible for me to think straight. Perhaps he won't notice that I didn't say I loved him either.

Oh, Christ, he knows how to drive me crazy. He pulls my jeans down, then kicks off his own, and then at that last second before he enters me, at that moment of incredible, aching longing, I wonder why I'm *not* in love with him. Is it possible that I am, but I don't recognize it? Right now, *this* is all I need; *this* is all that counts. Just do *this* to me, Jay, again and again. I'll never tire of it.

"Congratulations are in order, I hear, Strachan." Sandra is standing at the entry to my alcove.

"Um, yes. I'll be upstairs in a couple of weeks." I haven't seen much of Sandra in ages, mainly because I've been going out to lunch a lot more, so avoid seeing her in the lunch room, but also because she hasn't deliberately sought me out for anything.

"That's good new for you, isn't it?" She gives me a small smile. "I've been meaning to stop by, wanted to say 'good luck', you know."

"Thanks, Sandra." I can't think of anything else to say.

"All this time you've been here – even before me, and we've never really talked. Funny that."

Is she mad? Has she forgotten how miserable she's made me over the years?

"Oh, well, it happens." Why can't I be a bitch now? Why can't I tell her how much I've always dreaded seeing her? But I can't. If you can't say something nice, say nothing. Isn't that right?

"Jay says you've written a book, too. I'm impressed. I had no idea."

She seems uncomfortable, which is odd for Sandra. I can't figure it out.

"Mm, well, it has a ways to go yet. I'm hoping someone might publish it."

"Yes, Jay said…. God, how amazing is that! We had a novelist in our midst and didn't know it. You must be pleased with yourself."

"Yes, I am." I'm uncomfortable with this new Sandra.

"Perhaps you'll autograph a copy of it for me when it's in print."

I laugh. "Oh, that's way off yet. It could take more than a year, even two."

She examines me then, in that old Sandra way, but it's not unkind. "You're looking very nice, Sandra. I like the new you."

"Thanks, Sandra."

She turns then, but glances back. "I was surprised to hear that you and Jay were seeing each other."

"What?"

"You and Jay. He mentioned it to me. It wasn't meant to be a secret or anything, was it?

I stare at her. Why on earth would Jay be talking to her about us?

"We're friends now, yes."

She gives me that little smile again. "Good friends, I hear. Don't worry, Strachan, I won't spread it around."

"Well, that's good, then. Thanks."

"See ya," she says, waving her hand over the top of the screen as she walks away.

157

TWENTY-ONE

"We used to date, Strachan." Jay doesn't look the slightest bit embarrassed. "Just for a couple of months. There was nothing much to it." He hasn't even sat down yet. I pounced on him as soon as I opened the door.

"And that's why you told her, because you used to date? That's stupid."

"Look, she was bad-mouthing you…being a bitch. I was listening to her rattle on, and I just lost it, and told her about us. I said she'd better start treating you with respect because Dylan was grooming you for bigger things." He grins. "I tell you what, her face went bright red. I've never seen her so shattered."

"How friendly were you two?"

He shrugs. "The usual. What do you think?"

"You had sex with Sandra." My voice is flat.

He shrugs again. "It was just over a couple of months. She was too much for me, with her bitch-attitudes. When she started trying to dictate what I did in my spare time, I dumped her. She's a control freak. She was like a spoiled child."

"It took a couple of months to find that out."

He leans forward, closer to my face. "Yes, Strachan. It took that long. She was on her best behavior in the beginning."

"Good fuck, was she?"

He stares at me. "Shit, are you saying you're jealous? This was years ago!"

"She's the one person at work who made my life impossible. I can't stand her, Jay." I turn my back on him, and fiddle with the coffee maker.

"And I can't stand her either. I have to be polite at the office, but that's it."

I look at him. "Yet you told her about us. I can't bear to think you've made love to her the way you do with me."

He puts his arms around me. "I've never made love with anyone the way I have with you. Don't you know that?"

I chew my lower lip. "I wish I didn't know about her, Jay. I'd give anything not to have this image in my head."

"Strachan, listen to me. You're all I care about. Don't mess it up for us. It's all in the past." He tries to kiss me, but I move away.

"Leave me alone for a while, please, Jay."

"You want me to go?"

"Yes. I need to get my head around it."

"Jesus, Strachan, you're making far more out of this than it deserves."

"Please, Jay. I'll see you tomorrow."

He stands there silently looking at me. I've never seen this crumpled expression on his face before, and I consider reaching for him, but I don't.

"What do you mean, you can't trust him?" Katie is very angry. "Hell, Strachan, it's not like you caught him at it with her. He said it happened years ago. He hasn't been screwing around on you. What's the matter with you?"

"It's just the thought of them together. I can't bear it."

"Jealous! You! I can't believe it. Ms. Cool who never wanted to get involved."

"I can't help it."

"You're going to lose this guy, if you keep this up."

"I probably will." I've already come to terms with the idea.

She shakes her head. "You stupid bitch. You'd let a nice guy get away from you because of some fucking pride thing."

"I'm dreading seeing her again, as well. I swear I'll say something to her."

"About what? She's past tense. Can't you get that through your head?"

I look directly at her. "Katie, I don't think I've been this miserable since Mum died. I feel as if my world just collapsed around me."

She pulls me to her, and strokes my back. "It's just that he's your first, Strachan. You've invested so much in him. But he's not a saint and he never claimed to be. You have to forget all of this.

Don't lose him. I'd never seen you so totally happy until he came along."

She's right, as usual. I've never been so happy. But somewhere in the core of my soul, if I have one, I think, like my mother before me, I shouldn't expect it to continue, because regular, continuing happiness isn't meant to be part of my experience.

This is why Celia found me. Because she's exactly the same.

August 14, 1943

"Oh, Alex, it's been a whole week!" Celia knows she sounds like a whining child, but is incapable of stopping it. (And she hates the smell of the phone mouthpiece.)

"I know that," he replies. "But I just can't. You have to understand how much pressure all of us are under up here. Just because you don't see it in Boscombe, doesn't mean it's not going on. I'll try to get down there next week, but I can't promise anything."

Celia's camp is purely a supply depot, with no air field. They deliver stores, laundry, even refuse, and sometimes ferry brass from camp to camp. They have the formal title *Aircraft Woman 1st Class*, or ACW, yet they rarely see aircraft, other than occasional dog fights, when everyone rushes out to watch. The girls all acknowledge what the *Auxiliary* in Women's Auxiliary Air Force means: 'Helpers'; that's what they were, their duty title, *Aircraft Hand General Duties*, or AHGDs. They felt hardly more involved than Land Army girls. Some complained that they didn't always feel like they were part of the war at all, that they could have done the same thing as contract workers, without having to wear those ill-fitting uniforms – well, it wasn't the uniforms so much as the shoes. Celia was proud of her uniform, even if it was on the big size, but nobody – not even Pamela – would wear those shoes on civvy street.

"I'm fed up with it, Pam," Celia says, when she gets back to the hut. "There's something wrong with him."

Pamela looks at her before speaking. "Well, you know what I think about it. Perhaps the novelty is wearing off."

Celia glares at her. "You mean having it off with Alex, don't you? Why can't you say the words?"

Pamela blushes. "I'm sorry, Celia. It's not something that I can speak easily about. My parents have always been very firm with me. And school, of course."

"Oh, don't explain. I shouldn't get upset with you. It's Alex I'm annoyed with."

"Perhaps he'll still make it down here."

"No, he won't. I could tell by his voice."

The hut door opens then, and Marion and Lucy come in, their faces solemn, but their eyes bright.

"You'll never guess what happened," Lucy says. "That bastard Kilpatrick is dead. Bloody good riddance, too."

"How?" Celia imagines him being strung up by a horde of men, mutilated. She has read Emile Zola's *Germinal*, and has never forgotten the mob scene, with that penis spiked on the pole.

"Driving back to camp, wasn't he?" Lucy sounds triumphant. "Got caught in an air raid. His lorry rolled over on him." She smiles. "He probably wasn't anywhere near the bombs, but just got the wind up, lost control and went into a ditch. They didn't find him until next morning. Hope he took a long time to die."

Celia isn't sorry that he's dead, but she's relieved it wasn't the way she'd briefly imagined it.

Lucy looks sharply at Pamela. "What the bleeding hell are you crossing yourself for? He doesn't deserve it."

Pamela drops her eyes. "All men belong to God," she says quietly.

"Well, if you really believed all that cod's wallop, don't you think he'd more than likely be with Lucifer? God wouldn't bloody-well want him." She walks to her bed and begins changing her clothes. "I'm out with my new major tonight. I'll have an extra good time, knowing that bugger is dead."

Pamela picks up her hairbrush and begins to smooth some wisps of hair back into her bun. She looks over at Celia. "Shall we go to the pictures? There's a good one on tonight. Bob Hope, *Road to Morocco*. I'd like to see it."

"Yes, let's," said Celia, standing up. "I could do with a laugh. If you're nice, I'll buy you a shandy on the way home."

Flight Sergeant Kilpatrick is never mentioned again.

It's odd how different New York smells to Toronto. I can't figure out what the smell is, but I suspect it's connected to the Hudson River. At first, I thought it was something to do with the age of the city, because Toronto is about one hundred and fifty years younger than New York, and its subterranean structures wouldn't have built up as much gunk. But the first drainage and sewage systems would have been installed at much the same time in both cities, surely, so it can't be that. Whatever it is, this strange sulphur-like odor is always with me, and yet Jay doesn't smell it at all. He laughed and said that smelling things that aren't there is a symptom of insanity, or a brain tumor. Hmm.

Of course, I've more or less forgiven him for Sandra. Katie's talk seemed to set me straight, and I couldn't let the New York opportunity slip by because of my pride.

We have this great room at the Algonquin on West 44th, just around the corner from Times Square, Broadway and Shubert Alley, and a whole array of bars and restaurants. Jay says Fifth Avenue is the same distance the other way, but I told him I'm not much of a shopper; he said he's taking me there tomorrow anyway.

I think this hotel must be quite expensive, because our suite is beautiful, and there are amazing gift packs of things in the bathroom and these soft terry robes and thick, thick towels. I'm trying to get over the feeling that I'm trespassing.

One thing that really excited me at the front desk was this little sign saying that writers get a discount, and they don't have to be published, but just need to prove they have a work in progress. Jay asked them if they would offer that deal to me, because he could go online to show them my manuscript; he has it stored at an external site, for safety's sake. They said fine. How cool is that? I felt like a real New York writer, just for a minute. And Jay didn't do it to save money, I know that. He did it to make me feel good.

I get to sit at the famous round table for coffee this morning. The waiter obviously enjoys telling people about it, although he must have repeated it hundreds of times. To think Dorothy Parker sat right here! Well, in fact, this isn't the original table, the waiter told me. It was replaced in the 90s. It doesn't matter to me. The floor where my feet are is the same floor where Dorothy Parker's feet rested back in the 20s. That's satisfying enough.

Seeing Jay outside of his usual surroundings is interesting. He seems more confident, even a little brasher, talking to people. It's as if New York gives him a jolt of energy that Toronto doesn't. Well, I hope it's just that. Already, within one block, two guys asked us if we wanted some snort. In Toronto, you could walk miles and not have that happen.

I'm kidding about Jay. He doesn't do dope, although he did way back. The guy's too successful to risk everything on instant gratification. Besides, that's what sex is for. We have been instantly gratifying each other a good deal since we arrived. It feels like a honeymoon. The only things missing are the wedding rings.

August 20, 1943

Celia is shocked by the way Alex looks, but tries not to show it on her face. It's only been a fortnight since she last saw him, but he is haggard, his cheeks quite sunken, and his color isn't right, although she can't work out how it's different. 'Ashen' is the word that comes to mind.

"Why didn't you tell me how bad you've been feeling, Alex? Didn't you think I'd understand?"

They are in the little pub near her camp, and the place is almost empty; it's a spectacular summer day, and everyone is drinking in the beer garden at the back.

He takes a sip of his Scotch. "It's not something a chap can talk about."

"But you look...so exhausted."

"So I'm told. Mother had a go at me about that."

Celia blinks. "You've seen your mother?"

He looks at her, somewhat surprised. "I went home after this last big push. I should have mentioned it."

"You can't see me, but you can go home?" Her face is stony.

He studies her. "Celia, I don't think you realize what's been happening. You can't even guess at what we're all going through. I can talk to my father and mother about it, because I'll always be a boy in their eyes, but I can't be like that with you. A chap's supposed to be strong, to be above it all, isn't he? Well, I'm not, blast it! I've never been like this before in my life. I can't eat or sleep. I just keep thinking about what happened to all those poor bastards."

Celia is shocked to see tears welling up in his eyes. "It was terrible, Alex. The story was on the BBC news, although it was only later we heard how many of our planes went down."

Bomber Command dispatched 597 aircraft on August 17 and 18, of which Alex's was one. They attacked the German rocket research centre at Peenemunde on the Baltic coast. Forty aircraft failed to return (not mentioned at the time), but the German V-2 rocket program has been delayed by approximately two months.

Well, bully for them, Celia thought when she heard, only forty planes lost for an extra two piddling months. Of course, she had already heard from Alex by then, and knew he was safe.

"And it was like a bloody abattoir's on the runway for the ones who did make it back." Alex drags almost angrily on his cigarette and she sees his hand shake. "I've seen that before, but not with so many, and especially not with so many who were friends." He looks at her despairingly. "I don't know if I can go through it again, Celia."

"You must take some medical leave, Alex. A lot of you must be feeling like this. I can't believe the M.O. won't understand."

"We're needed now more than ever." He finishes his drink and stands up. "I'm going to have another. Are you ready for one?" Her own glass is half full.

"No. I'm all right." She watches him as he walks across to the bar, his gait awkward and slow, like an old man's. A shaft of sunlight illuminates him as he stands waiting for his drink, and he turns his face towards the window, as if warming himself.

"Do you believe in God?" he asks, out of the blue, as he sits down again.

She considers this for a moment. "I was Christened in our local church, but then everyone does that, don't they? My mother and father aren't really church-goers, and I'm like them, I suppose. I enjoy the hymns at Christmas, and I've been to a couple of services with Pamela, because she likes the company. But I don't really believe in it all." She had never examined her beliefs until she befriended Pamela.

"Well, I don't believe in anything. My parents are very anti-church – they call themselves Secular Humanists. They believe in mankind. But Hitler's a person, isn't he? Do they believe in him?

Not bloody likely! I wish I could believe in something, Celia. It must be a comfort."

She needs to hold him close to her. She longs to stroke his hair, and kiss his sad mouth. "Can we go somewhere tonight? It's been so long."

He looks at her with a small frown. "I don't know if I'd be much good."

"Just to hold each other, that's all. I don't expect you to make love to me."

They find a Bed and Breakfast on Walpole Road, in Boscombe, a house that Celia has passed hundreds of times. She's always said she would never stay so close to her own home with Alex, but now her misgivings don't seem as important.

They lie on the bed, its covers thrown back because it's so warm, and hold each other. Alex's head is on her chest, but he makes no move to caress or kiss her. She reaches down and strokes him, her own breath quickening at the sound of his gasp. She believes he will turn to her soon, but instead he allows her hand to complete things, his guttural response ugly in her ears, sounding more like the groan of a wounded animal, than the joy of ejaculation.

"I'm sorry," he says finally, reaching for a towel on the bedside table.

"It's all right. It's nothing." She kisses his mouth, but he doesn't respond. "I love you, Alex."

"We can try again in a little while, if you want."

But they don't. Alex falls asleep in her arms. An hour later she gently extricates herself, but continues to watch him. This is the first decent sleep he's had for days, she guesses. It would be a pity to wake him just to please her.

TWENTY-TWO

"They've sold the house on the other side of that old place, did you see?" Jimmy is sitting on the front steps, painting the hand rail. "They're putting up a high-rise apartment block."

I look over my shoulder. There's a large redevelopment sign in both the gardens of *my* house and the one next door. I came home by cab from grocery shopping and so I didn't see it until now.

"That's a doctor's office, isn't it? I wonder why they sold." My mind is racing, trying to figure out how much time I have before everything is snatched from under me.

"He died. The doctor." He slaps some more paint on. "Eighty-two. Should have retired years ago."

"Did you know him?"

"Only to say 'hi' some mornings." He looks up at me. "Hope you've done with all your drawing."

"Mm, guess so." It's ridiculous to think he believes I'd take this long over a drawings. "How long before they pull them down, do you think?"

"It all has to go to City Hall for approval. They have to send these notices out telling anyone who might get their noses out of joint about the plan. They gotta give 'em time to respond. There won't be too many arguments. Those places are an eyesore."

"Will I get a notice?"

"No, it goes to the building owners. Tenants don't have any say."

"So how would I find out what's happening?"

He fixes his eyes levelly on me. "Why do you wanna know? There's nothing you can do about it now."

"Curiosity. I like that old place. I'd just like to know that they're doing something nice over there, and when it's going to happen."

"You could phone City Hall – their building permit department, I guess. Couldn't hurt."

"Thanks, Jimmy." I wriggle around with my bags and start up the steps. I look back at him. "Hey, Jimmy, I was in New York last weekend."

He looks up. "Oh, yeah? Where'd you stay?"

"The Algonquin."

He rolls his eyes. "Oh, sure. Very hoity-toity."

"It was wonderful. New York is amazing."

"I guess. I haven't been there since 1972. It was pretty wild then. They say it's all cleaned up now. Guess I wouldn't like it today." He goes back to his painting, but then turns back again. "Hey, Strachan. What do you see of that nice lady you were with that night?"

"Ida?" I grin. "Nothing, Jimmy. But I could phone my friend, if you like, and maybe get her phone number, if you're that keen."

"Just saying, if you were to get it, I might ask her out – just coffee, is all, the first time. Unless she's married."

"I forgot to ask, but I don't think she's married. My friend would have mentioned it, I think."

"Okay, then," he nods at me. "So do it. It's a long time since I took a lady out. You can see she's a lady, can't you?"

I nod. "She's a very nice lady, Jimmy." I watch him for a moment as he slicks on the jet black paint. "Do you believe in ghosts?"

He stops and looks up at me. "That's an oddball question – is she into that stuff? I guess I do, if you wanna know. My parents were from the old country, and they brought me up that way. There's something in it, that's for sure."

"Yes, well...I'm glad you have an open mind about it, because Ida *is* quite interested in the subject."

"Oh, yeah? Well, I've got quite a few family stories up my sleeve to keep her entertained, if she's interested." He calls after me as I open the door, "What about you, Strachan? Do you believe in them?"

"I never used to, but Ida set me straight." It really is close to the truth, isn't it?

Jay puts an envelope on the table in front of me. We've just finished eating, so he must have hidden it until now.

"Surprise," he says, grinning.

Inside is one piece of paper, a legal looking form, and I look up at him. "Is this to do with Celia?"

"No. This is for Alex."

I stare down at the paper, my breath shallower suddenly. Is it possible I'm about to start patching Celia's sad life together? Because it is a sad life, from what I've seen. She's in love, but it seems doomed, although I've no idea how that will happen.

Jay bends closer to me as I look at the document. "Alex's branch of the family still lives in Winchester – at least, his descendants do," he says, pointing at one section. "Glenn did all this" – he waves at the page – "because he said it was quicker than explaining to me how to do it. First he got the original family address from this census – and this is the last date available – 1911 – and then he looked up a site that lists phone books that go back forever, and found phone numbers for the family. The Briard name is still listed today. The family still owns the same house, Strachan. And Glenn's certain about it, because they're the only Briards in Winchester."

Patsy and Harvey's house, then Alex's house, then – who, now? Alex's son? Alex's grandson? It would mean Alex survived the War. A warm excitement flows through me. What would it be like to speak to a real Briard, who might know more of Alex's history, particularly relating to Celia? I concentrate on the page in front of me, which says *Census of England and Wales, 1911,* at the top. It has Harvey's and Patsy's names, but no Alex, because he wouldn't have been born then. It shows their ages, and the date they were married, and describes Harvey as a company director, but no mention of Patsy's occupation; I guess 'wife' didn't count. There's some other stuff – where they were born (both were originally from Salisbury – that's where Stonehenge is, I think), citizenship, and then, at the very bottom, Harvey signed it in a fine copperplate flourish. I'm looking at Alex's father's signature. It's quite moving.

I look up at Jay, who hasn't said a word the whole time. "This is incredible, Jay."

"I know, babe," he smiles, "and Glenn's been digging around at the Royal Air Force site and already sent a letter – they won't take emails there – asking for Alex's service record. Once we get that, we can approach Births, Marriages and Deaths, to fill in all his details."

"And what about Celia? What did he get on her?"

"Well, nothing, yet. It would help if we had a bit more on her. I need a surname before I can get anything else. Of course, if she married Alex, there'll be a marriage certificate, so it could make things easier."

I try to think if I've ever heard mention of her name. I concentrate, and then it comes to me. I remember the new sergeant-in-charge calling her back one day. I must have taken a rest in the writing at that point, because it was irrelevant to the story. I mean, I don't write down when Celia goes to the toilet, for God's sake, do I?

I remember, *"ACW Denning! Change those stockings immediately or I'll have you up on a charge!"* Celia was wearing rayon ones, instead of the regulation lisle.

"Denning, Jay. Her name's Denning."

"You knew it all along?"

"I guess...it just never registered. I don't write down everything. Sometimes I don't even remember *what* I've written until I see it later.. When it's stuff to do with just reading, or taking a bath, or something, I take a break. Even with my laptop, I need that now and then."

"Well, it looks like we're getting somewhere, doesn't it? I'll phone Glenn later. Poole isn't that big a place either. Perhaps her parents will be on the census there."

"They won't," I say. "Celia's mother was from Poole, but her father was from London. They didn't meet until 1922 – so that's no good."

"But we'll get her birth certificate and war record. That should be enough to get other certificates, like marriage or death."

I look at him. "It's a bit sick, really, what we're doing. Don't get death certificates, Jay. I don't want to know when they died. It's cold-blooded, talking about them like this."

"Well, I understand how you feel. I won't have Glenn request them if you'd rather not. But just remember that it's evidence of lives lived – all of this. It's all that's left when people have forgotten about us. It happens within a couple of generations. Unless you have someone like Glenn, who's dedicated to it, none of us really knows much about family members who died before we were born, do we? We're doing something – well, *you're* doing something – to keep their memories alive. They'd thank us for it, if they could."

And I know he's right. Perhaps this is the reason Celia has me writing her history, just to make sure she's not forgotten. I feel very calm as we walk back from lunch. Something is happening at last. Soon we could have answers to everything.

The nice thing, although he would deny it, is that Jay must definitely believe me now, with no niggling doubts. Celia's story isn't just a figment of my imagination.

October 1, 1943

"I'm worried about you, Celia. Is there anything I can do to help?" Pamela sits down beside her and massages her back as she lies on her side on her bed.

Celia looks up at her. "I haven't seen Alex in over a month, Pam. His mother wrote to me and said he was a lot better, but I need to see him."

"Poor chap. A lot of them go through it, you know. He'll be all right. Just give him a bit of time."

"He was terrible the last time I saw him. I could hardly stand it. He cried, Pam. Do you know how that made me feel? He didn't look like my Alex any more."

"You're not the same girl I first met here, either, Celia. You were so bright and bubbly, full of excitement, and happy. This war's changed you, too. It's taking its toll on everyone." She glances around the hut at some of the other girls who are busy trying to get the radio speaker to work, joking and giggling as they fiddle with the wires. Gladys hasn't returned to camp, and no one is quite sure where she is, but a friend came by to take her things *and* her record player. They are now forced to listen only to the radio piped in from the admin hut. "Well, perhaps not everyone has been affected, but most of us have." Pamela says, sighing.

"If I could just see him. That's all I want."

"At least you know he's safe, and you *will* be able to see him again. Lots of girls have lost their chaps for good."

"I know you're right. I should be grateful." Celia struggles into a sitting position. "It's Friday night, Pam. I don't want to go home to Mum and Dad. They fuss over how I am, and I know it's worrying them. Can we do something tonight, just you and me?" She bites her mouth, fighting back tears. "It's my birthday! I'm twenty today." she blurts out. *(I stop for a moment from my typing. Got it! I can't wait to tell Jay.)*

Pam is clearly shocked. "Oh, poor dear, your birthday? I didn't know. You've said nothing. Happy birthday, Celia." She hugs her. "Of course, we'll go somewhere. What would you like to do?"

"A pub? Would you go to a pub with me? I need somewhere with lots of people enjoying themselves, somewhere that makes me feel I'm not alone."

Pam is hesitant. "I suppose it won't hurt. I've never been inside a pub, you know. I've been in a beer garden, though, so I suppose it's not much different."

"I'll tidy up," Celia says. "My hair's a mess."

"In half an hour, yes?" Pam stands up. "I have to find the Sergeant first. My mother sent me some nice soap, but I haven't seen the parcel yet. She might have it over there."

"Pam?" Celia looks at her with reddened eyes. "I don't know what I'd do if you weren't here. You're a good friend. You always make me feel better."

Pam smiles. "Silly. I'm here now." She pats Celia's cheek. "If you try really hard, you should do what I do, and just pretend we're back in the dormitory at school, young girls having a nice time."

Celia realizes that Pamela has no idea that she was an ordinary day girl at the Grammar. In any case, there's no harm in pretending. Celia did read all those girls' books, after all. She's almost forgotten about them. At one of those schools, Celia and Pamela would have been "chums" and had lots of "jolly fun", having midnight picnics in the dorm with food from the hamper someone's parents had sent. Perhaps it *was* possible to play make-believe.

She tries to put out of her mind the Daily Mirror article she'd read a week earlier that announced the deaths of 36 schoolgirls in the night time bombing of their boarding school near Wimborne Minster, half an hour from Boscombe. Of course, the bombers hadn't intended to bomb a school. They were trying to reach Portsmouth Harbour, but there was no harvest moon that night, no *Bombers' Moon,* as they called it, which would have guided them more certainly to the real target.

*

October 3, 1943

"I've made you a lovely cake," Celia's mother says, as she hugs her. "Happy birthday for Friday, love."

"You're not looking very well, Celia," her father says. "Are you sleeping all right?"

"Not really." She smiles at him. "I've been worrying about Alex."

Her father shakes his head. "Mum told me he was at home, resting up. Poor sod. Not easy doing what they do these days."

Celia looks at the cake set in the middle of the table. "It's lovely, Mum. How did you manage that?"

"I got the recipe from that lovely Marguerite Patten on the BBC. Grace next door gave me an extra egg from her ration, and I had two saved, and Peggy on the other side gave me some flour and some marg. But the best thing was getting a pound of sugar from some chap Dad knows. His son's in the Merchant Navy and gets his hands on things like that. It was cubes, of course, but it dissolved easily enough. I put in lots of vanilla to cover the taste of the marg, too. It tasted all right in the mixing bowl."

"You went to a lot of trouble…" Celia looks at her mother, noticing that she looks drawn, and that the frown line between her eyes is deeper.

"I loved doing it, really," Marie says. "It felt like before the war."

Celia turns to her father. "And how are you, Dad? Nothing too nasty lately?"

"Some Hun machine-gunned the Esplanade last week. No one hurt, but he left some lovely holes in a lot of buildings."

Celia hasn't told her parents about the hotel in Bournemouth. "They do it just to be bastards," she said.

"Celia!" Her mother's mouth drops open. "I've never heard such a thing from you before! Don't bring that kind of language home here!"

"Oh, Mum, if that was the only thing we had to worry about in this war, we could count ourselves lucky."

"It's awful, hearing you say words like that." She looks at her husband. "Aren't you going to say something, Bert?"

He sighs. "No, Marie, I'm not. You've no idea what this girl has been going through lately. If she wants to swear, if that helps, then let her."

"I know a few other ones, Mum. Do you want to hear them?" Celia grins.

"Oh, stop it! Keep this up, and you won't get any cake."

"A funny thing did happen the other night, though," her father says. "I was coming home, pedalling along, and this other air raid warden flew by, and I thought, "Hello, mate, I'm not letting you get away with that", so I chased him. As we got to Sea Road, I passed him, and I cheered as I went by. Then I looked back and saw he only had one leg. He was pedalling with one leg! He had a crutch tied on the back of the bike. I felt a proper fool, you know. But he was nice – he just laughed and waved." He sits down in his chair, smiling at the memory.

"It's nice to hear something that's got a bit of humour in it for a change," Marie says.

"Well, except for how he must feel being one-legged, it *is* funny!," he says.

After tea, they sit in the back garden in deck chairs. Her father lights a cigarette, but Celia doesn't; they don't know she smokes. It's mild for October, and Celia and her mother wear only cardigans over their frocks.

"Beautiful evening," her father says. "Red sky, too. It will be nice tomorrow."

'Red sky at night, sailor's delight.' Celia remembers the rhyme. She also knows that the red sky they are looking at is from the flames at Portsmouth Harbour. It's been bombed the last three nights in a row.

But she doesn't mention it to her parents.

TWENTY-THREE

"You're enjoying the new work?" Jay asks, as we eat lunch. "It's okay, I guess. We're working on a script for that new organic makeup range – you know, that one from Australia – *Koalee*? It's a bit different with the Australian angle – we're not creating anything new, because we have the original material from the Sydney ad agency. All we have to do is make it more acceptable for a North American audience. But it's a good way to get comfortable with the work."

"And Kelly's good to work with?"

"Oh, she's very cool. But it's odd the way a TV script looks, only on half the page, after seeing Nell's layout for *my* book. I have this urge to make all the type aligned to the left. But I'll get used to it."

He puts down his fork. "I have some news about Celia." He pulls a note from his pocket. "Are you ready for this?"

I look at him and swallow hard. "Go on."

"As you said, she was born October 1, 1923, and the family's address was Palmerston Road, Boscombe, Hampshire. Her full name is Ethel Celia Denning – I guess she didn't like the 'Ethel' – poor kid, who could blame her? Her father is listed as a cabinet-maker, and her mother as a housewife. Father was thirty-five and her Mum was 26." He smiles then. "Don't look so serious, Strachan. You should be happy. Glenn's dropping off the birth certificate later, but he thought we'd like to know what was in it."

"It's hard to take in, isn't it? Hearing about her as if she's real."

"Oh, she was real all right. Glenn will go after her service record now, and see if she got married, as he's doing for Alex." He strokes my arm. "Happy? You're getting the answers you needed for the book."

I stare at him. "The weird thing is that it doesn't seem to have anything to do with the book, Jay. This feels more like you've found a relative of mine. The book seems unimportant. Now, it's just that I have to know what happened to them."

Ethel Celia Denning – how nice to know her proper name. It's odd to say it, but this must be how an adopted child feels locating a biological mother. I'm somewhat muddled by the idea. Celia would be old enough to be my grandmother, wouldn't she? Old enough to be a great-grandmother, in fact. I'm beginning the construction of a family tree that isn't even mine.

October 23, 1943

"You'll like my Dad, Pamela. Mum's all right, but she gets a bit over-anxious. She fusses a lot."

"All mothers are like that, silly," Pamela says.

She is a little out of breath. Celia rides her standard-issue bicycle everywhere, but Pamela rarely leaves the camp, except to drive a lorry. "How far now?" she asks.

"This is our road, but it's right up at the top, near the railway line. Not too far." She glances at Pam. "You all right?"

"Oh, yes. I needed a bit of exercise." She stops speaking to concentrate on her pedalling. And breathing.

"Mum and Dad ride bikes everywhere now, too. They enjoy it, as long as there aren't any bombs or shrapnel falling! Do your parents ride bikes? They must need them living right out in the country." Pam had told her they lived on the outskirts of a village three miles from Bath, surrounded by country lanes and hedgerows.

"Well, Daddy has the car, of course, because of his war work. Mummy doesn't go out too often, only to help out at the primary school – her volunteer work, you know, for the war effort. She walks there most days."

"What sort of war work does your father do?" As soon as Celia says it, she regrets it. *Walls have ears*, she's reminded. "Whoops, Pam – I shouldn't have asked."

"No, that's all right. He's working for the Ministry of Food. Nothing too hush-hush. He's a farmer, after all, so he was a good fit."

"Big farm?" Celia turns to her house, and brakes.

"We're here? Oh, good." Pamela is relieved. "It's quite big – the farm. More than he can handle alone. Our laborers were called up, so now we have Land Army girls. I don't think Mummy appreciates that too much. Some of them are a bit cheeky." She dismounts and follows Celia up the path to the front door.

Celia hesitates and glances back. "I can't get used to not closing the gate behind me. It's been drilled into me all my life. It's peculiar, not having one."

"They took if for the metal, did they? They raided Daddy's barn, too."

"They probably used it to make these bikes," Celia says, laughing. "They certainly don't look like anything you used to see in bike shops."

Celia's mother appears at the door. "There you are! How nice. I heard you coming." She steps forward and smiles at Pamela. "And you're Pam. Lovely to meet you at last, dear." Pam holds out her hand, which Marie looks at for a second, before taking it, unused to such formality.

"Pleasure to meet you, Mrs. Denning," Pamela says.

"Dad!" Celia continues into the house."Come and meet Pamela."

He comes out of the sitting room, still wearing his glasses, newspaper in hand, but Celia knows he's gone to some trouble to impress her friend. He's freshly shaved, and wearing his best waistcoat.

'Welcome! Welcome." He bows slightly to Pamela, sweeping his hand towards the sitting room. "Come in, come in."

"Let me take your coat, Pamela," Marie says.

Pamela looks around the room. "You have a lovely home," she says.

"Thank you," Marie says, reviewing her work. The furniture gleams from the polishing she gave it that morning, and there are some hydrangeas – fading, but still pretty – in a glass vase on the window sill. The table is already set for tea, and she's used her best china.

"When did you join up then?" Celia's father asks, settling back in his armchair.

"Now don't sit there, Bert." Marie interrupts. "I'm bringing the tea in now,".

"Oh, right, dear." He sits down at the head of the table and gestures to the girls to sit either side of him.

"I joined up in 1940. After Normandy." Pamela shakes out the little linen serviette and places it on her lap. "I gave up my place at university to do it."

"University? Oh, very commendable." He picks up a plate of sandwiches and holds it out to her. "Cucumber. The last one from our garden."

"Pamela's family lives in Bath, Dad. We've been there, haven't we? I remember Uncle Joe driving us there, after we'd been to Stonehenge."

"Years ago, yes. You would only have been about six. Nice day out, that was. Don't have those anymore."

Marie returns from the kitchen bearing the teapot. "Pamela was at the university. Bert, before she joined up." She begins pouring the tea.

"I know, she was saying."

"You must be a very clever girl, Pamela," Marie says.

"Oh, not really. Daddy wanted me to do it."

"And what will you be when you're finished?" Bert asks. "I suppose you *will* go back and finish, won't you?"

"Oh, yes, as soon as the war's over, when the next term starts." She sips her tea. "I don't know what I'm going to do, yet, when I'm finished. I was reading English, second year – Medieval Studies – when I left."

Marie smiles. "Goodness, that sounds very clever, doesn't it?"

"But what will you *be*?" Bert persists.

Pamela raises her eyebrows and shrugs. "I'll have a Bachelor or Arts degree in English." She smiles at him. "I won't *be* anything – like a solicitor, or a doctor – if that's what you mean."

"Oh," Bert says, looking disappointed. "And what do you do with that…Arts degree? Can you be a teacher?"

"I could, but I'd have to get a teaching diploma at a teachers' college before I could do that."

Bert digests this for a moment. "What do you *think* you'll do?"

"I'd like to work at the BBC, in fact. They take on graduates and train them in all aspects of broadcasting. I'd have to have a decent result though, or they won't even look at me."

"I never knew that, Pamela." Celia gazes at her. "You hadn't mentioned it before."

"It's just an idea. Mummy thinks it would be fun, but Daddy would like me to go on and get my Master's and then a PhD, so I can get a university posting somewhere. Daddy's very keen on the academic life. He didn't finish, you see, when he was young, because of the Great War. He resents it still. By the time he came back, he felt he was too old."

'Well, it all sounds like a lot of work to me," Marie says. "I felt bad enough sending Celia off to do that course in shorthand and typing. But she seemed to enjoy it We said to her," she glances at her husband, "didn't we Bert? It will never go to waste. Whatever happens in this funny old world, you'll always be able to get a job."

Bert looks at her. "You worked, love. You never had any bother getting a job."

"It's not the same. Anyone can work in a shop." She runs her hand over the tablecloth in front of her, a smoothing motion, brushing away nonexistent crumbs. "I always thought it would be nice to work in a library, but my father just laughed at me when I told him. But there," she looks around at them, smiling, "different times, weren't they? Young women can do almost anything they want today. You girls are very lucky."

Celia and Pamela exchange smiles, both undoubtedly thinking about the escapades of some of the girls back at camp. If only Marie knew.

"Ida was so pleased to be seeing you again, Strachan." Nell offers me one of her home made cookies. I don't get many of these, since Mum died, although I try making them myself, but they're never quite the same.

"Well, me too," I say. "I want to fill her in on all the stuff that we've found out about Celia. But can we wait until she's here? Otherwise I'll just be repeating myself."

"Of course, won't be long now."

'*Won't be long now..*' - the constant reassurance back in the war, when everyone said it with such optimism. Nell sits down next to me. We're on her beautiful balcony overlooking the city in the distance.

"This must be nice in the early morning," I say.

"It is. I often sit out here with my coffee. When Mother was alive, it was our nicest time together. Sometimes birds land on the railing, too, and Mother loved that. She had a peculiar passion for birds."

"You still miss her?"

"Now and then, when I'm doing something that we always did together." She waves her hand at the table. "Like this."

"How come you never married, Nell? After your friend died, I mean."

"One word: Mother. She was so emotionally dependent on me, and I suppose I was on her, truth be known. I went out with a few men over the years, but I always felt awful leaving her alone in the apartment. Silly, really. We were very close, of course. Being the only child, I expect."

"My friend, Katie, and I don't want to marry. We made up our minds years ago."

"Even though you and Jay are so close?"

"It doesn't have anything to do with that. Katie and I just have the feeling that it spoils things, relationships, if it's made formal. It's all a load of crap, the whole thing, isn't it, when you seriously think about it? Just an ancient superstition that we blindly follow. What gives society the right to say that a couple is or isn't legally-joined, or – worse – for the church to say that it's until they die, like some horrible mythical curse? It's outrageous in this modern age."

"Perhaps. Some seem to thrive on it, the convention of it. And I believe there are some legal aspects that could be important. That's what the gay rights people have been fighting for."

"Legal-shmegal. Not me, or Katie. *And* Katie wants a baby without a husband!"

"Oh, my goodness," Nell says. "How brave of her."

"She has a very good job, makes lots of money, and they have a good parental leave system in place. She says she'll take a year off, and then go back to work. They have daycare in her building, as well, so she'll be able to see the baby whenever she wants."

"What's her work?"

"She's a production assistant with a TV station." I don't bother to tell Nell which one, because she only has basic cable herself, eschewing hundreds of others as an unnecessary expense.

"What a remarkable girl," Nell says. "She's certainly thought it out. But first, of course, she'll need to get pregnant."

I grin at her. "She's working on it, believe me."

Ida arrives then, a flurry of electric-blue in her acrylic suit and matching shoes. No hat today, but she has a bright blue barrette holding back the top of her hair, a surprisingly girlish look.

"This is so exciting, Strachan, hearing your news," she says, puffing as usual as she sits down. "To think you'll actually be able to identify her properly. In all these years, I have to admit, no one has ever been able to do that with any of my other presences."

"We have her birth certificate, Alex's father's census record from 1911, and we'll be getting both his and Celia's war record soon. Alex's family owns the same house that was listed in this 1940s phone book, as it is today in the current one – I don't have the number yet, but I might be totally brave when I get it, and phone them." I sit back, a bit out of breath myself.

"How amazing! Fancy speaking to a direct descendant." She frowns. "Of course, Alex could still be alive. How old was he?"

"He was twenty-five when Celia met him in 1942. So he'd be over ninety now. Not too many people live that long, do they?"

"But it's possible, isn't it?" Celia leans forward. "Can you imagine how it would feel for you to speak to him – a character from your book?"

I think about it. I've always believed he was dead. "I can't."

"It would make a fascinating piece of publicity for the book if you did find him, wouldn't it? He could corroborate everything you've written."

"I never intended saying that the book was based on fact. I don't want to bring the attic into it at all."

"I know, I know. But think how people would react to it, if you did, and if you had Alex as proof."

"Well," Nell speaks up in my defence, "as Strachan said, he probably isn't alive. That would be too much to expect."

"But the one thing I really need," I say, "that I think might be the hardest bit of information, is finding out why Celia is talking to me in a house in the middle of Toronto. Why here?"

"A lot of people immigrated after the war," Ida says.

"I guess. Jay thinks we should be able to get something from British, or even Canadian, records on her, but I can't believe we could find out that easily."

"And if she married someone else, her name will have changed, so that would make it even harder," Nell says. "It might not have been Alex..."

I sigh, suddenly wishing we could just be sitting here talking about the weather or the latest books. "Jay's asked his friend to search for a marriage certificate. It will all take time, waiting to see if he has any luck."

"Nell says you were going to take a picture of the room. Have you done it yet?"

"I tried once, but the light was too poor, and I couldn't even tweak it with my program, to get it clear enough. I'm waiting for a bright sunny day."

"And where are you up to with the book now?" Ida says, her mouth full of cookie.

"Alex is on medical leave, suffering from traumatic stress, or whatever they called it then, and Celia is just getting on with things, waiting for him to come back. We're nearing the end of the war, so it can't go on for much longer, can it?"

"But you'll just go right on writing in your little attic, until it's all resolved one way or the other?"

I grimace. "They're going to pull the house down soon. The land is being redeveloped for an apartment block. I found out from the building department at City Hall that planning permission isn't "in committee", as they put it, yet. But, once it is, they then have to allow interested parties to examine the plans, in case they want to protest it. It takes about three weeks for that. If no one puts up a fight, it will go ahead." I look dismally at them. "I figure I could have a couple of months, tops."

Nell touches my hand gently. "Then we must all hope that Celia is forthcoming with the rest of her story as swiftly as possible, or that you find out more about her from your other research."

"Yes," Ida says, "that's right. If the worst comes to the worst, you'd be able to finish the book without her." She looks at each of us in turn, blithely unaware of our saddened faces. "I don't think I've been this excited over anything for a long time. It's made such a difference in my life, really."

"We all need something to break the routine now and then," Nell says. "It's certainly broken mine."

Ida laughs. "I've been feeling all girlish and silly this last little while, ever since that night in the attic. I've felt like picking up the phone to you a couple of times, Strachan, to ask you how it was going."

"You should have, Ida. I wouldn't have minded."

She pats my hand. "Oh, you've got enough on your mind. I'm just a silly woman with too much time on my hands."

I look at her tentatively. "Ida..." I hesitate, "...this might sound odd, but there's this man, Jimmy – he takes care of my apartment block...He wants to meet you."

"Meet me? How does he know me?"

"The night when you were leaving after your visit, he saw you getting into the car. He seems to have quite a crush on you, just from that one time."

"A crush on me? How silly." But she looks pleased as she says it. "What sort of man is he?"

"Well, he's from New York originally. He's fairly quiet. About fifty, I'm guessing. The fact is, at one point he had a drinking problem, but he seems fine these days. He's either separated, or widowed. – I'm not sure which, but he definitely has no women in his life that I know of. I think he's shy. Anyway, I like him. He's a gentle sort of guy. "

"I don't know what to say." She smooths her hair, which is already totally controlled from her generous use of hair spray. "What does he want to do? –Take me out somewhere?"

"He just wants your phone number so he can introduce himself. You could see if you hit it off. His eyes light up when he talks about you, Ida. I think it's sweet."

She smiles. "Well, I suppose there's no harm in just talking to him, is there?" She pulls a notebook from her bag and scribbles down her number and hands it to me. "But let him know I'm no pushover, Strachan. I'll only talk to him if he's a complete

182

gentleman. I've been on this planet long enough to know what some men will get up to on the phone while you're talking to them. I'm not having any of that. You tell him." She ignores Nell's startled expression.

Ida knows about phone sex. How naughty. I look at her with renewed interest. And it's funny that she used the word, 'gentlemen', when he had called her a lady. Perhaps there's hope for these two. *Strachan, the Matchmaker*. I like the sound of that.

TWENTY-FOUR

November 5, 1943

"I hope you like dogs, Celia. We have five of them." Pamela pulls her bag off the rack as the train pulls into Bath Spa Station.

"I do," Celia says, struggling with her own things. "But you never mentioned them before."

"Oh, didn't I? They're Daddy's dogs, really. They're certainly not what you'd call lap dogs."

As they make their way along the platform, Pamela suddenly stops and jumps up and down, wildly waving her arm. "Mummy! Mummy! Over here!" She rushes forward, with Celia trying to keep up.

"Darling!" A tall grey-haired woman in a brown tweed suit moves forward and clasps Pamela to her generous bosom.

Pamela steps back after a moment. "Mummy, this is my friend, Celia."

'Mummy' turns to Celia. "My dear, what a pleasure it is to meet you. Pamela has told me so much about you."

Celia is conscious of a strong, earthy odor, as she steps forward to take the woman's hand. She sees then that Pamela's mother has very dirty finger nails. "Thank for inviting me here, Mrs. Mayall."

"No, no. It's our pleasure. Adrian is dying to meet you too, but he won't be home until later. And you must call me Bridget, dear." She looks at her daughter. "It would have been so nice to have a bonfire tonight, to celebrate Guy Fawkes, wouldn't it? But it's not to be, once again."

"Of course," Pamela says, "I'd forgotten. Never mind. We'll definitely be having one next year. It's my favorite thing. Is it yours, Celia?"

"Mm, it's fun. We had a bonfire in our back garden every year, and some of the neighbours would join in."

"Now we just have to put up with the bonfires that Gerry makes for us, don't we?" Bridget says dryly.

They have reached the car, a Bentley, Celia thinks.

"Just throw everything on the back seat. There's room for all of us in the front," Bridget says.

"It's a beautiful car." Celia can smell the same earthiness she'd smelt outside.

"Lucky to have it. Adrian got a ride to work today, especially, so that I could pick you up."

And then the landscape is so remarkable for Celia that she can't speak. She is mesmerized by the lush green pastures that curve like an undulating ocean swell, all punctuated with wooded areas and sheep, and toy-like villages that look as if they are still in the 17th Century.

"This is the most beautiful place in the world," she finally says.

"Yes," Bridget says. "It is jolly nice, isn't it. Take it for granted most of the time, don't we, Pamela?" She swings the steering wheel left then, and turns into a long driveway, with shrubs and tall trees on either side. "Nearly home!" she says gaily.

And then they reach the end of the drive, and Pamela's 'quite big' house confronts them. Celia's mouth falls open.

"Pamela! This is your house? *All* of it?"

The house is Elizabethan, she thinks, an enormous multi-angled and timbered brick building, covering three floors, with dozens of leaded windows, and tall chimneys, the roof tiles green with age, and all of the woodwork, including the huge front door, bare of stain or paint, and reduced to an ancient, modest grey.

They have stopped, and Pam and Bridget are out of the car, reaching for the bags.

"Come on, Celia," Pamela says, laughing. "Stop gawking. Come inside for tea."

Celia looks at Pamela, and then at the house. "You never said, Pamela," she whispers, watching Bridget walk up the steps. "You should have said."

Pamela looks hard at her. "Be honest, Celia. You wouldn't have come. You're always going on about social inequities in this country." She squeezes Celia's arm. "Well, I can't apologize for it, whatever you think. This is my home."

185

To Celia, Pamela's house is old enough, grand enough, to have been the home of Henry VIII, and she says so.

Pamela smiles. "Well, he didn't *own* it, but he did stay here quite a lot, as a matter of fact." She giggles. "It belonged to one of his mistresses."

Celia wonders what her mother and father will say when she tells them. Her mother had confided to her, as they left that last time, that she was worried that perhaps the cucumber and fish paste sandwiches hadn't been quite good enough.

Celia had whispered back that Pamela wasn't snooty like that. Pamela was just like her.

Now, as they enter the huge lobby, dark with panelling and heavy furniture, with brooding portraits on every available wall space, she sees how wrong she was.

For the first time, she wonders what Alex's family home looks like.

She is ushered into the sitting room, a vast space with several separate seating areas. Tables and cabinets proliferate, trinkets, photographs, vases, and what-nots sprinkled liberally on every surface. There is a huge fireplace, almost large enough to stand in.

But the second thing that Celia notices, the really surprising thing, is the messiness of the room. In all her years, Celia has never seen a more dishevelled, untidy place. Every sofa and armchair has beaten down, grubby and decidedly threadbare cushions, and there are newspapers strewn on both the floor in front of the sofa near the fire, and on two of the armchairs. A large water bowl, obviously for the dogs, sits beside the coffee table, and the remains of a huge bone, deeply gnawed, lies nearby, along with one well-chewed Wellington boot. To the left of the door from the hall there is a box full of split logs, despite wood already piled up on the hearth, which also accommodates a two-foot high pile of newspapers. The side tables have brimming ashtrays and long forgotten tea cups and saucers. The floor is dirty, with muddy marks on both the tiled floor, and on the huge rugs that demarcate each area of the room. Dog hairs cover every soft surface, as far as she can see. She sits down gingerly on one of the armchairs at Bridget's command, trying not to stare.

That earthy smell, associated with both Bridget and the car, now reveals its source. Next to the grand piano, handsome despite its fading veneer, are four huge baskets of potatoes, unwashed, the scent of the soil permeating everything.

Bridget sees her look. "Oh, silly to have 'em there," she says. "I've run out of room in the kitchen, and they looked so jolly awful in the hall, when you have to open the door to someone. You should see the back scullery." She laughs. "You can't get into it at all." She seems to consider something, then says, "The storage shed is full. Bumper year. I've been pulling them up for days. Never seen anything like it." She sits down heavily on the couch.

Celia realizes that neither Pamela nor her mother seems to find the rest of the room in need of explanation.

"Be a love, Pamela. Go and make some tea, there's a pet." Bridget reaches over for a cigarette and lights it, inhaling deeply. "Bloody awful morning, actually," she says to no one in particular. "The kitchen drain backed up and I can't seem to clear it."

"It's a lot of house to take care of," Celia says. "Is it only you, then?"

"Cleaning girl we had joined up. I can't get anyone else, although I offered it to her grandmother, but she turned me down. Told me she was involved in some war project of her own." She sighs. "In the old days, people clamoured to work here, really. Thank the Lord we still have Doris to do the evening cooking." She smiles at Celia. "Too old for war work, but she's a treasure in the kitchen."

"Perhaps Pamela and I can help you with the cleaning." Celia glances around the room.

Bridget follows her look and frowns. "This room? Oh, no, Ceila. This room is always a wreck. Mainly the dogs, of course, but neither Adrian or I particularly fuss. It's just us after all."

Celia can offer nothing more. Her mother had gone to great lengths to get her own house ready for Pamela's visit, even though the house was always kept neat and tidy. Her mother was dedicated to it, keeping it dust-free, and well-swept. It's hard to imagine how shocked Marie would be to see this room.

"Kettle's on," Pamela says, flopping down on the couch next to her mother and kicking off her shoes. "Where are the dogs?"

"Oh, I put them in the stable. They'll be all right out there until Daddy gets home."

"We used to have horses," Pamela says to Celia. "Gone now, of course. Confiscated for war duty, they said. Daddy said two of them would have gone to the knacker's yard, they were so old." She drops her head for a moment. "I loved those horses. I grew up with them."

"I'm sorry," Celia says. "That's awful."

"Ah, well," Bridget says, "we have to sacrifice just about everything to help get this war over and done with, don't we?"

They go to the kitchen to have tea at the big scrubbed wooden table in its centre. There is no space for the tea things, and they spend several minutes moving breakfast dishes to the sink, books and newspapers to one side, and wiping the surface, before sitting down. Again, Celia can't believe the state of the room. She has read stories about girls who lived in ancestral homes, but those houses were always beautiful, with polished furniture smelling of good wax, shining brasses and silver, and great vases of flowers everywhere. She has seen no flowers so far.

Pamela takes her for a walk after tea. They don't go too far from the house, because they are both weary from the train journey, but Pam points to various copses and fields in the distance to illustrate the full extent of the property. No wonder they'd needed horses, Celia thinks. She finds herself irritated with Pamela now, strangely hurt that she'd been told nothing of Pamela's economic status. From all her reading, Celia had concluded years earlier that the wealthy had always taken advantage of the less privileged. She had loved Dickens when she was at the Grammar, but her reading had evolved to include even more contemporary writers who deplored the lack of opportunity for so many. The only thing that somewhat excuses Pamela, in Celia's mind, is the fact that her friend is so nice, and, in the short time they'd known each other, had never been condescending or superior in any way. All the same, Celia feels her cheeks becoming warm as she thinks about her own family house in Boscombe, with its tiny front garden, and equally small rooms, and remembers how Pamela complimented her mother about it.

Pam's father, Adrian, is just entering the house, waving goodbye to the Morris driver who'd dropped him off, as they return. He turns to Pamela. "Hello, my darling girl!" He pulls her to him and holds her for a moment, then stands back to look more closely at her. "You all right, dumpling? Not too overworked?"

"I'm fine, Daddy," Pam says. "Meet Celia, my friend from camp."

"My dear, a pleasure to have you here." He takes her hands in his, and looks into her face. "Bit of a long trip. Tired, are we?" He releases her hands. "Come on in and get warm. The sun's almost gone."

He is a tall man, lanky in build, with steely-grey hair, cut very short, so that he looks to Celia for all the world like one of those German officers she's seen in films. She had noted Pamela's resemblance to her mother, the same height and figure – except for Bridget's impressive bosom - and they have the same color hair, but she sees no similarity in this man's face. But she immediately likes him, with his direct gaze and the way his eyes seem to warm as he looks at her.

"You enjoying the WAAFs, Celia?" he asks, as they go into the kitchen. Bridget has just filled the teapot again, and places it before them.

"Yes, most of the time," she replies. She's a little in awe of his voice. She can't decide if he sounds like Rex Harrison or Noel Coward, but his accent is definitely very posh. Oddly, she doesn't hear that plumminess in either Pam or Bridget.

"Terrible time we're having, aren't we?" he says, biting into a sandwich his wife has made for him.

"It's supposed to be over soon," she says.

"Yes, of course. That's what they're saying." He wipes his mouth with a linen serviette, and Pam almost smiles. In all the mess and general grubbiness, sitting at this untidy, stained table, he uses a serviette.

"Pru says we'll be in Berlin soon," Bridget says, pouring tea.

"Pru? Bloody woman. What would she know?" he says.

"Heard it at the post office."

"Should keep their mouths shut, those people. Loose lips, and all that…"

"There's something definitely on, though, Adrian. Mrs. Montgomery's son works at the Admiralty, and he hinted at something big this month."

"Bloody hell!" Adrian slaps his hand on the table. "Don't these sodding bastards know we have to keep mum about all of this?

I can't believe it." He shakes his head. "I've a good mind to report him."

"But you've heard it, too, haven't you, dear?" Bridget seems totally oblivious of her husband's anger.

"It's possible," he mutters. He looks up at them all. "That's all I'm saying." He turns to Celia. "I suppose your father gets just as angry over it all, doesn't he? It makes a man feel like a fool, that's the thing. We're not out there, doing our bit, are we? My leg got gammied up in the last war, and I couldn't go. But it's hard on chaps that stay at home." He glances at his wife. "We're like a bunch of women, sitting around having to listen to gossip."

"Nonsense." Bridget kisses the top of his head. "You love being somebody important at the Food office. I can tell by the way you walk when you leave in the morning."

He ignores her, concentrating on his sandwich.

"I'm going to run a bath, Mummy," Pam says then. "Is there hot water?"

"Yes, darling." Bridget smiles indulgently. "I got the boiler going long before you were due. There'll be enough for Celia, as well, when you're finished."

As they go up the wide staircase, Celia studies the oil portraits lining the walls. She sees Adrian in a few of them, at least his likeness, because most of the paintings obviously are from much earlier centuries.

"Are these people all your ancestors, Pam?" she asks.

Pam glances back. "Oh, yes. The family dates back to the Doomsday Book."

Celia considers this, realizing that everyone alive dates back to that time, *and* before, but she understands the distinction in Pamela's words.

"Were they all famous?" They have reached Pamela's bedroom, which is about eight times the size of Celia's at home, and filled with enormous pieces of furniture, for all the world like rooms she'd seen once at Hampton Court.

"Famous?" Celia throws her bag on the bed. "I suppose some of them were." She guides Celia out of the room and across the hall. "You're here, all right?"

Celia's room is equally large, furnished in the same heavy and ancient furniture. Pamela jumps on the bed and spread-eagles on her back.. "Oh, it's good to be home! I'll probably be all grouchy on Sunday when we go back."

Celia laughs. "I can understand why. Your house is marvellous, Pam. I can't believe you never told me about it."

Pamela slides off the bed. "I wanted us to be friends first," she says. "If I'd told you too soon, you would have avoided me, admit it."

"I'm not sure. Perhaps." Celia studies the other girl. "I've never met anyone who lives like this." Although she wasn't sure about Alex.

After they have their baths, they set their hair in hairgrips, allow it to dry and then brush it out, happy with their appearance as they put on their prettiest frocks (their uniforms happily banished to a wardrobe). Finally, with a little powder and lipstick applied, they go down to the dining room to have supper, as Bridget puts it. It's like no supper Celia has encountered before; at home, it usually consists of a piece of bread and jam and a cup of cocoa. This table is spread with a large assortment of food, and looks more like the lunches that Celia's mother lays on most Sundays, depending on what's left in her ration book, except there is far more of everything here.

Celia has never started a full meal at nine o'clock at night before, either. Her mother would disapprove, pointing to the possibility of nightmares later, eating so much so close to bedtime. The five dogs, large and friendly, are now 'in', released from the stable, and sharing the dining room with them. They constantly look for food scraps, and are so easily accommodated by all three Mayalls that they keep circling, like wolves in the wild, Celia thinks. But they don't bother her, recognizing that she is an outsider, unfamiliar with either their eating habits or preferences. After a while, Celia becomes used to them excitedly rushing past her, although the noise of their claws on the floor boards is irritating, but no one else seems to notice.

Towards the end of the meal, just after ten o'clock, there is a small tap at the door, and a white-haired elderly woman pops her head around it.

"Excuse me, M'Lord," she says, in a worn voice. "I'm off now. Was there anything else you wanted doing?"

He beams at her. "No, Doris. We'll see you tomorrow. You're son's waiting, is he?"

"Outside, M'Lord," She bobs her head to the girls and then **to** Bridget. "Good night, Lady Bridget."

The rest of the meal is a haze for Celia. They finish their puddings, spend time in the sitting room listening to the wireless, and finally Pamela's parents bid them goodnight. She and Pamela now stand outside their respective bedroom doors, and she puts voice to the questions that have been buzzing around in her head.

"Your father is a Lord, Pam? Why didn't you tell me?"

Pamela studies her carefully. "A Baronet, actually." She gives Celia a small smile.

Celia stares at her. "What does that mean, exactly? Is he in the House of Lords?"

Pamela shakes her head and shrugs. "No, he's not involved in that. It's not a very important title – at the bottom of the pecking order - but it's hereditary for daughters, so I'll be Lady Pamela Mayall one day. Silly, isn't it?" She sighs and moves closer to Celia and puts her arms around her. "I'm sorry, Celia. You mightn't have known, except for Doris. I forgot about her. Mummy and Daddy don't make a fuss about it. I would have told you eventually."

"But I called your father Mr. Mayall, and your mother, Mrs. Mayall. Why didn't they correct me?"

Pamela steps back from her. "It *was* correct. 'Sir' or 'Lady' is the formal address. Only tradespeople, or house staff (when we've got them) use it. My parents aren't like that, anyway, even if it wasn't so. My father's title means hardly anything these days. I mean, we're not hugely rich. It costs a fortune running a house like this, and we don't earn that much from the farm. The taxes alone on this place are almost the value of the house." She takes Celia's hand. "We can talk more comfortably in my room."

'There's no need," Celia says. She wants to go to bed, to get to sleep quickly. The day has exhausted her.

"Tomorrow, then." Celia pats her cheek. "Don't think less of me, Celia, for keeping it from you. I don't have many friends. You're my *best* friend, actually."

Celia sees her earnest face, so ordinary-looking, without the prettiness most girls want so badly at her age, and she is moved by it.

"You're my best friend too, Pam."

Pam has tears in her eye. "Oh, thank you. I'm so pleased you said that." She squeezes Celia's hand. "Good night, Celia."

"Good night, Pam." Celia turns to her door, and then spins around. "Pam? Doesn't that mean you have some kind of title too?"

Pam grins at her, her hand on the doorknob. "No. I'm just plain old Miss Mayall, not even an Honourable one. Daddy is *Sir Adrian Mayall, 4th Baronet, of Uxton House* – this house. But once you get to know him, you'll see that he's quite ordinary, Celia. Truly he is." She opens her door. "See you in the morning. Any time is good. Daddy's away by eight and Mummy usually gets up just after he's gone. Sleep in, if you can."

But Celia finds it difficult to sleep, despite her tiredness. The meal she's eaten is not agreeing with her, more meat than she's had in months, and she hears and feels her stomach's protests. She hopes she'll be able to find the bathroom in the dark, if she needs it.

She still can't take it all in – her rather mousy friend a blue blood. Of course, she wasn't any different to Celia. People were people, after all. But Celia has read books and seen films about girls like Pamela. They go to posh schools, then grow up and go to West End parties, drive fast cars, and spend time abroad, and then they become maids-in-waiting at the Palace, she was sure. How is it that such a girl can be her best friend?

It truly is a funny old world, with this war on, she thinks, as she finally falls asleep.

TWENTY-FIVE

I spent too long in the attic last night. It was after one a.m. when I got in. Rupert shunned me completely, and slept the night on the couch. It's a bit like we're married, the way he carries on.

But I need to do more over there now, with the time so limited. I thought that last night's work would reveal the ending of Celia's story, but all it did was take me on a tour of a grand estate. I'm disappointed, and wonder whether these new pages are even relevant.

Jay's coming by later. He said he couldn't stay, but wants to drop off more documentation from his friend's research. I don't know what I'd have done without that guy. Certainly, I couldn't have found so much – if any – information on Celia.

I find myself thinking about this publishing quest all the time now. At the beginning, it was fun, imagining my book sitting in a book shop, possibly right near the front door. I pictured myself walking up to someone who was browsing through it, and telling them who I was. But it all seems rather foolish and unnecessary these days. I find myself sadder than I've been in weeks, lethargic about most things, including work, although I try my best not to show that to Kelly.

The new salary is amazing, and I bought some new things for myself and for the apartment, but, when I looked at it all at home, I couldn't see the point to it at all, and wondered why I'd bought it in the first place.

Nell says it's natural for me to feel this way, that I've been on this emotional ride with Celia, and it was bound to rub off on me. But I'm so *not* Celia, and it's unfair to carry her burden around, perhaps forever.

Ida went out with Jimmy last week, just to a rather over-priced coffee and dessert place nearby. She reported to Nell that she liked him very much and would be seeing him again. I've never been a romantic – how many times have I said it? – but it's the one good thing that's come out of all this. Ida and Jimmy. Who would have thought it?

Somehow, over these next few weeks, before the demolition crew moves in across the road, I have to end Celia's journals. I've even scribbled down a few things that I could use to end the story myself, if that becomes necessary, but they don't ring true, and I'm not satisfied with them.

I spent last weekend with Patty, blotting out my miseries with the delights of being around Sarah Margaret. She is a joy, and I hated leaving on Sunday morning, but I know I have somewhere to go now, when things get too much. Even Patty saw my sadness, and seemed concerned. She assumed I was having a problem with Jay, but there's nothing wrong there.

Jay seems to take pleasure in being with me even more than in the early days of our relationship. I sometimes feel guilty when I'm with him, because I am demanding, finding that sex is the one thing that makes me forget what's going on with Celia.

In fact, the last time Jay was here, after we'd made love the second time that night, he commented on it. He tried to assure me that I meant more to him that just the sex. As he spoke, and I nodded my understanding of that, I was secretly thinking that sex is the *only* thing I need from him right now.

Looking at his face, wondering what it is about him that attracts me, I decided that it's a vulnerable quality there, a little boy look, although he doesn't really look like a little boy at all – but it's the expression in his eyes. Writers usually describe their heroes as having a strong face, a strong jaw – that kind of thing. Well, Jay has a vulnerable face, not weak, not mealy-mouthed, nor effeminate, but revealing a kind of fragility. I don't think I'm in love with Jay, but I'm not sure. I certainly don't want anyone else in my life right now. But his face…I do love that.

November 15, 1943

Celia takes the phone from the Sergeant, her hand trembling. Only an emergency allows such a privilege.

"Hello?" Her voice sounds strange in her ears.

"Celia? Harvey Briard, Alex's father. Sorry to alarm you. I pulled a few strings to get to you. Just wanted you to know that Alex returned to camp today."

"He's back?"

"Not doing too well, though. You might not hear from him. He's been very withdrawn, talking about how relationships were a waste of time with the war on. But at least you know he's back, and not fretting away here at home."

"Thanks, Harvey. I do appreciate it. He is a bit better then?"

"Over the worst, but not himself. He looks God-awful. Hope you don't mind that I phoned you, put you in a panic. Patsy asked me to do it. She said you must be worried about him."

"Thank her for me, will you?" She can't think of anything else to say.

"If you do hear from him, or write to him, act as if nothing's wrong, there's a good girl. He's a bit ashamed of himself – can't think why. All those poor blighters taking off every day and night not knowing if they'll return – they should realize how proud of them we are. It's a hell of a job, and nobody begrudges them being fearful or anxious."

"They are all so brave," Celia says.

"I'll sign off, then. You all right? No other worries, other than my son?"

"No, everything's going all right. It's a huge relief to hear about Alex. Thanks again."

"Toodle-oo, then. Look after yourself." He hangs up, and she stares at the receiver for some time before replacing it in the cradle.

"Thanks, Sarge," she says. Her Sergeant has remained in the office the whole time.

"Everything all right – not bad news?"

Imagine her predecessor giving a damn. "No. Good news. Thank you."

All she has to do now is wait for Alex to call.

"Guess what?" Katie stretches out on Strachan's sofa, kicking off her shoes.

I look at her more closely. "Are you pregnant?"

Katie smiles broadly and reaches her arms way above her head. "Yes! Yes! Yes!"

"Oh my God, Katie. You've done it! How do you feel?"

"How the fuck do you think I feel? I'm over the moon! I'm beside myself! I'm drunk with it!"

196

"How many weeks?"

"Six, we think. Have to have proper tests, of course." She sits up then, and reaches for the coffee I've made her.

"And your friend? How's he taking it?"

She looks at me with what can only be described as shyness. I've not seen that expression on Katie's face before. "He loves it. He wants me to marry him, Strachan."

I blink. "Katie? That was never the goal. You always said you just wanted the *baby*, not the father too."

"Oh, Strachan, I wish I could describe how I'm feeling. It's not just the baby; it's Kyle. At first I was all business as usual, loving the sex – he's really good, by the way – doing it as much as possible. I exhausted him that first couple of weeks, in fact. All we ate the whole time was pizza and ice cream, to keep our strength up. Oh, and lots of beer. He likes a beer. But we were so randy, just couldn't seem to stop, and that was fine with me. I figured, if I wasn't pregnant after all that, I'd never be." She stops to take a breath.

"But then I realized that I enjoyed him *after* the sex, you know, when you're just lying there, recovering. He's so interesting – the things he talks about – and I found I was liking him more and more, and wanting to hear everything I could about his life, what music he likes, what movies, you know."

"You're in love with him," I say, finding the words peculiar, addressed, as they are, to Katie.

"I am. I really love him." She sits back, and beams at me. "I didn't even know it, but I've been waiting for him all my life."

"Oh, Katie, it's so odd to hear you talking like this." I sit down next to her and put my arms around her. "But I'm glad he's making you so happy."

"You'll like him, Strachan. He reads a lot, like you, and he knows so much stuff. And funny! He cracks me up, and it's enormously sexy, and I hadn't considered that before."

"And you said 'yes', to marrying him?"

"Yep. We're going to do it in September – haven't booked the date yet, but we will. Nothing fancy, right? I'm not into that bridal crap – you know me. We thought somewhere outside, in one of those gardens where they allow ceremonies, with the leaves starting to fall, and everything golden and beautiful." Her eyes shine as she speaks.

"I'm so happy for you, girl. I know we always said marriage is a load of shit, but it *does* work for some people, and you're so smart, I know it will work for you." I half believe this, as I say it. I find I *want* to believe.

"No drinking tonight, of course," she says. "I'm going to have this baby by the book." She looks at her coffee. "And I'm cutting back on this, too. Just two cups a day from now on."

"Katie without booze? That's novel," I say.

"But it's not hard to do. Now I have something else to worry about." She pats her flat stomach. "I'm going to consider what this little devil needs from now on."

"Have you told your mum and dad yet?"

"Of course not! You were first. We've been hanging out together for so long, you were the first one I thought of – I mean, after I'd told Kyle. I'll tell my parents the next time I'm up there. There's no rush. Have to make sure this is real, first." She pats her stomach again. "I mean, things could change. The first three months are the riskiest, I've heard."

I frown. "And if something does happen, if you're no longer pregnant, you'll still get married in the fall?"

"Of course I will! Kyle and I are committed, whatever happens. I love this guy, Strachan, with or without a baby."

I kiss her on the cheek. "Oh, you! Nothing is going to go wrong. You and Kyle and your little boy or girl are going to have a wonderful life together. It was time for you to have this. To think, if Patty hadn't had Sarah Margaret, the whole thing might never have started. Remember how you reacted when she was born?"

"I know. It was you. You had this goofy look on your face the whole time you were describing it. I got caught up in that too. Women are meant to have kids, aren't they? And it all just hit me then – why wait?"

I smile at her. "I don't know about me. I don't know if I'm meant to. I like the idea of Sarah Margaret, but I can't honestly picture me doing it. There's a huge amount of work involved with a baby, and I'm not sure I could handle it."

"Well, first decide how you feel about Jay, whether he's a contender, and then start considering motherhood, once you've decided."

"Jay? Oh, we're so not like that," I say lightly.

"Really? Had me fooled," she says.

"It's just sex, honestly."

"And he's never said anything about getting more serious?"

"Well, he has, actually." I stand up to take the cups to the kitchen. "But I have too much on my mind, what with the book and the new job, to consider anything else right now."

"Excuses, excuses." She levels her gaze at me. "Strachan, you silly bitch, you're scared."

"That's not true. I'm not scared. It's just that I like myself as I am. When I'm with Jay, I sometimes forget who I am. I act differently around him. Some other me emerges. I'm not sure I even like her much." *Hungry, lustful, greedy Strachan.*

"You'll learn to like her, Strachan. She's your grown-up self, that's all, and that's why you're afraid to let her move in."

I look at her, knowing she is probably right. Growing up, even at my age, is the most terrifying thing for me to face.

November 25, 1943

"They buggered up that Berlin run, didn't they? Did you hear?" Yvonne has just come off duty, and looks even more tired than usual.

"What Berlin thing?" Janine sits up on her bed, and puts her mouse back in its tin.

"Big raid on Berlin on Tuesday night and yesterday. One of the Yank blokes told me. We lost over 350 aircraft. They're saying it's one of our worst defeats yet, all just a waste of time."

Celia stands frozen beside her own bed, which she was straightening. "Do they have definite news yet – I mean, do they have details?"

She gives Celia a sad smile. "It's not looking good, Ceel." Everyone in the hut knows about her and Alex.

Celia grabs her cap and runs from the hut, slamming the door behind her. Of course, Alex wouldn't be among the losses. He's only just come back from sick leave; they wouldn't have sent him up yet. But as she reaches the NAAFI building, and races along the corridor towards the phone, she's sure she's about to vomit. The blood seems to pound in her ears as she dials the Briard's number.

Another WAAF, emerging from the canteen, looks at her oddly, then runs forward. Celia is aware of the woman speaking to her, but can't understand the words. She finds herself on the cold linoleum floor, but doesn't know how she got there. Patsy's words, broken and overly-loud – shrill, in fact – are etched in her head, even as the other WAAF is still speaking to her.

Missing in Action.

"There's nothing you can do, Celia." Pamela removes the wet flannel from Celia's forehead, takes up more water from the bowl on the locker beside her bed, then reapplies it, its coolness now starting to clear her mind somewhat.

"You should see the nurse and get permission for leave, and just go home. Being with your mother will help, you'll see." Pamela stares into her face, and Celia tries to focus on her, but she's too close. "Missing doesn't mean dead, don't you see? It's a good thing. Lots of chaps have made it back, or are in some POW camp over there. But they're alive, that's the thing to remember."

Celia tries to sit up.

"Where do you think you're going?" Pamela asks. "You're not ready to get up yet. You frightened us, fainting like that."

Celia then sees that the other girls are crowding around the bed, although she's momentarily forgotten their names.

"Give her some air, girls," Pamela says, suddenly aware of them.

"I need to see his father," Celia says. "He'll know more. Patsy didn't make much sense."

"Well, you can do that later. You're not going anywhere right now, all right?"

"I have his father's office number. If I can use the phone…"

"You'll stay there for a bit longer. Lucy's making you some tea, with lots of sugar, if she can scrounge some. And, anyway, it's after office hours. He wouldn't be there."

Celia looks up at Pamela's worried face. "You're a good girl, Pam. Taking care of me like this, but I'm all right now, I think. I can sit up."

Pam looks at her suspiciously. "I don't know. You're as white as a sheet."

But she helps Celia into a sitting position.

"I have to speak to him, Pamela, you see that, don't you? Help me back there, go on. Take me back to the phone."

The others fall back as Pamela grudgingly helps Celia off the bed. She takes her arm and carefully walks her to the door. The fresh air helps. Celia seems to gasp it in as if she were taking her first breath.

But there's no answer at Harvey's office.

Pamela looks at Celia as she hangs up the receiver, seeing the desolation in her face. "Well, you can call in the morning, can't you?" she offers brightly.

But Celia doesn't think she can wait until tomorrow.

"How far you going, honey?" The American Army Private doesn't look at her as he speaks, concentrating on steering through the darkened streets of the town. His was the first vehicle she flagged, as she stood beside the road, and he screeched to a stop immediately.

"I'm trying to get to Winchester," she says.

"Whoa, long way. I'm heading for Southampton, so that's half your trip." He navigates a corner carefully, then straightens the lorry, and quickly glances at her. "Were you waiting for a ride for a while?"

"Not too long. A few troop lorries went past, but they had a lot of men in them, and they wouldn't have stopped."

"Kinda late for you, isn't it?"

She gnaws at her lower lip. "I could be up on a charge. I slipped out without anyone seeing me." Pamela had started a long-winded conversation with the guards, asking them about their families, and would they be getting leave for Christmas.

He raises his eyebrows. "Didya now? No pass, eh? Well, keep your head down a bit, sweetcakes. I don't need the Provosts stopping me."

She scrunches lower in her seat. "They won't be looking for me until tomorrow," she says.

"Oh, well, that's a relief," he says, tapping out a cigarette from the soft pack he has, and lighting it, needing only one hand. He offers her one, and she almost snatches it.

201

"What's been happening to you, anyway?" he asks. "You look kinda wild-eyed. Was there an air raid round here?"

"No. No raid."

"What's your name? I'm Larry."

"Celia." She wishes he would stop talking, because she has so much she needs to concentrate on.

"Pretty name. My Mum's name is Cordelia. They sound the same. Celia. Cordelia." He speaks with the cigarette firmly planted at the corner of his mouth, so that his hands are free to change gears. "Do you live in Winchester?"

"No," she says.

"Oh." He glances at her. "You sure you're okay doing this? You don't look too good."

She wonders how he could know what she usually looks like, and finds herself smiling. "I'll be all right. I just need to get to Winchester."

"Sure. Once you're in Southampton, you shouldn't have any trouble getting a ride. I know a lot of guys there. You'll be fine."

She turns to him, seeing his face properly for the first time. He is about her age, barely twenty, she guesses. His fair hair is cut very short, recently, she guesses, in the assembly-line style of recruitment camp barbers.

"How long have you been over here?" she asks.

"A month – nearly five weeks. I haven't seen any action yet, but they say it's coming soon."

"What do you think of England?"

He laughs. "It's pretty, from what I've seen. Not the towns so much, but the countryside." He glances at her. "I'm from Buffalo. It's kinda ugly, too, I guess, but outside – like here – it's beautiful."

"Do you still live at home?"

"Oh, yeah. I was meant to start college this year, but that didn't happen."

"When you get back, you'll go then. Everything will be the way things used to be for you."

But she knows this isn't true. He will see things, hear and smell things, that he will never forget. If he's lucky, he won't die. But he will have nightmares, possibly for the rest of his life. Her father hadn't told her about his experiences in the Great War, but her mother had. Her father would wake up at all hours, in a sweat, and she would hear her mother in the kitchen making tea for him, to soothe him. Her mother said he would never be cured of it, the torment in his head. Celia wonders if she will ever be the same after her shock back at camp. She hadn't seen the carnage of Alex's plane, but she had pictured it. Imagination was a terrible thing, revealing images she might never physically see, but which were no less terrifying.

It's after midnight when she reaches Winchester. Her last ride was from Fareham, with a charming priest who was on his way back to his parish after ministering the Last Rites to someone. He was very cheerful, and chatted amiably during the whole ride, and she found it unnecessary to say much herself. Death couldn't be so bad, could it, if a man like this was so down-to-earth and apparently untouched by it?

She stands in the phone box holding a lighted match to see the directory. She hopes there's no warden around to see the alarming brightness in the darkened street. She finds the name, and wonders if she should call them first, but then decides against it. She memorizes the address, and walks to the edge of the road to wait for another lift.

"Celia!" Harvey opens the door almost immediately, in day clothes, so she knows he's not been dragged from his bed. "Oh, good Lord, girl," he says, taking both her hands, "come in to the warm."

She hadn't realized she is cold until she's sitting beside the fire, and then she notices that her teeth are chattering and she tries to control it.

"I'll get you a brandy," he says.

"Where's Patsy?" she asks, as she takes the drink from him. Its raw heat burns at her throat, but she drinks it all, reviving somewhat as the shock of it reaches her stomach.

"She's asleep. I had to get the doctor to come out to her. He gave her something. She's very cut up, naturally. We both are." He studies her from the chair opposite. "But how are you, Celia? I'm sorry I wasn't hear when you rang. I had to get Patsy's prescription filled, and then I...just curled up with her." He drops his eyes, then looks back at her. "What made you come here?"

"I didn't know if you'd heard more. Patsy didn't make much sense. I wanted to find out if you knew anything more than what she told me."

"We got the telegram before breakfast. Wondered who the buggery it was coming to the door at that time of the morning." He leans forward and takes her hand. "It's not over, Celia. You must believe that. He'll have been picked up by someone, taken to a cottage or somewhere like that. Lots of people helping us now, in these situations."

She watches him speak, and wants to believe him, but she sees that his own face is dreadfully drawn, the eyes raw, the lines around them deeper than she remembers.

He releases her hand, and drops his eyes again. "I have absolute faith in him. I want you to know that."

She knows that he saw her recognition of his grief. "Then we'll have to hang on to that, won't we?" she says, brushing her hair back; her bun has long lost its shape, and limp strands fall around her cheeks. "I *have* to believe he's alive. If he isn't, I don't know what I'll do."

"We all feel that way, Celia." He stands up to refill her glass. "Patsy was beside herself. She's normally a rock, but today she seemed to grow old in an instant. She sort of crumpled before me – not her body – her *being*. I've never seen her that way before, even when her mother died, and they were very close."

"It's almost unbearable, isn't it?" She sips her brandy. "I want to bang my head against a wall, or something, to make all the thoughts go away."

"You're all in, Celia. I'll get an eiderdown for you, and a pillow, and you can sleep on the settee here, near the fire, tonight. There's no point in going over it and over it. Gets us nowhere."

Yet he had been awake when she arrived. Pacing, was he? Weeping? "I am tired," she says. "The brandy's working. I might sleep."

"Good, good. I'll just nip upstairs and get the things for you..." he stops "– or I could make up the spare room for you, if you'd rather."

"No," she says firmly. "I'd like to stay down here."

"I'll see if I can find something else for you to put on. One of Patsy's nighties."

She sits staring into the fire, hearing him moving about upstairs, and she suddenly realizes how difficult things are for Harvey at this moment. She's thought only of herself, how *she* was feeling.

"There you are..." He appears with a blue flannel nightgown and hands it to her. "It might be a bit on the long side – I think Patsy's taller than you." He puts the eiderdown and pillow on the settee and then steps back, studying her. "All right, then? Anything you need? If you get hungry –are you hungry? (she shakes her head) – you can find something in the kitchen. The bathroom is at the top of the stairs." He glances around the room. "Well, then. Good night, Celia. Sleep tight, if you can."

She lies in the darkness staring at the ceiling, which is alive with the flickering shadows from the fire. She doesn't think she will every sleep again. She wonders if anyone has ever died from that.

TWENTY-SIX

"So it's all coming to a head now, is it?" Nell throws a scrap of her sandwich to some seagulls who are hanging around. We get a lot of seagulls here, even this far up from the Lake.

"I'm almost scared to write," I say.

"Nonsense, Strachan. This is what you needed. To finish the thing once and for all."

"I know you're right. But I haven't been feeling good – I told you. Lately, I've just wanted to stay at home."

She turns to me. "Listen to me. You just have to get this last little bit done. It will probably be finished within one or two more visits. Then you can say goodbye to the attic for good."

"But it's so much darker to write about now. I suppose real writers know that they're going towards a more demanding part of the book, and are prepared for it. But I don't know what's coming, and it's very stressful. I have this stiff neck all the time, and I never had that at the beginning."

"Be patient just a bit longer, dear. You've produced an amazing story, whether you feel responsible for it or not. People will want to read it, to see what those people all went through, and they'll enjoy it.. I know they still publish books about that time, and make films, but there aren't that many of them and I can't recall anything lately that is like Celia's story. It's quite different from the usual World War dramas."

"I can come over this weekend, if you want me," I say. "Jay's away, and I get fed up being alone now. I used to enjoy my own company, but not lately."

"Oh, that would be lovely. Come on Saturday. We can go out to lunch somewhere. I haven't been out for a proper lunch in ages."

"I meant to tell you – this is so weird – I tried to take more pictures the other night. I even used the flash on the camera, but the pictures still came out all dirty looking and fuzzy. I thought my camera was broken, but I took a perfectly good one of Rupert, quite late at night, and it was fine. What do you think that's about, Nell?"

She eyes me for a moment. "I suppose we should ask Ida. It is odd, isn't it? It seems the room really doesn't want its Celia-look revealed. The way things are now, the only proof you've got about that room is the book." She folds her empty lunch bag carefully and puts it in her purse. "To anyone else, the only paranormal thing about it all is that you managed to write the story. If you're the only one who's ever seen it that way, some people might say that you did it without Celia – that you made it all up. You can't prove you didn't research it, can you?"

"But I wasn't going to tell anyone else about the room, anyway. Nobody else will ever know about it. It's just that I would have liked you and Ida, Jay and Katie to see it, to know that it's real."

"Well, Ida felt a presence, didn't she? I trust Ida's judgement. You don't have to convince me how it really happened."

But Nell doesn't say that she trusts *me*. If Ida wasn't involved at all, would Nell still believe me?

December 18th, 1943

"Say you'll come, Celia. Please." Pamela puts her arm around Celia's shoulders and squeezes her. "Mummy insists. There'll be other people there – some nice chaps, too. Mummy says the servicemen she's billeting are all perfect gentlemen, and very entertaining. They'll take you out of yourself. Take your mind off things."

"I don't know Pam," Celia replies. "It's too soon, I think. I just don't feel like socializing."

"But of course you don't, and that's the very reason why you should make the effort. You need to get back to a normal life. You can't just keep hiding away here, or at home."

"I'll think about it."

"Just Boxing Day, and you'll stay overnight. I know you'll want to be at home for Christmas Day."

In fact, she's not looking forward to spending that time with her parents. She knows there will be false joviality, far more food than usual and she has no appetite, and they'll have to wear those silly paper hats that come out of the Christmas crackers. She knows

207

she will go, of course, because her parents will need her there for their own celebration to be complete. They will want to study her, too, test her, to see how she's coping. But her parents and her Aunt Nell, who attends every Christmas, at least will avoid asking how she is feeling, for fear that she might tell them and spoil the festive mood.

She thinks she's done quite well, considering. After the initial shock of hearing about Alex, she seems to have numbed, gradually losing the images she initially formed in her mind – first, of his broken body beside those of his crew mates, and the unrecognizable Halifax, and then – later, more optimistic – Alex being tended by some nice Belgian housewife, who feeds him soup, and tells him in broken English that her son has gone to find some resistance group who will advise the War Department that he is all right.

And now she has stopped thinking about him completely, as if she never knew him. It's easier to be the overly-serious, pensive girl she's become, who rarely smiles, and never laughs, someone who's boring at a party, that you wouldn't want to have a drink with…a girl without history, uninspiring and dull, but safe from further assault.

She knows she looks awful. Several people commented on her pallid skin, her lifeless hair. She was never vain, accepting that she was pretty enough, and that she would age more or less like her mother, arriving at middle-age reasonably nice looking, and not too overweight. But now she's stopped using lipstick, washes her hair only when it becomes completely unmanageable, and no longer applies Ponds face cream before going to sleep at night. No point now, is there? Who is there to notice?

"We're okay, aren't we, Strachan?" Jay and I are in bed, as usual, and he has his arm around me, his head at my neck. "You seem so preoccupied lately. You don't laugh the way you used to."

"It's just the book, Jay." I wriggle from his arm, and sit up. "It's really worrying me now."

He slides out of bed and begins to dress. "Better if you start thinking about what's going to happen after the book sells. Because it will. You'll be expected to promote it, too, get out the message that it's worth buying."

He has a fine body, nicely toned, but not in that self-indulgent, narcissistic way. I like the tan line above his buttocks (momentarily wondering how he got it) and the way the muscles twitch as he pulls on his shorts. Other girls must have observed him exactly this way, but I'm not jealous. All those other women have played some part in making Jay what he is now – sexually experienced, comfortable with himself, unselfconscious. I'm grateful.

"I can't imagine ever being able to do that," I say, considering whether or not to entice him back to bed. "I even hate having photographs taken. It's not something I'm looking forward to."

We go back to the living room, me only in a robe, because I'm still nurturing the thought of another round of love-making. He puts on another CD – Diana Krall, his favorite.

He sits down next to me on the couch. "You didn't answer me, Strachan. Are *we* all right?"

"I guess. Nothing's changed, has it?" But I know it has.

His mouth tightens then, and I can see he's becoming angry. "Fuck it, Strachan! You know how I feel about you. I don't know any other way of showing you that. But you – you never say or do anything to acknowledge it. I know you love the sex, but it's screwing my head to think that's all we have." He pulls me around to face him. "What do you expect of me? Do you just want me to keep seeing you for a quick fuck? Is that all it is?"

I study his face, those gentle eyes now hard. "You need to be patient with me for a bit longer, Jay. I don't know what I feel. The book – Celia's life – seems to consume me. I've never told you this, but when you leave, when all I should be thinking about is you, how we've just been, it's Celia I return to. She's in my head all the time. Sometimes I think I'll go mad if she doesn't leave me soon." I know I'm about to cry, but I try to ignore the start of the tears, hoping they'll stop.

"It's unhealthy, Strachan. You know it." He stands up. Usually, when he sees my tears, he wraps himself around me. "Whatever this thing is that took hold of you, it has to leave eventually. Get the fucking book finished, and then get back to me."

I frown. "What do you mean? Get back to you…"

"I think we should take a little break. I think you need time to get this project finished, and I don't see that I'm helping much by interrupting that flow. You need your mind clear for the book. All I'm doing is creating more stress for you, forcing you to deal with me and my hang ups." He stands up, thumbs in his jean pockets, a pose that usually turns me on.

"I don't want that, Jay. I need to see you. You make a huge difference to me. You don't add to my stress, you relieve it."

He smiles at me sadly. "You know what, Strachan? A vibrator could do that."

December 26, 1943

Pamela's house is filled with Christmas, in every corner, on every surface. Candles and wreaths; a tall tree at the French windows decorated with huge red bows, tinsel and sparkling balls; there are trays of drinks, bowls of nuts, mince pies and even sweets. Celia wonders how many ration books they used up, but Pamela whispers that her father pulled some strings. Men with some power, Adrian *and* Harvey, who had been able to phone her at the Flight Sergeant's office that day, with no difficulty at all.

"Come in, darlings," Bridget says. "I'm so glad you decided to come, Celia. I was delighted when Pam said you would."

There are perhaps a dozen people in the sitting room, and Celia is momentarily startled by so many faces brightly looking at her. Adrian takes her arm, and leads her to a chair near the fireplace.

"Everyone! This is Celia who's at camp with Pamela in Boscombe." He turns to Celia. "You won't remember everyone's name, but–" he points around the room, "–over here we have John, Archie, Paul, and my sister, Janet, and her husband, Peter. And over here–" he indicates the group around the piano, "–Bob, Alan, Gary, Jock, and Stephen."

They nod to her, some giving her a little wave.

Adrian continues, "The boys here are all Air Force chaps, Celia, Canadian contingent. All a bit dodgy when they first got here, from injury or exhaustion, but they're almost recovered with all this good country air, right chaps?"

She is surprised that this statement doesn't somehow stab at her, reminding her of her pain from the month before, but instead she instantly feels huge affection for them, wanting to talk to each of them, to hear their stories, to find out how the War has treated them. "Hello, all," she says, waving back.

She is suddenly feeling much better, more like her old self, and doesn't understand it.

"He'll be back, Strachan," Katie strokes her face. "Men get funny like this, but it won't last. He'll get his first decent hard-on, and he'll be picking up the phone."

"I think I've hurt him a lot, Katie. I didn't see that."

"Look, you've been upfront with him the whole time, so he knew what he was taking on. It's just their egos, isn't it? They can't bear to take a back seat to anything else." She pats her visible stomach, using any excuse to do that, these days. "This baby is not going to change a thing for me and Kyle. I've already talked to him about it, because I was reading this article. He just had to understand that a baby is demanding, and needs constant attention, but that it doesn't mean he'll be less important in my life. Marriages break up over it, Strachan. Men just can't deal with the competition. I'd have thought, from what you've told me about him, that Jay was smarter than that." She sighs. "But then they're all just big kids, really, aren't they, needing Mummy's undivided love?"

"I can't phone him, whatever happens. There's nothing I can say. Until the book's done, nothing I'm doing will change." I look glumly around the room. "That's if things ever change, even after it's finished. Perhaps Celia will be with me for life."

"Crap, Strachan! You'll be back to normal soon. Jay would be a real ass-hole if he didn't come around." She shrugs. "It's possible that's why he's had bad relationships before. Perhaps he's just too demanding."

"But he's not! Except for the way I distance myself from him sometimes. In every other way, things are perfect."

"Nothing ever stays the same, girl. We contantly have to be on the lookout for those changes when they come. He's probably resented the book much more than he's said, but you didn't see it."

"I don't think you're right. *I've* changed, that's the thing. And he doesn't like me this way."

I don't like myself much, either, so I know where he's coming from. The great fear is that I might never be happy with me again.

"When will you be going home, Stephen?" Celia asks.

They are alone at the breakfast table, the first to come down. Pam's house has been a haven for her, washing away all her old negativity, and presenting her with renewed optimism.

"Waiting for transport, really. Could be a while."

She likes his accent, the softened consonants, the rolling 'r', the fullness of the vowels.

"You must miss it."

He frowns, looking at her. "Not really. Glad to be out of it. Nothing noble about what I saw."

She grins. "I meant home."

"Oh, sorry." His laugh is short. "Thought you meant the War. On my mind the whole time. Can't seem to get rid of it."

"And where are you from?"

"Toronto. All my family's there."

"I've heard it's nice, very modern."

"Yes. I suppose it is. Some old buildings of course. But it's not that old a city, really." He gets up and goes to the side table to get the coffee pot.

"Your family must be happy you're going home." She would like to ask about his "condition" as he'd referred to it yesterday, when they sat next to each other at lunch. She doesn't want to know out of some altruistic need, but to better understand how a damaged mind functions, and wants details of his nightmares to compare with her own. Strange, she suddenly realizes, that she didn't have one last night.

"Mum was crying the whole time I talked to her, when I first knew I was going back. Dad didn't say much. But then Dad never does. He lets Mum do all the talking."

"And will you return to your old job?" She knows he's older, perhaps thirty-five, and guesses he left a career behind.

"Hope so. No reason not to. The docs told me my episodes were only related to flying and airfield ops. I'm a teacher. I doubt there'll be any terrors there for me, other than the kids themselves."

"What do you teach?"

"High School English. A downtown school. Privileged bunch, most of them. It's right in the heart of one of our more affluent neighborhoods."

Others have moved to the table now, and she smiles around at them. "Good morning, everyone. Did you sleep well?" She wishes she hadn't said that then, thinking about Stephen's personal demons, but it's too late.

Celia, herself, feels wonderful. It's the first time in ages that she hasn't woken up with that old feeling of dread.

The decision to come to Uxton again was a good one, it seems. She'll tell Pamela after breakfast.

"I just wondered if you got those records from Glenn," I say. It's the perfect excuse to talk to him.

"Not yet, Strachan." Jay's voice is the same, although a bit cooler-sounding, almost businesslike.

"Oh, I just wondered. Anyway, how are you?"

"I'm fine. Busy as usual."

"Of course. I was wondering if you wanted to come over tonight. It's been six weeks. Rupert misses you." What a totally dumb-assed thing to say.

"Nah. Can't tonight, sorry."

"Oh, well." I search for another topic, something to keep him on the line, but fail. "Let me know when that paperwork arrives."

"Of course I will. I know how much you need it."

He makes it sound as if it's all I need. "Right, then. See you, Jay."

"Yeah, see you, Strachan." The line goes dead.

What is 'being in love' anyway? Has anyone set up any guidelines, a set of boxes to check to see if you score high enough to qualify for it? I stroke Rupert's soft head, loving the way he responds to it, needing me. I've fucked up whatever Jay and I had, regardless of the score on that imaginary survey. I used to think of myself as unlovable, and perhaps I cannot see myself any other way, and deliberately cultivate it.

At least I have Rupert.

*

213

February 19, 1944

"I don't know if this is right, Celia," Stephen says, his voice rasping, as if his throat is dry. "You hardly know me. You don't know how I can be." He is breathless now, awed by her, and his hands reach for the buttons of her blouse even as he protests.

They are in his room, where they are meant to be listening to *Itma* from the BBC. The others are downstairs playing Whist, two groups sitting at separate tables. The sitting room looked a bit like a gentlemen's club, she'd thought, as they excused themselves. Only Pamela gave her an extra long look, she saw.

His body is a magnetic thing, compelling her to touch him as they kiss for the second time – if it can be considered a second time, rather than a briefly interrupted continuation of the first. She surprises herself, not with her boldness in reaching for him, but in the explosion of longing she has for him. She is driven to look at him – all of him – to revel in his instant response to her. He flops back on his elbows now, watching her as she begins to unfasten his trousers.

"Let me, Stephen," she murmurs. "Let me do this."

"Oh, Christ," he mutters, "just do it!"

And although Tommy Handley continues with his puns and silly voices, he is unheard by either one of them.

Soon Alex pulls her to him, and rolls her onto her back, and she is amazed at his power. She'd thought of him as a wounded thing, an infant in need of succour, but now she sees that he's completely in charge. He is demanding, even rough.

Celia wouldn't have it any other way.

TWENTY-SEVEN

March 4, 1944
      "It has nothing to do with me, Celia," Pamela says in a quiet voice. "You can tell me to mind my own business, if you like." They are in the stable, making room for more potatoes, Celia raking rotting straw, and Pam sweeping. "It's your life. I just thought I should say something, that's all, otherwise you wouldn't know."

"He's perfectly fine, Pamela," Celia says. "There's nothing about him that worries me. He's told me about his nightmares, but then so many of us have those, don't we?"

"It's more than that." Pamela sits down on an up-ended bucket and studies her. "When these attacks come, he's beside himself. He barely recognizes anyone. While he was in the hospital, after he first got back, they had to restrain him – you know, tie him to his bed. That's what his C.O. told Daddy when Stephen first came here."

Celia looks at her, unmoved. "He's a nice man, Pam. If these spells were like that, he's not having them now. He would have said something."

"They're triggered by planes, don't you see? That's why he came here, because we don't see any. He can't be anywhere near an airfield where they're coming and going. He might have been able to get a ride back to Canada if he could fly. As it is, he must wait for a spot on a ship. It could be months before that happens."

Celia strokes her shoulder. "Don't worry about me, Pam. I'll just have to keep him away from planes, won't I? And if I can't, I'll deal with it then. "

"It's odd how quickly you've become involved with him, isn't it? So soon after Alex?"

Celia tightens her mouth. "Alex isn't here, is he? Even his parents think he's dead."

"But the telegram didn't say that – it didn't say 'presumed dead', did it? It's just that you've got it into your head that he must be. I've heard a couple of stories of chaps turning up months later, who'd been hiding somewhere, or were so affected by the things that had happened to them that they couldn't remember who they were." She picks a piece of straw from the top of one of her boots. "I thought you'd wait for him forever, the way you felt."

"I don't have forever. I need someone now. Being with Stephen seems to blot out everything and I forget there's a war on. I need that comfort, Pam. I know you don't understand what I mean, but once you've been in love, it's impossible to be without it. I ached for it, Pam, night after night. Well, Stephen made that go away." If I were honest with her, I would try to explain that it's safer for me, having Stephen. He's damaged, isn't he, so they won't want him back? There is no possibility of this man being snatched from me.

"You're so different to the girl I used to know, Celia," Pam says. "You've become rather hard, to be honest, and you even look older. I wish you were that earlier Celia. She used to make me laugh all the time."

Celia sees that she is close to tears, but doesn't move towards her. "The War did it, Pam. Perhaps, when it's over, we'll all be able to laugh at things again."

Pamela stands up, and takes her arm. "I need a rest. We'll do a bit later. Let's go and make a cup of tea."

"He's perfect for me, Pamela. Honestly. I want to be with him all the time. It's hard having to go back to camp each Sunday."

Pam flashes her an impatient look. "You said that about Alex, too."

"I know I did. I meant it at the time. But things change."

March 25, 1944

"Jesus, Celia, try not to be away so long next time. I nearly went mad." Stephen's head rests on her breasts; her blouse is still unbuttoned and her brassiere and vest is pulled up, wrenched aside in his eagerness for her. He nuzzles her gently, seems to refresh himself from the scent of her.

"I can't always get leave, Stephen. There's a lot on, these days." She repositions her hips, sliding from under him, wincing as she does. There will be bruises tomorrow. There are often bruises. She welcomes them, smiles when she finds them.

His hand slides down between her legs again, and she closes her eyes.

"I can't seem to get enough of you, honey." His voice takes on the thick hoarseness she recognizes and loves. "It's like I can't quite reach you – the heart of you – you're always a little beyond me. I want to be suffocated by you," he moves his fingers, "and be trapped here." He rolls back on top of her then, and she opens her eyes and looks into his. Whether it's sweat on his face, she's not sure, but he looks as if he's crying. She lifts herself to meet him, urgently, and they both make that same soft, animal sound of surprise.

She has often heard girls in her hut, the Cockney ones, say, "He gave me a right seeing-to, he did," meaning that a man made love to them forcefully, aggressively, but it's always said with a smile. Celia understands this completely. Stephen does the same thing the instant they are alone in odd places where no one can see them, barely giving her time to get her knickers off each time, roughly pushing her legs apart and then almost beating her with his body. Stephen knows all about giving her a right seeing-to.

"What caused your illness, Stephen?" She has a small idea of his ordeal, but needs to see if he can tell her about it. It's important that he share it with her.

"I don't much like talking about it." He drags on his cigarette. "Not as bad as it was, but it's till there."

"I thought it might help to tell me about it."

"The doctors said the same thing. 'Talk about it as much as you can,' they said. But it's hard."

She strokes his face with her hand, touching the little scar at the side of his mouth. "Your plane landed back at base all right, but it was badly damaged, wasn't it?"

"Yes." He takes a deep breath. "We started out from home with full cloud cover, but by the time we got to Bremerhaven, there was a full moon, and little cloud." He shifts his position so that he is completely on his back, staring up at the dark of the stable roof.

"We were attacked over Bremerhaven by Messerschmitt 109's and Focke-Wolfe fighters – dozens of our planes were going down. We were badly hit, I knew, and I turned back. Then, just over Vilhelmshaven, we came under fire from a flak installation, and a shell hit close to the starboard wing. If it had ignited the fuel tanks, I'd have lost both left engines. I was thinking we'd been lucky, when I saw that Milt, our radio operator, had been hit, but I couldn't tell if he was alive or dead – I just had to get the plane home somehow. We were going straight into the sea from twelve thousand feet when I managed to pull us out at a thousand feet. We struggled back to England and landed at 150 miles an hour with no brakes. I tell people I stood at the Pearly Gates that night, but St. Peter said, 'Not yet, Steve. Come back later'."

He turns his face to her. "After I landed her, when I got out, I saw them. All dead. Every man, Celia. Guys I've been flying with for over a year. Milt Carruthers, our Canadian wireless operator – from Guelph, he was – lost half his head. Jerry Dixon, our front gunner – also RCAF – from Vancouver – his guts were spilt out. Bill Torrence from Manchester, the mid upper gunner, and Mike Williams, our Aussie rear gunner, were so mashed up I couldn't recognize them as a human beings. Colin Edwards, from Bristol, our observer and bomb aimer, had no legs. It was like the back of a butcher's shop. Blood and flesh all over the tarmac as we pulled them out." He shudders, turns to put out his cigarette, and reaches for another. "And all I got was this," he said, touching the insignificant scar. "I found out later that we lost 31 Halifaxes that night and 235 men. But I made it, didn't I?"

Celia listens carefully, recounting his words in her mind. Odd that she feels no repulsion at this description, especially that bit about those two gunners, who probably had to be hosed out, as that poem said. She is breathing faster, of course, because it's really so horrible, isn't it? She can almost smell the blood. But he'll need soothing now, won't he? He did very well, recounting it for her. She can't imagine how difficult it must have been for him, but he is in pain, obviously. She must show him how much she cares about him, mustn't she? Prove that only she can make him feel better. She's so good at it now.

April 24, 1944

"Where on earth have you been, my girl?" Her father stands at the front door. "We thought something must have happened to you. Your mum's been frantic."

"I'm sorry, Dad," she says. She kisses his cheek and slips past him to put her arms around her mother. "I've been so busy – not many days off."

"But you still *get* leave, don't you?" Marie fixes her eyes on her. "It's not good enough, Celia. I know you have a lot on your mind, worrying about Alex, but you should come home regularly. At least you could have left a message with Mrs. Johnson next door (*they had no telephone*). She wouldn't have minded – just to say that you were all right. It's hard on us, not knowing."

"I've been spending the odd weekend at Pam's, Mum. It's so quiet there, and no air raids or anything. I feel so much better when I go."

"Oh, of course you would." But Marie is hurt. "It's only natural you'd want to get as far away from things as you can." She tries to smile. "We understand, don't we, Bert? She's been through a lot."

"I bought some Spam for you to try, Mum." She digs around in her bag. "One of the girls is seeing an American chap, and he gave her a whole case."

"Oh, lovely! How nice of him to do that. I'll say one thing for them, they're very generous, aren't they, the American boys? Marjorie's girl over the road got six pairs of nylon stockings from her fellow. Beautiful, they are. I've never seen anything like them before."

Celia wonders if her mother has any idea what Marjorie's girl probably did to warrant the six pairs of nylon stockings, then decides that Marie believes that such gifts are offered from simple affection, in gratitude for the innocent company of nice English girls. She glances at her father and knows immediately by his face that he's under no such illusion.

"I met a nice chap at Pam's house," Celia says, as she sits down in the sitting room.

"You what?" Her father is shocked.

"He's billeted there until he gets passage back to Canada. He's awfully nice. I've been spending a lot of time with him." She keeps her eyes lowered as she slips off her shoes.

Her mother stops in the middle of putting the tablecloth on, so that it lies half-on, half-off the table. "What are you talking about? What about Alex? It's only been – what – five months? Where's your head, madam?" She calls Celia madam only when she's very annoyed.

"Five months – five years. I can't wait around forever, can I?" Celia unbuttons her jacket and flops back in the chair, looking directly at her mother. "What have you got for tea, Mum? I'm famished."

Both Marie and Bert stand there, just as they were when she first mentioned Alex. She frowns at them. "What? Don't look at me like that. There's a bloody war on, isn't there? Here today, gone tomorrow? Did you think I'd just sit around waiting for him to come back?"

Her father walks over to her, and stoops to put an arm around her shoulders. "Sweetheart, listen to yourself. Whatever's come over you? You love Alex. You told us that. You can't just chuck him to one side like an old sock."

She shrugs his arm away, and stands up to finish putting the table cloth on. "I can. I have. I've got Stephen now."

"A Canadian you said?" Her mother frowns at her. "And what happens when he goes back? What will you do then?"

She faces them squarely. "I'll marry him."

Marie turns quickly, hiding her face. "I'll bring the tea things in," she says.

Her father looks hard at Celia, trying to control his anger. "You're going to marry a man you hardly know and go and live in Canada? Just like that? What about me and your mother? Don't we even get a say in it?" He sits down on his chair, shaking his head. "It will kill your mum if you go to Canada, Celia. Think hard on it. You're all she's got – all *we've* got."

"I have thought about it, Dad. Once I'm settled, you could come over, too. Everyone's talking about how nice it is, and that it will be easy to immigrate if you have a family member already there. Stephen says it's very beautiful, and you can earn good money. It's modern, and forward-thinking. You could find a lovely job, and start a new life. England's over, Dad. It will take years to rebuild it to what it was." She stops to help her mother with the cups and saucers. "I have thought about it, you see?"

"You want us to leave England, just like that?" her father says.

"What's that?" Marie stares at her. "You expect us to go, too?" She shakes her head. "I'm sorry, dear. If you want to marry this bloke and run off to the Canada, you go ahead and do it. But don't expect us to follow you. England's my home. I thought it was yours, too, but it seems I was wrong. I'll never leave here. If I can stick this rotten war out, the rationing, the bombings, having to work half days when all I want to do is take care of my house and the garden, then I'm certainly not going to give up on it when the war's over." She looks at her husband. "Right, Bert?"

He nods, staring at Celia. "She's right, Celia. I'm not going to move now, at my time of life. If Gerry couldn't do it, you certainly won't"

And the rest of the day is spent in almost total silence. Celia changes her mind about staying overnight. They don't argue with her.

June 3, 1944

RCAF Pilot, Sergeant Stephen Andrew Mercer and WAAF Leading Aircraft Woman *(she's been promoted)* Celia Denning are married at St. Clement's Church in Boscombe today. She attended the attached infants' school as a child, and loves the old church. She wears a simple, short-skirted bride-like dress that she'd had made from a piece of a parachute that one of the chaps at Uxton had given them. He'd been hanging onto it for his own bride, but as no one seemed imminent, he thought it a nice gesture to part with some of it. She has a small wreath of white roses on her head, and six more roses tied with a white silk bow, which her mother had saved from when Celia was a child. Pamela gave them a nice set of luggage, more for Celia than Stephen, who has few possessions in England. In any case, he will leave separately to Celia; she will be assigned passage on a ship specially fitted out for transporting War Brides when the time comes.

Marie and Bert have a nice spread for them at the house afterwards, and Pamela is there, which is nice, and Mr. and Mrs. Johnston from next door, and Doug Adams, an old friend of her father's. None of her mother's friends is there, which is odd. Adrian and Bridget can't attend because of their own responsibilities in Bath, and the billeted airmen aren't able to make the journey as far as Hampshire. It's a quiet little reception, with Pamela doing most of the talking.

When they leave for Brighton for their two nights' honeymoon, getting a lift to the station from Doug, Celia sees that Pamela is crying. Marie isn't crying. She and Bert stand at the empty place where the garden gate used to be and wave without enthusiasm, their faces expressionless. As she turns to look out of the back window at them, she knows that things will never be the same again. Well, of course, they can't be, can they? She is a married woman now.

"It's not happening now, dear, so you shouldn't be so upset. It was all so long ago." Nell places a cup of coffee on the table in front of me. It's too hot to sit outside on the balcony today.

"But how could she, Nell? It was such a lovely story. Celia's spoiled everything."

"But that's life, Strachan. Things are never so pat, ending happily. You're one of the smartest, no-nonsense women I know, and I'd have thought you'd be more pragmatic about it." She goes to the kitchen for something, probably her home-made cookies as usual. She knows I have a weakness for them.

I fan myself with a paper napkin. Nell hasn't put her airconditioner on yet. It's funny how no one outside of Toronto understands how hot it gets here in the summer. They think Canada equals snow. But the hot, thick humidity of the Bayous, in the deep south of the United States, snakes its way up to us every year. My grandmother hated it, Mum told me, became miserable with it, and constantly longed for England. But I've heard that Britain gets very hot now, that the climate has changed. Everything changes, over time.

"But you think this is it, with her marriage?" Nell puts the plate of cookies in front of me.

My appetite has been bad lately, so I'm surprised at how good they look to me, and I take one, still warm from the oven. "What else can happen? I guess she'll finalize everything here in Toronto, as that's obviously where she's headed." I take a big bite of the cookie. Oh Lordie, Nell knows how to please a girl.

"Perhaps there'll be a lot more about her life here."

"Oh, shit. I don't know. I'm just getting so tired of it all. I loved writing about England, seeing all the place names, and the way people were. I don't imagine Toronto was that interesting in the Forties."

"Well, of course it was. Different to England, but a very vibrant city even then, I think. A lot of famous people came from here – I can't think who, off the top of my head, but I know there's a lot."

"*Came* from here'…did you hear yourself? Not '*were*' here, or '*lived*' here. That means they must have left to go someplace else, in order to claim they '*came*' from Toronto."

"Oh, Strachan, I can't deal with you when you're in such a mood. Now you're fed up with Toronto."

"I'm grouchy, I know. Sorry, Nell." I finish off the cookie and take another. What the heck, Jay liked my accommodating hips.

"I think you need to take a break from the writing for a bit, if you can. It's all becoming too real to you, and that can't be healthy." Nell sits down next to me on the couch.

"I can't, Nell. Those bulldozers, or whatever the hell they use to knock perfectly good houses down with these days, will be in any old day. Each morning, when I'm leaving for work, it's the first thing I look for – signs of activity across the road."

"Then you'll just have to get down to it, and write the ending before they arrive…*if* that's what you want. Or you could write the ending your way. That wouldn't be so bad, would it?"

"I've been thinking the same thing. It would be so easy to remove all reference to her marriage to Stephen, to have Alex suddenly return. A nice happy ending. I've thought about it a lot."

Nell raises her eyebrows at me, but doesn't speak.

I sigh. "But I know I can't," I continue. "It wouldn't be right. Celia wants *all* of her story told, warts and all. It wouldn't be fair to deprive her of that – at least, the memory of her. When people read the book, if they do, they'll get the truest accounting possible. That's the only way I'll ever be able to put the thing to rest."

She leans over and hugs me then. "You are such an honorable girl, dear. It's one of the first things I noticed about you – your total honesty. Whatever happens, you're always truthful about it, even if you don't come out smelling like roses. You seem unable to deliberately mislead people. That's a gift."

"Or a curse. And – since this book – I've learned more and more about how to omit the facts – which is a sort of lie in itself, isn't it? Don't ask, don't tell? You know."

'Well, the book is different. You were afraid of looking like a crazy person. But no one thinks that now."

I smile. "*Now*, Nell?"

She smiles back. "To be honest, as we're discussing honesty, I thought you were a tad eccentric, when you first told me about how you wrote the book. But you weren't doing any harm, I thought, and the book was so nice. But it really wasn't until Ida agreed with everything that I decided you were as normal as I am." She sits back. "There. Now you know my little omission of truth, too."

"You didn't have to tell me, Nell. I've known for ages."

Tonight I am going to stay in the attic until the book is done. Tomorrow is Saturday, and Jay's out of town, so I can stay until dawn if I have to. One way or another, this will be my last visit over there.

I think.

TWENTY-EIGHT

June 5, 1944

In their room at the Arcadia Private Hotel in Brighton, which they leave only to eat and to allow the bed to be made, Celia and Stephen make love so many times that her hip muscles are sore as they pack to leave, and it's decidedly uncomfortable for her as she walks down the two flights of stairs to the lobby. Their room looked out over the sea, but they barely glanced at it.

"Good morning, Sergeant...Madam," Mrs. Pettigrew, the hotel owner, comes out from behind the desk. "Need help with the bags? Shall I order a taxi for you?" She has undoubtedly seen many couples like them, exhausted, their eyes puffy from lack of sleep.

"Yes, a taxi, please," Stephen says, glancing through the front door. "What's going on out there?" There seems to be more traffic than when they had arrived.

She follows his look. "Supposed to be hush-hush, but you'd never know it with all those army vehicles out there, would you?" She drops her voice, unnecessarily; they are the only ones in the lobby. "I know one of the chaps in charge of our Air Raid Wardens, and he told me there's an invasion planned for somewhere along the French coast in the next day or two – by land and air, he thinks – our biggest push yet to take it back from Hitler, at last. All our boys will be out over the Channel somewhere today, doing exercises – a rehearsal for it. They'll be dropping dummies as if they're paratroopers, things like that. It hasn't gotten going yet, but we should see quite a lot of your chaps flying over in a little while."

Stephen looks back at Celia and she sees the fear in his eyes.

"Can you hurry up with the taxi, please, Mrs. Pettigrew," she says. "We really are in a bit of a rush..."

June 7, 1944

Everyone has heard about Operation Overlord – D-Day, as it came to be known. It's rumoured that Churchill himself had wanted to go, to spur the troops on, but King George received this news with some shock, and quickly squelched the idea. In a meeting with Mr.

Churchill, he told him *he*, as the King, intended to land at Caen – his Kingly duty. When a stunned Churchill told him that was impossible, that he likely would be killed, His Majesty had fixed the Prime Minister with a quizzical eye, and Churchill got the message. *Neither one* could go.

Both the BBC and the newspapers now reveal that Allied air forces flew a total of 14,674 sorties during the first 24 hours of Operation Overlord, for a loss of 113 aircraft, many by friendly fire. Fighter cover for the invasion beaches was provided by nine squadrons of Spitfires, while Typhoon and Mustang fighter-bombers of the 2nd TAF flew armed reconnaissance missions further inland. Such was the Allied air supremacy that the *Luftwaffe* only flew 319 sorties in the same period.

June 8, 1944

An attack by Typhoon and Mustang squadrons yesterday decimated the German 7th Army armoured division which was moving towards the Channel coast.

June 10, 1944

First use of the new 12,000lb deep penetration bomb ("*Tallboy*") by No. 617 Squadron against the Saumur rail tunnel in France occurred yesterday. The tunnel was totally blocked, thus preventing German armour moving by rail to the D-Day beachheads.

June 11, 1944

Over the forty-eight hour period from the night of June 8, Allied aircraft were deployed to temporary airstrips in Normandy.

Not long now, everyone says. Nearly over. All be over in a couple of months...

Celia, listening to the radio, lying on her bed staring up at the hut ceiling, wonders if Stephen has heard all of the latest news yet. She glances around the room at the other girls going about their various chores – shoe polishing and brass cleaning, hair setting, and stocking darning, reading, and gossiping. Janine is cleaning the little strip of linoleum that surrounds her bed. Sarge is very particular about everyone's little strip.

It will all change for them soon. They'll go home to families who've hardly seen them over the past four years, perhaps to sweethearts who've long allowed for the likelihood of infidelity, unfaithful as they've been themselves with some tart in Soho, or the wife of that farmer who billeted them in Gloucester. They will go home and try to put it all behind them, the frights they've had – both from the bombings, and the possibility of an unwanted pregnancy, or a dose of the clap – back to their factories, shops, or schools, and try to be as they were before.

But they can never be the same, not after the things they've seen – the craters where once houses or a school stood; the bus filled with workers blasted off the road and left pierced into the side of a block of flats by the force of a bomb landing nearby; the high street shops in Poole strafed by three Messerschmidts on their way home to Stuttgart, or Nuremberg, killing many mums, some with toddlers, as they tried to find things they had enough coupons for; and the sad looks on the faces of boys as they said goodbye, but who never returned, despite how long the girls waited outside the barracks.

And they will never be the same after the things they've *done*, with those same boys, most no older than they were, even as some of the girls remain virgins, because there were those alternative things that they did, that they learned how to do in a hurry.

Someone has put a jam jar filled with cowslips on one of the window sills, and Celia smiles. Even with everything that is happening around them, someone has thought how pretty the cowslips would be sitting on a window sill in their hut.

"It's good of you to bring them over tonight, Jay. You could have waited until tomorrow, given them to me at the office." I open the package and put the enclosed pages on the coffee table.

He is still looking at me, I know, and I long to look back at him, but I'm afraid of what I might see there.

Before me is Alex's birth certificate, and Celia's, and – incredibly – Celia's marriage certificate. I gave Jay the news about her wedding only a few weeks ago, so hadn't expected it. Celia's service record is here, too, and it's quite lengthy, so I skim-read it. There are many notations, including one about that fiasco when she took off from camp without a pass, to make that journey up to

Winchester. It seems so long ago, my recording of that night. I look up at Jay, who's no longer gazing me, but at the papers.

"Alex's service record, Jay – couldn't Glenn find it?"

He looks hard at me. "I have it." He pulls some papers from his pocket. "I wanted to tell you about it first."

"He *did* die, is that it? She was right all along?" I feel tears prickling.

He shakes his head. "He didn't die, Strachan. He was captured and held in Bremervörde POW camp – Stalag X-B, near Bremerhaven – until June 1945. It was one of the worst camps of World War ll. Glenn filled me in. The rescue forces found their own men, of course, but there were also Russians, half-dead, who'd been treated like animals because they weren't under the auspices of the Geneva Convention, and they also found hundreds of civilians, starved, dying, dead, more or less stacked in these huts. Like the things we've heard about Jewish death camps..." He looks at the paper. "Alex was in a very bad way, some kind of infection from a poorly treated wound he'd got when he first went there. He stayed in Germany after the camp was liberated, in hospital, and then convalesced there, too. He didn't get back to England until Autumn 1945."

"He survived the War." It's all I can say.

"He was pretty sick and emaciated when he got back, and was in hospital in England for a long time, too. Rheumatic fever." He leans over and hands the pages to me. "It's all here. I thought it was best to tell you about it first, because it's not the best news, really. He survived, at least, but – Strachan, listen to this – he wasn't demobilized until September, 1946, from the English hospital, and it looks as if he didn't physically leave the hospital until even later than that. Apparently the powers-that-be just overlooked a lot of those poor bastards."

"And Celia didn't know he was back."

"If you look at her record, she was discharged in January, 1946. I asked Glenn about it. He says there was a fuck-up with the whole demobilization thing after the war. So many people to process, and they tried to do age seniority/longest service first. Alex should have gotten out before Celia, but didn't. By the time he was back in civvies, Celia was probably here, I'm guessing."

"Whatever date it was, she'd married Stephen in '44, anyway. It didn't make any difference." I stand up and go to my room, and gaze out at the attic window. My head is buzzing from this latest information. Jay has followed me and now stands beside me.

"Will I ever finish this book, do you think, Jay?"

"Sure. It might feel like you're going at a snail's pace, getting to it, but you're almost there. It won't be—"

I put a finger on his mouth. "Don't say it, Jay. For Christ's sake don't say '*it won't be long now...*' I am just so fed up with that expression."

He takes my hand with the silencing finger and kisses it.

I stare at him. "What's that for?"

"Because you are the kindest, most generous girl I know. Because you care so much about these people, who are nothing to you, really. Because you've been doing all of it – going through it with them, by yourself. —Oh, fuck, Strachan..." He pulls me to him then, and holds me very tightly, and I can feel his heart pounding.

"I've been so lonely, Jay." Tears slip down my cheeks, and he kisses them away, like a daddy with his child. The truth is, I'm crying for Alex.

"Come over here, you." He pulls me to the bed. "Christ, I love you, you damned idiot. I've been going crazy."

"I thought you'd never come back, that I'd screwed things up for good..."

He pulls my dress over my head, and pushes me back on the pillow, although I am still trying to unfasten my bra. "Hey, hey, it's okay. There's no rush, Strachan. We have all the time in the world," he says, as he cradles me to his chest.

But this proves to be a slight exaggeration. In what seems no time at all, he's whipped off his own things, and mine, and we're back doing what we do best. It takes my mind off Celia and Alex, of course.

June 26, 1944

Pam has free tickets from her father for Jack Hylton's review, *Hi-De-Hi*, and can't resist it, especially as it's due to close within three weeks. It would take their mind off things, she thought, although nobody likes going to London now – such a sad-looking place - and Celia protests, but Stephen is in Bristol for the night anyway, getting his three-monthly assessment by his doctor at Bristol General, and Pam talks her into it.

Celia thinks he'll get the all clear this time. His nightmares have been less frequent, when she's with him, at least. At first, she had tried to wake him during what she saw as his bad episodes. His body would suddenly stiffen beside her, waking her up, and then he would always shout the same thing, 'Start outer port engine!'. He would begin tossing, gently at first, but eventually shaking so badly that she wondered why he didn't wake himself up. He would be bathed in sweat, his eyes wild when he finally opened them, taking a minute to recognize her. She would hold him, whispering that everything was all right, until he fell asleep again. He hasn't had that nightmare for over a fortnight.

She and Pamela take the train to London. Everyone's been talking about the show for months, and saying how good it was. But first they have to get to the theatre, past bombed-out buildings, huge piles of rubble all that's left of them, and they just keep talking and talking about anything but the war, trying not to peer into the gaping holes that were once shops and flats and theatres.

Hi-De-Hi is a delight to them, with its costumes and the music, the wonderful stars – people they'd read about but had never seen in the flesh. Celia can't wait to tell her mother about it. And there was no air raid tonight, just as the girls at camp had assured them. Hitler was too busy bombing Russia these days, wasn't he?

They are still chattering about the show as they walk back to the tube station, taking a short cut through a side street. Pamela is just recounting one favorite piece in the show, when they hear a strange noise, a loud, deep, droning motor sound, unlike the usual lorry or bus, and they look up and down the street. It sounds for all the world like a huge tractor moving along, coming closer and closer to them, yet there's nothing there, other than a cyclist, who also turns to look back, then up. The noise increases, and Pamela is clearly frightened, following the cyclist's gaze, but there's still nothing to see. In any case, she grabs Celia's arm, but the noise stops, and they smile foolishly at each other, and begin to walk on. They laugh as they see the cyclist pedalling furiously away.

"I wonder what it was?" Pamela says, and then she suddenly frowns, stops and grabs Celia's arm again. "Doodle bug!" she screams, and throws herself at Celia, slamming her up against a wall.

"What?" Celia says, staring at her, the wind slightly knocked out of her.

And then the V1 rocket reaches its unknown destination, the noise of its impact deafening, the vibration of it felt long after it has exploded.

Pamela goes to the kerb, after a minute, and sicks up all the licorice allsorts she'd consumed at the theatre. Celia had thought she'd eaten far too many.

They stop in a pub on the way to the station to have a quick brandy. The barmaid tells them the "buzz" bomb hit Croydon - her sister lives near there and has just telephoned. Celia has heard about the V1 rockets, of course – the "Doodle Bugs" – but not in detail. Pamela knows far more about them from her regular chats with one of the radio op girls, but she hadn't known what they sounded like, until now.

Later, Celia would read that Evelyn Waugh, the writer, had said they (the V1s) were *as impersonal as a plague, as though the city were infested with enormous, venomous insects'*, and she would shudder, remembering that night.

It was to be the last time Pamela and Celia would go to London to see a show.

"I don't understand, Strachan." Katie lowers her considerable self onto my sofa. "I thought you already knew Alex survived, because the phone number is still listed in his home town."

"It is, but I started to believe that Celia was right – I don't know why – I thought perhaps Harvey and Patsy had more children, and it was their new offspring living there. That's not impossible. They were quite young. Celia figured they were only in their early forties. Women do have kids then, don't they?"

"I don't know if they would have done that deliberately back then, because they didn't have all the testing we have today." She smiled. "Of course, they wouldn't have known what to test for – in fact, come to think of it, they probably didn't even think about age being a problem for the baby."

"Well, that's what I figured, anyway – or perhaps they adopted. Christ knows, there must have been enough orphans around after the war. But I really did believe Alex was alive all the time, right up until Celia got married, and even his parents thought he was dead..." I look sadly at her. "I gave up on him, Katie. Just like she did."

"It's almost finished, isn't it? What will you do with yourself when it's over?"

"Dunno, really. You're going to think I'm really nuts, but I was considering going over to England and trying to meet some of the families. Nell thinks it would be a good idea. It would help with the book, too, if I get it published. I could claim that's where I got all my research material from, right in England. I wasn't looking forward to being questioned too closely about how I know so much about it."

"Makes sense to me. And you deserve it." She smiles. "If I wasn't such a blob, I'd come with you."

"You're going to have enough to do soon, without flitting off to England."

"But Jay will go with you. He'd love that."

"Maybe. He's not sure if he can get away. I did ask him. I'm not sure how I feel about traveling alone."

"What about Nell?"

"I've got weeks of vacation time, but I'm not sure about Nell. She's pretty vital to the company." I laugh then. "Can you imagine it? Me in England? Going to all those places I've been writing about?"

"And face-to-face with one of Alex's descendants?"

"Oh, I know! Weird, eh?"

'Well, I think you should go. Perhaps England holds the answer to all of it."

"Oh, Katie. Wouldn't that be amazing? I'd finally be able to wake up each morning without thinking about it – I'd have the answer to that big *Why*?" I reconsider. "Even better, the *Why Me*?"

"Oh, that's easy. You showed up. No one else did."

*

232

I sit in the attic just looking around tonight, really studying at it, stamping it all in my mind. I've decided to take the record player and 78s when I finally leave here for the last time. They've come to represent all the work I've done on the book. Years from now, if I hear one of the melodies, it will instantly take me back into Celia's life.

For the first time I take a closer look at the calendar. It has a permanent sepia-colored picture of the founding Dominion Bank building, but with a little tear-off pad below it representing each month. The month that's uppermost now is August. How odd that I hadn't noticed this before. If Celia *was* in this room, she stopped tearing those months off after July, 1947.

I'm not in the mood for writing – not that it requires much effort – but the sitting still for hours at a time isn't good, and I think I have permanent carpal tunnel syndrome in my right wrist, because it sure hurts a lot at times, especially working with the small keyboard of the laptop, although I've become quite proficient with it. I manage to produce about twelve pages, some of it – most of it, really – involving things that happen in Celia's hut, but I'll probably omit that later. A lot of the hut dialogue just goes on and on and has nothing to do with Alex, although it sometimes is an interesting and even funny read, when they're not talking about war stuff.

A couple of weeks ago I was determined to make it my last visit here. What a joke. I think I'm still hovering somewhere around the end, but there's no guarantee of that. Any sort of sound of heavy equipment outside my window in the morning has me jumping to the window to see if it's *Them*. So far, so good.

But Celia is definitely on borrowed time.

TWENTY-NINE

September 30, 1944

"Gerry's been at it again in London, did you hear?" Janine sits on the edge of Pam's bed, and helps herself to a piece of home-made cake. "There's been so many bombs falling, and our boys don't let too many of their bombers through, do they? It's all a bit peculiar, if you ask me. My dad says it's not bombs at all, but they've just learnt how to send over doodle-bugs without making any noise."

"Could be, couldn't it?" Pamela nods. "Monica in radio ops said the same thing, and she hears everything, doesn't she?"

Later they will learn that these are the V2 rockets, Hitler's silent and deadly final assault on London.

"She should be more careful," Janine says. "All it takes is one big mouth to get her into real trouble."

"Well, she only talks to me. She knows I'm safe." Pamela smiles.

"I'm just saying." Janine reaches for more cake. "Your mum's n'alf clever, Pammy, the way she makes things like this."

"Well, Daddy's a farmer, so there are a few perks with that – you know, eggs, butter, a bit of local jam now and then. And Mummy saves all our sugar rations – we've all stopped having sugar in our tea – just so she can bake now and then."

"How's your hubby then, Celia?" Janine offers a morsel of cake to her pet mouse, which is in her blouse pocket.

"Oh, he's doing well. He's working in Bath now, some government office to do with weights and measures – all beyond me. But he seems to be enjoying it."

"Hard on you, though, being apart all week."

"Used to it now, aren't we? Stephen's trying to find a little flat for us right in Bath, so I don't have to travel as far. It's unfair to Pamela's parents anyway, with him still living there."

"They don't mind – I told you," Pam says. "They think the world of both of you."

234

"Well, it's not right, all the same." Celia is quite looking forward to the time when she and Stephen no longer have to be careful where they are when they make love, or how loud they become. Sometimes Celia is forced to stuff a corner of the pillow in her mouth, to stop from crying out. She wonders if such vocalizing is normal, as she's not heard of other women responding this way, but has no one to ask about it (well, no one she'd consider asking about it.)

"Dad says the War's just about over now. Now we've taken back Belgium, Holland's next." Janine puts her mouse back into its tin, but doesn't fasten the lid tightly, so that its nose can still be seen, a tiny quivering pinkness. "He says we just have to get one more winter out of the way."

"One more winter?" Celia says. "What – six or seven months? Is that all?"

"Yanks are saying it. That group at the pub, the ones flying the new Lancasters, well – they sing this song at the end of the night...you know the one..." She sings with a sweet soprano voice, *"We'll Meet Again..."*

Celia stares at her, her mouth a little open.

Janine stops singing and laughs. "Course, they sing it with a sort of Ivan Novello la-di-da voice – you know – they're so funny."

"Iv*or* Novello," Celia corrects her gently, swallowing hard.

"What? Oh, is it? - Yes, him, that's right. Very posh, anyway."

"I don't think he wrote "We'll Meet Again," Celia says. "He wrote "My Dearest Dear". Do you remember that one?"

Janine puts her head on one side. "Oh, love us – I remember it – it was from that show "The Dancing Years", wasn't it? Everyone was going on about it. Lovely music that. A bit of a pansy isn't he – the Novello chap? Some of the lads called it the "The Dancing Queers." She giggles.

Celia doesn't reply. On reflection, the whole production was over-sentimental nonsense. Strange she hadn't realized it before. Even Alex hadn't commented.

It's the first time Celia has thought about Alex in months.

"Look, if you're uncomfortable about it, just say," Nell says, passing the cookie plate to me. It's out-and-out bribery, of course.

235

"I don't mind, if you're happy," I say. "I almost don't care, to be honest. I mean, we have to show it someone at some point, don't we?"

"She's only an assistant at this agency, but she was telling me that she's usually the one who gives the thumbs-up on new manuscripts anyway, screening them for the agent. I thought she could just give it a quick look, and see if we're on the right path."

"If you want to do it, go ahead. Anything we can do to get the ball rolling, right?"

"I've known her mother since high school, and Kerry's a lovely girl. A lot of writers would jump at the opportunity, I think."

"Then go for it. The quicker we get going on it, the better." I look squarely at her. "I'm tired of it, I told you. I'll be glad to see the back of it."

"But you'll still try to find the people in England?"

"Oh, of course. I have to follow through with that now. That will be the final point of *closure* – isn't that how Hollywood puts it these days?"

"And Hollywood might want to make a movie of it… Imagine that." She smiles.

"Jesus, Nell! Don't say that! I want it over and done with."

"From what I've heard, once a book's film rights are sold, you're more or less guaranteed never to have anything to do with it again, so you're safe."

But it's a tempting thought, all the same, the idea of a movie. I try to imagine what actors would play Celia and Alex.

Nell laughs. "I know what you're doing. I did it too. Kate Winslett and Colin Firth, I thought."

"Jude Law and Kate Beckinsale," I say, laughing.

Nell frowns and shakes her head. "I don't know who she is…" She smiles then. "I don't get to the movies, you know. Long time since I last went."

"Trust me, she'd be a candidate. The 'Kates' definitely win. But Jude Law would be a lovely Alex. Colin Firth could be Stephen."

"Another cookie?" Nell holds out the plate.

I must say I'm not feeling as bad about the idea of a movie as I first did.

December 15, 1944

"It's perfect, Stephen," Celia says, peering from the window out into the gloom. Bath's famous Royal Crescent is just across the road, more or less, but is invisible now. "It sounds posh, doesn't it? Royal Avenue?"

"Considering the rather unprepossessing houses along here, yes, it does. I won't tell, if you won't..." he says, putting a finger to his lips. "I'll pick up some bits for it, and we can dump this lot...all a bit nasty, isn't it?" The settee and one armchair are decidedly dirty, and the springs are gone judging by the lumps in the seat and there are cigarette burn marks everywhere. "Bedstead's okay. I'll buy a new mattress somewhere, that's all. We can spend Christmas Eve alone together for the first time."

"It's a shame, having to buy new things, when we'll be off to Canada soon."

He studies her. "Who says it's soon? Could be a long time yet."

"Oh, just one of the girls. She thinks it will be over by spring."

"She's been listening to those Yanks, I'll bet. They're always tooting their own horns."

"Her father said it." She doesn't understand why Stephen is so critical of the Americans, when he sounds so much like one himself, although he denies it.

"Oh," he says, raising his eyebrows, "then it *must* be true..."

"You shouldn't be so nasty, Stephen. He could be right."

"You think I'm nasty, do you?" He pulls her into his arms and buries his face in her neck.

"You never listen to anyone else's opinion." She allows him to walk her backwards to the settee, where she falls onto it.

Stephen drops to his knees on the floor beside her, and undoes her tie.

"Is it your opinion that there's a distinct likelihood of a certain randy chap getting a quick leg-over before heading off to Uxton?" He pulls off her jacket and begins to unfasten her blouse.

She laughs at him. "I'd say it was very likely."

"There, then," he says, pulling off her skirt, "I bow to your superior knowledge, and concur with your opinion on the matter."

237

The flat is at the top of the house, and there is a great feeling of abandon in being alone up there. When Celia cries out this time, he doesn't cover her mouth with his hand, as he sometimes does, and his own voice blends with hers, a bass note to her soprano. If neighbours do hear them, no eyebrows are raised. All kinds have rented this flat, after all, even two chaps, according to the landlord, who were even noisier in bed, although he didn't mention that.

Nothing surprises people anymore.

I've made up my mind, this time. I have enough food, drink, a pillow and blanket, and I'm just going to stay here from tonight, right through tomorrow – Saturday – until Celia's story is finished. I'll need to run home to use the washroom, but that's the only reason I'll leave. I told Nell what I was planning, in case she phoned and couldn't reach me. Jay is in Vancouver all week, and I asked him not to call me this weekend, and explained why. Except for Katie, who's been so busy with her own plans these days, no one is likely to miss me.

I set out some snacks and a couple of cans of drink on the table, and sit back, laptop all ready, and wait for the words. For some reason, this reminds me of that first time I came here, when I longed for a pen and paper. I can feel the dialogue buzzing at the back of my mind, and I can see what Celia sees. I need to save this memory, make sure it's not fleeting, or quickly forgotten. Tonight, so late in the summer, will be one of the last I'll spend in this strange room. Outside it's hovering at around 78 degrees, and it's also very humid, but in here it's comfortable, perhaps 70 degrees. I can't explain that, but then I can't explain anything about this room. I feel my head nod for a second, and know the writing will start soon. It's a pity I never got a picture of this attic with its pretty wallpaper and furnishings. I would have liked something concrete to look back on, years from now, when I tell someone else about it, perhaps Katie's child, or little Sarah Margaret, when they're old enough to be interested. They wouldn't think me such a weirdo if they could see a picture, right?

It's been hard for me, coming here, but I had no choice, of course. The attic made me do it. Those nights when I tried to ignore it, I was absolutely miserable, and when the light was out for all that time, I thought I'd go mad. After this weekend, I'll go back to being the girl who loves staying home with her cat, fussing with her apartment, drawing pictures, and not needing much more than that. Of course, Jay's in my life now, so I'll never be quite the same as before, but I've remained true to myself. It was a battle at times, but I came through. Strachan, honey, - man or no man - you've remained your own woman.

April 30, 1945

"Celia?" Pam sits down next to her at breakfast. "Did you hear?"

"What is it?" Celia stirs her tea. She wonders if she could go back for more jam. Everyone seems to be using rather a lot on their toast.

"They've started bringing out the POW chaps. That's all bomber command is doing now, just providing transport home."

"So?" Celia says brightly.

"I thought…you know, perhaps Alex…"

Celia turns to her. "For God's sake, Pam. Forget about Alex. If the Red Cross had come across him, don't you think Patsy and Harvey would have heard by now?"

"There have been some unusual cases, though. A couple of chaps who weren't even listed as missing turned up from a camp in Belgium."

Celia finishes her tea, stands up and reaches for her cap. "I'm married now, Pam, in case you've forgotten. I don't have time to mess about worrying about every POW under the sun, do I?" She gazes down at her. "I'd have thought you could be a little more thoughtful really, what with Stephen demobbed and getting a berth on the *Aquitania*. How do you think I feel about that? I'm going to be wretched when he's gone."

"Oh, Celia, I'm sorry, pet." Pamela jumps up and puts her arms around her. "I know how hard it all must be for you. But you'll be going soon." She steps back to look into Celia's face. "I'm truly sorry. I just can't stop thinking about Alex, that's all. I know it's really none of my business, but it's just so sad."

"You're a big old soppy twerp, aren't you?" Celia pats her back, and turns towards the door. "As if you don't have enough to worry about, taking care of yourself, without taking on everyone else's worries."

"Not everyone's – just yours," Pam says quietly.

"Well, stop it. I'm perfectly all right. Forget about Alex, Pam. Leave him for his mother and father to grieve over."

"I don't know how I'm going to feel when you're gone, Celia." Pam tucks Celia's arm into hers as they walk back to their hut.

"We'll both hurt, of course. I've come to rely on you so much. But we'll send lots of letters. It's going to be really hard for me leaving Mum and Dad, too. But thousands of girls are doing it, Pam. Making new lives in different countries. We just have to cope, don't we? If we want to stay with our men, of course, and I certainly want to stay with Stephen. Give it a year, and perhaps you can come over for a holiday…once everything is back to normal, and people can take holidays again."

Pam looks at her. "You're right. Daddy spent his holidays in North America a number of times when he was younger. His father considered it part of his education, he says. Perhaps Daddy will encourage me, as well, even if it is expensive."

"There, then. All settled." Celia leans over to her and kisses her cheek. "Stephen says Toronto is the greatest place in the world to be young. Lots of jazz clubs, and shows and stage plays. We'll have an amazing time, won't we? We'll have to see if Stephen knows any nice young men to show you around. I mean, when *I'm* not available. I'll have Stephen and the apartment to take care of, you know. "

For a moment, Pam thinks that Celia sounds a bit like a little girl, talking about setting up her nice new tea set, having friends over for pretend tea. Pam used to make believe that way, up in her own playroom, surrounded by her dollies, and she recognizes the dreamy expression on Celia's face. "Just think," she says, "By the time I manage to come over there, *if* I do, you could have a baby."

"Oh, I don't know about that," Celia says. "First things first. I'll have enough to do, just making a nice home for Stephen."

"It's lovely though, thinking about a baby." Pamela opens the door to their hut, and lets Celia go first. "You'll make a lovely mummy."

Celia looks at her sharply. "Why do you say that?"

"Well, you know, lots of things. You read a lot, and you love music, and you're so much fun – all things that children need."

Celia smiles. "That's not me anymore, Pam. It used to be. I don't seem to be as much fun as I was. But that's you, now, isn't it? You're the one always trying to make *me* laugh."

Pam pushes her playfully. "Oh, you! You'll get back to the way you were. Once this War's behind us…" But, even as she says it, she's not sure it's true.

May 8, 1945

"Celia! Celia!" Marie struggles through the crowd on the street outside the house, forced to stop as she is hugged by someone she's never seen before. "Celia," she finally reaches her daughter, "come inside quickly. Mr. Churchill's about to give his speech."

"Pshh," Celia makes an impatient sound. "I'm not coming in to listen to that. It's over, Mum. No more bloody speeches, or boring news bulletins. I never want to hear another word about it."

Mr. Johnston grabs Celia's hands and tries to jitterbug with her, but his wife pulls him away. "George, behave yourself!" She laughs at Marie. "One boozey toast too many, I think." She takes his arm and steers him towards the house. "Is Winnie on now, Mrs. Denning?" she calls back.

"Just about to start, yes." Marie turns to Celia. "Come on, love. Dad wants you to come in. You know how much he thinks of Mr. Churchill."

Celia shrugs, and winks at the young man who's grabbed her around the waist and trying to spin her. "Sorry, Romeo," she says, as she extricates herself, "better find someone your own age." She follows Marie back to the house, threading her way between the tables - surprisingly laden with food - that line the street, their colorful array of tablecloths fluttering in the breeze. The young man stares after her. He's known Celia since they went to school together - they were in the same class right up until she went to the Grammar. He was certain they were the same age.

"I don't know how you'll be able to hear anything with all that racket outside, Bert." Marie closes the window in the sitting room, and turns the volume knob on the wireless.

"Don't twiddle with it, Marie," Bert says. "I had it just right. If you sit down and be quiet, you'll hear it clearly enough."

The three of them sit in the living of the Denning house, on Walpole Road, Boscombe, in the County of Hampshire, and listen to

241

their Prime Minister address a grateful and somewhat tipsy nation. As his sober voice and carefully-modulated words fill the room, their faces – including Celia's – are filled with wonder, almost disbelief.

'Yesterday morning at 2:41 a.m. at Headquarters, General Jodl, the representative of the German High Command, and Grand Admiral Doenitz, the designated head of the German State, signed the act of unconditional surrender of all German Land, sea, and air forces in Europe to the Allied Expeditionary Force, and simultaneously to the Soviet High Command. 'General Bedell Smith, Chief of Staff of the Allied Expeditionary Force, and General Francois Sevez signed the document on behalf of the Supreme Commander of the Allied Expeditionary Force, and General Susloparov signed on behalf of the Russian High Command...'

Celia sighs, and then, as her parents don't seem to notice, slips out of the room, and stands looking out of the kitchen window. The sky is a magnificent blue, with puffs of fairytale clouds, and the garden is very lovely, as if no war had existed.

Over. It was over. All the people could go back to their homes, to their own countries, to their wives and children. The street lamps would come back on. They would never hear another air-raid warning, although they would never forget its sound. They could turn their air-raid shelters into sunken gardens, or fishponds. She uses the tea towel to dry her eyes, then drinks a glass of water before returning to the front room.

... 'Today this agreement will be ratified and confirmed at Berlin, 'We may allow ourselves a brief period of rejoicing; but let us not forget for a moment the toil and efforts that lie ahead. Japan, with all her treachery and greed, remains unsubdued. The injury she has inflicted on Great Britain, the United States, and other countries, and her detestable cruelties, call for justice and retribution. We must now devote all our strength and resources to the completion of our task, both at home and abroad. Advance, Britannia! Long live the cause of freedom! God save the King!'

It wasn't one of Winnie's longest speeches, but it's so moving in its simplicity, so incredible to hear after all they've been through, that

Marie allows tears to roll down her cheeks unheeded. Bert fumbles for his own handkerchief and blows his nose loudly as the broadcast ends. When they look over at Celia they see she is dry-eyed, her mouth a thin line.

She looks back at them without expression. "Well, that's that, then, isn't it?"

Bert stands up. "I think I'll make a fresh pot of tea."

January 17, 1946

"Harvey got some petrol, at least," Patsy says. "I must say it's nice to have a car at our disposal again. I ruined so many stockings, riding that old bike they gave me."

"And Patsy doesn't have to do war work anymore." Harvey smiles at his wife. "She can stay home and take care of the house properly now."

"Well, there are still things I'll be involved with. So many homeless people now, you know. I'm part of our local committee involved in providing housing and clothing, and the like. Some of these poor chaps came back to nothing – flats they had that got confiscated by the landlords – or they upped the rents. All terribly immoral, but apparently not illegal." She pours more tea for Celia. "And that's not even counting the people who lost their homes to the bombings. They're talking about using old military huts as temporary shelter – did you hear?"

"The Nissan huts, yes." Celia looks around the room. The last time she was here she had been almost insane with grief, the evidence of it perfectly hidden from view. How well she'd coped. "They're easy to transport, I suppose."

"And you're not just a tiny bit sad to be leaving England?" Patsy says.

"Well, of course, there's Mum and Dad, my friend Pam – we're very close. But this is a new age now, isn't it? Time to start afresh. Like those early immigrants who founded America and Australia, places like that. I'm a modern day pioneer, really."

"Well, we both hope you'll be very happy there, dear. Canada is a lovely country, once you adjust to their winters." Harvey takes a cigarette from a silver case, and then, an afterthought, offers her one. She shakes her head. "I was in northern Ontario the last summer before I graduated,' he continues. 'A man's country, at least

243

then. Kayaking, and camping out, learning how to live off the land, even taking part in an Inuit tribal ceremony – although I don't recall what that was about. All changed today, I suppose."

"Stephen says it's still like that in the Far North. It's only the southern parts of Canada that are really developed."

"Really?" He seems happy with this. "Too harsh up there I suppose for most city people. Who knows, some day I might go back, just to check it out."

Patsy leans forward. "Anyway, Celia, we know where you'll be. The moment there's any word, we'll let you know."

Celia looks at her with curiosity. "Any word…?"

"When we hear about Alex. We'll send you a telegram, or telephone you if we can, to let you know."

Celia smiles. "Oh, of course." She glances at Harvey, and then back to Patsy. "You still have a lot of optimism, do you?"

They look at each other. "Of course we do," Harvey says. "No reason not to. Tons of chaps coming back now, and some of them weren't even on the Red Cross lists. Yet another bloody cock-up by the authorities, that's all."

"So you must think I'm awful, not waiting for him…" Celia has always wondered how they felt about her marriage, other than the usual platitudes they'd offered at the time.

'But you don't have to feel awful about it, dear," Patsy says. "It's not as if you were engaged to Alex, after all. So many romances during this war, and no one needs to feel guilty about them. It was a way of coping, wasn't it? Dealing with the fear and loneliness?" She pats Celia's hand. "You'll have a lovely life in Canada and Alex will come home and get back to university and get on with his own."

"He certainly wasn't ready for marriage, you know," Harvey says, reaching for an iced cake, putting his cigarette to one side. "Too much on his plate, what with getting his degree, and then medical school and his internship. The last thing he needs is the responsibility of a wife." He sits back, taking a small bite of pink icing. "But, of course, you knew that, didn't you?"

Celia looks at each of them, sees their open faces, the warm eyes. "As a matter of fact, he never mentioned marriage to me at all," she says. He hadn't told her he was going to be a doctor, either; she hadn't asked what he was taking at university, but assumed that, like Pamela, he simply wanted a B.A. to help with future career plans, or simply for the sake of education. They were that kind of people, after all.

"There, then." Patsy laughs. "So you've no need to feel guilty, do you? A wartime romance, wasn't it? Something to remember when you're old and grey."

But Celia thinks she sees a tiny look of relief in Patsy's eyes, as she says goodbye.

On her way home to Boscombe, Celia wishes that Stephen could be sitting next to her. Nice, dependable Stephen, with his need for her clearly defined, his feelings always unambiguous. When Stephen said he loved her, he meant it for all time. When he married her, he meant forever. It was important to know where you stand with people. Stephen could be trusted.

THIRTY

May 26, 1946

Toronto is just as Celia imagined. From the very first warm day that she stepped outside to go for a walk alone, she felt at ease, enjoying the peace of the place, the unbombed buildings, the wide roads and the trees and flowers everywhere, the unhurried walk of the pedestrians.

Stephen gave her money and she quickly found Eaton's and Simpson's, wondering at the amazing variety of clothes that were available without coupons. The women she saw seemed more outgoing, looking directly at her, equals, not dropping their eyes as English women did, and the sales girls were very friendly, almost casual, and not at all snooty. It was to do with their confidence, she felt. The British were a conservative, reflective people, on the whole, wary of offending, of speaking out of turn, conscious of their class. The English regimen of the queue at bus stops and shops wasn't evident in Toronto, either, where a more hit-or-miss approach seemed to prevail. Your turn came in the end, people seemed to think, and it wasn't worth formalizing it. The men didn't lift their hats to women as they did at home, sometimes just raising two fingers in a semblance of a salute.

Celia liked this relaxed way. People said "Hi" to her as she walked along. In England, perhaps someone she knew by sight would say a stiff 'Good morning," but never a stranger. She now understood why Stephen was the way he was. He was a Canadian through and through.

His parents were equally friendly, although she saw little of her mother-in-law, perhaps on weekends, as the family home was in Rosedale. The Jarvis Street house belonged to Stephen's father. He used the ground floor for his accountancy practice, with his desk and filing cabinets in the front living room, and his secretary's space in the original dining area. There was a fine, brass sign beside the front door, announcing his hours of business.

The upper floor – bedroom, kitchen, bathroom and a large sitting room, were Stephen's – had been his since he began teaching; the house was only a stone's throw from his school. Celia took a lot of pleasure in redecorating these rooms, and Stephen applauded everything she did. She intended to spruce up the two attic rooms at some point, as well, in case they had overseas visitors one day, but there was no immediate hurry, as no one had indicated any plans in that direction.

Stephen was the happiest she had ever seen him, and seemed to be completely over his illness. Not that many planes went over the city – the nearest airport was miles away, so there was no way to judge how he'd be in that situation, but she was confident that he was better.

She became an excellent cook for him, producing some lovely meals that would have impressed her mother. Her greatest pleasure was to have some little appetizer all ready for him when he came in from school. She would take his coat, and offer him his slippers, then, once he was settled in his favorite armchair, she'd produce the Hors D'œuvres – perhaps boiled eggs with the scooped out yolks spiced up with chutney and mayonnaise and piled back on top, or smoked oysters on little crackers spread with cream cheese, things like that – and his favorite gin and tonic, of course, the latter with a tiny sliver of lemon floating on it. You couldn't get lemons in England, at least, not when she was there, but Canadians got all sorts of exotic fruit and veg that came up from the southern states of America. You could buy almost anything at the grocers.

Of course, it has been a difficult winter for her. She'd never experienced anything like it before, even that time when she was small, when her parents had taken her to Scotland for a week. Cold as that had been, it was nothing compared with Toronto in mid-March. Stephen told her she was lucky to have missed February entirely – always their worst month, he'd said. But she had a new woollen winter coat with a hood, and fine zip-up long boots with very thick treads on the soles; she hadn't slipped over once on the icy pavements.

She watched the children pulling each other along on sleds, and thought what fun that would be. Stephen said there was a park nearby where even adults could ride their toboggans down its steep slopes, but she would have to wait for next winter now and the arrival of perfect 'packing' snow, as he called it.

By the time Celia saw her parents again, and Pam, she surmised that she would be an excellent skier, as well, because Stephen enjoyed skiing.

The only thing that isn't quite right in Celia's new life is the lovemaking. Once she and Stephen had settled down to the routine of it – for naturally he expected it every night – she realized that it had become somewhat repetitive. She searched the health and wellness section of Riverdale Library, which was quite close, trying to find books on the subject, but seeing only dry encyclopaedic tomes about each stage of pregnancy. She thought it odd that there was nothing about how you got pregnant in the first place. She considered asking the librarian, but the woman looked somewhat forbidding, and gave the impression that she had never had sex in her life.

Eventually, when Celia grows more comfortable with it all, she plans to ask Stephen if he might try something a little different, just to break the monotony. In all the times they have made love, she's never suggested anything, despite believing that there are one or two other things she might enjoy. For instance, Stephen barely lingers at her breasts, which are extremely sensitive to the slightest touch, and she longs to keep his hands or mouth there, but he's always in such a hurry to get to the main business. Stephen is still rather rough with that, which she quite likes, but it's all over far too quickly. If only she had the courage – the audacity – to ask him to take a little more time. That would help enormously, she thinks.

October 31, 1946

Halloween is quite different to All Hallow's Night in England. Everyone gets involved in it, buying sweets – candy – she must remember that – for the Trick or Treaters, decorating the doorways to look like witches' hovels or haunted houses, and even the most sophisticated adult wants to feel like a child again. Celia waits until she hears her father-in-law closing up his office for the night and takes her box of decorations downstairs.

"Keep the candies coming, now, Celia. I don't want eggs smashed on the door when I get in tomorrow." But he is laughing. "What, will you just sit on the staircase waiting for the little devils?"

248

"Perhaps," she says, smiling. "Or I'll just keep my ears open for them upstairs."

"It's nice that you want to do this, Celia. Stephen can be a bit stodgy about it. Too much the school teacher, I suppose. They tend to take themselves too seriously. Not that we accountants are much better." He kisses her cheek. "But I don't have to tell you about Stephen – you know him." He wraps his scarf around his neck and pulls on his gloves. "Have a nice night, dear. See you tomorrow."

She's amazed by the number of children who ring the door bell. As soon as it's dark, they appear in little groups, crying "Trick, or Treat!" as she opens the door. The big punch bowl she's using to hold the candies is soon almost empty, and it's not yet nine o'clock.

She runs upstairs to their sitting room. "Please go and get more sweets at the corner shop, Stephen. They throw eggs at the door if you don't have anything to give them."

"So let them," he says. He studies her as she stands in the doorway, the long black frock she's wearing catching the light from behind, so that her legs are silhouetted.

"Please, Stephen? It's my first one. I love seeing their faces. Some of them are really quite scary, too." The doorbell rings.

He stands up then, and walks to her. "Just ignore them. They should be home in bed by now, most of them, anyway." He puts his hands on her breasts, watching her face.

"Stephen!" She steps back, but he moves closer to her. In fact, she loves what he's doing. The doorbell rings again.

He pushes past her to the top of the stairs, and flips the switch that turns off the light on the front porch, and the one in the downstairs hall. After a certain amount of scuffling and giggles, the children leave.

"Easy as that, see?" He returns to her, and pulls her into his arms. She waits for him to touch her again, but this time he only concentrates on pulling her skirt up, and reaching for her underwear, pushing her back against the arm of the sofa.

"Aawhh…isn't that good?" he says, then, his voice rasping. "We haven't done it in here before, have we?"

She would just have to remember to buy twice as many candies for next year, she thinks next morning, as she scrubs the dried egg yolk off the screen door.

January 20, 1947

The attic looks so pretty with the new wallpaper. Mr. Mercer Senior, Stephen's dad, gave her a charming little desk and chair that wasn't being used in his own suite downstairs. Mrs. Mercer insisted that her husband bring over a tiny sofa from their basement, which she reminded him would only go moldy if it stayed down there too much longer. He and Stephen managed to tie it securely into the trunk of the Buick, although Mr. Mercer was naturally nervous, as the car was only six months old. Mrs. Mercer gave Celia a lovely hand-crocheted blanket for Christmas, which was perfect tossed over the back of the sofa. The best thing of all in the room, of course, is the Gramophone that Stephen bought her for her birthday. It was exactly like Gladys's back at the camp, and Celia had smiled at the memory, but quickly dismissed it. He bought just one record, some boogie-woogie thing, but he told her where she should go to buy more, and gave her some extra housekeeping money to choose what she wanted.

From then on, Celia spends most of her time in her private space. She writes all of her letters here, makes up her shopping lists and menu ideas, and reads her library books. She keeps her photograph album up to date, to show her parents one day. She spends a lot of time gazing through the window at the street below and at the old apartment house across the road. She regularly sees the tenant in the window exactly opposite her open her windows, and they've waved to each other once or twice. She looks like a nice girl, and Celia wonders where she works, as she seems to be out all day, and apparently lives alone, for no man has ever stood at the window. Celia wonders how it would feel to live by herself, just doing things when she felt like it, with no rush to start dinner, or to wash the dishes, but simply read or listen to the radio late into the evening. She imagines having the girl over for coffee, chatting about clothes and hair styles. Sometimes, when Celia is feeling a little anxious over something Stephen has said or done, she finds that she envies the girl her apparently solitary state. But, on most days, with her favorite music playing (she bought "*The Dancing Years*" – the only thing she could remember in the music shop), she thinks that she's never been so happy in all of her twenty-three years, and envies no one.

April 1, 1947

Sometimes she sleeps up here now, in this little attic. She doesn't intend to, but finds that she just nods off, sitting on the sofa, listening to the music – not too loud, because Stephen has a different taste in music, and also needs quiet to mark his students' essays.

He is becoming more despondent with her these days, badgering her about having a child. He tells her he needs a baby to prove that she loves him. She has an inkling that her resistance is because she's not sure if she wants a Canadian child. She loves Canada, of course, and it's a perfect place to raise children, she knows, but she has this image in her head of a sweet English boy or girl, polite and neat, relatively quiet, and mindful of their elders. Canadian children are so boisterous and loud, she's noticed, and are occasionally rude to their parents. But she sometimes wonders what a child with Alex would look like.

Stephen's lovemaking is no longer pleasurable to her, knowing what to expect – the sameness of it, his roughness, although she pretends to enjoy it. Each night, she slips away from him when he's finished with her, takes her douching apparatus from the bottom of her underwear drawer, and sits in the tub to use it. The warm washing of his juices from her body is always a pleasurable experience. She doubts Stephen will ever enter her body with such gentleness or – even more startling – trigger that same depth of response from her. She wonders if other women use it simply to pleasure themselves. She would never do that, of course.

July 15, 1947

Celia fingers the corners of the page as she reads. Patsy has such exquisite taste in everything, and even her stationery is a soft pink, with a tiny green border. She has to read the letter three times, before it finally sinks in.

'*He is amazingly well in spirit, but his poor body is still recovering. He was so badly treated by the Hun, of course. No doubt he will write to you himself when he's settled in a bit more.*'

She starts from the top of the page once more.

'*Harvey and I wanted you to be the first to know that Alex was delivered back to us on the 4th of June , safe and sound at last.*

He had no documentation, and had been so ill that he was unable to identify himself, although his memory is back to normal now. Needless to say, the Red Cross were unable to locate his family until he, himself, was capable of giving them our address and telephone number.'

Celia stops and gazes out of the window. The girl across the way is drying her hair at her own window. After a moment or two, Celia looks down at the page again.

'We both know how much Alex meant to you, and we thought you would want to know that he survived that terrible war. No doubt your own life is so different now, and this news will serve to close that earlier chapter for you, once and for all.'

She wipes away the splotch of tears that falls.

'Alex is delighted that you came through the War safely, and that you have found your soul mate in Stephen. He wants to assure you that he will always be your dear friend, and that you can always count on his support at any time.

Wishing you well for your future,

I remain,

Yours very truly,

(signed) Patsy Briard."

She walks over to the calendar on the wall, tears off the July page, circles the date with a flourish of her pen and puts it into the envelope with Patsy's letter. Then she goes downstairs to start Stephen's dinner. Hamburgers tonight. Stephen enjoys her hamburgers.

"We'll spend the whole summer there," Stephen says. "It's a lovely old place, right on the water."

She removes his plate, and puts his coffee in front of him. "It sounds nice," she says.

"Well, you've never really seen the countryside, have you, since you got here? Last year was useless for me, trying to get on top of things at Jarvis, but I'm ahead of the game this summer." He sips

252

his coffee. "Dad has a motor boat, too. You'll be able to drive it yourself. You'll like that."

"It will be nice to spend more time with your parents." She stirs her coffee.

"I know. How silly is it that you hardly get to see them except for Sunday lunch?" He looks hard at her. "Are you all right? You look a bit washed-out."

She touches her face with her fingertips as if she'll be able to feel the source of her imperfect appearance. "Just a bit tired. I did too much in the garden this morning." Patsy's letter is now carefully pressed between the pages of her Webster's Dictionary.

"Oh, Celia – I keep telling you. Just let that guy that Dad hired get on with it. You don't have to do anything out there."

"I know that, Stephen. Ron is very helpful, but it's not the same. He just mows the grass, and pulls the weeds. I want it to be a proper garden."

"Well, I don't want you doing it. It's hard work, messing around with garden beds, all that bending and stooping. You'll never get pregnant working like a laborer out there. You should spend more time with your feet up. That's what Mum thinks."

"And what if I don't want to have a child yet, Stephen?" She finally said it.

"What do you mean?" He begins to chuckle, then stops. "Are you saying you'll *never* have a baby?"

"I don't think I'm ready. I sometimes still feel a bit like a child myself."

"That's only because you're on your own here, without your mum around. Girls need their mothers. It's only natural you feel a bit lost."

"I just can't picture it – a baby, I mean. I've tried, Stephen. I look at pictures of babies, and try to imagine holding one of my own, but I can't. I suppose some women just aren't cut out to be mothers."

He stands up then, his face a deep red, and she can see the vein throbbing at the side of his temple.

"Well, you are, so that's that." He speaks very quietly, but she knows it's because he is trying to control his rage. She has seen him this way before, when she hadn't felt very well, but when he insisted on having her anyway.

She stares back at him, and wonders if she looks as defiant as she feels. "I don't think I can be forced to get pregnant, Stephen."

"Well, we'll just see about that, shall we?" he says, shoving his chair back under the table. "I want a child, Celia. It's my right." He strides out of the room, and she hears him slam the front door.

She sighs then. He won't be back for hours, she knows. Perhaps she can convince him she's fast asleep when he gets home.

But it makes no difference to him at all.

Later, after she's certain he's asleep, she fumbles in the bottom of her drawer for the chintz bag containing her douche. She frowns, and quietly takes out most of her underwear and nighties and stacks them on the chair, but the bag isn't there. She walks back to the bed, barely able to make out his sleeping face in the darkened room.

Now what, she wonders, as she begins to strike him with her fist on his shoulders and back, sobbing loudly, cursing him. He groggily spins around and grasps both of her hands in one of his, and with the other hand he hits her squarely across her cheek, and she collapses beside him.

"For Christ's sake, Celia! Enough!" He pulls her to him. "Can't you see how much I want this baby? You're driving me insane. I need a child, don't you see? It's the only way I'll ever feel that you're really mine."

She struggles to sit up, and he hits her in the face again, very hard, and she falls back. As he pushes her legs apart, his eyes are glazed with rage. "I'll show you, you bitch," he says. "You *will* get pregnant."

"Strachan, do you realize what time it is? What on earth's happened?" Nell's voice is full of concern. It was unfair of me to phone her at this time of night.

"It's over, Nell. I finished it tonight."

"Really? How do you know? What's happened?"

"I just know, that's all. I stayed in there another two hours, just napping really, waiting for more to come. But it didn't. She tore off the month of July. I knew I'd finished."

"So how does it end?"

I take a deep breath. "Celia's going to have a kid, Nell. With Stephen. She doesn't have anything else to say. And she heard that Alex is all right, and it didn't seem to make any difference to her."

"Oh." There is a long pause. "Alex came home." She says it with such a sad voice. "So she stayed with Stephen."

"Easy enough to check. There'll be a birth certificate for the kid, right?"

"But she didn't want a child – you told me that, remember?"

"I know, but he forced her. Life goes on. You said it yourself. We don't always get the happy endings, do we?"

"We'll talk tomorrow. You sound exhausted."

"I've been over there since Friday night, Nell. I told you. Marathon writing."

"Try to get some real sleep, dear. At least now you can resume a normal life."

"I brought the record player back tonight, and the records. Nothing else, though."

"Funny girl. That lady's desk is worth far more than that record player, according to Ida."

"I wasn't thinking of its dollar value. I just needed to have it, something of Celia's."

"And the book isn't enough?" Nell laughs mirthlessly.

I sleep through the whole of Sunday, more or less without waking, except to pee, until around 5 o'clock on Monday morning. Rupert has been giving me some very strange looks, as if he thinks I'm sick, but he enjoyed the protracted snuggling, all the same.

I'm feeling okay as I leave the apartment. From here on, it's just me. I'm content to leave Celia to some publisher, if they want her. I'm about to sprint for the bus when I'm aware of a loud mechanical sound, and, even as I turn to its source, I know what it is.

They're pulling Celia's house down.

THIRTY-ONE

Dylan shakes his head. "Well, it's a bit soon after taking on the new job. A month? What does Kelly think?"

"She says she's fine with it. She says this is the slackest time, Dylan – the real work doesn't start building up until late October."

"I guess if she's okay with it, I am. Who do you know over there?"

"Oh, just people connected with the Second World War. I've been researching them for my book, you know. I'd like to put faces to the names, if possible." It is such an easy lie, but I blink after I say it, but I don't think he saw that.

"And how's the book doing? Any feedback yet?"

"Nell's doing all the leg work for me – she knows someone who works for an agent. I'm just going to leave it up to her."

"If you end up making any serious money from it, you're going to have to cut her in, from what I've gathered. She did all the formatting for you, too, didn't you say?"

"She's the kindest woman, Dylan. I couldn't have done any of it without her."

"Well, hang loose, sweetie. Don't go getting involved with any English guys, now. You'll have Jay coming down on me."

"Are you a relative?" the clerk asks me, looking at the form I completed.

"Um, yes, he's a second cousin on my mother's side." I'm a kind of writer, aren't I? Writers know how to lie. I'm not sure I really needed to, all the same. It's just writer's research, after all.

He takes my debit card and swipes it through the machine. "It will take ten to fifteen business days to process." He looks at the form again. "You've left the date blank, eh? All you have are the years."

"I don't know the date – or the exact year. I just figured it would have been somewhere around 1948. Is that okay?"

"I guess." He scribbles something on the form. He smiles. "If there was a child during this time, we'll have a record of it." He places my form in a tray at the side of the counter. "If you don't hear back in a couple of weeks, don't worry. It sometimes takes a bit longer." He gives me a look that suggests I should fully understand bureaucratic delays.

"Thanks." I smile at him. He has no idea how this one birth certificate affects everything I've been doing, how it's the result of all those nights I spent writing in Celia's attic. I can wait a little longer.

"So you've finished," Jay leans over and kisses me. He seems unaware of Kelly's widening eyes.

"I have. And if I haven't, it's too bad. They pulled the house down."

Kelly looks directly at me then, her face a question mark.

I laugh. "It's okay, Kelly. No bodies in the basement or anything like that. It's the house I was researching for my book. They're building a high-rise on the land where it stood."

"And you don't need it anymore – the house?" She knows a little about the story, but no details.

"Well, as I said, if I did, it wouldn't do me any good. There's just a hole in the ground now."

"We'll celebrate tonight. I'll take you somewhere very expensive." Jay is genuinely happy that it's over, I know.

I look at Kelly. "I guess you figured out that Jay and I have been dating."

She shrugs. "I didn't until just now. You covered your tracks well."

"It wasn't deliberate, was it Jay? It just seemed the responsible thing to do – you know, not broadcast it all over the office."

"No one gives a shit about that sort of thing, Strachan," she says, turning back to her computer. "It's when the person you're dating is married you have to be careful."

Just for a split second, I think I see some irritability on her face. Kelly, you sneaky bitch, are you screwing around with

257

someone here? I look at Jay with raised eyebrows, who shrugs, and waves goodbye.

"Everything okay, Kell?" I say, feeling a bit mumsy for asking, but hating to see her upset. She shakes her head, dismissing the question. As I try to concentrate on the work in front of me, I can't help wondering. Not that it's any of my business, but I'm curious, is all.

Come to think of it, it was always curiosity that got me into trouble in the first place throughout my life. I'm just your average nosy-parker – oops, watch the English idiom – your average sticky-beak – oh, hell, where did *that* come from? One of Alex's Aussie crewmen used to say it, didn't he? For the life of me, I cannot think of the North American equivalent for someone who's overly interested in other people's affairs. This is sad, really. I'm losing my Canadian cultural heritage, the jargon of my peers, and next it will be my identity. Or has that already gone?

"You'll be here for the wedding, right?" Katie is only in her fifth month, but sticks her stomach way out now. I know what five months of pregnancy looks like, and she's exaggerating.

"Of course. I'm booking for the end of September. You know I wouldn't miss your wedding day."

"Well, just a thought. You've been a bit distracted lately."

"Look who's talking. I never hear from you these days."

"Well, whatever, I'm glad the book's done. It was turning you into a bear."

"I know! It was no fun for me, either."

"Do you think you'll find a publisher?"

"Well, there's always self-publishing, if I really need it."

"Oh, Strachan, don't go there. After everything you've gone through for this story, you have to do it right."

"A book in the hand is worth two unpublished manuscripts in the drawer..." I say. In fact, Nell had said it first.

"You can't do it yourself. The book will lose all credibility."

"I'm teasing. Nell wouldn't let me, anyway. She doesn't believe in vanity presses. Huge ego-stroking, she thinks. I'm not convinced, though. I think she's a bit out of touch."

"Really? So you're checking it out?" Katie shakes her head. "Whatever you decide, it's your book." She looks around the room.

"It will seem strange not being able to call you whenever I want, Strachan, when you're in England."

I laugh at her. "You can call me there, silly. And, anyway, you don't call me now. It's nearly always me."

"Oh, silly, I do. It's just that I get tied up with Kyle, when we're not working. He often has different shifts to me, you know. It can make things hard."

"Perhaps you'll stop work completely after the baby – I mean, I know you're taking time off, but it would be nice if you could just be a mum and a wife full time."

"What an odd thing to say, Strachan. You, of all people."

"Is it?" I frown. "I guess I've changed my thinking about some things."

"Only since this book. You're taking on more and more of the Forties sensibilities, girl. Staying home to be a mum and wife – what does that sound like?"

I laugh. "I never thought about it. You could be right. That Celia has a lot to answer for with all her house-cleaning and cooking, everything ready on time for when the master gets in." I suddenly feel a stab of sadness, talking about her so casually.

"You'll soon get back to who you were before the book."

"D'ya think? Sometimes I feel like I'm changed forever. I don't curse the way I used to – did you notice? Celia only swears when she's really upset. I used to swear just to emphasize stuff. It wasn't necessary, really."

"Well, I'll be cleaning up my act for the baby, too. It's not good to have kids saying 'fuck' before they even know what it means, right?"

"Right! And that's really, really young, these days – what – six, seven?"

We sit quietly then, listening to Wolfgang Haffner playing softly in the background. Katie reaches for her juice.

"We'll always be best friends, won't we, Strachan?" She looks at me with surprisingly moist eyes.

"We're more than that, idiot. We're more like sisters. No matter what we say or do, we'll always be close."

Celia said exactly the same thing to Pamela, that day in 1946 when she boarded the '*Mauritania*' at Tilbury Docks. Pam had cried too, just like Katie's doing now.

259

"Soppy twerp!" I say, offering her a tissue.

Poor Katie has the weirdest look on her face. Of course, too late, I realize what I said. I wonder if I'll ever lose this new-found vocabulary.

I stand just inside Nell's office door. "Knock, knock," I say.

She looks at me, her face lighting up. "Oh, Strachan, what's happening?"

"Something a bit strange, in fact." I put the birth certificate on her desk.

She scans it quickly. "Oh, that's that, then. They had a baby, as you said."

"Take a closer look at it, Nell."

She picks it up and studies it, squinting a little, then looks back up at me. "Oh, my God. Strachan! It's not Celia. Stephen had this child with another woman!"

Typewritten on the extract form is:

'*Stephen Andrew Mercer, teacher, aged 40 years, and Marion Alice Mercer (nee Walsh), aged 24 years, both of the City of Toronto, registered the Live Birth of a daughter, Celeste Irene, on May 28th, 1951, at Wellesley Hospital, as witnessed by...*'

Nell puts the paper on her desk and we both continue to gaze at it, then at each other.

"What do you reckon, Nell? Are you thinking what I'm thinking?"

She nods, and then stands and silently hugs me. When she steps back, I can see her tears, and then I'm a bit blinded by my own.

"Celia left him, Strachan. She went back to England."

THIRTY-TWO

It's not as if I'm a jet-setter. The only time I've flown before today was when I went down to New York with Jay, and that was only an hour in the air, which hardly counts, really. This flight, far more complicated it seems to me, knowing where to go at the airport, what papers I needed at the ready, where to wait, gate numbers, all that stuff – well, I find it a bit overwhelming. I'm a grown woman, used to doing things alone, taking care of myself, but I'm just a little lost, sitting here, waiting to board. I'm not the only one traveling alone, and that makes me feel better, but the other single travelers looks more assured somehow, sipping their coffees or their water, reading, checking their cell phones, playing with their laptops. I envy them their cool.

"First time overseas?" The older lady next to me peers into my face.

"Um, yes." How could she tell?

"You looked a bit nervous. I thought it was either your first flight or that you simply hate flying."

"First time alone," I say.

"Oh, nothing to it. By the time you come back, you'll be an old hand." She smiles at me. "Ask me how many times I've flown."

"Oh, how many times?"

"Over two hundred – I've been everywhere." She checks her face in a hand mirror, fiddles with the corners of her mouth. "I can't seem to get enough of travel. There's always one more place to visit."

They announce our boarding then, and we sit forward waiting for our seat numbers to be called. She is ahead of me, and I nod to her as she walks away, and follow her with my eyes. I wonder if all those other flights of hers were alone as well. There is something sad about an ageing and unattached woman embarking on yet another trip. Is she running to something more exciting, or simply escaping something terribly dull? Her own life, perhaps? I shiver as I join the line. I'm glad I have Jay now. Everyone needs someone, don't they? I mean, other than family and friends? I never used to feel this way.

It's an understatement to say I'm impressed with London. It really is an amazing city. The buildings seem more solid, more in-your-face, than the ones at home, and the streets are so very crowded, and the traffic is appalling. I see famous bridges, and St Paul's and Westminster, but they all blur as my cab navigates the alarmingly narrow roads, barely missing jaywalking pedestrians. I didn't come here to do the tourist thing, anyway, but I need a base while I'm in England, and all trains lead to London. The hotel is okay, and handy to Big Ben – or the Elizabeth Tower, as it was renamed in 2012, which no one uses - although I can't see it from my room. In fact, I can't see anything of interest from my room, just the backs of scruffy old office buildings.   The place looked posher on their website – all fine furniture and fancy drapes, but, close up, everything is just a bit shabby. Not the price though. London is expensive.

I decide to grab breakfast before I shower and sleep. It's only 8:30 am, but I know I won't function until I get a little more rest. I didn't sleep on the plane at all. I don't recall the New York flight being so full of odd noises. I guess I was too caught up in the adventure and being with Jay to notice the creaks and rattles of the average passenger plane. Of course, the flight from Toronto to New York took only an hour, just time to lift the undercarriage, pass out the drinks, and lower the undercarriage again.

My waiter is nice. He stands just a few yards away from me the whole time I'm eating. Not so close that I'm uncomfortable, but enough that I only have to raise my eyes to him, and he swoops over. I don't usually eat a big breakfast, but this one was spectacular. English Full, they call it. I know I am.

"Any idea how I get to Bath from here?" I ask him, as he tops up my coffee.

"Mm, let me see, Madam. I believe you want Paddington Station. Bristol train I think. If you give me a minute, I can confirm that, and give you times. When were you thinking of going?"

"I was going to make it later, after I'd taken a nap, but I'm wide awake now. In an hour, say? Gives me time to freshen up."

And so it is that at 10:05 am, I am sitting in First Class of the Bristol Express on my way to Bath. I chose First Class so that I can compare it with the commoners' section another time. Only Britain would still have a class system for its trains, right? Well, that's not true. Even Via Rail practices it (I went to Montreal once). The steward (oh, my!) grudgingly accepts my excuse not to eat another breakfast, and pours me a coffee in the daintiest of porcelain cups, and then whips out a bottle of champagne and holds it up for me to examine.

"Goodness," I say. "I just got off a plane."

"Oh, well, then, Madam, this is just the thing for you. Put a spring back in your step."

By the time I emerge from Bath Spa Station, I'm well-sprung.

"Yes, miss," the cabby says, "I know Uxton. Twenty minutes from here. What part?"

"I'm not sure. A very large house. Uxton House?"

"Oh, the manor, of course."

The view from the cab is breathtaking. I remember how impressed by it Celia was that first time, driving with Bridget and Pamela. It really does look like a folk art painting. I pull my camera out and take a quick shot of it through the window. Silly, I suppose. I'll have plenty of time to take pictures.

I considered phoning them first, but didn't have the courage. One thing was certain – based on their historic connection, the current Mayalls will still be here, unless they've met with some Royal Displeasure.

As we enter the drive and the house comes into view, I am shocked by my reaction. *It feels as if I am coming home.*

I fumble with the money, but I'd practiced with it on the train, so was confident enough. I tip the driver the way I would in Toronto, but he seems exceptionally pleased, so perhaps it was a bit too much.

I glance at him as I take my bag out. "Could you just wait a minute, in case no one's at home."

He grins at me. "Oh, I wouldn't worry about that, darling. House this size, there's bound to be someone around." But he waits anyway.

A middle-aged lady in a grey pants suit opens the door to me. "Good Morning. May I help you?" She has a different accent to the cab driver. West Country twang, Pam used to call it.

I fix her with a calm and professional gaze. "I hope this doesn't sound too rude, as I have no appointment, but I'm hoping to find the family of Sir Adrian and Lady Mayall who lived here in the 1940s." It comes out way too fast.

"Oh? May I ask what it's in reference to?"

"I'm a writer. I've written a lot about this house, and its earlier occupants. I expect to have a book published soon. I thought, as I'm in England, it would be nice to meet the present family."

"Come in." She indicates a seat in the huge lobby. "Just wait here and I'll see if I can fetch someone for you."

I turn back to wave goodbye to the cabbie, take a deep breath, and step into the hallway of Uxton House, just as Celia did over seventy years ago.

Nothing has changed. Peering through into that enormous sitting room, I picture them all in there. Pam and Adrian, Bridget, the recuperating flyers - John, Archie, Paul, Bob, Alan, Gary and Jock, Pam's Auntie Janet and her Uncle Peter, and...Stephen. Poor sad Stephen, with his wretched, empty eyes. They seem to all stand there smiling back at me.

"Julian Mayall-Bryce." The voice makes me jump, and I spin around.

I take his hand, and am immediately struck by the strong face, not handsome, but certain in its features, compelling somehow. He is perhaps fifty, I'd guess, with steel grey hair, cut very short. Put him in a Nazi uniform and he could be German, Celia had thought about Adrian. He appears to be about the same age as Adrian was back in 1944.

"Strachan Marshall." I'm not sure what to call him.

"You've written a book about my family, have you?" He ushers me into the sitting room and I find myself sitting in the very same chair (I swear!) where Celia sat that first time. But this room is a little tidier – not much, but there are no boxes of logs or baskets of potatoes strewn around.

"I don't have a publisher for it yet, but I have high hopes, as they say."

"You wrote about my grandfather and grandmother, of course." He looks up at the hovering lady in the pants suit. "Any chance of another coffee, Marjorie?"

"Of course, Mr. Julian."

Not 'Sir' Julian. How odd. He's dropped the title. I suppose that's easy enough to do if you don't want it. "It's not just about *your* family, in fact," I say. "There are other people from the same time frame. I got to know them so well through writing about them that I thought I should come over and follow up on their later lives."

"Canada?" He kicks off his wellington boots, and puts his feet up on the coffee table. There's a hole in the big toe of one sock.

"Yes. Toronto."

"Nice city, Toronto. I spent a summer there my final year. Supposed to have made a man of me."

"Kayaking and camping, and Inuit ceremonies?" I can't resist it.

"How do you know that? Is it so common?"

"I guess." I smile at him. If I ignore the big screen TV on the far wall, and the cell phone that rests on the table in front of him, I can almost believe it's the Forties again, and I'm sitting with Adrian.

"So what's your book? Non-fiction? Fiction?"

"A bit of both, really. Poetic Licence. It's a bit complicated."

"Right up Mum's alley, that sort of thing."

I stare at him, and he sees my frown.

"My mother's name is Pamela – is she in your book, too?"

"She's still alive?" I say, and realise that my eyes have filled up. And that's why he's just plain old Mister.

He springs around the table to me, and offers me a handkerchief. "My God, woman, I had no idea how important all of this is to you. Of course she's alive. Can't get rid of her, can we?"

"I'm really sorry," I say, handing him back his handkerchief. I didn't know people still used handkerchiefs.

Marjorie arrives with the tray of coffee things then, and that gives me time to grab my mirror and repair a bit of the damage around my eyes. I know, never wear mascara when you're involved in some emotional journey, but I didn't think.

He hands me my coffee. "Mother will be back soon. You can talk to her yourself. I'll get out of your way, if you like, so you can have a little weep in peace."

"No, I'm fine now." I smile at him as proof. "Can I ask who your father is? I thought I knew everyone from that time."

He laughs. "Mother waited until it was almost too late, actually. After the War she went back to University, and then went on to get her PhD. She always said it was her father's idea, but she was born for academia. Even today, she still reads everything she can get her hands on. Agri-science. Did you know about that?"

"I don't even know what it is." I shrug.

"Oh, studying the soil, plant growth, farming practices – organic farming, of course. She's one of the original crusaders involved in efforts to eliminate chemical farming practices that started after the War, under the auspices of the Soil Association." He looks out of the window at the fields that surround the house. "Of course, this farm was part of Mum's experiments," he nods, "and we were one of the first to have the official organic symbol for it. It's become the standard for the EU." He grins. "I'm not assuming for a moment that you have the slightest idea what I'm talking about, but think of my mother as a very early Greenie, yes?

"Anyway, she met my father, Grayson Bryce, at some conference - also an organic farmer with property in Shropshire. His father was a Labor MP in the 20s. Gentlemen farmers they called them, but there's nothing gentlemenly about running a farm, believe me – nothing but cow shit and horse dung. No one thought Mum would get married. She was always very independent. But something clicked. She was over forty when I was born. Risky business, apparently, but I seem to be all right. Father died ten years ago, but she's over that now."

"Who's here?" The woman's voice, loud and demanding, reaches them from the hall. "Get my bloody boots off, Marjorie. Feet are killing me." After a certain amount of scuffling from the hall, a tall elderly woman appears in the doorway. Julian has already strode to the door to take her arm, and I stand awkwardly.

Lady Pamela Mayall – Pamela Mayall-Bryce now - instantly recognizable, the mousey-colored hair now a dazzling white, her face less plain in old age, but strong and resolute – very like Julian's – glares at me.

"What's all this about then?" she says, sitting on the sofa and pulling me down next to her. "Sit, sit, or I'll get a crick in my neck."

"Strachan Marshall, Mum. She's written a book about the family." Julian pours coffee for her, but she waves it away, still staring at me.

"A book? What book?" She leans closer to me to study my face. I want to squash her to me, tell her that her best friend is back, but I can't, of course.

I have no idea how I'm going to explain the book to her. Julian was fine, not too concerned with the why's and wherefore's, but this woman, sensible as always, and ever so slightly looking like her own mother, Bridget, seems to be peering into my soul.

God spare me.

THIRTY-THREE

The first thing I see when I open my eyes is the wedding photograph of Katie and Kyle which I'd put on the bedside table the night before. As the sun creeps over the frame, she seems to beam at me, laughing as she grasps Kyle's arm, and his face is full of the same joy. My beautiful Katie, soon-to-be-Mummy Katie, with her sweet guy. The sight of her picture there reassures me this morning.

I've slept in this room once before. Well, not me, but Celia. I recognized it as soon as Marjorie opened the door for me last night. It was all I could do not to say, "I know," when she told me where the bathrooms are located. Have to watch that kind of thing.

Pamela and I sat up talking until after ten o'clock, long after the dinner things had been cleared, and Julian had taken off for the pub. Somehow I told her everything I knew, but suggested a huge amount of reference material available on the Web, and wartime anecdotal resources through the BBC. She accepted it easily. I did feel guilty, of course, because she deserves the truth. I didn't mention Celia or Alex, because I didn't think I could get away with that. But I questioned her about her own friendships during the War, and she talked about them, without naming them.

As we finally said good night, she darted (yes, she darts) to the bookcase and returned clasping a book, "*The Living Soil*", by E.B. Balfour. "You must read this, Strachan," she said. "It's what we're all about. You can't write a history of my family without knowing about Lady Eve Balfour." She smiles then. "If you have any kind of interest in this life we have here, you need to know about organics. Julian has only one passion," she tapped the book, "and it's this." She studied me for a moment. "Well, up until now," she muttered.

That Pam, always so astute.

I will have to tread carefully now, for this last part. I'm heading for Winchester next, to find Alex's house – or the house where he once lived.

Breakfast didn't go down as easily today, whether because of jet lag, or good old-fashioned nerves.

"She's over ninety, Nell. But you'd never know it. She's as sharp as I am, and almost as fast on her feet. Now I wish you'd come with me, just so you could meet her." I have so much to tell her, but I'm a bit worried about the cost of the hotel phone call.

"How amazing you must feel, Strachan. All this time writing about them, and I'm sure you never imagined you would get to talk to any of them."

"I'm going to hang around London today, just to take a bit of a break from it – it was very draining, meeting her – you know what I mean? But tomorrow I'll try to find Alex's house. I can't believe it will be as smooth for me there as it was in Bath, though. I mean, it was almost too easy, Pam being alive."

"Get back to me as soon as you find out anything, all right? I'll be on tenterhooks until you do."

"England is beautiful, Nell. Did I say? I meant to, if I didn't. Once you get out into the countryside, it's hard to remember how tiny this island is, and how huge its population. There are all these little villages, and the meadows and hedgerows, like something out of a Constable landscape, and it all goes on forever. It's as if time has stood still."

Which, in a way, it has, for me.

A man opens the door. He peers at me short-sightedly. "Yes?"

"Mr. Briard?"

"Who wants to know?"

"My name is Strachan Marshall. I'm over here from Canada. I've just finished writing a book about the Second World War, set in the Boscombe area. In my research (*now the lies begin*), I came across the name Doctor Alex Briard, from here in Winchester, and I wondered if you were related to him." It all comes out in a rush.

I've already guessed who he is. The morning sun catches the top of his head as he stands there. I remember Celia noticing the light falling on Alex's fair hair, although this man's hair is totally

269

white. I think he must be around sixty, far too young to be Alex, anyway, but just the right age to be Alex and Celia's son. I wish I could put my arms around him and kiss his cheek.

"My father," he says simply, without expression. "Come in. I'll make us some tea."

When you've spent almost a year writing a book about people that you grew to love, that you wept over, it's difficult to say goodbye to it all. When they pulled the Jarvis Street house down, it seemed to help at the time. It was final, irrevocable, as they say. Coming to England has proved that wrong. The house may be gone, but it was just bricks and mortar, after all. The lives there, the anger and grief, the dreams – they lived on, after all.

As Martin Briard talks about his parents, about their life in England after the war, I am humbled that Celia gave me the opportunity to be a part of it all. I was just a rather ordinary, rough-around-the-edges Toronto girl, who got into mischief in her teens, and had an uncomfortable relationship with her own mother. I was never taught how to love, how to be affectionate. I learned a little of that from Patty and her lovely baby, from Katie with her optimism and pure joy in her life, in her delight with sex, and from Jay, who showed me how nice guys can be – I could have done much worse with my first real affair.

And then Celia invited me into her world, and showed me what love was really about. She showed me how fragile life is, how easily things change. I'd never understood real pain before – oh, some when Mum went, and Dad, or course, but I was unfinished myself, not fully capable of experiencing loss as deeply as Celia did. I used to think Celia wanted me to know *her* story, to fully understand why she was the way *she* was, but over these past weeks, especially since I got to England, I've come to the conclusion that Celia wanted *me* to have a better life, that she had to show *me* how I could live *my* life to the fullest, and not make do. Don't settle, they say. I was very settled, until the attic.

I watch as Martin reaches out a well-worn hand to turn the pages of the photograph album on the table.

"And here they are the day they got married," he says, peering at me over the top of his glasses, tapping the photograph with his finger. "It almost never happened, you know."

I wriggle a little closer to him on the sofa, and squint at the picture.

"She was a divorcee. Shocking thing back then. My paternal grandparents would have nothing to do with her at first, or with her family. My father told me once that they thought she was a tart, just out for anything she could get. Terrible snobs, my grandparents. They didn't think she was the right sort, a bit beneath him. They came around in the end. She was a lovely girl, Mum was. Well, of course I'd say that, wouldn't I? Father died in 1997, and Mum followed a year later. I don't think she could face being without him."

Celia and Alex stare back at me, some sort of official building behind them. She is wearing a pale blue suit, with a blue hat with a white flower on one side of the crown. She has white shoes, bag and gloves. I have never seen her look so feminine or so utterly beautiful before. The little crowd around them are all recognizable too, of course: Adrian and Bridget Mayall; Marie and Herbert Denning; Lucy and Janine from Celia's old camp, both clutching toddlers beside them, with their own husbands, I guess, there as well; Pamela and her Uncle Peter and Auntie Janet; one or two others I don't know; all gloriously happy, all with that terrible War firmly behind them.

I take the album from the table, and find myself turning the pages back, and back again.

"You have a good look, dear." Martin stands up. "Bit of history there, you'll see. I'll just go and freshen the tea, and see if I can find a bit of cake in the tin."

My hand stops turning the pages when I see a picture of Celia and Alex alone. They are standing beside an old inn, with hedgerows, huge lilac trees, and a sweep of fields behind them, and I know instinctively it's the pub where they stayed, where Connie fantasized about her husband coming home. I feel my eyelids droop and shake my head to try to wake up. Jet lag, I suppose, still hanging over me.

May 4, 1948

"Don't you two be late back now," Connie calls to them. "My Harry will be in a right state if you're not here when his hot pot

271

is done." Harry had been a sergeant in the Catering Corps and considered himself something of a chef.

"We'll be here," Celia says, laughing. "We wouldn't want to miss his hotpot." She looks up at Alex, grinning. "Would we, darling?"

"Stop teasing!" Alex says, steering her through the gate and out onto the grass pathway. "I've been wanting to do this for the last hour," he says, kissing her very thoroughly in the shadow of the lilac tree that grows there. He releases her, and studies her face. "I thought Harry would never finish telling us about his war experiences, did you? I was getting desperate for you."

"I think they're just lovely. I'm so glad he came back to her."

Alex kisses her again, but lightly this time, and puts his arm around her waist as they head off for their walk.

"Oh, Alex," Celia says. "Look at the lilacs. Have you ever seen so many blooms, so heavy on the trees?"

"Only in my head," he says, softly. And then he begins to sing *"We'll Gather Lilacs"* – the latest hit Novello song that he loves, and this time she joins in with him.

Connie looks up from bringing the washing in from the line, as their voices reach her from the distance. "Harry, hark at them! Do you hear them singing, bless 'em?"

Harry pops his head out of the back door. "Do I? I can't think of a nicer way to end an afternoon, can you, love?"

He returns to his hotpot, humming the overly-romantic song, from that overly-sentimental show, *"Perchance to Dream"*, written by that sensitive, effeminate composer, Ivor Novello, and he has no idea of its significance. He simply recognizes that it's pretty.

"Are you all right, my dear?" Martin is staring at me.

I brush the tears away. "It's just exactly as I always pictured them," I say truthfully, as I close the album. "It's the way I hoped they would be." At last I can tell Nell that the book is truly closed, that she can include this last tiny part, the most important part of all, in Celia's story. They had almost fifty years together after the war. "I'm so sorry," I say to Martin, trying to mop my eyes with the paper napkin clutched in my hand.

"Goodness, you certainly take your research very seriously," he says, sitting down. "It's been a long time since I had a weeping woman in my house, to be honest." He leans forward. "Bit of cake, dear? It's Carraway."

I don't know if Jay really understood, but he was okay with it, finally. Deep down, I think he always knew we wouldn't stay together. It *was* love, of sorts. When you have no one in your life, and someone treat you as sweetly and considerately as Jay did me, it's only natural to believe you're in love. But I never said it to him, never used those words. In all the times when it might have been appropriate, after making love fervently, he would say it, but I would not. I don't think you should take these things lightly.

Getting the residency for England could have been tricky, but apparently my grandmother, Anglophile that she was, insisted that my mother's British Patriality was registered with the UK High Commission in Ottawa, soon after her birth. Of course, I knew nothing of this until I was wailing to Patty about how much I needed to return to England for good. She thought I knew about it. (Once again proving that she and Mum always talked and I was never included.) In any case, this means that I, too, have the right to enter Britain based on what's called "Double Descent", on a UK Ancestry Visa.

I had a terrible time dealing with Rupert. I couldn't leave him, could I? But it was hard to imagine the poor thing stowed in the luggage section of the plane. I talked to his vet, and did a lot of online research, and in the end, there was no choice. He was coming with me, whatever happened. I had to start all these tests on him months before his trip, so that he wouldn't have to go into quarantine in England. I wept as they sealed him up in his carrier. I don't think I've ever felt so awful, like a monster, really.

In the end, he was fine. He wouldn't leave my side for the first couple of days, but then he discovered how wonderful Uxton House is, with so many nooks and crannies, and he must be overjoyed now he's forgotten the flight. They *do* forget, don't they?

And my lovely Katie had a little boy on December 15th, just in time for Christmas, which she never really enjoyed as a season, but went crazy for this time. The kid was just over a week old, and she had a tree, with gift after gift for him. I sat there watching her as she talked to him, her little Luke, and it took a lot of effort on my part not to break down in front of her. He is the happiest, sweetest child, which is testament to her theory that good sex produces the best babies. I hope I will be as lucky. It was tough leaving them when I headed back to England in the spring, when Rupert was ready to travel, but at least I had reason to be there during one of the most perfect times in Katie's life.

Dylan wasn't surprised. He thought I'd leave after the book was published anyway, that I'd be too big-time to work nine to five once my name was known. In fact, the book isn't published yet, although it looks as if we have a couple of outfits interested. Nell seems to enjoy the role of manager, which is funny, because there's really nothing to manage. I doubt this story will ever be on the New York Times book list, but Nell is the eternal optimist.

I'm digging up potatoes in the side garden, with Pamela cleaning, sorting and separating them. She keeps up a non-stop, one-sided conversation the whole time she works, addressing the potatoes:

"You, you bugger, we'll have you, then," she says. Or, "You can keep your green bits, and all those eyes. You can be next year's seeds." Or, "Call yourself a spud? You look more like one of those turdy-looking French truffles."

I don't quite understand why Pamela is so comfortable with me. I've looked into those rather watery, pale blue eyes of hers, to see if there's some kind of recognition there – that she sees a bit of Celia in me. But there's nothing. She told me it was good to have another 'gel' around the place. That'll do.

As for Julian. Oh, my…what can I say about Julian? If I knew that I *wasn't* in love with Jay, then I certainly know that I'm totally *in* love with Julian. I think I knew from the first day I saw him, standing in the hallway with mud on his boots and his face. I felt he'd been waiting for me. Which he was, really.

He consumes me. If he's not around, I go looking for him. If he's at the pub, I go and join him. If he's on the loo, I knock on the door. If he leaves on the tractor, I run after him for one more hug. It will have to stop soon, I know, or I'll drive the poor bloke away. But he loves me. *Me!* He says the reason he never married was because he'd never met anyone who could hold his interest for more than five minutes. He says I make him laugh. Well, he makes me laugh, too. I can only add that it's a good thing that Pamela is a bit hard of hearing, because late at night, what with the laughing and the noisy old bed we make love in, she'd never get a decent night's rest, poor soul. Of course, it's also a very large house.

I don't know if we'll marry. Katie asked me the same thing. It's different today, isn't it? Built into my psyche is some odd alarm system that says that marriage spoils things. I hope I'm wrong, as I am trying to get pregnant which means we'll need to be married for the poor kid eventually to inherit the estate. Not that I care about the title – it's bizarre, isn't it – in this day and age? Laws passed down since Henry Vlll. And Julian doesn't seem to give a toss one way or the other, but it *is* part of his family history, after all.

Julian thinks I'm mad, but after we make love, I put my feet up on the back of the bed (you know, the usual four-poster monstrosity – hard as a rock, and probably riddled with woodworm) and keep my body in a sort of semi-perpendicular position for about an hour, to help the sperm find their way home. Apparently it helps.

Pamela has gone to the local Organic Farmers' meeting tonight – she's still secretary, for God's sake. I don't know where she gets all her energy. Julian and I are alone in the sitting room. He's rubbing my feet, which I like, now I've established that there's nothing perverted about his enjoyment of it.

"Julian…" I lift my head to see his face better.

He looks down at me with that lovely expression he has."What is it? Why are you frowning?"

"Do you really love me?"

"Of course I love you, silly. I love every bit of you, even your big arse – *especially* your big arse. That's how much I love you."

"It's just that there's something I need to tell you. I've been trying to find the right time." I pull myself up into a sitting position. "But you have to hear me out before you say anything, all right? And you mustn't laugh. Please don't laugh at me."

"I promise I won't. Go on. I'm all ears."

He does have rather large ears, *a la* Prince Charles. It's our little joke. Big-Arse Strachan, and Big-Ears Julian.

"Well…you know my book…"

THE END

Music Titles:

"The Dancing Years" by Ivor Novello, Chappell & Co. Ltd., 1939

"Warsaw Concerto" from the RKO film, "Suicide Squadron, 1941, by Richard Adinsell, Keith Prowse & Co. Ltd., 1942

"Cornish Rhapsody" from the Gainsborough film, "Love Story", by Hubert Bath, Keith Prowse & Co.,, 1944

"Pine Top's Boogie Woogie" by Clarence "Pine Top" Smith, Vocalion Records, 1928

"Down the Road a Piece" by Don Raye, Columbia Records, 1940

"How High the Moon" by Nancy Hamilton and Morgan Lewis, from "Two for the Show", 1940

"Concerto in F" by George Gershwin, 1925, published New World Music Corp., 1927

"We'll Meet Again" by Ross Parker and Hugh Charles, Dash Music Company Ltd., 1939

"My Dearest Dear" from "The Dancing Years" by Ivor Novello, Chappell & Co. Ltd., 1939

"We'll Gather Lilacs" from "Perchance to Dream" by Ivor Novello, Chappell & Co. Ltd., 1945

"All the Things You Are" from "Very Warm for May" by Jerome Kern and Oscar Hammerstein, 1939

"I'll Be Seeing You" by Sammy Fain and Irving Kahal, Williamson Music, Inc., 1936

"As Time Goes By" by Herman Hupfeld, Warner Bros. Inc., 1931

Book and Poem Titles:

"The Fountainhead" by Ayn Rand, Bobbs-Merrill Company, 1943

"The Grapes of Wrath" by John Steinbeck, The Viking Press, 1939

"Far from the Madding Crowd" by Thomas Hardy, Cornhill Magazine, 1874

"The Living Soil" by Lady Eve B. Balfour, Faber & Faber, London, 1943

"Death of The Ball-Turret Gunner" by Randall Jarrell, 1945 (Publisher unknown)*

*I took a liberty with Randall Jarrell's poem by mentioning it in an earlier period than its actual publication date, but it was so perfect for that particular point of the novel, and I couldn't resist this tiny manipulation of the truth.

www.ingramcontent.com/pod-product-compliance
Lightning Source LLC
Chambersburg PA
CBHW030355020726
47493CB00003B/827